HAV3N

TOM EASTON

First published in 2012
by Andersen Press Limited
20 Vauxhall Bridge Road
London SW1V 2SA
www.andersenpress.co.uk

2 4 6 8 10 9 7 5 3 1

British Library Cataloguing
in Publication Data available.

ISBN 978 1 84939 418 5

Printed and bound in Great Britain by
CPI Group (UK) Ltd, Croydon, CR0 4YY

PART 1
THE END

The Hilton, Heathrow Airport, London
12 October, 7.43 a.m.

Rory Chambers stared at himself in the mirror and rubbed the back of his neck. He felt awful. His greying hair was dry and flaky, his skin sallow and waxy. He must have drunk too much last night, he told himself. How else to explain the dry mouth, the thumping headache, the nausea?

He took a shower, standing still, face upturned to the stinging hot water. The back of his neck tingled and he rubbed it again, feeling a spot developing there. Trying to squeeze it between finger and thumb caused a sharp pain and he decided he'd better leave it alone.

Wandering through into the bedroom, Rory flicked on the TV. They'd been banging on about bird flu the last few weeks: *AV3N*. In the last couple of days everyone had suddenly got very excited and the boffins were talking about the virus having combined with a human flu strain. Death rates were soaring. The anchors looked earnest, but didn't they always?

He coughed, feeling phlegmy, and turned the TV off. Media hysterics. He didn't have time to worry about a little cold. So what if a few grannies and sickly kids died? 'That's natural selection in action,' he said to himself, sniffing. Survival of the fittest. Pandemics were there to clear out the chaff.

His hand had found its way to the back of his neck again. The spot felt huge, and tight. He squeezed, and this time the thing burst. Warm fluid crept down his back. Inspecting his hand, he recoiled at the sight of a black, viscous mess coating his fingers. *What the hell?* He grabbed a tissue and dabbed the spot gently, wincing. Then he coughed again, his chest rattling.

'Come on, Rory,' he told himself. 'Get it together.'

He was on his way to a big meeting in New York, a huge meeting for him. If he pulled off this deal he'd be able to buy a yacht so big it would make Abramovich's look like a pedalo. He couldn't be sick for this, simply couldn't.

'I just have to get on the plane, then I'll take some pills and sleep it off,' Rory muttered to himself as he hauled on his trousers.

The coughing proper started as he was checking out. The procedure took a good ten minutes as every time he tried to say something to the pretty young receptionist, he exploded into a fit of hacking coughs, drawing up phlegm. She tried not to look disgusted as she handed him tissue after tissue. Eventually she just passed him the box and took a firm step backwards.

Rory staggered out into Terminal 4, blearily examining the boards for his gate. He'd checked in online the night before and carried just a bag.

Gate 13, the board told him. Unlucky for some.

Please allow 10 minutes to walk to your gate.

It took him seventeen, as he kept having to stop and gasp for air. His breathing was by now ragged, and the back of his neck itched and scratched like crazy. He was running a little late so he tried to speed up, but he stumbled, and burst into another fit of coughing as he passed an Asian family looking for Gate 9. They recoiled in distaste and he mumbled an apology.

On arrival at the gate he stood swaying for a minute. The lights hurt his eyes and the back of his neck was agony now. The flight attendant held out her hand for his boarding pass; then she shrank away, horrified, as she caught a look at his sweating face.

'What's wrong?' he tried to say as she swam in and out of focus, but it came out as 'Wassra?' He felt cold and hot at the same time, and suddenly, for the first time since he could remember, Rory Chambers felt very, very frightened. A warm trickle of urine ran down his leg as he sank to his knees, feeling an enormous cough rise in his chest. A security guard swam into vision and the last thing Rory saw, as he coughed up half a liquidised lung, spraying it over the guard and half the passengers in the lobby, was this poor man's face and torso suddenly turn bright pink.

Then the darkness claimed him.

1

Judith Pirbright pressed the red button and replaced the phone handset on its shoe. She did it carefully, as she did everything. It wasn't that she was overly neat, or obsessively tidy. Just that she seemed to think hard about everything, as if constantly trying to remember how exactly it was that one made a cup of tea, or turned on the television, or wrote a birthday card. It drove Josh mad. He liked the way his father did things. Casually, gracefully, almost without thinking. Which was strange when you considered what his job was. His father should be the perfectionist, the one who watched what he was doing. The careful one.

'Was that him?' Josh asked, though he knew it was.

His mum nodded, then turned to face him, refusing to meet his gaze across the cold kitchen.

'Well?'

Judith breathed in deeply, as if she were about to blow Josh away with her next sentence. *Hell*, he thought. *Maybe she is.*

6

'Your dad thinks we should set up barricades half a mile outside the village, on both roads,' she said.

'Barricades?'

'We need to block the roads,' Judith explained. 'Stop anyone from coming into the village.'

Josh nodded, trying to appear calm even though his insides churned. He was used to it now; his stomach had been churning since the state of emergency had been announced the day before.

His father had phoned from his laboratory in a remote part of Suffolk and spoken to Josh's mum for twenty minutes while she'd stood and listened quietly, just saying 'OK' from time to time. After the phone call had finished she'd sat for a few minutes in silence, before pulling herself together. She'd been careful with her words, but had left Josh and his twin sister Martha in absolutely no doubt just how big this was.

Now, suddenly, it seemed to have got just that much worse.

'It's that bad?' he asked.

She nodded. 'He told me to be honest with you . . . with both of you. It's actually very bad indeed. Much worse than the government said yesterday.' She sat down and Josh wondered if he should go over and . . . what? Put a hand on her shoulder? Hug her? They weren't a touchy-feely sort of family. He stayed where he was, telling himself that he had to stay strong. They all did. Hugs could wait.

7

'How did he sound?' he asked.

Judith looked up at him, disturbed. 'He...didn't sound like himself. He was almost gabbling. He's under so much pressure...'

She tailed off and Josh's stomach lurched. His father, Michael Pirbright, was not a man to let pressure get to him easily. If he was panicking, there was something to panic about.

'I can't put up barricades by myself,' he said. He sensed Martha appear in the doorway, knew she would be listening intently, and he could hear she had stopped breathing so as not to announce her presence. Martha liked to know what was going on. She listened, she read, she watched – it was why she did so well at school; not that she was clever, just that she paid attention. Josh, by contrast, tended to act first and think later.

'No,' his mother agreed. 'He said we need to tell everyone in the village. Make them aware of how serious it is. He said we need to make them listen, whatever it takes.'

She paused. He waited, knowing there was more.

'Otherwise people will try and let...others through. We can't let anyone back in. Not even loved ones. No matter how they beg. If we let them in we could all die...'

Josh's head reeled. His thoughts turned immediately to his friends in the villages and towns nearby, his grandparents in Scotland, his cousins in Kent.

Were they now building barricades of their own? Or were they trapped without? Or worse still, had they already succumbed?

'How long will this last? Did he say?'

His mum paused for a moment before shaking her head. 'I don't know, Josh.'

'Dad will come back, won't he? He'll be OK, in his lab?'

This time the pause was longer. 'There's always hope,' Judith said.

Martha's blonde cloud of hair, so like his own in colour, bobbed and she was gone. Back to her room to write in her diary, no doubt: *Dear Diary, Today the government disappeared and the world fell apart.*

Josh felt sick. Just four days ago the Department of Health had released a statement saying the bird-flu strain AV3N had combined with a human strain, creating a new, deadly virus – HAV3N. The BBC showed pictures of the molecular structure of the virus, saying that there'd never been anything quite like it before.

The science was lost on Josh – Martha was the scientific one, the analytical one. He had never done well in science, or maths for that matter, and there was no chance of him following in his father's footsteps. Michael, to his credit, never expressed disappointment in Josh's supreme lack of scientific *nous*, but encouraged him in his interests in photography, or motorbikes. However, the fact that their father would heap praise on Martha's always-excellent results in chemistry or physics made Josh feel he was falling a little short of his father's expectations.

Within hours, the BBC reported, the virus had spread across the globe and now reports started arriving of deaths in the thousands. Most people in their village, Josh knew, had decided to stay in their homes, as advised, while schools and colleges were immediately closed and the trains began running a reduced service – none at all by the curfew today. Maybe two dozen villagers commuted to work in nearby Guildford, or London – about an hour away by train – and some had driven to work as usual, airily declaring it all media hype, another swine flu. But those people were now trapped in the cities since all travel had been forbidden when the state of emergency was declared.

Things were so desperate that the army had orders to shoot anyone not complying. But Josh had heard on the radio that many people were ignoring the instruction to stay put, desperate to escape the death trap that London or the other cities had become; they were risking the bullets to try and get back home to their loved ones.

'He said we should man the barricades with any guns we can gather,' his mother continued quietly. 'Hunting rifles, shotguns. I know Mr Mitchell has one he uses for pheasants...' Josh could hear her picking her way through the minefield her sentences were laying down, leaving him to blunder in.

'So if the commuters try to return...?' he began, before trailing off.

She nodded.

'And what about Dad? He just waits at the lab? Is there any chance of his team coming up with a cure? A vaccine?' He immediately reached for his mobile, thinking to text his father, then remembered that the signal had been shut down the day before.

His mother's eyes filled and she looked away, through the window over the sink, out into the gloom of the October afternoon. 'He said there's always a chance. He said he thinks he's close to something. We need to do what we must to keep ourselves alive in the meantime.'

'He's going to come home?'

Judith turned, her blonde hair backlit by the picture window behind. She ignored his question. 'Go now, Josh. Go and get Sam. Then meet me down at the pub; that's where everyone seems to be congregating. I need to tell everyone what your father just told me.'

'What about Martha?' Josh asked.

'I'm going to ask her to wait here, in case your father phones again.'

Josh nodded, then went out through the front door and onto Highland Terrace. He paused for a moment, breathing in the earthy scents of autumn. Brown apples and wet leaves. How strange to think the countryside would just carry on doing its thing, whatever damage this virus might do to their lives. The trees would still grow apples even with no one around to eat them. Leaves would still fall and hedgehogs would sleep beneath them. It didn't seem fair. He should have drawn comfort from the thought that life would go on whatever became of the human race. But at the moment, he was finding it all but impossible. Surely such an apocalypse should affect every form of life. Not just humans. And stuff the hedgehogs.

He walked three houses down to the Hilfenhaus' rose-covered cottage and hammered on the door. It was opened by a girl a couple of years younger than he and Martha, pretty and pale with dark hair and a mass of freckles radiating out from her small nose.

'Hey, Kitty,' Josh said, trying to sound upbeat. 'Is Sam here?'

She smiled. 'I thought you'd come to see *me* for a minute.'

Josh smiled despite the situation. Kitty had always liked him, or pretended she had. He was never sure if she was serious or not and the uncertainty had been going on for so long now there was no way back. Anyway, even if he did like her in that way, she was his best friend's little sister.

'Sam!' she yelled, then retreated into the house, still watching Josh with a half-smile. 'Come in,' she said.

Usually Josh would have charged up the stairs and

12

burst into Sam's room, but today it didn't seem right. Today it seemed formality was required. Josh took a seat in the sitting room until Sam wandered in, looking pale. Josh couldn't remember his friend ever so sombre; Sam didn't usually take life so seriously. Never got too bothered by anything. Always the first with a joke. Just maybe not today.

'Hey,' Sam said, ducking his strawberry-blond head in acknowledgement.

'Is that all you've got to say?' Josh asked, rolling his eyes. 'Civilisation might be about to end and all you can think of to say is "hey"?'

Sam's face cracked into its familiar grin. 'Gotta save my energy.'

Josh smiled back, despite the churning inside. Thank God for Sam.

'Does Kitty know what's going on?' he said. 'She didn't seem all that worried just now.'

Sam shrugged. 'Dad told her it was all media crap, then went off to work yesterday so she stopped worrying. You know what Kitty's like; if it's not on a reality TV show it doesn't exist.'

'Have you heard from him?' Josh asked gently.

'He called last night, said he's staying with a friend in London until it blows over.'

Josh said nothing. They'd both watched the news. Things were bad in London.

Sam went off to the kitchen to get drinks and Josh turned his attention to the TV, which was showing scenes from the capital – it was like watching a disaster movie. Troops lined the streets. There didn't seem to be any civilians. But then the shot changed to a different street and Josh saw a crowd of people arguing with soldiers at a checkpoint. As he watched, a figure at the back of the crowd, standing a little apart, stumbled and fell.

'Where's the government?' Josh muttered.

Sam came back with Cokes, and Josh told him what his dad had said about the barricades.

'Does your father keep a gun?' he asked.

'Think so,' Sam said, shaking his head at the scenes on the TV. The soldiers were now pushing the crowd back, then one fired a gun into the air and the crowd turned and ran, trampling each other. 'Yeah, you know what? There's a shotgun in the garage.'

The boys slipped through the door into the garage. Once there, Josh lifted a canvas cloth to have a peek at Sam's dirt bike: a Suzuki, a good one, if a little old now. It was similar to his own. Most weekends they took their bikes out to a track in the Bourne woods. He wanted nothing more than to head out there right now and forget this was all happening. But the bikes would have to wait.

Part of him still clung to the tiny mad hope that this might all be a media blow-up, the way they'd told themselves it was just three days ago. His mum had told him the old boys in the pub were still saying it, though some were only saying it now because they had sons or daughters in London and wanted to believe it.

Sam found the shotgun, wrapped in oily rags. He broke it to check it was unloaded and sent Josh to a set of drawers to hunt for the shells. Josh found a box of twelve, with two missing.

'Those were the ones he used to test it worked,' Sam said, peering at the box contemplatively. 'Never used it since.'

'Why'd he get it?' Josh asked. 'Not many grizzly bears in the Bourne woods.'

'He reads the tabloids,' Sam said, shrugging. 'All those headlines about feral youths and Eastern European criminal gangs targeting rich folk in the shires. Load of nonsense, of course. And once he'd got the gun he just forgot about it.'

He handed the gun to Josh. 'Go on, you do it,' he said. 'I wouldn't know where to start.'

Josh slid a shell into each barrel, enjoying the sensation of working something so simply designed, yet so effective. He'd been taught to handle a gun by his grandfather, who shot clay pigeons because 'they make less mess than pheasants'. He'd only fired one once, though, when he was a few years younger. The recoil had made his arm ache for a week, but he could still feel an echo of the thumping thrill the blast gave him. He checked that the safety catch was on before swinging the barrels back up with a satisfying, tomb-door *clack*.

They kneeled and stared reverentially at the weapon for a few seconds more until Josh said, 'Come on, let's go. Mum said to meet her at the pub.'

The two boys hurried out the front door and headed down to the Wheatsheaf. But when they arrived they found they were late. Judith was already there – Josh could hear her shrill voice from outside. He guessed the regulars were proving a little hard to convince.

He stopped for a minute and took a deep breath, steeling himself. How had it come to this? Why was it up to him and his mum to do something? His heart pounded in protest.

'What's the plan?' Sam asked.

'First, get their attention,' Josh said, slapping the cold steel of the gun's barrel.

Without stopping to think too hard about what he was doing, he stormed in through the door, just as pub regular Clive Mitchell was speaking:

'Look, Judith, many of us in this village have family in London. For all we know they're battling against all odds to get back home to us, and you want to put up a barricade to stop them? Are you suggesting we carry guns? That we—'

Josh didn't give him time to finish; he swung the barrel upwards and fired, once, into the dried hop boughs hanging from the ancient oak ceiling. As the gun kicked hugely in his hands he suddenly worried that the blast would punch through into the floor above and whether there might be someone up there who might be hurt. Looking to see the result of his shot would betray his uncertainty, though, so he kept his head level, sweeping his gaze across the assembled, shocked pub regulars. Thomas Butcher, the landlord, had ducked down behind the bar. Most of them just sat, or stood still, staring at him, unable to believe what he'd just done. He saw Judith standing to one side watching, clearly shocked but able to give him a weak nod of encouragement.

'We need to put up barricades, now,' he said as calmly as he could manage. He could hardly hear himself, what with the ringing in his ears from the shotgun blast.

No one moved.

The only flicker in the pub was from the television set, which no one ever watched, but which was always on, muted. Now it was tuned to the rolling news coverage of the crisis, exactly as Josh and Sam had just been watching. Josh couldn't help but glance over at the screen. A helicopter shot over what looked like Trafalgar Square, showing images of hundreds of people, some lying down and apparently dead, others running as the army tried to kettle them. Then the camera shot changed. A soldier stood in a deserted London road, bin bags of rubbish lying strewn against the gutter, the street cleared to allow lorries to roar through, carrying bottled water or stocks of the useless drug Tamiflu in a brave but doomed attempt to actually help people.

Josh noticed everyone else in the pub was looking at the TV now too, following his gaze. As they watched, a lorry swung wide and ran over a bin liner, and suddenly it was obvious that these weren't sacks of rubbish. There, on the national news, on a live feed from the centre of the capital, they watched the great black tyre of a ten-tonne lorry run over one of the bin liners and crush the head of a corpse inside. The skull exploded like a melon hit with a mallet, spraying red and grey matter across the street.

The assembled drinkers, as one, breathed in sharply. *That should do it*, Josh thought, through rising nausea. He swallowed a bit of sick that had crept up into the back of this throat.

Then he saw the soldier on screen cough and rub his neck.

'We can't let anyone back in,' he said, looking at Clive. Mitchell was an opinionated loudmouth. Every pub has one. But no one talks that much unless they have listeners. Josh knew he had to get Clive moving; the rest would follow.

Clive pointed a fat finger at Josh. 'We'll stop them coming in tonight, quarantine them, but if they're still OK in the morning…'

'We'll let them in, then,' Judith said. 'Michael tells me that once someone has contracted the virus, it strikes within four hours.'

'And where is Michael?' Clive asked. 'Hiding in his lab?'

'He's working on a vaccine,' Judith said quietly.

'C'mon, Mr Mitchell.' Josh was gesturing ever so slightly with the shotgun.

Clive got the message. He hopped heavily off his bar stool and looked around.

'Reg?' he said to an elderly man. 'What do you think?'

Reg Walker, who Josh thought he'd heard had been in the army, nodded and stepped forward.

'I think the boy's right,' he said. 'And I think we need to do this now. Amir, we'll need you.'

Amir Mansoor, who Josh remembered worked for the council in Guildford, stepped forward and followed Clive and Reg out of the pub into the cold evening. Josh scanned the rest of the crowd. His mother's face was unreadable. Then he saw Mark Rogers. The Rogers' house was just across the road from Sam's, and Mark had been at Josh's school until he'd left at the end of Year 10 to become an electrician's apprentice.

'Mark, we could use your van to move stuff?' he suggested. Mark paused, perhaps not liking being ordered around by someone four years his junior, but then nodded and followed the others.

'We'll set up headquarters right here,' Judith said firmly. 'We'll keep checking phones, radio and television. If anyone has any useful information, then they are to bring it here first.'

After that, the adults took over and shouldered Josh and Sam aside, as if embarrassed they'd needed to be pushed into this by teenagers. They worked fast, and by the time the light had begun to fade, the two barricades had been set up.

Reg and Clive had taken charge. They and a dozen or so men had constructed the barriers, choosing similar, narrow parts of the respective roads. First they parked four small cars in a row. Sam grinned with delight as he was allowed to ram a commandeered Clio into the hedgerow; he and Josh had decided to help out on the Guildford Road blockade. Josh guessed that was because Sam's dad was most likely to come back the other way, if he was still alive; Sam wouldn't want to be pointing a gun in his own father's face.

Their team consisted of Reg, who it turned out had served in the Falklands; Clive, who was a builder by trade; Josh; Sam; Mark Rogers the electrical apprentice; a lorry driver named Tucker; and a man Josh didn't know but who everyone called Mad Pete. Clive told him Pete liked dressing up as a Saxon on weekends and re-enacting battles in Kent. Martha had asked if she could come too but Clive had shaken his head.

'So much for gender equality,' Martha had grumbled to her mother. 'First sign of trouble and the men take charge of everything.'

'Come on, Martha,' Judith had said. 'This is not the time to have that fight. I need you here at Headquarters anyway.'

They piled wooden pallets, mattresses and sheets of roofing materials over the cars, leaving a ledge at the back to allow them to peep over the top. Mark's electrical van was parked a dozen metres behind the barricade, packed with food, ammunition, blankets and torches. There was a way through each of the barriers too, in one door of each car and out the other.

A motley collection of guns had been assembled, as well as one crossbow provided by Mad Pete. The men laughed at the crossbow until Pete fired a bolt through a car door from ten metres.

Just after 7.00 p.m. a message came from the village to tell them the BBC had stopped broadcasting and landlines had now also gone dead.

Little Sheen was a tiny village of just over one hundred people. Set in the heart of the Bourne woods, and accessible by just two winding roads, it tended to have few visitors. The local community liked it that way, though the teenagers – which, right now, amounted to only Josh, Sam, Martha and Kitty – found it dull and escaped to Guildford or London whenever they could. The village was one of those that tended to win awards: *Surrey's Prettiest Village, 1991; England's Tidiest Town (runner-up) 2003* – that sort of thing. It would have won more if people could have been bothered to enter more often. Now it seemed it might be too late to add to the trophy cabinet.

Sam's family, the Hilfenhauses, had lived here since before he was born. The Pirbrights were relative newcomers, having moved here thirteen years ago, when Josh and Martha were toddlers. They had moved for the schools – the nearby junior school was one of the best state schools in the country – and when Michael Pirbright began a new job at a laboratory in Suffolk, they'd decided to stay, which meant that Josh and Martha didn't see their dad as often as they'd like; he was sometimes away for weeks at a time.

Josh, Martha, Sam and Kitty had all been to the local school – though it had been boarded up for the last ten days, since the beginning of the outbreak, when it had seemed it was just another bird flu.

The first car arrived around 8.30 p.m., driving slowly into the glare of a couple of searchlights Clive had found somewhere. The car was driven by Simon Gardener, whose wife Susan was waiting anxiously for him in their home. Josh didn't know much about the Gardeners – no one did. They'd only moved to the area a year ago and had spent most of their time overseeing the renovation of their massive farmhouse on the southern edge of the village.

Simon saw which way the wind was blowing and got out of the car about a hundred metres down the road. He walked towards the barricade, blinking against the lights. Hands held high, like a defeated soldier in a war film.

Clive was already shaking his head.

'You can't come in, Simon!' he shouted when the commuter was within earshot. 'I'm sorry, but you'll have to go back.'

'Don't be ridiculous,' Simon called, trying to sound cheerful. 'I haven't got it. I'm perfectly healthy.'

Josh could hear the fear in the man's voice. He'd come from London. What terrible things must he have seen?

'I've had one hell of a journey. Bloody trains,' Simon continued, trying to joke his way through. Josh saw he still had his tie on. You had to give the man respect for that.

'You're not coming in, Simon,' Clive repeated firmly. 'And before you even think of it, there's a blockade on the London Road too. And we've got sentries in the woods. They'll shoot on sight.'

Josh wasn't sure if this last bit was true – there certainly hadn't been any discussion about this – but Simon seemed to believe it, though his shoulders sagged.

'Can I see my wife?' he asked.

Clive shook his head, and then called out, 'No,'

as he realised that Simon wouldn't be able to see him against the glare. This they had discussed. 'Go and get back in your car, reverse a hundred metres up the road.' His voice sounded hoarse with all the shouting in the chilly air. 'We'll bring out food and water and leave it at a safe distance for you.'

Simon nodded and turned slowly towards his car.

'If you're still alive in the morning,' Clive added, 'you can come in. Then you can see your wife.'

Simon stopped as he listened to this, and then carried on. Josh thought he saw the man stumble as he reached the car, but whether this was from exhaustion, despair or something else, was impossible to tell.

'Someone needs to take him supplies,' Clive said, without moving.

'No,' Mark said quickly. 'We need to keep well away.'

'We're taking him food, Mark,' Reg said firmly.

Josh hesitated; should he volunteer?

But he was too late.

'I'll do it,' Sam said. Clive nodded and went to the car for food and coffee.

Josh saw Reg pat Sam on the shoulder and found himself wishing he'd spoken sooner.

Then they all watched as Sam walked a hundred metres along the road, carrying a Thermos, a water bottle and a Tupperware container full of cheese-and-pickle sandwiches.

'Don't get too close!' Mark shouted. 'He's getting too close,' he hissed at the others nervously.

Josh felt a lump in his throat as he watched his friend approach the car. *Be careful, Sam*, he thought.

Sam left the food in the middle of the road and retreated, even as Simon got out of his car and trotted towards him. Sam walked hurriedly backwards, trying to get a good look at the man, stage-lit by the searchlights on the barricade and backlit by the headlights of his own car.

Simon's figure appeared to glow with an unearthly intensity and Josh, heart in mouth, saw Sam stop for a second, seemingly fascinated. But then the shining Simon raised a hand to his mouth and Sam hurriedly turned and jogged back to the blockade.

'I thought I saw him coughing,' he said as he returned. The men nodded grimly and Pete checked his crossbow again.

15 OCTOBER, 7.30 A.M.

As it happened, the crossbow wasn't necessary. Simon died in the night. They'd taken it in turns to keep guard on the barricade, ensuring there were always at least three of them, armed and awake.

Tucker the trucker said he'd heard coughing from Simon's car. When dawn finally broke, they could see the car door open and Simon's body sprawled out in the road. His head lay in a pool of blood expelled

25

during his last, lung-busting moments. They'd already gathered from the news reports that the final throes of the disease were fantastically painful, sending the victim into paroxysms of agony, but they'd heard nothing save a few coughs. HAV3N had claimed Simon Gardener without much fuss.

'Do we just leave it there?' Josh asked Clive, not specifying whether he was talking about the car, or the body.

'Yes,' Clive said. 'We'll leave it. If anyone else comes, it'll help slow them down.'

The crew were working three-hour shifts. Josh had taken a break around 10.00 p.m., returning at one in the morning. He went off again at 4.00 a.m., grey-faced and exhausted, but returned later along with his mum and Martha, who had been running an all-night coffee and sandwiches service from the kitchen in the pub, or HQ as it was now being called. As they got to the barricade, they saw that another car had arrived in the early morning – Mrs Fletcher was now lying in the road with a crossbow bolt through her throat.

'She just came running,' Pete said by way of explanation. 'We told her to stop.' He stared at Josh as he spoke, a note of panic in his voice, some underlying chaos within him that he was struggling to control.

'There was nothing else we could do,' he added.

Josh spoke as calmly as he was able. 'You did what you had to.'

Josh's mum's BMW crept down the lane quietly

again just after seven thirty in the morning, bringing fresh coffee and news. Judith got out and Clive came over to chat.

Sam wandered across to the car too, and Martha wound down the window. They smiled at each other. They'd always got on well, Sam giving Martha gentle cheek while she'd tut in mock disapproval at his puerile jokes.

'Hi, Sam,' Martha said now.

'Hiya,' he mumbled. 'Thanks for the coffee.'

'You're welcome,' she replied. 'It's a cold night out here.'

'I know,' he agreed.

'The power's gone off,' she told him.

'Probably a fuse,' he said. 'You were playing your stereo too loud again.'

She grinned. Sam knew very well Martha wasn't that into music, and she certainly never turned up the stereo too loud – she was more likely to be found with her nose in a book. 'Yeah, that's probably it,' she said.

Their conversation was interrupted by Josh and Pete, who came over to talk to Judith, to get the news. She updated them on the other barricade, where she and Martha had just been, reporting that no one had tried to come through that way.

'I'd guess the other road's blocked further down,' Pete said. 'Simon wouldn't have come from the Guildford direction otherwise.'

'Simon Gardener?' Judith asked. The men glanced at each other uneasily, then Clive told her what had happened.

'Oh God, that's awful. Susan's beside herself,' Judith said. 'She keeps popping round to ask if I've heard anything. I'd better tell her.'

'Don't, Mum,' Josh said. 'No point, really.'

When everyone turned to look at him, he shrugged. 'Well, let's face it; we're probably all going to get it anyway, so no point making her more miserable than she has to be.'

'Josh!' Martha said. 'That's a terrible thing to say.'

'I agree,' Pete said. 'We don't know we're going to get it.'

'No,' Judith agreed, shaking her head. 'And regardless of that, Susan needs to know the truth. She needs to grieve, even if she is going to follow him soon enough.'

'Judith,' Clive said kindly. 'If Susan finds out her husband's body is lying across the Guildford Road, crawling with ants, what do you think she's going to do?'

The twins' mother considered this, then nodded briefly. 'Good point, I'd better keep schtum for now. Anything else?'

'Mia Fletcher... is dead as well,' Clive said quietly. Martha saw her mum close her eyes and lean against the car for support; she and Mrs Fletcher had been friendly, and Martha sometimes baby-sat for the Fletchers' daughter Ellie.

'That poor little girl,' Judith breathed softly. 'And poor Bryan.'

Josh and Martha looked at each other, unused to seeing their mother broken like this.

After a moment, though, she straightened, stiffened, a look of quiet determination on her face. She forced a smile and went to collect the empty coffee cups.

'Tough cookie, your mum,' Sam said to Josh.

He nodded. She'd considered the best way to deal with it and carried on. People react in different ways, he thought. But they were all going to need to be a little harder from now on.

If they survived for long enough.

5.30 P.M.

And so it went on. The villagers relieving one another every three hours. They ate lunch on the barricades, trying not to think about the dead bodies a few metres away. They drank coffee, talked and waited. It wasn't until the early evening that a third car turned up. A blue Audi.

'Who is that?' Clive asked.

'I'm not sure,' Josh said, peering out into the grey morning.

The barricade at that time was manned by Clive, Josh, Sam and Reg Walker.

Reg climbed up on the barrier to see.

'Les Rogers,' he said. He gripped his old service revolver and checked the safety catch. 'Get up here with that shotgun, Sam.'

'That's Mark's dad,' Sam said, as he clambered up to join them.

The car slowed as it passed Simon's body and then sped up again, swerving past Mrs Fletcher's prone corpse. Clive waved furiously, showing his gun, but the car didn't stop until it was just a dozen metres from the barricade.

Sam was still holding the shotgun at that point, and he lifted it half-heartedly. His mouth was dry. Though he'd been holding the gun off and on for quite some time now, suddenly he was pointing it in the direction of another human being. Part of him wished it had been Josh's turn with the gun.

Les Rogers sat in his car, glaring at the blockade. Eventually he got out and stepped towards them.

'That's far enough, Les,' Clive called, pointing his hunting rifle at the newcomer's chest. 'I don't want to shoot you, but I will if I have to.'

Les looked at him. A great bear of a man, he was not the sort of guy who let others push him around. He ran his own business, something to do with plumbing, in Basingstoke. A self-made man and pleased with himself for it. He always drank too much at village social occasions, roaring with laughter to begin with, arguing aggressively with his cronies as the day wore on.

'Bollocks, you will!' he shouted up at Clive.

'I don't care if you haven't got it—' Clive began, but Les cut him off with a dismissive wave of one hand.

'Of course I've got it,' Rogers spat. He rubbed the back of his neck, as if to demonstrate, wincing as the bubo burst. He showed them his palm, now smeared with black, sticky liquid.

'Then what are you doing here, man?!' Reg shouted. 'You'll kill us!'

'You've all got it anyway,' Mark's dad shouted, then doubled over as a coughing fit enveloped him. 'We're all dead,' he continued once it had passed. 'The only question is how we spend our last few hours. You may wish to sit on a pile of mattresses, playing with pea-shooters. Personally, I want to eat a pork chop, drink some twelve-year-old single malt, see my son, then make love to my wife one last time.' He paused to grin madly at the heads peering at him over the parapet. 'Then I shall despatch my wife and son as painlessly as possible,' he carried on, 'before turning the gun on myself.'

The four defenders stared at him in amazement.

Les Rogers smiled in the silence and took another step forward.

'You're not doing that, Mr Rogers,' Sam said in a firm voice, stopping the man in his tracks.

Rogers squinted against the weak morning sun.

'Is that little Sammy Hilfenhaus? With a bloody big gun too! Allowed to come out with the men, are we? They must be desperate.' He coughed again and spat on the floor, a great wad of red mucus. As he dipped his head, they saw the sticky black bubo on his neck, glistening in the searchlights.

'You're not coming in,' Sam repeated.

'And who's going to stop me?' Rogers asked. He took another stride towards them. Then there was a roar and the top of his head tore itself away and covered his Audi windscreen with a fine spray of gore. Curiously, his eyes remained untouched and Les Rogers appeared to be watching Sam with quite some considerable surprise as his body first swayed, then collapsed slowly backwards with a wet crunch, as what was left of his skull hit the ground.

Everyone except Josh remained transfixed by the corpse for some time, as if expecting it to stand and come towards them again. Josh was looking at the smoke curling out of the barrel of the shotgun in Sam's hands.

'*I'm* going to stop you,' Sam said firmly. 'That's who.'

2

Judith finished replacing the batteries on the old portable radio and twiddled the tuning knob.

'Still nothing,' she told Martha. The DAB had stopped working when the power went off that morning. Judith had taken her time lighting candles around the house.

Even before the DAB had given up it had been broadcasting nothing but a pre-recorded and rather vague message from the BBC. '*Stay in your homes. Do not attempt to travel. Wait for further information from the government.*' That sort of thing.

'What did we pay all those taxes for, if the government's just going to collapse at the first sign of trouble?' Judith asked.

Martha coughed behind her. Saying nothing.

'And as for all that licence-fee money we hand the BBC ... the least they could do is tell us what's going on. Surely three thousand people can't have called in sick?'

Martha coughed again.

'Hand over your mouth, darling,' Judith said

33

sharply. She twiddled the knob again, thought perhaps she'd picked up a signal, and went back. But no, there was nothing there. 'I'll try long wave.'

'Mum,' Martha said quietly.

'Though if I do find something on long wave they'll just interrupt it for the shipping forecast,' Judith continued.

'Mum,' Martha said, louder. 'It's getting bigger.'

Judith turned round, but squeezed her eyes tight shut as she did so, delaying until the last possible second visual confirmation of her worst nightmare.

'Look,' Martha said, impatient now.

Judith opened her eyes. Martha stood with her back to her mother, holding up her thick blonde hair. On the nape of her neck lay a glistening, purple-black bubo.

Judith took her daughter's arms and moved them away. She turned her round and hugged her tight.

'I'm sorry, Mum,' Martha said as the older woman shuddered with great, silent sobs. They stood clenched tightly together for a few minutes. Judith's sobs gradually weakened, and Martha felt her mother's muscles tensing again. Martha admired her; she was a strong woman, attractive and smart. But this also meant sometimes she could seem a little hard. She had never been one to overdo the emotion. Not like Kitty's mum, who perhaps went too far the other way, and wasn't the sort to handle a crisis well.

Judith stood back and forced a smile. 'Come on,

let's get you to bed, young lady. I'll dose you up and we'll see if you can't sleep it off.'

'Mum, I'm not a toddler. I know what this means,' Martha said, a pale, thin hand wandering towards the nape of her neck.

'We don't know anything,' Judith said quickly. 'Your father said there's always a chance, and he knows better than anyone else.'

Martha looked back at her mother and smiled her sad, placid smile. 'Dad's a hundred miles away,' she said.

Judith paused as she seemed to be considering what exactly would be the best way to deal with a daughter who'd be dead by morning.

'Up to bed,' she said firmly. 'I'm your mother and I know best.'

6.03 P.M.

'We can't leave the body lying there,' Clive said. 'Mark will be here for his next shift in an hour or so.'

Sam had gone for a walk up the road towards the village, to clear his head. Josh had offered to go with him but his friend had wanted to be alone. 'Maybe we should tell Mark not to come back?' Josh suggested.

Clive shook his head. 'He'll find out soon enough and won't thank us for keeping it from him. No, we wrap his dad's body and put it in the Audi. If we get through this, we can bury them all properly.'

Josh found it comforting that the no-nonsense Clive was still thinking they might get over this. Maybe there were villages and towns all over England – the world, even – doing the same thing, barricading themselves, trying to hold the disease at bay? Maybe his dad would find the vaccine, save them all? Josh was trying not to get his hopes up too much, though he so desperately wanted to see his father again. He wanted his father to see him as well, standing firm on the barricade, protecting the village.

'Risky, though, isn't it?' Mad Pete asked, looking out at the body lying in its pool of darkening blood. 'Touching it? Moving it? Won't we catch it?'

'Riskier just to leave it there,' Reg replied. 'We need to clear it... *him* away from the barricade.'

Pete nodded. Josh had noticed that when Reg spoke, which was quite rare, people listened. He gave off a sense of authority. Clive talked a lot, but Josh got the impression people didn't entirely trust his opinion.

Nonetheless, nobody moved. They just stood, watching the pool of blood slowly expand across the road.

Then Sam, grey-faced and quiet, came back up onto the barricade.

'I killed him,' he said. 'I should clear up.'

Clive shook his head at first. But Sam insisted.

'I'll help,' Pete clapped a hand on Sam's shoulder.

The two put on face masks and took a floor sheet from Mark's van. Passing through the barricade they laid it out over the body, Sam focusing on the shoes, unable to look at the head. Together they rolled the heavy corpse over, wrapping it securely. Then, with difficulty, they drag-pulled it into the passenger side of the still-idling Audi.

Pete reversed the car a hundred metres down the road, being careful to avoid Mrs Fletcher's body, and then came trotting back and peered up at Clive and Reg who were watching them from the barricade.

'Do you think we should stay out here?' Pete asked. 'We might be contaminated now.'

Clive thought for a while. 'No,' he said. 'Let's face it; since Les Rogers turned up, spraying his germs, all of us here are likely to get it. It's them in the village we need to protect. Come back in. Have a coffee.'

Sam was grateful to get into the warmth of Mark's electrical van, parked a dozen or so metres behind the barricades. He and Pete were both shivering, and not just from the cold. As the engine idled quietly so as to not wear down the battery, Sam churned things over and over in his head. He had actually just killed a man.

The two sipped coffee from a Thermos as they listened to Pete's iPod through speakers, anxious for some form of familiar comfort.

'You know how we didn't tell Mrs Gardener about killing her husband?' Sam managed. 'So as to avoid upsetting her?'

'Yes,' Pete replied.

'Well, can we also not tell Mark it was me that shot his dad in the face?'

Pete paused for a second or two. 'Yeah, I think that's probably fair enough,' he answered. 'We'll just say one of us did it and leave it at that. What happens on this barricade stays on this barricade.'

'Thanks,' Sam replied.

He looked at the others perched on the road block. He saw Reg slapping Clive on the shoulder and Josh laughing at something one of them had said. Even at a time like this, people could still make each other laugh. Sam knew Josh was terrified underneath, just like him. But Josh always seemed to be in control. Always knew the right thing to say, and when to say nothing at all, a trick Sam was yet to learn. Having something to do, holding a gun in your hand, it made it seem you were in control, Sam thought. That you had some power to stop what was coming. Whatever you do, don't stop to think about the reality. Don't let your mind wallow in the certainty of impending death.

'Watch Mark with his gun,' Pete said. 'He's jumpy. Always messing with it, fiddling with the safety catch. He's going to kill someone if he doesn't calm down.'

Sam nodded.

'Sorry,' Pete said. 'He's not a friend of yours, is he?'

'No,' Sam said. 'He lives over the road. My sister thinks he's fit – I think he's a loser.'

Pete grunted by way of a response.

'What's this music?' Sam asked, trying to take his mind off the knot in his gut.

'King Crimson,' Pete replied. 'You don't know this album?'

Sam shook his head and Pete rolled his eyes in disbelief.

'This just happens to be one of the defining albums of the late sixties, man,' he said. 'This album basically created the genre of progressive rock.'

'Uh-huh,' Sam replied diplomatically.

'Without this album,' Pete continued, warming to his theme, 'we'd never have had Jethro Tull, or Supertramp, or even Pink Floyd.'

'A tragedy,' Sam said, trying not to grin.

'That's right, a musical tragedy,' Pete agreed, nodding furiously. 'Imagine no Pink Floyd...' He trailed off, shaking his head in horror at the idea.

'Dad has...had some Pink Floyd,' Sam said, taking a sip of the rapidly cooling coffee.

'I'm sorry...' Pete said awkwardly. 'About your dad.'

Sam nodded, unwilling to speak for fear the tears would start. *Damn!* He'd been trying not to think about his father. Now he had this picture of him standing in his study, listening to records with his big, goofy earphones, eyes closed, miming along to the music. Playing air guitar. Sam used to peep round the door, laughing at him and loving him for not caring how ridiculous he looked.

'I thought at first it was a load of shit,' Pete said after a long pause.

'Pink Floyd? Yeah, me too.'

Pete shot him a wounded look. 'No, I mean this HAV3N thing. I was sure it was just the tabloids getting all hysterical again.'

Sam shrugged. 'Yeah, Dad said the same thing – that's why he went to work. Lot of people did.'

'Yeah.'

'Every year they're panicking about something, Dad said, even before bird flu. Swine flu, and before that CJD and before that AIDS and before that something else.'

'Bastards,' Pete muttered.

Sam looked out his window into the hedgerow, where a robin bustled in and out of the branches, engaged in some mysterious avian activity. If you stopped thinking for a minute and just looked through a car window, you could almost pretend everything was normal and the world wasn't drowning in blood-flecked sputum. That he hadn't just killed a man.

'My brother Jim got it,' Pete said after a while. 'He was one of the early ones. Lived in London, you see.'

Sam didn't reply, waiting for the next bit.

'Spoke to him on the phone on Tuesday. He said

he felt a bit lousy. Armpits hurting, big spot on the back of his neck. Coughing down the phone at me.'

It was a familiar story now. The news had been regularly describing the symptoms for a couple of days before the newsreaders started to get it too. One, Miriam Bennett, had actually insisted on staying on air even as the disease ran through her. The floor manager had finally dragged her off the sofa when she'd coughed up a foetid, brain-sized lump of oesophagus and collapsed unconscious over the *BBC Breakfast* coffee table, scattering wax fruit.

'When I phoned back that afternoon Jim was dead,' Pete went on. 'I spoke to his girlfriend, who'd started coughing too. She was just mental with fear. It was horrible. Screaming at me to come and help. I had to hang up on her in the end . . .' Pete trailed off, staring into the middle distance.

'There was nothing you could do,' Sam told him gently. Now it was his turn to feel awkward. Everyone had lost someone.

There then followed a long silence. Sam desperately tried to think of something else to say. But there was nothing. In the wing mirror, Sam saw Mark approaching on his bike, heading down the lane towards them. What was already the most terrible day of Mark's life was about to become a whole lot worse.

Pete coughed.

'You OK?' Sam asked after a few seconds.

'Fine,' Pete replied. But then Sam noticed, out of the corner of his eye, that Pete's free right hand shifted from the crossbow in his lap and up to the back of his neck, rubbing something there. Then he coughed again.

6.43 P.M.

In a brief hiatus between racking coughs that felt as though they were tearing apart her lungs. Martha lay staring at the lilac-tasselled light shade which she'd had since she was a baby. She'd paid no attention to it for years. But now she could barely move there was little else to focus on. She wondered if she should tell her mother it needed dusting. There was a tiny spider web floating in the air, half-detached from the tassels. When you're seriously ill, your world contracts to what you can feel and what you can see. Martha's world had become coughing and lilac light shades.

She felt trapped. Though she was covered by nothing more than a thin, sweat-soaked sheet, she felt compressed, squashed. As though the devil was sitting on her chest. Her armpits and groin ached and burned. Even if she'd had the strength to move she'd learned not to do so. The briefest movement was pure agony.

Martha had followed the spread of the disease closely. She had always planned to follow in her father's footsteps, into science – biology or chemistry – and she had chosen her A-levels accordingly. Well before the sudden surge in infections over the last few days, Martha had been convinced this was bigger than the government or the media were suggesting. She'd found watching the news distressing, and reading some of the doomsday predictions on the internet had left her terrified. Martha had phoned her father and he'd tried to reassure her.

'We're working on a vaccine now, love,' he'd said. But there was something in his tone which didn't sound right to her. And he'd told her he loved her so many times. It was like he was saying goodbye.

Trying to avoid discussion of it, and with school closed, she'd found escape down at McGoverns' farm on Wycliffe Lane where she earned pocket money feeding the lambs and collecting eggs from the hysterical chickens.

Two weeks ago Martha had arrived at the farm on a grey Saturday morning to find they'd slaughtered all the chickens, calming their hysteria permanently. The bodies had been stuffed into thick black bags and were piled high in the barnyard; they were awaiting collection by a truck that would take them to be burned according to the standards established by the Emergency Disease Control Act.

But it was too late by then. The disease was already widespread amongst bird populations: chickens, turkeys and, of course, pigeons who were spreading it everywhere. Curiously the avian strain of the disease was not nearly so virulent as the human strain. Most birds survived, carrying the virus as they moved, or were moved, around the country. Killing the chickens was like shutting the stable gate after the horse had bolted and the stable had burned down. The cull had been done so the government could be seen to be doing something.

A waste of time and a needless loss of animal life. But that was what governments did. That's what humans did. Martha had shrugged inwardly and carried on helping with the sheep.

Now she coughed again, gingerly turning to one side to spit a clump of noisome lung tissue into a bowl left by Judith for precisely this purpose. As she moved she felt the bubo crack again and the warm trickle of fluid slide down the side of her neck. Martha longed to escape her disease-ravaged body, if only for a few seconds, just to catch her breath. She felt like the little spider web on the light shade. Half-detached, needing nothing more than a nudge to break free and float off to who knows where. If only she could detach herself from her physical form. Was it possible? If she stopped fighting and let go? Would she just unhook and float away? Maybe if she willed herself to stop breathing...

But she was interrupted by the return of her mother with fresh sheets and the faintest scent of lavender and she decided to hang on for a little longer.

Cold dread gripped Sam's guts as he watched Mark
ride up, cheerfully enough, and park his bike. Clive
went off to meet him while Reg and Josh stood,
uselessly, on the barricade, unsure where to look.

Clive laid his rifle down on the ground and stood
face-to-face with Mark. The older man spoke for a
while, and then placed a hand on Mark's shoulder as
the young man's knees suddenly buckled. Then
suddenly Mark straightened and was up onto the
barricade in a flash, looking along the road. He tried
to climb over, evidently intending to head out to his
father's car, but Josh and Reg held him back, trying
to calm him down. Mark spun to Reg. He said something, but Reg shook his head.

Mark spoke again, this time loud enough for Sam
to hear.

'*Who?*'

'Oh, bollocks,' Sam muttered.

But then Pete coughed again loudly and Sam
realised they had more pressing concerns. He got out
of the car. Mark glared as he approached, a slightly
deranged look in his eye.

'Was it you?' Mark spat. 'Did you shoot him?
You've been swinging that gun around. Got a bit
trigger-happy maybe?'

'You can talk,' Sam replied hotly. 'You—'

'Now, now, you two,' Clive called. 'Mark, maybe

you need to head back to the village, be with your mum. You're in shock.'

'I'm not going anywhere,' Mark replied coldly. 'I—'

'Pete's got a cough,' Sam interrupted.

There was a pause as everyone digested this.

'Any other symptoms?' Reg asked.

Sam hesitated before responding. '...Yeah, he's got one of those black zits on the back of his neck.'

'Shit, crap, damn!' Mark said, punctuating his words with slams of his palm against the cab of the flatbed truck he stood on.

Pete still sat in the van.

'It's huge,' Sam went on.

Sam and Josh exchanged glances as Mark continued to swear and beat the top of the truck. They hadn't had much of a chance to speak during the chaos since Sam had shot Mr Rogers, but each drew comfort from the other's presence.

'We're *all* dead now. Dead!' Mark hissed, on the verge of tears. 'It's your fault,' he spat, pointing a finger at Sam. 'I told you not to get too close to Simon. You went too far. Now Dad's dead...' he trailed off and slumped to his knees, sobbing silently.

Sam just shrugged. 'We've all got it anyway,' he said quietly. 'What difference does it make?'

'That's not helpful, Sam,' Clive said.

Mark looked down at Sam. 'It *was* you, wasn't it?'

'It doesn't matter who it was,' Reg said, stepping in. 'Any one of us would have done it. We have to protect the village. Your dad admitted he had it.'

Mark jumped down from the barricade and over to his bike where he picked up Clive's rifle. He clutched it closely, hand squeezing the stock as though it were Sam's throat he had hold of.

'What are you doing?' Clive asked.

'Calm down, Mark,' Josh said, just loud enough to be heard.

Mark looked over to him.

'*He's* been sitting there in that van, *my* van, with a . . . with an infected,' he said. 'If Pete's got it, then so's he. We ought to finish them both off. Remember,' he said, turning to Clive, 'we have to protect the village! If my dad had to die then so should they.'

Reg sat on the barricades, still clutching his revolver, watching the exchange with a sad look on his face. If Mark tipped over the edge and violence ensued, Josh was worried that Reg would be little help, Falklands or not. He, however, had Sam's shotgun. And now he lifted it slightly. Not in a threatening way, but just to remind Mark that he wasn't the only one armed.

'No one's finishing anyone off,' Josh said. 'We stay cool, OK?'

'Mark's right,' a voice called from behind them. Pete had got out of the van and he took a few steps towards them, swaying slightly. He coughed like he had a throatful of marbles and sat back against the car to rest before speaking again.

'You need to finish me off,' he said. 'I'm going downhill quickly. I'm no use to you now.'

'Let's do them both,' Mark said, looking at Sam as Josh stared at Pete in shock.

'No!' Josh cried.

'No,' Pete agreed. 'Sam's not showing symptoms. No point in doing this earlier than necessary. You might need him on the barricade. Remember, we still have a job to do here. We must defend the village.'

'Still thinking like a Saxon warrior, eh?' Sam raised a smile from Pete, which was all too quickly snuffed out by another bout of racking coughs.

'Come,' Pete rasped dramatically, when he'd finished. 'Let it be done.'

'Now?' Sam enquired. 'You don't want a last cigarette, or something?'

'I've given up,' Pete said. 'Bad for the lungs.' He coughed again. 'But do me a favour, will you?' Croaking, he looked Sam in the eye.

Sam nodded.

'Use this, eh?' Pete said holding up his crossbow.

Sam raised an eyebrow.

Pete shrugged. 'Warrior's death, y'know?'

Sam nodded again and walked over to take the weapon.

'Leave this to me, lads,' he called to the others.

Josh stepped forward, not sure how he could be of

help, but wanting to stand with his friend. Reg grabbed his shoulder. 'Don't get closer than you have to,' he said.

Mark glared at them, for now holding his tongue as he watched to see what would happen.

Sam hefted the crossbow. The stock was smooth and he could sense the power of the twisted cable, stretched taut. A steel bolt lay snugly in its oiled groove straining to fly.

'Ready for this?' he asked.

Pete nodded and shuffled round to the side of the van to stand proud, facing his executioner directly.

Kitty sat cross-legged at the end of her bed staring at her laptop. The only other light came from a church candle burning on the pine chest of drawers at the other end of the room. She frowned at the white page on the laptop's screen. PAGE NOT FOUND. That was all there was on the internet. Not that she was actually *on* the internet, of course. It was just the screen her browser displayed when the broadband company had screwed up again and cut off the feed.

She hit BACK and got Bebo. But this wasn't a live page, either. It was just the last page she'd looked at before the networks had all collapsed. She read her friend Daisy's final status update again:

Feel rlly bad now. Coff n coff. Bits cmg up. Yuk!!!

All her friends were the same. Swapping symptoms. Kitty hadn't really been worried for herself.

She never got ill. It just didn't occur to her that she might get the disease too. And at first people weren't too concerned. But when the death rates started soaring and even the broadsheet newspapers started suggesting it was time to panic, no one on Bebo was talking about anything else. Suddenly your friends' status updates became compulsive reading and the 'OMG! I've got HAV3N!' group quickly hit the million members mark.

Most of Kitty's friends lived in Guildford, which was where she herself went to school. Guildford had been hit by the disease hard and early. Most of her friends had gone down with HAV3N before the internet had crashed. *Stay inside*, they warned her. *Not trying to be funny, Kits, but you do NOT want to get this. It is mingin'.*

She hit back on the browser a few more times and found a cached Twitter page, which was, of course, mad with #HAV3N tweets. Everyone saying the same thing. A mass tweet of coughing and death:

I'm really worried now about this. Where's the government?

I have these weird boils under my arms. I can't get NHS Direct on the phone even.

I'm signing off now, can't stop coughing.

Where is all this Tamiflu they promised us?

WTF! The boil just popped. I have black goo running out my sleeves.

Trains not running.

Have taken 3 packets of Beechams in contravention of instructions lol!

Anyone else having trouble with broadband?

Police just on voicemail – what's new, though?

O2 services out.

Not being melodramatic or anything, guys, but I think I'm going to die.

Have you SEEN the traffic jam on the A40? I've been stuck outside World of Leather for 3 hours!

This is bad. Really bad.

Describe your own death in 140 characters or less.

Kitty's father had told her not to worry. That it would blow over.

'This happens every year,' he'd said as he'd jammed papers into his briefcase at the breakfast table the day before yesterday. 'The papers go bananas about the latest flu virus, then forget all about it after a while until next year.'

Then he'd kissed her on the top of her head and was gone.

Deep down, even then, Kitty had known her father was wrong. She'd been fighting the fear ever since. She didn't say anything to anyone, though. It was better to say nothing, to pretend she didn't know what was happening. That way she could act like everything was normal. And maybe, if she did, her dad would turn out to be right. Maybe it *would* all blow over.

She flicked back further through her recent history

looking for the memory of the page she wanted. There, Facebook. And just a few days ago, when HAV3N really *was* just a background worry, like climate change or terrorism, that was when she'd received the personal message from him that had burned itself into her memory and would stay there longer than it would on the laptop, which was nearly out of battery.

You going to the Harvest Festival next week? Maybe see you there? Xx J.

OK, so it wasn't a date. And even if it was it was only the Harvest Festival, which the whole village went to. But it meant he was thinking about her. Maybe she was just imagining it, but it seemed like maybe lately Josh was showing a bit more interest in her. Or was that just wishful thinking? Sending her that message told her one thing at least. That he liked her enough to want to hang out. It meant something, didn't it? He'd sent two kisses. Which boys generally didn't do.

She'd really been looking forward to the Harvest Festival.

Her laptop battery light went red and she tutted. It couldn't be as bad as Sam had said, she told herself for the hundredth time. *They'll get the lights back on soon and I'll be able to recharge the computer.* She snapped the lid shut and stood up, stretching like a cat, trying to lose the knot in her belly as she looked at the photograph in a wooden frame on her dresser.

It was a picture of her, Martha and Sam, atop a hill on some hike her father had dragged them all on last summer. Kitty loved that picture, because she and Martha looked so happy, despite having been so tired at the time, and so sick of their hair being blown across their faces. Sam could be seen in the background raising his arms in the air as he shouted defiance into the wind. The photograph had been taken by Josh, which was why he wasn't in it and why it was so good. It seemed to capture them all so well, the flying hair, the grinning girls and the shouting Sam fixed for all time. Captured just as they were.

She walked to the window and looked out in the direction of the barricade where she knew Josh and her brother were. She could see nothing in the coal-dust darkness. She shivered, and not entirely from the cold seeping through the single-glazed sash window, plucking at her body warmth. There was something coming, something she wasn't convinced she was ready for.

'Are you sure about this?' Sam asked, uncertain now that it looked like he might actually have to go through with it.

Pete nodded. 'My life is forfeit, brave yeoman of Surrey. I go to join my Gods.'

Sam blinked and raised the crossbow. 'Okey-doke,' he said. They'd moved Mark's van a dozen metres up the road, away from the barricades, and had laid sheets and tarpaulins down, ready to wrap Pete's body afterwards.

'Right in the head, OK?' Pete croaked, pointing to his forehead. 'That way it'll be quick.'

Sam hesitated, suddenly worried he might mess this up. 'How quick?' he asked.

'Don't worry, it's a twelve-inch-long, steel-tipped, solid aluminium bolt, half an inch in diameter,' Pete replied. 'It'll be quick enough.' Then there followed thirty seconds of hunched-up, rib-cracking coughing. Sam shuffled closer a few paces so as to reduce the chances he'd miss. Pete leaned forward, forcing his red-rimmed eyes open, staring death in the face.

Sam paused, willing himself to pull the trigger. He knew it was the right thing to do. Pete wanted it, anyway. Better this than drowning in your own corrupted lungs. And yet he couldn't quite bring himself to...

'Do it!' Mark screamed from behind him and Sam jerked in surprise, squeezing the trigger instinctively. But the jerk caused his aim to waver and the bolt missed Pete's forehead and instead hit him twenty centimetres lower down, in his throat. The bolt ran straight through, jerking his body backwards and pinning him to the side of Mark's van. Sam stared in horror as the very-much-alive Pete thrashed and twitched, unable to free himself from the pinion. His mouth opened in a gurgling scream as rivulets of blood poured from it. The hole in his throat was a gurgling mess of gristle and blood-spattered, broken windpipe. Sam looked uselessly down at the spent crossbow in his hands. Even if he'd had another bolt, he didn't know how to re-load.

But then there was a crack and Pete slumped dead against the van, a neat bullet hole in his left temple.

Sam looked up to see Reg holding his revolver with a steady hand.

'Sorry, Sam,' Reg said. 'I should have stepped in earlier.'

There was silence as they stood and stared sickly at the bloody, torn corpse. Mark walked off without a word and climbed the barricade, facing away from them, looking down the road towards his father's car. Sam was first to break the silence.

'OK,' he said. 'This is another thing not to tell the others about.'

Josh sank to his knees, trying not to let the tears come, because once they started they'd never stop.

Sam felt surprisingly OK; it was as though having survived the most horrific experiences and done this...this terrible thing, he'd decided there was nothing else to do but laugh. Or maybe he was just hysterical. 'Reg,' he said. 'When it comes time... y'know?'

'Don't worry,' Reg said grimly. 'When it comes time, I'll do us all.'

Refusing offers of help, Sam cleared Pete's body away. First he had to pull the dangling corpse forward, off the shaft of the bolt and onto the road surface where he had laid a couple of sheets and a heavy canvas. He wrapped poor old Pete up and dragged him to the side of the road. It was dark by the time he'd finished, the car headlights doing little to ward off the sense of impending doom the night brought with it. Sam washed his hands with bottled water and tried not to think about what he'd just done as he turned to the others, smiling weakly.

'Well done, Sam,' Josh said softly.

'Yeah, good for you, Sam,' Clive added. Reg winked. Mark said nothing, he stood atop the barricade, looking out into the floodlit road.

'What was that?' Reg said, suddenly, cocking his head. 'Did you hear something?'

They all listened for a minute, then Mark spoke. 'I can't hear a damn—'

'. . . Shhh,' Josh cut in.

'Don't shush me, you little—'

'Shut up, boy,' Reg called sharply. 'Listen.'

Then it was there, and Josh wondered how he could have missed it before. In the distance, across dark fields of stubble towards Guildford, they could hear the regular, if faint, sound of an engine of some sort.

'It's a car,' Josh said.

'No, it's harsher than that,' Reg replied thoughtfully. As they listened, the sound grew louder and developed into a thudding beat.

'It's a motorbike,' Sam said from down below. He and Josh looked at each other – nobody in the village apart from them rode bikes. 'It's the army, maybe?'

'Maybe,' Reg replied doubtfully. 'Where's it coming from?'

They listened carefully a while longer; the bike's engine roared and revved irregularly, suggesting the rider was on rough terrain.

'Over there,' Josh said, pointing out into the fields.

'It's a dirt bike,' Sam said.

'Avoiding the barricades,' Reg said.

'Clive!' Reg called. 'Get in your car and head to the village. Find out what's going on, if you can, then come back and report.'

Clive nodded, apparently having ceded authority to Reg. As he got into his car and reversed quickly away towards the village, the men turned to look at each other. In the harsh glare of the headlights from Mark's van, they looked pale and defeated. No one had anything to say. They were all thinking the same thing. That maybe, just maybe, the motorbike offered hope.

But as the sound of the engine gradually died away, it was replaced by the rather more unwelcome sound of Sam coughing.

Coughing hard.

Kitty decided to head down the road to visit Martha, which her mother had expressly told her not to do.

She wanted to see her friend. Though more than two years her senior, Martha had always been nice to Kitty, including her in her games and confidences. As the only teenage girls in the village, the two saw a lot of each other, especially as their respective brothers were inseparable. The two girls were very different, however. Though Kitty looked up to Martha, she sometimes found her a bit straight-laced, since while Martha loved nothing more than a quiet night in, reading, Kitty would rather have been out with her mates in Guildford, or at a friend's party.

As it happened, Kitty's mother had actually forbidden her from leaving the house altogether. She'd meant it too, as Kitty's protests had been met not with the usual World of Shouting but the much rarer Sit-down Earnest Chat. 'Do this for me,' her mother had asked her, red-eyed. But Kitty had never been one for following orders. She stopped halfway down the stairs, listening for her mother, but heard nothing. Maybe she was out, Kitty thought. At church, perhaps? Her mother, Monica, had been spending a lot of time there since losing contact with her husband.

Kitty slipped downstairs, unnoticed, and snuck out the back door. She was careful to close the catch quietly, a trick she'd learned from Sam long ago. Whilst Martha would never have left the house after being specifically told not to, Kitty had a rebellious streak in her. She made her way down to the end of the garden and let herself out through the sagging wooden gate that led to the path which ran behind the gardens of Highland Terrace. Few adults came this way, the path being overgrown with nettles and brambles. Kitty's calves were soon wet from the weeds as she hurried along in the darkness, her way lit only by the occasional white glare from a battery-operated security light. She opened the Pirbrights' back gate and entered the garden. The swish of uncut grass and the rustle of her gilet at first obscured the sound of the voices, but as she rounded the shed she noticed them and stopped. She recognised the sound of Martha's mother's voice.

'I wouldn't get too close,' Judith Pirbright said. 'If Martha's got it, I might too. I'll leave the pack on the table if you want one. Bit late to be worrying about cancer now.'

Kitty heard the flare of a match and smelled the sharp tang of cigarette smoke; she blinked in surprise. Feeling she was intruding she shrank against the rough wooden side of the shed.

'God, I needed this,' her mum said. Kitty's eyes widened. Her mother, smoking? 'Do you think that's it, then? It's all over?'

'Michael said there's always a chance, but when I last spoke to him there was still no vaccine. The way he was talking...I don't think there'd be time to distribute it anyway. He's working on an antiviral too, apparently, but...'

Kitty heard the crackle of her mother's cigarette as she drew on it.

'How's Martha?' Monica asked.

'Not good,' Judith said.

'Oh, Judith, I—'

'No, stop,' Judith said. 'I can't start crying now. She needs me strong.'

'What are we going to do?'

'Michael said there's always a chance,' Judith repeated.

'And it's everywhere? America too?'

'Yes. He lost contact with his counterparts in the US two days ago.'

There was a pause. Then Judith spoke again. 'Nothing from Ben?'

Another pause, longer this time, broken eventually by a strangled sobbing sound. Kitty's stomach tightened in fear.

'Oh, Monica,' Judith said. 'I'm sorry. I'm so sorry.'

'Look,' came her mother's voice, after a while. 'I've got to go. Kitty will be wondering where I am.'

Kitty slid down onto the ground, her back to the shed. She curled up into a tight ball as the bubble she'd been trying to hide within finally burst. It was worse than she'd thought. Her friends weren't going to recover. Martha was going to die. Her father wasn't coming home.

She sat there for a long time, hearing the Pirbrights' back door shut as Judith went inside.

A light rain began to fall, tiny darts pricking Kitty's skin. She cried silently.

But then, a sound. A throbbing, irregular growl. Mechanical. It seemed to be coming from behind the house, out towards the fields and allotments. Louder and louder as the machine approached. Was this the army? The government?

Then the garden gate crashed open and she was first dazzled by a light and then half a second later deafened by the roar of a motorbike charging past her. She stood and peered round the corner of the shed, her clothes damp and clingy. The bike came to a stop and the rider dismounted. A few moments later the back door banged as Judith came running out and stopped, staring in amazement. The rider stood for a moment in the glare of the security light. It was a man wearing shiny black leathers and a silver helmet, which he removed as Kitty watched.

'Michael!' Judith cried and ran forward to greet her husband.

Then, in the distance, Kitty heard her mother screaming her name. Backing away reluctantly, she left the scene of the reunion and hurried home, her mind whirling.

A small part of Martha was still rational, still alive and still grounded in reality. That part of her had been sitting and observing as her visions became ever-more lurid.

Mostly these waking dreams were influenced by books she'd read and films she'd watched recently. There were unicorns and vampires, a dancing dwarf and Galadriel from *Lord of the Rings*. Jimmy McNulty from *The Wire* had even come to visit at one point. There was also a lot of fire. Burning hats and flaming hairbrushes, that sort of thing. She was hoping this didn't suggest her post-death destination was to be downwards rather than up.

She tried to explain this to her mother who sat by her side, holding her burning hand. But as she was telling the story, her mother was suddenly gone and Martha's hand dropped to the sheets. With fading strength she turned to the window and saw the glare of the angels arriving for her. She heard the thundering hooves of the horses they rode.

She felt the urge to cough again, but had no strength with which to do it. She could hear her own, rasping breath now that the horses had gone quiet.

It was time to die. When angels came to get you, the sensible thing to do was quit while you were ahead and let them take you. Martha closed her eyes and relaxed, accepting death's grasping claw. But then she heard footsteps and a familiar voice speaking her name. She tutted inwardly and forced her eyes open again.

Another vision, as impossible as the last. Her father couldn't be here – he was in his lab, working to try and stop the disease. Nobody was allowed back in the village. But there he was, standing by the bed, looking down at her with love, concern and guilt. Martha smiled and managed a croaked, 'Love you, Dad. But I have to go now,' and she closed her eyes again.

'You're not going anywhere,' her father said, and she felt, through all the aches and agonies, the pinprick of a needle in the crook of her elbow. Then she lay back and let death claim her.

When Sam had finished his coughing fit, he glanced up to see Mark's rifle pointing at his head. Even in the poor light of the headlights he could see the electrician sweating, terrified either at the prospect of catching the disease from Sam, or of having to shoot him.

'Now, look,' Sam said nervously. 'I appreciate you and I might have our differences...'

'I'm gonna fire,' Mark announced.

'No, Mark,' Josh said as calmly as he could.

'He's got it!' the panicked Mark screamed.

'We've *all* got it, you idiot. What's the hurry?' Josh replied. 'He's not a zombie, for Christ's sake.'

But Mark kept the barrel aimed at Sam's face. Sam reached up to scratch the back of his neck, and stumbled a little before managing to steady himself.

'Go on, then,' he said, defiant. He hawked and spat a huge oyster onto the road. It landed a few centimetres from Mark's foot, causing him to flinch and shift backwards a few metres.

Mark's finger tightened, and Sam tensed, wondering if there'd be time to hear the crack and see the muzzle flash before ... well, before what? That was the question.

'Don't do it!' Josh screamed, but Mark ignored him and began to squeeze the trigger.

Suddenly they were drowned by the flood of approaching headlights, and Mark squinted against the glare, having lost his target. In an instant Josh was on him, knocking the barrel upwards. He heard a crack and the whistle of a bullet in the thin October air. Mark, larger and heavier than Josh, knocked him to the road and punched him in the face; the rifle went clattering across the Tarmac. Then Mark was up and made for the gun, but Reg was there and kicked it into the hedgerow. In his peripheral vision Josh could see the newcomers get out of their car.

Mark wasn't finished. With a grunt, he body-checked the old soldier. Josh, winded, lay helplessly watching the men struggle, then Mark twisted back towards Sam, and Josh saw that somehow the older boy now had hold of Reg's revolver. Again Mark aimed at Sam, his face twisted in fury, blood trickling from his nose.

Josh dragged himself to his feet and again lunged for Mark, who crumpled with the blow and they were sprawling in the ditch, struggling for the revolver. Then the gun fired between them and Mark grunted, relaxing his grip. Josh felt warmth on his chest. He raised himself up from the oddly intimate pose they had ended in, to see blood pumping out of Mark's thigh. The electrician stared back at him with hate, already shivering in shock as blood flowed from the wound.

Then a tall figure arrived and grabbed Josh by the shoulders. Josh looked up at him blearily.

'Dad?' It was impossible. How could his father be here? Someone brushed past them, on the way to attend to the groaning Mark.

'Stay back!' Sam called out, interrupting. 'We're dead men walking here.'

'I have medicine, Sam,' Josh's father said, looking over at him.

Sam peered weakly at Michael.

'Lemsip Max just ain't going to do the trick, Mr Pirbright,' he said, then coughed up a wad of mucus by way of demonstration.

'Let me help you,' Josh's father said to Sam. 'You'll feel better.'

At first Sam eyed him doubtfully, but he nodded and smiled as Mr Pirbright showed him the syringe he was carrying.

And it seemed Sam found his faith, for he then held out his arm and Michael plunged in the needle. Josh watched Sam's knees buckle as he fell forward, into the waiting arms of Michael Pirbright.

*

Kitty heard a knock at the door downstairs and then the hurried padding of her mother's feet on the wooden floors as she went to answer it.

Moments later Monica cried out, 'Kitty! Come here, Kitty!' She ran downstairs to find her mother and Mr Pirbright, who was still in motorbike leathers, supporting an apparently unconscious Sam. Kitty had never seen Mr Pirbright in anything other than a collared shirt, and for a moment he looked exactly like Josh, just back from a ride in the Bourne woods. Kitty hadn't told her mother that she'd seen Mr Pirbright's arrival at his own home.

'He'd contracted the virus,' Pirbright said breathlessly as they manoeuvred Sam to the stairs. Kitty gasped as she saw her brother properly and took an involuntary step back.

'It's fine,' Pirbright said. 'I have a vaccine, combined with powerful antivirals. I've given him a heavy dose,' he explained. 'He's likely to sleep for a long time as his body fights the virus. He'll be weak when he wakes up.' They made their way up the stairs slowly and laid Sam on his bed, Monica taking off his trainers.

'Keep an eye on him, try to get fluids into him,' Mr Pirbright said. 'But I think he should be just fine.'

'How's Martha?' Kitty asked in a little voice. '...And Josh?'

Mr Pirbright turned to her and smiled. 'Josh seems fine. Martha was very ill, but we caught it just in time. She's going to be OK.'

Kitty sighed with relief and sat on the side of Sam's bed, taking her brother's limp hand in hers. How clever of Josh's dad to find the cure. She hardly dared hope that they might be able to find her own father, somewhere in London, and give him the medicine too.

'That's wonderful news,' Monica said. 'Had anyone else...got it?'

Michael nodded grimly. 'Four were lost on the barricades, three more dead that we've found so far in the village, and a few showing symptoms. Those who were on the barricades are now setting up a clinic at the Wheatsheaf for the healthy to get a dose, and we're organising a couple of teams to go door-to-door with the vaccine.'

'How on earth did you manage to organise everything so quickly?' Monica asked, her eyes shining with admiration.

'Disease control is part of my job,' Michael replied morosely. 'Or at least it was. We received training for this sort of thing. Never thought I'd need it.'

'How lucky we are to have you coming to save us,' Monica said. 'Like a knight in shining armour.' As she said this she looked down at her sleeping son, and in so doing missed Mr Pirbright's reaction to her comment.

'Lucky...' he said quietly and Kitty saw Mr Pirbright close his eyes. For a second a look of exhaustion clouded his face. Exhaustion and horror. Just what had he been through?

Mr Pirbright, realising Kitty was watching him, recovered his composure. He smiled and winked. Then he reached into his pocket and handed Monica a syringe and a tiny bottle. 'Just jab it in a buttock and push the plunger, OK?' Monica nodded. 'Five milligrams each for you two, just as a precaution,' he said. 'You might feel light-headed afterwards, so take it easy. Come and find me if there are any other side effects.' And with that he left, clumping down the stairs in his heavy motorcycle boots.

Monica ran to the top of the stairs and shouted after him, 'Thank you, Mr Pirbright! Are you sure there's nothing we can do to help?'

But the only response was the sound of the door slamming downstairs.

Monica came back into Sam's room, smiling for the first time since her husband had left the house two days ago.

They took turns sitting by Sam's bedside that night, occasionally dabbing his forehead with a wet cloth – there wasn't much else they could do. Kitty slept badly during her mother's shifts, crying silently from time to time, haunted by visions of those who hadn't been so lucky. Her father, her grandparents in Dulwich, her friends from school. Were they all dead? As she lay there in the small hours, listening to the creaking of the old timbers, she clung to a faint hope – that maybe the vaccine Mr Pirbright had brought had been distributed all over the country. All over the world. Surely the government would have done something? The army? The Americans?

'Please make it all OK,' she said, clutching Red Ted and squeezing her eyes shut. Mercifully, her thoughts turned to Sam and how Mr Pirbright had saved him and the tears stopped for a time.

3

16 OCTOBER

In the morning, while Monica and Sam slept, both snoring softly, Kitty was disturbed by another knock on the door and she trotted down to answer it. It was Mr Carter, who lived next door. He was wearing a suit as though off on business, which Kitty found odd.

'Hello there, Kitty,' Mr Carter said. 'Could you tell your mother there's to be a meeting, in the church at nine a.m. sharp?'

'What sort of meeting?' Kitty asked.

'Oh, you know, about what to do next. Supplies and what-not.'

'Someone needs to stay and look after Sam,' she said.

'You'll need to do that,' Mr Carter said. 'The meeting's only for grown-ups.'

'Oh, OK. Do you know if the vaccine was distributed everywhere?' she asked. 'It must have got to London.'

'I'm afraid I don't really know,' Mr Carter answered. 'Mr Pirbright seems to be in charge, God bless him. He came over early this morning and asked me to go door-to-door telling people about the meeting. It'll all be made clear there, I think.'

Extracts from the minutes of the meeting of Little Sheen Parish Council St Andrew's Church 16 October

Previous minutes
Due to the exceptional circumstances, the minutes from the previous meeting were declared irrelevant and not read out.

Emergency resolution
Following the tragic death of council president, William Everidge, Michael Pirbright was voted for by a significant majority to take over as interim President.

Two attendees, Reg Walker and Bryan Fletcher, voted against the motion and asked that it should be noted that they opposed the idea that the Parish Council should form the interim administrative body. They called for an entirely new, secular government to be formed, free of the trappings of the church. Their proposal was overruled with further discussion on the proposal to be deferred until the current state of emergency should have passed.

Monica Hilfenhaus proposed a vote of thanks to Michael Pirbright for returning to the village with the vaccine and the antiviral medicine. Without his heroic actions, we would most certainly all have perished. The proposal was unanimously passed.

The incoming president then gave an address, recorded and reproduced here in verbatim:

Thank you all for coming at such short notice. Before we begin, let me assure you that all of those showing symptoms and who received the vaccine last night have made recoveries. Those in whom the disease had reached an advanced stage received the combined vaccine and antiviral medication. They are still sleeping, but there is no reason to think they will not make a full return to health. Mark Rogers, who was accidentally shot at one of the barricades, is also recovering, I understand, though in need of antibiotics. Mrs Stephenson is investigating availability. Indeed, our thanks to Jenny Stephenson whose nurse's training proved invaluable last night at the emergency clinic.

Thanks also to Emily Green, Harry Waldock, Bryan Fletcher and Howard Carter who have spent the night knocking on doors, distributing the vaccine and checking for the sick and dying. Many lives were saved last night due to their efforts. The group is heading out again this morning to search for survivors in neighbouring farms and villages. If there were to be survivors, they are most likely in isolated areas, cut off from other people. There is a limited supply remaining of the vaccine, which will be usable for another week or so and which the search party will take. The antivirals are less stable but should be good for another couple of days, and frankly, if we haven't found anyone alive within two days, we're not going to find anyone.

Some of you have asked about the possibility of the army or government sending help. To that I say the rapidity of the disease and the scenes we have witnessed on television, and those that I myself witnessed on the difficult journey back here, would suggest that we should not count on any outside assistance reaching us any time soon, if ever. The discovery of the vaccine which saved us was an incalculable stroke of luck. Unlikely to be repeated by any other laboratory in the world.

Before I throw the floor open to questions and suggestions, let me just make one final plea. That we keep calm and carry on. We must invoke the Spirit of the Blitz. Obviously things won't be exactly as before, and frankly we shouldn't want them to be. But life carries on. It is important for all of us, but mostly for the children, that there be an air of normality.

That's enough from me for now.

Jenny Stephenson, Interim Health Officer, spoke, calling for a trip to be made to a hospital or pharmacy to stock up on medical supplies. In addition to the antibiotics needed for Mark Rogers, there are at least two diabetics in the village who need supplies of insulin.

Amir Mansoor, Interim Chief Engineer, has made an inspection of the village water supplies and is of the opinion that running water can be restored. Mr Mansoor needs to investigate further and will make a trip to the Southern Water facility near Compton in the next few days. Mr Mansoor wished to stress that he is a qualified structural engineer, so water supplies are not his primary field but that he would do his best.

Clive Mitchell, Interim Procurement Officer, volunteered to lead a foraging trip to Guildford to collect supplies, particularly dried goods for storage. The president agreed, though suggested the trip be delayed until the next day, suggesting it was best to keep the barricades up for another twenty-four hours.

Bryan Fletcher volunteered to form a burial party and dig graves for the seven dead. Monica Hilfenhaus asked if they needed to be buried outside the village for health reasons but President Pirbright assured the meeting that due to the availability of the vaccine, the danger had now passed. Reverend Halfdene, the vicar, said he would lead a service of remembrance and that he expected everyone to attend church this coming Sunday (18 October).

It was proposed by Monica Hilfenhaus that all households should pool their food supplies and that these be shared out amongst all the villagers until the foraging party should return with more. This broadened out into a general discussion about food supplies for the coming winter. It was agreed that a party should be put together, involving the children, to bring in what remained of the year's harvest as soon as possible. Most of this year's harvest is complete and properly stored, but there will be plenty of fresh fruit and vegetables to be found on surrounding farms. Livestock is to be rounded up from surrounding pastures and brought closer to the village. David McGovern volunteered to organise this.

Finally, Reg Walker asked why the surviving four teenagers of the village hadn't been invited to this first meeting. President Pirbright replied that, though the teenagers in question were nearing adulthood, there was still an imperative to protect them from the harsher realities of what we are facing. He expressed concern that two boys had been allowed on the barricades, and went on to suggest that in the longer term consideration might need to be made to protect the four teenagers from the usual perils of young adulthood. When pressed on this point by Reg Walker and Bryan Fletcher, President Pirbright remarked that it was a discussion to be held at a more appropriate time and the subject was dropped.

16 OCTOBER, 10.06 A.M.

When Josh woke up, Pete's crossbow was resting against a wall in his room. He remembered grabbing it in the confusion, before someone had bundled him into a warm car.

The walls of Josh's room were covered in photographs, some enlarged, mostly black and white. A keen amateur photographer, he had a roll of film in the Canon camera on the dresser full of aerial shots of Sam on his motorbike. Josh doubted now they'd ever get printed. Shame, there were some he'd been excited about seeing.

Lying in bed, listening to the cackling of crows in the fields behind the house, he recalled the events of the previous night. Soon after his father had turned up at the barricade, and before he'd had a chance to protest, he'd been injected with an enormous needle.

'What is this?' he'd asked.

'Vaccine, and antivirals,' his father had said as they roughly rolled up his sleeve. 'You'll sleep a long time. You need rest.'

He'd been ordered to bed by his mother upon returning home and sleep overtook him almost immediately, though it was anything but restful, packed with images of death, decay and violence.

This was the first time Josh had had to stop and think, to get his head around what had happened and what was to happen next.

No more college, was the first, insufficient, thought. Josh considered his friends, presumably all dead now. His grandparents, his aunt, uncle and cousins. All the people he'd ever known. All gone? There was a hollowness there, a gaping maw of uncertainty.

And what of the rest of the world? The news reports had made it clear nowhere had been unaffected. But maybe some little islands? Or remote communities in Alaska? Surely some must have escaped? Others must have discovered the vaccine? Not just his own father? But even so, billions must have died. A planet full of corpses. He pushed the thoughts away before they engulfed him.

He stumbled downstairs into the kitchen, rubbing his eyes. Judith gave him a brisk hug, checked him for buboes and made him eat some foul muesli and over-ripe fruit. He could see she was preoccupied by Martha, still in bed in her room, still deathly pale.

Josh was allowed to look in on her briefly. He stood in the doorway, his mother behind him, her hand on his shoulder. Martha looked tiny and fragile under a thin sheet.

'She's fighting back,' Judith said gently. 'She's tough.'

Josh didn't say anything for fear his voice might crack. He wiped his eyes and closed the door.

Turning to his mother he hugged her tightly. 'We've been lucky, haven't we?' he said. 'We're all going to make it.'

Judith nodded, her chin bumping against his shoulder. 'Thanks to your father, yes.'

Downstairs, Josh learned he'd missed the village meeting, but Judith told him that he hadn't been invited to that anyway.

'Why not?' he asked.

'Your father decided it was best,' she said tiredly. His dad had apparently popped in briefly earlier to check on the children, before leaving again almost immediately. Josh's mother told him Michael had been a whirlwind of activity – he'd stayed out at the pub the night before, organising the vaccination and only come back in the small hours, anxious and complaining of a headache. He slept fitfully for just a couple of hours, then was up and back out, organis-ing again, briefing, discussing, listening, arguing with people. After the meeting he'd moved the centre of operations from the pub to the church, setting up a command centre there, saying it was 'a more appropriate environment'.

To Josh's frustration, his mother refused to let him leave the house.

'It's your father's orders,' she told him. 'He said all children and teenagers were to stay indoors for twenty-four hours until properly recovered.'

'But I feel fine,' Josh said. 'I didn't even have any symptoms.'

'Look,' Judith said. 'Your father thought he'd lost you and Martha – so did I. He's terrified something might happen to you. He hasn't said much, but I get the impression he saw some awful things on the journey back. Let's just do what he says for now.'

'Can I at least go and visit Sam?' he asked, but Judith shook her head and went off to check on Martha.

Josh spent most of the day peering out the window, watching people passing back and forth carrying boxes of food and bottles of water. As it turned out he began to feel tired soon after lunch and went to sleep on the sofa. He hadn't slept well during the night despite, or perhaps because of, the drugs in his system. His sleep had been racked by nightmares: Pete's thrashing death, Les Rogers' swaying corpse, Sam coughing and staring down the barrel of Mark's rifle. He woke in the evening to the sound of voices in the kitchen, his parents talking. Feeling groggy, he lay still under the blanket his mother had placed over him, listening.

'You should ask Josh if he wants to go to the pub,' his mother said. 'After what he did on that barricade. You should be proud. He needs to be there, with the others.'

'I just don't think we should start off by letting children drink alcohol,' Michael said. 'Is there a chance perhaps this new world could be a little more sober than the last?'

There was a slight edge to Michael's voice. He sounded as if he were angry and trying to suppress it.

'Who said anything about alcohol? He can have a Coke,' Judith replied. 'He should be there, at least, with the adults.'

'And Kitty? Should she be there too?'

'Well, that's up to Monica, but why not?'

'No, I think the children should stay indoors. Look, I was in there earlier, some of the men are quite drunk. The conversations are not appropriate for... for Josh.'

'A bit of blue language isn't going to—'

'Judith, I said *no*.' Josh was surprised. His father rarely raised his voice. He must be tired.

'Fine,' he heard his mother say. 'You just go, then.'

Josh closed his eyes as his father swept through the room and kept them closed until he heard the door shut.

Though still cross about having been made to spend the previous day indoors, Josh realised that his body had needed the time to rest. His mind too. Last night he'd slept much better, and this morning he felt fit and fine.

Sam and Martha were still bed-bound, and Monica Hilfenhaus wasn't letting Kitty leave the house. Josh felt a little lost without his friends.

After a quick breakfast, he went down to the church to see what he could do to help. On the way, he passed the pub and popped in there to see if he could learn anything, but he was pretty much ignored. Some of the men were drinking, even at this early hour, and a couple looked like they'd been there since the last time he'd walked in carrying a shotgun.

There was more useful activity in the church. Clive and Reg had out maps of the area and were identifying useful sites. Farms, garden centres, supermarkets. He floated around but no one seemed to want to talk to him.

Through eavesdropping, however, he learned that the men were planning an excursion to Guildford to stock up on food and bottled water and to look for survivors. As they'd suspected, London Road was impassable – at the junction with the A3 there had been a massive pile-up involving dozens of cars and to shift that lot would take weeks. The decision was made to strike for the Tesco at Guildford. The only concern was that it was on the far side, meaning they'd have to drive through the town, which could be difficult.

Josh wandered about the church and eventually found his father in his makeshift office in the vestry. They hugged briefly. His father looked exhausted, with panda eyes. His hair was greyer than Josh remembered.

'Have any more cars arrived?' Josh asked.

His father shook his head.

'And the search party? Mum told me there was a search party yesterday.'

Michael shook his head a second time. 'They didn't find anyone alive, Josh,' he said.

'There are bound to be some survivors, though, aren't there?' Josh asked – he so needed his father to nod this time.

'They visited every farm, hamlet and village for twenty miles around,' Michael replied sadly. 'They steered clear of Guildford, Farnham and the other larger towns, apparently.'

Josh felt an empty darkness open within him. 'They haven't given up hope, though? Have they?'

'They're extending the search,' Michael said. 'But we shouldn't hold out too much hope, Josh. And frankly, we have more pressing concerns. We're running low on food and fresh water.'

The taps had run dry two days before.

'There's always the river,' Josh suggested.

There was water in the River Wey which ran close to the village.

'It's not safe,' Michael replied. 'Won't be for a few weeks. There may be dead bodies in it, upstream.'

Josh thought this unlikely. If you had a racking cough and a neck sprouting buboes, nipping down to the Wey for a quick swim would be pretty low on your list of priorities, he felt. But he didn't say anything.

'Can I go to Guildford with the foraging party?' he asked instead.

Michael shook his head. 'I'm sorry, no. Too dangerous.'

'But I helped out on the barricade,' Josh protested.

'We didn't know the full situation then,' his father said, squeezing his eyes shut and pinching the bridge of his nose.

'Headache?' Josh asked.

Michael nodded.

'Sit down, Josh,' his father said. Josh sat and Michael perched on the desk, looking down at his son.

'Josh,' he began. 'It seems likely, that ... we here in Little Sheen could be the only survivors.'

'In the country?' Josh asked, shaking his head.

Michael fixed him with a steady gaze, his eyes dark and clouded with some inner turmoil. 'In the world, Josh.'

Josh stared back at his father, unable to compute this information. His mind reeled.

82

'Which means,' his father continued slowly, 'that you, Martha, Kitty and Sam, may be the only four teenagers on the planet.'

Josh shook his head again, rejecting what he'd just been told. 'We can't be the only ones,' he said. 'Have you tried the radio? What about the government in their bunker?'

'We received notification from the bunker some time ago that those inside were showing symptoms. It had got inside, Josh. They're all dead. This virus is unlike anything seen before, trust me on this. It's airborne, waterborne, extremely infectious, and very long-lived. Nowhere on the planet can have escaped.'

'But surely it's worth trying?' Josh said, and he thought he noticed just a glimmer of annoyance in his father's expression. A brief look heavenward.

'Of course we'll try, Josh,' Michael said. 'But like I said, I just don't think you should hold out much hope.'

Josh nodded dumbly, his mouth dry. Just a few minutes ago he'd harboured dreams that some of his friends and extended family might have escaped. No longer. Could it really be that everyone... *everyone* else was dead? Presidents and popes? Rock stars and celebrities?

Michael went on. 'There are little ones: toddlers, small children. And there are a few, like Mark, in their twenties. But more than two thirds of the village are over forty.' He watched his son carefully as he spoke, as though he were testing Josh, looking for the right reaction.

'You are the future leaders of this village. Of this entire world.'

Josh swallowed. He didn't want to be a leader. He didn't particularly want to be a follower, either, for that matter.

'I need you safe, Josh,' Michael said. 'I need you here, in the village, by my side. Do you understand?'

Josh nodded.

Just then David McGovern, the farmer, came in clutching some papers, and Josh realised the interview was over. He slunk out, feeling a little numb, sat on the stone wall next to the church and watched as the convoy pulled out. It was led by Clive's truck, followed by Mark Rogers' van, now driven by someone else and with blood spatters cleaned up. After that came two four-wheel drives with trailers. But then the final vehicle, an old Land Rover, stopped alongside him. The window wound down and Reg's face peeped out.

'C'mon, then,' the old soldier said. Josh hesitated, his father's words still fresh in his mind. He didn't want to disobey his father, but on the other hand he felt he had to do something. And if his dad wanted him to be a future leader? Well, he'd show what he could do. He grinned and jumped in.

As they sped off after the other vehicles, Reg said, 'I was younger than you when I joined the army but

I was man enough to fight.'

'Thanks, Reg,' Josh said.

Reg looked over at him and grinned. 'And if you weren't a man before what happened on that barricade, then you are now.'

Martha woke and was blind. She lay for a long time trying to remember. Just listening and thinking. She could hear her mother downstairs, clinking cups just like always, but she knew something wasn't right. Apart from being blind, that was. She lifted a hand slowly to her face. Her arm felt so heavy, like someone had strapped weights to it. She ran her hand over her face; her skin was spotted and dry but felt otherwise normal. Then with enormous relief she felt her eyelids and realised they were simply glued shut with encrusted sleep.

She had a vague memory of her mother periodically dabbing at her face with something soft and warm whilst she'd been drifting in and out of consciousness. Martha reached over to her dressing table and encountered what felt like a bowl of water and some cotton wool. She sat up, and with difficulty, and after a great deal of gentle dabbing, managed to unglue her eyes. She blinked blearily around the room. Everything looked the same, except that there were no standby lights on her stereo, or the TV or PC. Everything seemed quieter too, no electrical hum, although she could still hear some birds outside. She swung her legs over the edge of the bed and thought about standing up. She had no idea how much time had passed, but she realised that she'd been extremely ill. Close to death.

Something had come. But she couldn't remember what. A bright light? Angels? Her head swam as she stood and she was sure she would topple, but after a few moments her vision cleared and she shuffled to the door. There were no voices downstairs but she could still hear her mother in the kitchen. She gripped the banister tightly as she descended, one step at a time.

When she walked into the kitchen her mother had her back to Martha but must have heard her daughter enter. Judith turned round, an expression of vindication on her lined, tired face.

'What happened?' Martha asked.

'A miracle,' Judith replied instantly. 'It was a miracle.' She smiled at her daughter, risen from the dead.

12.03 P.M.

Josh heard sheet metal scream as the truck in front bulldozed a Rover off the road and into a shallow ditch. He could see the dead driver's head lolling as the car bucked and juddered towards its final parking space. They'd encountered a few cars on the six-mile drive into Guildford, mostly parked by the side of the road, the driver-corpses slumped at the wheel or lying a few metres away in pools of dried black blood.

Some cars, though, had stopped in the middle of the road and had to be shouldered aside by the heavy lorry at the head of the convoy.

'Keep your eyes peeled for signs of survivors,' Reg said.

Josh looked over at him. 'Dad seems to think we won't find any,' he said.

Reg frowned. 'I wouldn't want to go against your old man, Josh, but... well, I'm just not sure we should give up so easily.'

Reg's optimism cheered Josh somewhat. 'What am I looking for?' he asked.

'Oh, you know. Smoking chimneys, faces at the windows, that sort of thing.'

As they sped up again they passed an old Cortina, its windscreen obscured from the inside by a thick coating of dried, bloody mucus, presumably painted there by a hugely powerful final cough. Josh was perpetually surprised by the violence of the disease. So much blood. It was as if they'd been preceded by a madman with a sniper rifle picking off innocent motorists as he'd passed.

They didn't speak much as they drove, not after they'd seen the first few stopped cars. But Josh suddenly remembered Mark and asked Reg what had happened to him.

'He's stable,' Reg replied. 'Shot in the thigh, as you know. Jen Stephenson says she thinks he'll recover as long as there's no infection. We're to look out for some antibiotics while we're in Guildford, insulin too if we can find any.'

As they entered Guildford town centre, the congestion grew worse and they were stopping every hundred metres while Clive's heavy truck cleared the road ahead.

'We'll only need to do this the once, of course,' Reg pointed out. 'Once the route's clear we'll be able to get here much more quickly.'

It took them another hour to get into the town centre and Josh was relieved to see the streets were mostly empty – he'd been convinced the pavements would be lined with rotting corpses. Whilst the convoy stopped to clear another car up ahead, they pulled alongside an army checkpoint, deserted apart from the body of one poor soldier, slumped still clutching his weapon. Reg pulled on the handbrake, hopped out and walked over to the body. Josh followed.

'Poor sod,' Reg said as he crouched over the corpse. 'Can't have been more than eighteen.' Josh stood back a little. The young soldier's face was pale and puffy, his lips cracked and drawn back, giving him an expression of snarling anger, as though he were furious at a world so cruel as to create something like HAV3N. Blood had run from his mouth and nose and dried in a dark puddle on the pavement. There was a faint scent of something unpleasant, though in the cool weather the corpse hadn't yet started to rot.

'Isn't there a risk of infection?' Josh asked.

'Now you've had the vaccine, you don't need to worry about that—' Reg looked away as he was interrupted by a shout from Clive Mitchell, who was driving the vehicle in front.

'What are you doing, you old fool? Get away from that body!' Clive called, but Reg ignored him. He gently lifted the dead soldier's arm and slipped the rifle out. He did the same with the ammunition clip, then stood and gave a quick salute to the young soldier before turning to stow the weapon in the car.

The convoy had started to move again. 'C'mon, Josh,' Reg called, now back in the front seat. Josh tore his gaze away from the dead soldier and tried not to be too obviously hasty in getting back into the comforting old leather smell of the vehicle.

12.13 P.M.

When Sam awoke it was with a start. He raised himself onto one elbow and lay for a long time trying to remember what had happened. His throat burned and he coughed experimentally. It hurt but was nothing like the raw, back-breaking strength of the coughs he'd been experiencing just before . . . well, just before what? He remembered the barricade, and a gunshot. Mostly he just felt utter confusion. His head was a mass of jumbled images of violence and blood. His bones ached and he felt like he might be sick.

He sat up, feeling weak and was thinking about lying down again when Kitty walked in. She stopped in surprise to see him upright. She trotted over and gave him a warm hug, then pulled back and stepped away.

'You need a shower,' she said, wrinkling her nose.

He grinned and looked at her, waiting for her to explain everything.

'You OK?' she asked eventually.

Sam thought about this. 'I suppose I am,' he replied. 'I feel like I've had a bad cold, but that's it.'

'Mr Pirbright brought some medicine,' Kitty said. 'That's what saved you.'

Sam squeezed his eyes shut, thinking it over.

Then it all clicked into place. He remembered the roar of the motorbike in the fields. He remembered the mad gleam in Mark's eye as he squeezed the trigger, then the glare of the headlights approaching. Mr Pirbright proffering the syringe. He remembered shooting Les Rogers, and Pete's horrible death. He groaned, suddenly feeling a lot sicker.

'So Josh's dad saved the day? Cut it a bit fine, didn't he?'

Kitty nodded. 'Yeah, but I don't know how many others are left to save. Some people have been going out looking for survivors, but Mr Pirbright didn't seem very hopeful.'

Sam paused. 'Any word from Dad?'

Kitty shook her head quickly and bit her lip.

'If there's a vaccine, though...' Sam said.

Kitty shrugged and nodded. Not speaking.

'So did they distribute the vaccine to the whole country?'

'I don't know.'

Sam mulled this over. 'There must be others,' he said. 'If they had a vaccine, there must have been others saved. I heard HAV3N hadn't spread so far in Africa. Remote towns in Australia? If we've got a cure for HAV3N, then the Americans must have it too.'

They looked at each other, thinking the same thing. That perhaps this wouldn't be so bad after all.

'Maybe they'll get the internet back on?' Kitty suggested tentatively.

'How's Mum?' Sam asked.

'I found her crying this morning,' his sister replied. 'She...she said Dad probably wouldn't be coming home.' Kitty looked down at the floor briefly, then back up at Sam, utterly miserable. The light from the open curtains glinted in her eyes as the tears welled.

Sam stood unsteadily, and walked over to give her a hug. Having someone else to comfort helped him to plug the wellspring of despair that threatened to overwhelm him. Her slight body shook as he held her tight. He could feel her tears soaking through his T-shirt.

'It's going to be OK,' he said. 'Everything's going to be OK.'

Apart from the occasional dead soldier and a couple

of stray dogs who eyed them suspiciously before slinking off, Josh was struck by how normal everything looked. He'd often be here in Guildford on a weekend, catching up with his mates, checking out the music stores or the camera shop. The streets were mostly clear. The presence of the soldiers and fear of the disease had obviously kept people indoors and put a stop to any thought of looting. The shopfronts looked normal in the watery sunshine.

The convoy stopped again as they headed up towards the town centre. Leaning out the window, Josh saw Clive's truck go into action once more, this time trying to clear two cars which had crashed into each other head-on and seemed to be locked together. It looked like it might take some time, so Reg pulled on the handbrake, settled into his seat with a creak of springs and shut his eyes. Josh envied the old man his ability to sleep at a time like this.

Josh's attention wandered. As he looked away he thought he saw movement in an upstairs window above a mobile-phone shop. He stared hard at the window for a while, but saw nothing else.

'I thought I saw something move in that window up there.' He nudged Reg awake.

The ex-soldier craned his neck to see. 'We're not going anywhere in a hurry. Let's check it out.'

He grabbed the little soft pack they'd been given. It contained two doses of vaccine and two doses of the antiviral medicine. They hopped out of the car.

Some of the other drivers had done the same, but to stretch their legs.

Reg tried the door of the phone shop and it opened. Josh followed him inside. The shop was empty, and dark. He paused as he passed a display stand featuring the latest slimline phone. A week ago he'd wanted this phone so badly he'd have walked to Portsmouth and back, barefoot. Now it was just a cheap piece of plastic. Utterly worthless.

Reg went through to the back of the shop and found a flight of stairs. Josh followed him. At the top was a locked door.

Reg knocked.

'Hello?' he called. 'Anyone in there?' No answer. He looked back at Josh, who shrugged. Reg smacked his palm against the door. 'Cheap,' he said. Then he shoulder-charged it. Three times. *Thump*, *crack*, *splinter*, and the door broke open.

They were immediately assailed by a foul stench. Josh coughed and clutched his jumper over his face. Reg winced and stepped inside the flat. Josh hesitated, but then followed.

The source of the stench was revealed as they went into the sitting room. The bodies of a couple lay on the sofa under blood-darkened blankets. Their faces were grey and bloated, eyes staring forward. Bottles of aspirin and vitamin C lay on the coffee table before them.

Josh looked up at a photo frame on the sideboard. It showed the couple on a beach, the girl being carried on the man's shoulders, shrieking with laughter, her curly blonde hair flying. They were long dead; he must have imagined the movement up here.

But as they stood, staring, something stirred to their left and Josh's heart lurched in panic. He stepped backwards quickly and tripped, falling on his bottom as a cat shot past and disappeared down the stairs.

Reg helped Josh to his feet and looked him in the eye. 'Are you OK?'

Josh nodded, though he felt sick. They hurried downstairs. The cat had disappeared. Josh shivered and climbed back into the car to warm up. He sat quietly lost in his thoughts, the fat, inhuman faces of the dead couple still vivid in his memory. Reg got back into the driver's seat and sat, saying nothing. There was nothing to say. There were billions more like that. The entire world. Seeing those two up close, though, it brought it all home for Josh. Everyone was dead. *Everyone*.

After ten minutes trying to separate the two cars, Clive walked back along the convoy, relaying a message. He came up to Reg's window.

'What are *you* doing here?' he asked Josh in surprise.

Josh shrugged. 'I came to help.'

'Kids aren't supposed to leave the village,' Clive told him.

'Is that what Dad said?' Josh asked, stung.

94

Clive nodded and Josh frowned. 'Yeah, well, I'm not a kid,' he snapped, and Reg chuckled.

'This way's blocked,' Clive said. 'We're to reverse and go up the high street. We'll stop there for a while; see what we can scavenge before proceeding to the supermarket.'

Reg nodded and began reversing slowly down the road to the bottom of the high street. There was a flimsy raisable barrier at the bottom to allow service vehicles to access the pedestrianised street. He gunned the engine and drove through the hollow aluminium tube of the barrier as if it were made of dried pasta.

Josh had walked up this ancient, cobbled street so many times before on Saturday-morning shopping excursions. But now, after seeing the dead couple, everything had changed. He'd never seen the street empty before, and this, for some reason, scared him more than anything else. You knew the human race was in trouble when it stopped shopping.

Reg crawled slowly along, past the bookshop, the old Angel Hotel and the pharmacy. He stopped under the great brass clock halfway up the street and turned off the engine. The convoy stopped behind him and people began getting out.

'Let's go shopping!' Reg said in a jolly fashion.

Josh got the impression Reg was trying to cheer him up, and he smiled as best he could.

'What are we looking for?' he asked the pensioner.

Reg shrugged. 'Anything that's useful, and nothing that isn't,' he replied.

Josh stood by the Land Rover as the men split up and began entering shops, mostly having to force their way in. Josh flinched at the unwelcome sound of breaking glass. He looked at the nearest shop. Jewellery. Nothing useful there. What good are diamonds when the world's ended? Looking up, he noticed the camera shop across the street. They had a new Leica in there he'd been mooning over for months. Could a camera be classed as a useful item? Maybe he could set up a dark room, start recording the new world in photographs. Quickly, he dashed across the cobbled street and tried the door. It opened, which he took as a sign he was doing the right thing. It took him just a few seconds to locate the camera he wanted, within a display cabinet. Looking around, he spotted a fire extinguisher on the wall and used this to break the glass. He reached in carefully and, not without a flash of guilt, seized the camera. Then he was out of the shop and back to the Land Rover, where he tucked the precious object into the glove compartment.

Looking up again, Josh saw Bryan Fletcher and Amir Mansoor, the engineer, carrying box after box of supplies out of the pharmacy and loading them into Mark's van.

'No antibiotics!' Amir called. 'That shelf was stripped bare.'

Clive walked past, frowning again at Josh's presence.

'Hey, Mr Mitchell?'

Clive stopped and grunted at him.

'Should we be looking for people? You know, in the houses? Might there be people hiding?'

Clive looked up and down the street quickly. 'If there is anyone around they'll come to us. We're making enough noise to wake the dead.'

Josh watched him walk off down the street, then shook his head and wandered to the next shop. He peered through the window – shoes. He knew this shop. He'd been in it with Sam on more than one occasion, deciding which pair of trainers they'd have if they had the money. There was a pair of red leather Converse in the window. *Not practical*, he thought to himself. We need practical footwear. He tried the door and this one opened too. He entered and went through to the back where they had the outdoors section. Ten minutes later he'd built a pile of boxes next to the Land Rover. Wellies, boots and walking shoes. Reg came back carrying a pile of books.

'Useful books,' Reg said in response to Josh's raised eyebrow. 'Look.'

He showed Josh a few.

The SAS Survival Handbook
Ray Mears' Game and Offal Cookbook
Car Maintenance for Dummies
Home Butchery Made Simple
The Home-Birth Bible

Modern Soap Making
The Self-Sufficiency Manual

'We'll need specialist farming books too,' Reg added. 'We could be stuck in the village for a long while yet so we'll need to become self-sufficient.'

They split up again and made some more 'purchases'. Josh got some Drizabone coats and thermal blankets while Reg spent the remaining time happily plucking useful tools off the shelves of the old-fashioned tool store on a side street.

'Let's move on out,' Clive called, soon enough. 'We can always come back another time. Our priority has to be the food and we want to be home before dark.'

Reg hopped back in the Land Rover and started the engine.

2.29 P.M.

The Tesco car park was one enormous traffic jam. In the last couple of days on air the BBC had reported people panic-buying, desperate to stock up on dwindling food supplies. Josh had gone on one such trip along with Judith, but they'd gone early, as advised by Josh's father, and before things got too mad. Fights were common – people had even been stabbed. A series of collisions had blocked the roundabout at the entrance and exit, effectively trapping hundreds of cars. Some drivers had attempted to mount the barriers and planters which bordered the car park. Relatively few carried the tell-tale blood cloud on the windscreen which suggested a victim inside. Perhaps most had abandoned their cars and walked home to die.

The convoy ignored the main car park and drove round to the loading dock. An articulated lorry was parked but there was enough space to back Clive's truck up to the bay. They forced entry and went into the main part of the shop. The scenes inside were as chaotic as out in the car park, bodies lying here and there in the aisles. But it was cool, and mercifully the smell wasn't too bad.

The shelves were largely empty. Packets of cereals and perishable foods scattered the aisles. There were no canned goods – those had been the first to be bought in a panic. The men grabbed a few items that had either been forgotten or dropped. A few bags of rice and pasta, some fruit which still looked OK, nuts and cured meats. Josh grabbed some snow boots he thought Kitty might like. Then grabbed some more, for Martha, so that it wouldn't mean too much. There wasn't really anything that jumped out at him that he thought Sam might like.

Reg filled a couple of boxes with baby foods.

'There aren't any babies in Little Sheen,' Josh reminded him.

'Your father told me to get some,' Reg replied. 'He seems to think there might be babies sooner, rather than later.' He raised an eyebrow and went outside to load the boxes.

It was a meagre haul, though. There was very little in the storeroom they found at the back, either. Apparently there had been no deliveries for some time and all the stock had been out on the shelves. The men picked about the aisles looking glum.

'Should we try somewhere else?' Amir asked.

Clive shrugged. 'We could, but not today – it'll be dark in a couple of hours.'

Josh wandered down the clothing aisle looking for items people may have dropped. Brightly coloured winter clothes lay across the floor. He picked his way through and saw a can of beans lying half concealed under a shelving unit. He stepped on a heap of clothes to get to it then leaped back in alarm as he realised the pile was solid. It was the body of a man, his arm reaching out towards the tin. Holding his breath and refusing to look more closely, Josh leaned over and grabbed the beans. The corpse smelled thickly of earthy damp and sadness, still a couple of days from putrefaction.

'Sorry, mate,' he whispered to the dead man. 'We need these now.'

The daylight was dimming as they went back out onto the loading dock. Though it was still some time before dusk, the clouds were thick and they could feel specks of rain being blown in through the open bay.

As they climbed back in the cars something occurred to Josh. He trotted over to the lorry parked up at the bay and inspected the rear doors. They were padlocked shut.

'I was just thinking the same thing, Josh,' Reg said, appearing behind him. 'I think I have a sledge-hammer in the Rover.'

'Hold on,' Josh said, on a roll now. He went round to the cab and swung open the door.

A man sprang out and lunged at him. With a great shout Josh fell back onto the floor of the dock, hands raised to ward off his attacker. But the man had stopped. Josh looked up to see the truck driver hanging from the open door, upper body free but held in place by his lap belt. The man's dead eyes stared back at him contemptuously and he had the same bared-teeth look Josh had seen earlier on the soldier. He gulped as the others came to see what the commotion was about.

'I wanted the keys,' Josh explained.

Clive went round the other side and clambered up into the cab, he released the seat belt and the driver tumbled out. Reg and another man dragged the body away while Clive checked the ignition. The keys were still there. They found a key that fitted the rear doors and upon opening saw to their satisfaction that the interior was three-quarters full with non-perishable foods. Canned goods, packets, dried peas and lentils. The sort of food that people had been stockpiling, the sort of food *they* now needed.

'We'll never get all this into our vehicles,' Amir pointed out.

'We don't need to,' Clive replied with a grin and a wink. 'We'll just take the lorry.'

Just before they pulled out, Josh remembered Mark. 'We didn't get any antibiotics,' he said.

'You saw the shelves,' Reg reminded him. 'Stripped. And that included the pharmacy.'

'But he needs them,' Josh said. 'I feel responsible.'

'You're not responsible for him,' Reg said.

The sound of starting engines echoed around the loading bay, interrupting their conversation.

'Wait here,' Reg instructed. He got out, wandered over to the lorry to speak to Clive.

'Clive didn't want us to go,' he said when he returned. 'But I insisted. We're going to split off from the main group.'

'Where are we going?' Josh asked.

Reg peered at him through the deepening gloom. 'To the hospital.'

4

There was a knock at the door and Judith broke off from bustling about Martha to go and answer it. Martha lay under a blanket on the sofa. The only sound was the ticking of the wind-up clock on the mantelpiece and the occasional cry of a crow in a tree across the road, muffled by the double-glazing.

'Just five minutes, OK?' Martha heard her mum say as Kitty walked in. 'She needs her rest.' Martha smiled, ridiculously happy to see her friend. She'd been numb since she woke, and Judith fussing over her had hardly helped.

'Your mum let you out finally?' she said to Kitty.

'Now Sam's awake she's forgotten about me a bit. She didn't say anything when I told her I was coming to see you,' her friend replied.

'Did she hear you say it?'

'Possibly not,' Kitty said. 'Where's the TV gone?'

Martha looked at the corner where there was now a TV-shaped gap.

'Dunno, I guess Dad must have moved it into the basement now it doesn't work.'

'You could watch DVDs on it,' Kitty said, unwilling to let it go. 'If they get the electricity back on.'

'Dad said there'll be no time for that sort of thing,' Martha said.

'I miss TV,' Kitty said. 'And my laptop. Finally something worth updating my status about and there's no internet.' Martha nodded – she didn't care much for TV, but she missed the internet. What was she to do now there was no more college? Maybe she should try and complete the course regardless?

Kitty sat next to Martha and wrapped her in a hug that said an awful lot. In contrast to the Pirbrights, the Hilfenhauses were a touchy-feely sort of family. Kitty sometimes gave off an air of being a little self-centred, but Martha knew her friend well enough to know that it was just front. Kitty was soft inside.

Just as well we like each other, Martha thought. *We may be the only teenage girls around for a while.*

Martha smiled. 'It's good to see you. Did you... were you ill?'

Kitty shook her head. 'I never get sick.'

'What happened?' Martha asked. 'Mum won't tell me anything. She says I need to concentrate on getting better. But I can't concentrate on that with so many questions in my head. Did the government come, or something?'

'I thought it was the Americans at first,' Kitty said. 'But then I realised it was just your dad.'

Martha rolled her eyes. 'Well, obviously I knew

Dad came. I saw him this morning when I woke up, but wasn't there anyone else?'

Kitty shook her head, 'No, just him, on a motor-bike.'

Martha frowned. 'That's odd.'

'Why?'

'Well, presumably Dad made the vaccine at his lab. They must have made loads. Obviously Dad took some and rode down to Surrey to save us, but there must have been other people at the lab who kept making more of the vaccine.'

'That's what Sam said too,' Kitty said. 'That means there might be other survivors.'

'Yeah, so why is Dad still here? Why didn't he go back to the lab to help distribute more of the vaccine?'

'Maybe he figured he'd done his bit,' Kitty suggested.

'That doesn't sound like Dad. It's just odd, that's all.'

'Why don't you ask him?'

'I will,' Martha said thoughtfully.

'Do you think they'll still have the Harvest Festival?' Kitty changed the subject.

'Um, I don't know, probably not,' Martha was puzzled by her friend's question. 'Why?'

'Oh, no reason,' Kitty replied.

'OK, time's up,' Judith said, bustling back in carrying a vase of late-season roses.

'Oh, Mum!' sighed Martha.

Judith placed the vase on the table and studied the stems as if she'd never seen flowers before and hadn't the first idea what to do next. She nudged one or two into a more pleasing position. 'Martha needs to rest, Kitty,' she said.

'Mrs Pirbright? Is there still going to be a Harvest Festival?'

Judith paused as she arranged the flowers. She'd organised the Harvest Festival for the last five years, ever since Mary McDonagh was moved into the nursing home in Godalming. Though a church event, it really was Judith's baby. She glanced up at Kitty.

'*Keep calm and carry on,*' she said.

'Eh?' Kitty replied.

'Never mind. Do you know, Kitty, I think that's an excellent idea,' she smiled. 'I'll suggest it when I see the vicar tomorrow. Now, off you go. Come back tomorrow for lunch if you like – tell your mum and Sam.'

Kitty grinned and got up, brushing her fingers across Martha's shoulder as she left.

3.23 P.M.

'Are you OK with this?' Reg asked. 'I can go on my own if you like.'

Josh shook his head. 'No. I mean yes, I'm OK. I'll come.' He stared hard at Hell's Traffic Jam ahead. They were still half a mile from the hospital, on the A3.

A thousand cars were crushed, some literally, along the slip road, roundabout and entrance road that led to the hospital. In the final couple of days, there had been reports of hospitals swamped with patients during the outbreak, despite demands that people stay in their homes. Most had tried to drive, probably transporting sick family members since there were no ambulances or paramedics to drive them. Even those who had somehow made it into the hospital were lucky to find a doctor or a nurse not already coughing or scratching the back of their necks.

'There's only an hour's light left,' Reg said, looking at his watch. It had taken them longer than expected to get here. 'I wonder if we shouldn't return tomorrow?'

'Mark needs those antibiotics tonight,' Josh said.

Reg shrugged. 'OK, we'll give it a go. We've got water and some food.' He reached into the back seat and grabbed the soldier's rifle. 'And this.'

They set off on foot. At least the rain had stopped now and a watery sunshine trickled through the parting clouds. It was easier to walk along the verge as the hard shoulder was packed with cars. There'd evidently been a few collisions as drivers had grown increasingly desperate and tried to barge their way through. Josh tried not to look into the cars as they passed, though through the corner of his eyes he could see most of them had two or more passengers, some in the back seat covered with blankets.

There were bodies in the road too. People had abandoned their cars and tried to walk, stagger or crawl to the hospital. Many hadn't made it. It was impossible for Josh not to glance at them as he passed. They lay in a variety of positions, some curled up into a foetal ball, others spread-eagled on their front, or back. The only thing they all had in common was the black halo remnant of their last great cough.

Reg stopped as they approached one – a large man wearing a red jumper. Josh followed Reg's gaze. The man's right trouser leg was torn, and a huge, bloody gash disfigured the calf. Flesh hung in gobbets and the wound looked recent, blood glistening in the evening chill.

'Something's taken a bite out of that,' Reg said. Then he carried on, whistling.

Josh stood watching for a few moments longer, horrified at the implications.

'Dogs?' he called out after Reg as he ran to catch up.

'Bingo,' said Reg casually. He stopped and motioned Josh to move ahead.

Picking their way through the cars was slow going and the sun was low by the time they reached the hospital forecourt. Here the cars thinned where someone had erected crash barriers to stop more from coming in. But the bodies increased in number. A dank, sickly-sweet smell hung over the access road which led up to the A&E department. Josh was reminded of the smell of the corpse in Tesco.

'It's been too cool for them to start putrefying,' Reg said behind him, breaking the silence and making Josh jump. 'But they're on the turn. Couple of days and this place will stink like the devil's own turd. Next time we should go round the back, go through a window.'

'*Next time?*' Josh said, grimacing.

He headed towards the main doors out of habit. Every time he'd visited the hospital it had been through those doors, for some minor cut or scald, or there was the time he'd cracked a rib falling off his bike. These doors were just how you got into the hospital, as far as he was concerned.

'Not in there!' Reg shouted. 'It's gonna be—'

But it was too late – the automatic doors slid apart, releasing a noxious stench that set Josh back on his heels. He fell over in his haste to escape and scrambled away. Reg stood, holding his breath and grimacing in revulsion at the piles of rotting bodies beyond the doors in the reception area. A few seconds later the doors slid closed and the tinted glass again hid the worst of the carnage inside.

'Did you notice anything unusual there, Josh?' Reg asked after a few seconds of silence.

Josh peered up at the old soldier in astonishment. 'You mean, apart from all the rotting bodies?'

Reg shook his head. 'Sort of, but you're not using

your head, Josh. We'd expect to find piles of rotting bodies in a warm hospital, after a plague.'

Josh shrugged, still not getting it.

'What is different about the bodies inside from the bodies outside?'

Josh looked back towards the hospital; a couple of corpses lay between them and the doors.

'The ones outside aren't as rotted?'

'Yes, why would that be?'

'Because the ones inside are in the warmth.'

'And how is it that the inside is warmer than the outside?'

Then Josh twigged. 'Oh. Because the heating's on.'

'And not just the heating, but what else?'

Another couple of seconds, and... 'The electricity. The doors opened for me.' Josh grinned up at Reg. 'They've got a generator.'

4.03 P.M.

Mrs McGovern came round later in the afternoon to see how Martha was doing. Judith didn't ask her in, but when she returned to the kitchen she explained that the farmer's wife had asked whether Martha would be able to resume her work down at the farm soon.

'I'd love to,' Martha said. She was washing dishes with water boiled on the oil-fired Aga. Doing something so domesticated at such a time seemed surreal, yet comforting. Billions of people had died, but there was still the washing-up to do.

'You won't be paid, of course,' Judith pointed out. 'Everyone needs to do their bit and the food will be distributed equally.'

'You sound like this has already been discussed,' Martha said.

Judith nodded. 'At that meeting yesterday. Under-eighteens weren't invited,' she added, raising an eyebrow.

'Hmm,' Martha said. 'That's not very democratic.'

'Actually,' Judith replied reasonably, 'that's perfectly democratic. You didn't get to vote until eighteen before this, after all.'

'And look how well that turned out,' Martha said, half joking.

'Come on, Martha, things are different now,' Judith continued. 'You need to get used to that.'

Martha looked at her mother, surprised by her reaction.

'Yes,' she said thoughtfully. 'I suppose I do. If I'm on the farm, what's your job going to be?'

Judith sighed. 'Your father thinks I should stick with the job I've got. Keeping the family together, supporting him in his new role.'

'How do you feel about that?' Martha asked as she finished the last of the cups.

'I made the choice to give up my career a long time ago, Martha. It was the right decision,' Judith said firmly.

Martha raised an eyebrow, but said nothing.

'Anyway, this isn't just about what's needed. It's about your father's state of mind,' Judith went on, carefully. 'He's been...upset. He hasn't slept well since he got back. He has terrible nightmares.'

'OK, I understand,' Martha said quietly. Martha remembered the dark visions she too had experienced, and she shuddered.

Judith turned to her daughter. 'Out there, in the village, he's a hero. He saved them all. They look to him to lead them. But he's frightened, Martha, and now he feels responsible for the future. He's terrified something might happen to you and to Josh too. Just at the moment, I think he needs my support.'

Martha nodded.

'In time,' Judith said. 'Things will settle down. You'll see.'

4.06 P.M.

Sam didn't tell his mother when he left the house. He suspected she'd have forbidden it had he asked, but she hadn't yet specifically told him he couldn't go out. His mother hadn't been coping well – she tended to burst into tears every fifteen minutes or so and spent a long time at the kitchen table leafing through the Bible, reading passages apparently at random. He made her as many cups of tea as he could, but eventually had to escape the house.

Sam had yet to cry over the loss of his father. At present there was a dull grey emptiness within him which he was skirting around. Kitty had wanted to be alone and was upstairs reading an out-of-date magazine, losing herself in her own way.

He was still feeling weak and occasionally nauseous, but in addition to wanting to escape the atmosphere in the house Sam was desperate to discover what was going on. He snuck out the back and wandered down into the village. In the gloaming, and without street lights, the village looked odd, huddled and frightened. Candlelight flickered tentatively behind net curtains in the houses he passed.

Sam saw Reverend Halfdene standing alone at the doorway to the church, backlit by an ancient kerosene lantern. He waved as he passed and the vicar hurried down the path to speak with him.

'How are you, Sam? It's good to see you up and about.'

'I'm feeling absolutely fine,' Sam lied. The vicar looked tired and worried. 'What's been going on around here?'

'A few of the men, Reg and Clive and some others, have gone on a foraging expedition to Guildford and to look for other survivors.'

'I want to go foraging!' Sam said.

The vicar smiled. 'President Pirbright feels it would be better if children didn't leave the village for the time being.'

'Children?' Sam said. 'I'm not— Hang on, did you just say *President* Pirbright?'

'Yes, he's the interim president of the parish council,' the vicar said. Over the road Sam saw a couple of men standing outside the pub, smoking. They were lit by a dim glow from within; oil lamps and the pub's fireplaces, Sam guessed.

'So he's the head honcho now, is he? Josh's dad?'

'And why not?' the vicar asked. 'He saved us.'

'Like Jesus,' Sam said.

Reverend Halfdene frowned. 'Apparently there are a couple of dissident voices,' he said, nodding his head towards the Wheatsheaf.

'Oh,' Sam said, turning to look again at the Wheatsheaf across the green. 'Politics already, huh?'

'Indeed,' Halfdene said. 'I do hope we don't split into two camps. The problem is there are a couple of people in the village who are rather firm atheists, plus a few of a different religion entirely. They don't think any new government should be connected with the old parish council at all.'

'What people?'

'Oh, Bryan Fletcher, Reg Walker, Amir Mansoor. That reminds me, I saw your friend Josh getting into Reg's car and heading off on the Guildford trip.'

'*What?*' Sam cried. 'Jammy git!'

'He might not think himself so lucky when his father catches up with him,' the vicar said. 'He was furious when he found out.'

Sam remembered something. 'Mrs Pirbright told Kitty she's thinking of going ahead with the Harvest Festival, did she mention that to you?'

The reverend stared at him. 'No, she didn't. Does she think that's a good idea?'

Sam shrugged. 'Sure, the harvest is going to happen anyway. We're gonna be picking apples and spuds and stuff, aren't we?'

'Of course, we've already been discussing that.' The vicar was half lost in thought. Behind him, in the vestibule some flyers and notices fluttered in the breeze. Lost kittens that'd never be found now, cake sales which would never happen, rooms to rent to no one but the dead.

'It would be good to do something normal,' Sam said. 'And that's got to happen in the church. If you want to get everyone in here, rather than in there' – he pointed firmly to the pub – 'then the Harvest Festival is the place to start.'

The vicar looked at him and smiled for the first time. 'Thank you, Sam. That's a wonderful notion.'

'Don't thank me,' Sam said. 'Harvest is a gift from God. I just do his work down here.'

Halfdene sighed at the blasphemy and disappeared up the street, in the direction of the Pirbrights' house.

Sam smiled to himself and wandered over to the pub.

*

'Before we go in, take this,' Reg said, handing Josh his pistol.

'I can't take this,' Josh protested. 'It's your service revolver.'

'You need a weapon,' Reg insisted. They were at the side of the main building, looking for a way in that wasn't blocked by human cadavers. 'And I've got this bastard, anyway,' he continued, slapping the stock of the automatic rifle.

'What do we need them for, though?' Josh asked as Reg tested windows. 'Everyone's dead.'

'We'll almost certainly find nothing and no one alive in there,' Reg admitted. 'But you never know. This is a hospital, with medicines and isolation wards. I just want you to think; to consider all the possibilities and prepare for them.'

'Like a boy scout,' Josh suggested, grinning.

'Like a goddamn soldier,' Reg told him as he located an unlocked window.

He slid the glass across and pulled himself up to peer inside. 'A doctor's office,' he said. 'Help me.'

Josh pushed the old man up. Surprisingly limber for a man in his sixties, Reg slipped inside and reappeared a moment later, helping Josh to climb in as well.

Josh looked up at the ceiling lights, surprised at how beautiful a neon strip light could be after only a couple of days of candles. Reg was searching through

116

the drawers, grabbing a stethoscope and a couple of bottles of pills. He opened the last drawer and chuckled happily. Reaching in, he grabbed a bottle of scotch, almost full. Josh rolled his eyes as Reg dropped it into his bag and winked.

'You know,' Reg said, 'you've done the village a big favour insisting we come for these antibiotics now.'

'Why's that?' Josh asked.

'Because Mark's an electrician. If we're going to sort a generator for the village, we'll need someone to wire it all up.'

'That's not the only reason we should try and help him,' Josh said. He frowned as he watched the old soldier turn and move towards the door.

They left the office and walked slowly down the hall. Reg's suggestion there might be survivors here had made them both a little jumpy. Though he knew how unlikely it was, Josh was convinced someone would leap out from behind every doorway or corridor they passed. Reg didn't seem in much of a hurry, either.

'We'll head towards the dispensary,' he said quietly. 'It's likely to have been stripped, but it's worth checking.'

'And if it has been stripped?'

'I have another idea.'

Sam sat quietly in the snug in the pub, unnoticed, listening to the adults arguing. Some people seemed to have taken up permanent residence there. Damp logs hissed in the great fireplace. Most of the men held pints, the women glasses of wine.

'Look, I've said it before,' Tucker was saying, his words slightly slurred. 'We need to concentrate on foraging for now, since winter's coming. Our first priority is to get enough canned food and medical supplies to last the winter. We'll plant in spring, on McGoverns' farm and what-not.' There was a murmur of agreement around the bar.

'We need to defend ourselves properly,' their neighbour Howard Carter replied to an equal level of murmuring. 'We need proper gates at the roads, and a fence surrounding the perimeter of the village.'

'For what?' Emily Green, who'd been Sam's teacher at junior school, asked. 'Who are we keeping out?'

There was a pause, before Mr Carter spoke again. 'Others. And wild animals.'

Emily laughed. 'Others? There are no others, you know that. You heard Pirbright here last night. The chances of anyone else surviving are virtually non-existent. The foraging party aren't going to find anyone. And, anyway, what wild animals?'

That's strange, Sam thought. What *had* Josh's dad said here last night? Could there really be no one else? *They'd* survived, hadn't they? There must have been more of the vaccine. He didn't want to ask, though. If he were noticed he might be told to leave.

This time it was the farmer, David McGovern, who spoke. 'Oh, there'll be animals all right. Without humans around to trap and shoot them, or to run them over, fox and badger populations will soar. The worst problem will be dogs, though. Pet dogs turned feral, travelling in packs. Starving. It won't take them long to go wild. If you want us to raise livestock here, we'll need a fence, and a strong, tall fence at that.'

This seemed to shut Mrs Green up. There was a general silence around the pub as the adults considered this unwelcome information.

'Besides,' Mr Carter said, 'a fence doesn't just keep people out, it keeps 'em in too.'

'Oh, don't start that again,' Emily said. 'After all that nonsense about the teenagers last night.' Sam was even more intrigued now. What had they said about the teenagers?

But then the door burst open. Judith came in and spotted Sam immediately, spoiling his cover. 'Where's Josh?' she asked.

Sam shrugged.

'You, get home,' she said to him. 'The rest of you, outside, the foraging party's back and they've brought a truck which needs unloading.'

'Good news at last!' Thomas Butcher the landlord said, clapping his meaty hands together. 'We can use the cellar here as a storeroom.'

'We're not storing it here,' Judith said sharply. 'It's going in the church. It will be distributed at the

Harvest Festival on Friday night, along with anything else the foragers come back with, and every last bit of local produce we can pick between then and now.'

Thomas looked for a minute as though he might argue the point, but Judith in this sort of mood was unstoppable.

Sam ducked out of the pub. Though he would have liked to stay to find out more about plans and squabbles, he was tired and didn't feel much like helping to unload the truck. He passed the convoy on his way home, parked on the Guildford Road. Grim-faced men stood around, some smoking and chatting in hushed tones, enveloped by the dank autumn evening.

'Is Josh Pirbright with you?' Sam called.

One of the men shook his head. 'He's gone to the hospital, with Reg Walker.'

'Jammy git,' Sam repeated. 'Wish I'd gone.' He turned to go and got a shock as he came face to face with Michael Pirbright, standing on the pavement outside the pub, his craggy features half in shadow and full of fury. It was clear he'd heard what the man had said.

'Oh, hello, Mr Pirbright,' Sam said. But Josh's father ignored him, spun on his heels and stalked off towards the church.

*

'Here we are,' Reg said, looking up at the sign over a set of double doors. '*Intensive care.*'

The floor was littered with bottles, papers and medical equipment. Josh saw a tray of surgical instruments upturned on a steel trolley. Should he take those? Would Jenny want them?

'In there,' Reg said, pointing to a room marked DISPENSARY. But as he moved towards it, there was a noise from the room to their left. A dull thump, but loud enough to make them freeze. Josh felt an icy hand grip his chest.

Reg hoisted his rifle and walked into the room slowly, checking behind the doors. Josh followed, self-consciously holding the pistol, pointing it well away from Reg. He stopped and watched as Reg approached a large perspex window that offered a view into a smaller room beyond. A sign on the door read ISOLATION SUITE. There was a hazmat symbol below it.

'Jesus Christ,' Reg said as he peered through the window. Josh didn't want to, but he forced himself to move forward to see, and Reg stepped back to allow him access.

Inside the room was a white-coated man, perhaps a doctor, lying on a bed. There were three other, unoccupied beds, one of them stacked with cans of food and bottles of water. The doctor, if that's what he was, was clearly still alive. His chest raised and lowered as he breathed raggedly. His face was mottled and his hands purple. His eyes were shut.

Josh stared for a long time before finding the courage to tap on the perspex. The man inside shifted slightly, a second or so after the tap. Josh repeated it, and he saw the doctor's eyes flick open. The man stared at the ceiling, his cracked lips moved slightly.

'The vaccine. Get the vaccine,' Josh said, his heart pounding.

'He doesn't look in great shape,' Reg whispered as he fumbled with the pack. 'He needs the antivirals too. Reckon he sealed himself in, hoped the virus wouldn't get through.'

Josh tapped again, louder this time. The man managed to turn his head slightly and looked directly at them, sending a jolt of fear down Josh's spine. He watched the doctor half raise himself and hold out a hand towards them. Then he rolled forward and fell from the bed with a muffled crash, out of sight. Josh leaned over to the door and rattled the handle; it was locked.

'What do we do?' he asked Reg.

The soldier inspected the door.

'Reinforced glass. He has to unlock it from the inside.'

'We have medicine!' Josh shouted through the glass. The doctor had raised himself onto his hands and knees and was crawling towards the window.

Josh could see the bubo on the back of the man's neck – it had burst and black ichor stained the neck of his lab coat.

'I'm not sure he's not going to make it, Josh,' Reg said. 'We're too late.'

'Martha was this sick...' Josh said. 'We can save him.'

The man had reached the wall now and slowly, painfully, dragged himself up so that he was face to face with Josh, the perspex window between them. His face was haggard and dripping with sweat. He looked to be in his mid-forties, dark hair, greying. He stared at Josh, a look of curiosity and astonishment on his sweating face. Then he said something, but it was too muffled to make out.

Josh lifted a hand to his ear.

'Vaccine?' the man repeated, loud enough to hear this time.

Josh nodded and the man's face suddenly flushed with hope. He placed both hands on the glass and smiled.

Then his torso seemed to buck, his mouth opened and the doctor disappeared from sight as the perspex turned bright red.

Josh rushed to the door, which had its own, smaller window. The doctor lay on the floor, dark blood leaking from his mouth as his heart continued pumping, driving it through his veins, out of the corrupted lungs.

Josh stood helplessly and watched the man die. Then Reg took his arm gently and led him from the ward. The soldier made Josh sit on a chair in the corridor for a while and gave him a drink of water.

'We tried, Josh,' Reg said.

'There might be more,' Josh said, shaking. 'There may be others we could help.'

'Perhaps,' Reg said. 'But, honestly, if a doctor in a sealed chamber couldn't escape the virus, then it's unlikely anyone else here did, either.'

'We should look, though.'

'We'll keep our eyes open, Josh. But we have a job to do here. A mission. We need antibiotics for Mark. We don't have time to search the whole hospital.'

'But—'

'Enough, Josh,' Reg said. 'There are people alive, back in the village. Our focus needs to be on keeping them that way. Not going off on wild-goose chases. If we come across a warm one, then we'll do what we can. But we're not going to waste time scouring the whole damn hospital, the whole damn country. Your father made it clear last night that he didn't think anyone else was going to survive this, Josh. And it seems he was right. The vaccine came too late. Right now, we're alive and I want to concentrate on keeping it that way.'

He headed off across the corridor to the dispensary, and after a moment, Josh followed, his heart pounding. Was this what it was like to be a soldier? If so, he didn't enjoy it all that much.

As expected, the dispensary was stripped and chaotic. Reg scrabbled about on the shelves and did find a box of insulin, but no antibiotics. A dead woman in a white coat lay in the middle of the floor, between the shelves. Her head was surrounded by the obligatory halo.

'Looks like she stayed at her post until the last,' Reg said. 'A lot of heroes are going to go unmourned.'

'What now?' Josh asked dully, trying to clear his head of its nightmare images.

'My son once got this cut on his shin, when he was a lad,' Reg began. Josh glanced up at him, the old soldier's craggy face suddenly softening as he spoke.

'I didn't know you had a family,' Josh said. 'Where are they...?' But he tailed off. What was the point in such questions any more? What did it matter where Reg's family had been when they'd died.

'My wife died in 2007,' Reg said, replying anyway. 'She was the lucky one, I suppose. Escaped all this. Resting in the new cemetery at Frensham, where she grew up, you see?'

Josh nodded, watching the old soldier's face soften as he spoke of his wife.

'My son and daughter grew up and moved away. I spoke to my daughter most weeks, but my son. Well, he's like me. Not too good at staying in contact.' He stopped speaking, staring off into space. 'Wish I'd phoned him a bit more now,' he said softly.

Josh said nothing. He wished he could go and, well, at least lay a hand on Reg's shoulder, but it didn't seem right, not when they were both carrying guns.

'Anyway, this cut,' Reg said. 'We didn't think anything of it. We just put some Savlon on and a big plaster and left it at that. But when we checked the next day, the cut had grown and gone all infected. It smelled strong, like almonds, and we knew something was up. So we brought him here. This was thirty years ago, mind, and it was all different, but I remember they took him straight to intensive care and put him on a drip that was nothing but antibiotics, in liquid form. They must have had gallons of the stuff there. Reckon they probably still will.'

Josh nodded and followed Reg as he set off down the corridor, following the signs to the ICU. They had to go up two flights of stairs, passing the bodies of a couple of white-coated hospital staff lying together at the base of the steps.

They entered the ward. Josh took a sharp breath as he noticed each of the beds had an occupant, then regretted it instantly as the stench assailed him.

'Bingo,' Reg said from behind him. Josh turned to see the old man rummaging about in a small room behind the nurses' station. 'There's a fridge here full of bottles, and some of these are antibiotics. There's other stuff here too. Bandages and insulin, and that.'

As Reg packed a box he found on one of the shelves, Josh walked over to the window, hoping to open it for fresh air. He peered out and down and saw something in the forecourt that made him stop and stare.

Something moving.

4.55 P.M.

'So what happened that night?' Sam asked. 'After they gave me the injection and I went to sleep?'

Kitty looked up at him from the game of back-gammon they were playing before dinner. Monica had dressed in black and, trying to keep constantly busy, was occupying herself by cooking an enormous roast. Mrs McGovern had come around collecting non-perishable food earlier in the day but had told Monica to keep any meat or vegetables she might still have. Since the electricity had gone Monica had kept her freezer closed, to keep it cold as long as possible, but it was getting to a point now where everything had to be eaten or thrown away.

'Might as well use it up,' she'd said as Kitty had stared, wide-eyed, at the size of the joint.

'Mr Pirbright brought you back,' Kitty told Sam. 'And they put you into bed. Then next morning Mum told me to stay and watch you, she had to go to the meeting.'

'She left us alone to go to the meeting?' Sam asked, surprised. 'It must have been important.'

'I think the grown-ups wanted to talk about it all,'

Kitty said. 'About what they were going to do.'

'And what happened when she came back?'

'She said we were going to have to work on one of the farms and start going to church every Sunday.' They usually attended church once a month at most.

Sam wrinkled his nose in distaste. 'I don't like the sound of that,' he said.

'Which? Working on a farm, or going to church?'

'Neither, really.'

'I can't believe everyone's dead,' Kitty said. 'Dad, Gran, everyone.'

'It can't be everyone,' Sam insisted. 'Some people must have survived. We did.' He heard a noise outside and went to look through the window. It was almost completely dark now and Amir Mansoor's Land Rover went by slowly, headlights harsh compared to the soft candlelight flickering through the windows of the houses opposite.

'Where's Josh?' he said to the empty world.

Downstairs at the hospital, in the doctor's office again, Josh and Reg watched the dogs intently through the window. In the dusk, the forecourt was lit by a dozen or so lampposts, which must have been powered by the generator. In the hard yellow light, a pack of half a dozen dogs snarled and skittered. One of the dogs licked the dried blood off the cheek of a corpse lying near an ambulance. They looked skinny and mean.

'They're just pets, though,' Josh said. 'They won't attack us, surely?'

'I wouldn't have thought so. Not yet,' Reg answered cautiously.

'What do you mean, not yet?'

Reg clucked his tongue. 'Just at the moment, they have enough food – we saw that on the way down here. But eventually that food source will run out and they'll get hungry.'

'And they'll come looking?'

'Yeah. And having been pets, they'll associate humans with food. Maybe not these particular dogs, but the whole country will be overrun with abandoned pets. They'll form packs and some of them will sniff us out.'

'And by then they'll have developed a taste for human flesh,' Josh said.

Reg half laughed, half choked. 'Well, I wouldn't have put it quite so dramatically but, yeah, that's about the shape of it. Come on,' he added. 'We'll give them a wide berth and we should be OK, but keep that gun handy.'

The dogs noticed Reg and Josh as soon as they began clambering out of the window. One of them, a black mongrel, trotted up to them and stopped a few metres away. The dog wagged its tail, but growled as Reg stepped towards it. The other animals stood still or walked in circles, ears down, watching the humans. Waiting. Josh felt like he was in a film.

'They're confused. They don't understand what's going on,' Josh said.

'They're not the only ones,' Reg muttered. 'Let's go.'

Slowly, painfully, step by step, the two made their way across the forecourt.

'I'm not scared of you, I'm not scared of you…' Josh repeated over and over as they went. He remembered the bit in *The Jungle Book* where Mowgli stares the wolves in the eye to force them to look away and so assert his dominance. He tried it now, but these dogs just stared back. The black mongrel followed them but the rest of the pack kept its distance.

'That one there is the most dangerous,' Reg said, indicating a mean-looking Alsatian Josh recognised as the dog that he'd seen licking the cheek of the corpse earlier. 'I reckon that one's already half-savage.'

Just as they reached the access lane that linked the forecourt to the main road the Alsatian suddenly rushed towards them, tail and hackles up. The others quickly followed, encouraged by their friend's bravery. Reg swung the barrel of the rifle towards the pack and Josh pointed the revolver, feeling foolish and scared simultaneously.

The pack leader stopped about a metre away. The black mongrel faced it and growled, evidently having thought the matter through and deciding to side with the humans.

'We can't shoot them all,' Josh said.

'We don't need to. If he comes any closer—'

But then the Alsatian leaped forward and Reg fired. It yelped as it was flung back and to the side. The dog twisted and scrabbled in the dusty road, crippled. Josh raised the revolver and fired once, both pleased and horrified to see the dog's skull crack open, stilling it instantly.

The rest of the pack fled, but the black mongrel stood firm and looked up at Josh approvingly.

'I think we might have found a fellow survivor,' Reg said.

Josh nodded and kneeled to introduce himself properly to the dog. He reached out a hand. The dog sniffed it gingerly, then gave it a lick. Josh scratched the dog between the ears.

'You're just a big softy, aren't you?' he said.

The dog woofed.

'Come on,' Reg said. 'The others will have gone by now.'

'Here.' Josh, handed Reg the revolver as they made their way to the car. 'Thanks for this.'

'Keep it,' Reg said, turning away. 'You'll probably need it again.'

Josh got back home just before eight. Reg dropped him off first before heading to the clinic at Jenny Stephenson's house to deliver the antibiotics.

'Hey,' Reg called as Josh hopped out of the Land

Rover, carrying the Leica and the boots. Josh turned to the old soldier. 'You did good,' Reg said.

'Thanks,' Josh replied, touched by the praise. He opened the back door with difficulty and the dog leaped out, sniffing to get a feel for his new home.

'We'll make a soldier of you yet,' Reg said, then released the clutch and and moved off slowly down the street.

I'm not sure I want to be a soldier, Josh thought to himself, watching the car go. 'Come on, boy,' he said to the mongrel and walked up to the house.

He let himself in and immediately saw his mother in the hall, as though she'd been standing there waiting for him. She glanced down at the dog and he could see her thinking how best to deal with this. Josh put the boots down and stroked the dog's head, to comfort it.

Judith walked over and gave Josh a hug. 'I'm glad you're safe, Josh, but if you ever do something like that again I will strangle you myself.'

'Sorry, Mum,' he said.

She looked up at him and pursed her lips. 'Your father wants a word with you. You think *I'm* angry...?' She left the sentence hanging and nodded towards the dining room.

Josh swallowed. What an idiot he'd been going off like that. Why had he convinced himself his father might be impressed? He walked into the dining room. His father was at the table, looking over a land survey map, a notebook beside him filled with his graceful, looping handwriting.

'Close the door,' Michael said, without looking up. Josh did so. He hardly ever saw his father angry – once, when Josh had muddied the carpet of a new car, another time more recently when he'd stayed out all night with friends and not texted. Usually it was Judith who did the telling off.

His father stood up and walked over to Josh. 'Are you hurt?' he asked. 'Any injuries?'

Josh shook his head.

'A scratch, an infection, a broken limb – these were minor ailments before, Josh. Now they can be a death sentence.' He stopped and watched his son, waiting for this to sink in.

'We can't guarantee continuing supplies of antibiotics,' he went on. 'They're not that easy to find, or to make without proper facilities. The same goes for other medicines. We're damn lucky we have Jenny Stephenson, but she's not a doctor, Josh.'

'You're a chemist,' Josh said quietly, wanting to mount a defence at least.

'I'm a virologist,' Michael snapped. 'And frankly, Josh, it was work in my field which created HAV3N in the first place. It's time we stopped relying on fancy medicines and started using our common sense.'

'Sorry, Dad,' Josh said.

Michael's nostrils flared. 'How could you be so *stupid*?' he spat.

133

Josh was surprised by the venom in his dad's voice. He hadn't seen his father like this before.

'I thought I was doing something helpful,' he said. 'I wanted to get involved.'

'I thought I could trust you,' Michael said, his voice getting louder.

'You can, Dad,' Josh said.

Michael laughed. 'I clearly can't. What's that?' he said, noticing the camera Josh carried.

'I got it in Guildford,' Josh replied, holding it up. 'I thought it might be usef—'

Michael snatched it from Josh's hand and flung it across the room. 'Time to put your toys away, Josh,' he shouted. 'Time to grow up and start using your brain.'

Josh's mouth opened in shock. He understood that his father was angry, but where was this nastiness coming from? He was like a different person.

'Get out!' his father commanded, and Josh slunk from the room, reeling with shock and guilt.

18 OCTOBER, 2.34 A.M.

Martha Pirbright watched her father running towards her through a forest of dead trees in a red desert. But they weren't trees, they were people. Victims of HAV3N. The dead reached out, their crooked, blood-blackened fingers brushing against her father's thin frame. Clawing at him, limply gripping his calves as he forced his way through the thickening crowd of living corpses. And however fast or long he ran, he never seemed to get closer to her.

She held out a hand in encouragement and tried to move towards him. Perhaps she could help him, draw him up and away from the dead forest.

But there were too many. And their hatred for her father was too strong. They blamed him for their deaths. 'Join us,' they whispered. 'Stay with us. Be one of us.' Her father wept as he ran. Great tears, which splashed and hissed on the hot desert floor.

Martha woke with a start and realised she was holding out a hand, stretched across the room, to where a faint after-image of her father remained, still running. Still weeping.

5

The next day it was Sunday. Fat clouds raced across the sky casting a gloom over the village that perfectly matched the mood.

Martha had heard it all the previous evening. She'd popped out of her room to see the white-faced Josh as he came up the stairs.

'I don't think I've ever seen him so mad before,' she'd said.

'He's tired,' Josh had said. 'I shouldn't have gone, at least not without telling Mum.'

Martha frowned. 'He shouldn't have yelled like that, though, Josh. That wasn't right.'

Judith rescued the camera and brought it up to Josh's room in the morning. He checked it over as she spoke.

'I've spoken to your father. He feels bad about what he said last night,' she told him. 'He was angry and scared.'

'It's OK,' Josh said. 'I understand; it was a stupid thing to do.' The camera seemed fine, he noted with satisfaction. Leica made them tough.

'It's not OK,' Judith said. 'But perhaps it's understandable. He's under stress.'

Michael nodded stiffly at Josh when he came down for breakfast, his way of saying sorry. The four ate together and gradually the tension between Josh and his father faded a little. After breakfast, they went into the sitting room. It was chilly, and Judith had got last night's fire going again earlier. They settled down as Michael told them his tale. He said he wanted to tell them all about the events of the last few days. Josh found himself staring at the nasty-looking cut above his father's right ear, which Mrs Stephenson had done a good job of stitching. He complained of a headache again and Judith brought him some painkillers. He took four, at which she raised her eyebrows, but she said nothing.

'When the first reports of the virus started to come through,' Michael Pirbright began, 'we suspected it might be a bad one. The rates of infection seemed to be one hundred per cent, which was a figure we didn't believe at first. No disease has a one hundred per cent infection rate. Some people always have a natural immunity, some people always manage to escape infection. But not this time.' He stopped, closed his eyes as if doing so might block out the memory. The fire crackled, a comforting sound which helped to smooth over the ragged edges of the pause.

'When the tissue samples came in we knew this was it, the dinosaur-killer. The worst thing was the speed at which the disease took over the body. We call it a Goldilocks virus: not too fast, not too slow. It gave the victim enough time to move around, even go to work or to school, spreading the virus further. There are some viruses which work much, much faster – some artificially created strains can disable and kill the subject within minutes. Those tend to die out quickly, as there just isn't the time for them to spread through the population. Those that act more slowly are less dangerous too. There's time for the blood to build antibodies, and time for us to develop vaccines.'

Michael paused to take a sip of coffee and rub his temples. He was grim and his expression pained. Josh watched his father intently. Normally so graceful and easy with words, Michael was speaking slowly, thinking about each word, more like Judith now.

'Where did this virus come from?' Martha asked. 'They said it was pigeon flu.'

Michael glanced at her. 'Yes, a hybrid between bird flu and human flu, but bird flu alone is not particularly dangerous; it kills thousands a year, but mostly the weak. Human flu is the same. But when you combine the two...' He stopped and stared off into the distance, remembering again.

'Dad?' Josh said, after a while. Part of him was still angry with his father over the dressing-down he'd received, but it was clear his father was troubled, and Josh felt a pang of regret for having caused him grief the day before. Judith laid a hand on her husband's shoulder.

'Do you mind if we don't talk about the actual virus any more?' Michael asked eventually.

'No, of course,' Judith said.

'It's over now. Eradicated. And with God's will we'll never again see the kind of society that allows these things to exist.' He held out a trembling hand, palm down, and closed his eyes.

Josh looked at Martha and raised an eyebrow. Michael was the believer in the family, and dragged them all to church from time to time, but the way he'd said 'with God's will' sounded a little...well, evangelical.

'How did you get back to us?' Martha asked, tactfully steering the conversation away. 'Where did you find that motorbike?'

'Just outside Stowmarket, a motorcycle shop.' Michael answered. 'I tried to drive at first, but the roads were jammed. Car after car, all with dead bodies in – families, children, businessmen, housewives, police, ambulance men. I even saw a stretch limo smashed through the central reservation on the M11.'

Josh thought back to his own experience in Guildford. The black halos, the corpse with the bite marks.

'I took an SUV from the lab and pushed other cars aside. Until I couldn't get through any further, then

I found the bike and that was much quicker. I took the M25. That was carnage, but there were gaps, long stretches where the hard shoulder was free. I ran low on petrol near Sevenoaks and I had to come off the motorway and go into town to get more. I siphoned some out of another motorbike. It was horrible.' Michael stopped again, shivering slightly. 'There were dogs. People had been fighting to get food. I saw an army checkpoint with bodies piled up in front, bullet holes in the dead. The smell was awful.' Judith glanced up at Martha, looking worried, as though wondering if she should stop her husband.

'I tripped and fell onto the pavement,' he said, his voice trembling. 'There was a dead baby lying there, in the gutter. Didn't see the mother.' He stopped and shuddered at the memory. 'I found a shovel and buried the poor little thing in one of the gardens. It was one little thing. Completely pointless, I know, but I needed to do something. It made me feel a bit better.'

'Did you see anyone alive?' Martha asked.

Michael hesitated, then shook his head.

'Did you look for survivors?' Martha said.

'There wasn't time,' Judith said, answering for her husband, who seemed pained by the question. 'There wasn't time to search for survivors. Your father did the right thing. He had to get here as quickly as he could.'

Michael's head dipped gently and he closed his

eyes. For a moment Josh thought he was going to burst into tears, but then he recovered and nodded briskly. 'That's right. I couldn't help everyone. I had to make a choice. I chose to come here. You were my number one priority.'

My God, Josh thought. *You poor man*. What hell his father must have been going through. The guilt . . .

Michael drew a deep breath and went on. 'I left the motorway at Junction eight and took B-roads. I couldn't face the corpses any more. I don't know whether it saved time, but at least I couldn't see any more bodies. Those black stains. The curled lips, grinning at me, snarling at me. The stench, oh my word, the stench!'

'How did you hurt your head?' Martha asked.

Michael laughed. A harsh, coughing laugh. 'I was answering a call of nature and was chased by a young bull. I spent my life analysing the dangers that microscopic life forms pose to us, I'd forgotten about the big animals that can hurt us too. I just saw a bunch of cows and didn't think they might be steers.'

'They do look different,' Martha pointed out.

'Well, I know that now!' Michael said. 'Anyway, this young bull ran right across the field towards me as I was trying to pull up my trousers. Then I tried to get through a barbed-wire fence, but my backpack was caught and there I was, crouched over, bum sticking out while this manic bull came charging towards me, followed by all the rest!'

They were all laughing now, the tension broken. For a moment it was like before. He was like before.

'Somehow I got through,' he said. 'But then found I had blood pouring down my face. That was just up the road from here. Near Compton, I think.'

'Maybe we should take a drive up there,' Josh suggested. 'David McGovern said he needed a good bull.'

Michael nodded approvingly. 'Good thinking, son,' he smiled.

Josh found himself looking at the floor, embarrassed at how pleased he was by his father's approval.

'So, we've heard what everyone's saying . . . do you seriously not think there are any other survivors?' Martha asked.

Pirbright glanced at his wife quickly, and suddenly the tension was back in the room. Again, Michael seemed to be thinking carefully how to answer.

'Honestly, Martha? No, I don't. Even Little Sheen, isolated and barricaded, was on the verge of succumbing when I turned up with the vaccine. I've seen the speed and intensity of this thing. By the time we find survivors, if there are pocketfuls, it will be too late. You've been to Guildford now, son, you've seen it for yourself. You know I'm right.'

Reluctantly Josh agreed.

Martha wasn't quite finished. 'But there must have been more of the vaccine? Weren't there other scientists there at the lab?'

Michael shook his head. 'No, it was just me at the end.'

Martha looked puzzled. 'But I thought there were lots of scientists there...'

'That's enough for now,' Judith said. 'Your father's tired, and we must get dressed for church.'

Martha shook her head, now bewildered. 'It doesn't make sense—'

'Stop, Martha!' her father snapped. She stared at him in surprise, taken aback by the abrupt change in him. A minute earlier he'd been laughing along with the rest of them. Now suddenly it was as if a door had slammed shut. 'That's enough. There was no one else at the lab, there was just me and that's the end of it.'

ST ANDREW'S C OF E CHURCH
SERMON, 18 OCTOBER

Rev James Halfdene:
Good morning, everyone, and thank you for attending our service of remembrance. The list of those villagers so suddenly taken from us has been posted at the altar. A more permanent memorial will be arranged in due course. Despite the solemnity of the occasion, it's good to see the church full. We haven't had so many people together in the building since we stopped doing bingo. It seems a shame that it takes an event such as we've just experienced to bring

people back to Our Lord's house. In fact, this will be the subject of today's sermon. The importance and the centrality of the church to this community.

But first, let's close our eyes and pray together for those of our flock who have left us to be closer to God. And not just for friends, family and neighbours, but for the uncountable millions throughout the world who we believe have succumbed to the virus and are now at peace.

I will read a verse from Genesis. In which Noah, a man righteous in his generation, is saved from the flood by God's word and by his own, intense labour.

Reading, by Monica Hilfenhaus, from Genesis, chapter 6

Sermon contd...
In recent years I fear there has been a tendency in the church to focus on trying to present a softer, more modern face of Christianity. We perhaps have tended to underplay all that business about God's wrath and the eternal damnation side of things. But we must face bald truths. We have been visited by an horrific plague of biblical proportions, and really only the Old Testament offers us any precedent. When talking of apocalypse, for let's be in no doubt that we have just come through nothing less, the Old Testament is the closest we have to a how-to-do-it handbook.

And the Old Testament offers us a glimpse of how we must respond. The story of Noah, who survived the flood; or Job who escaped from Sodom; or David, or Daniel, who each stood against apparently insurmountable dangers and triumphed through courage, resilience and, above all, faith.

For it is faith that allowed us to survive this plague. We do not know exactly why God chose to spare us when so many died. But we know he did spare us, and that there must have been a reason. We have been given a second life, a second chance, and we must treat that with humility and respect. We must stand together, doing God's work, reading God's words and abiding by them. All of them, Old Testament and New.

Now I know that not all of you are comfortable with the idea of any new authority having a religious stamp, as it were. There has been talk of establishing a rival authority. Don't get me wrong, I like the Wheatsheaf, I occasionally pop in to bless the beer barrels as many of you have witnessed. But a pub is no proper place for a seat of power. It would set us off on the wrong heading were we to establish our new government in a drinking house.

It is to the credit of those amongst us who I know to be atheist, and those who pray to a different god, that they too are here, part of our community. To you I say this: no one expects you to change your views in light of what has happened. But regardless of your views, you are welcome in this church. In return, those of us who are members of the Christian faith, those of us who are looking to that faith for support and succour at this time, would ask that you respect our beliefs too. We do not know if there are other survivors out there. But it does seem likely that we are the only community which has survived relatively unscathed. We have a moral duty to establish a council, or government if you will, according to basic moral codes which are universal, whether or not you believe they are the commands of God. We cannot allow the mistakes of the past to creep back in.

We will be holding the Harvest Festival here at the church on Tuesday evening from five thirty. Food will be distributed. Mr McGovern tells me there has been a good harvest this year, and for the immediate future at least there is more than enough food for everyone. Let us thank the Lord for that.

The parish council will meet here every Friday evening at seven thirty p.m. sharp. We'll ring the bells to remind you. It is hoped that all interested parties should attend. The meeting is open to the public, who will be invited to ask questions and pose solutions.

Now let us sing. 'How Great Though Art', page thirty-seven of your hymn books.

The wind had dropped when they left the church, and under the low clouds the day had turned out quite mild. None of the teenagers felt like going home just then, and Josh and Martha had noticed a certain coolness between their parents over breakfast. In fact, there'd been a bit of an atmosphere in the house for the last couple of days. There'd presumably been a row at some point.

Sam and Kitty came too, and the four wandered around the graveyard to the massive old oak which dominated that side of the church. There were a couple of flat slabs of gravestones there which made good places to sit.

Josh told them about the trip to the hospital.

'So were you scared?' Kitty asked, staring intently at him.

'Yes, but we had a job to do,' Josh replied.

Sam rolled his eyes. 'You're such a hero, Josh,' he said in mock adoration. 'If looting stuff is heroic, that is.'

'It wasn't looting,' said Josh. 'It was *foraging*.'

'I can't believe you were in Guildford, grabbing free stuff and didn't get me those new Converse,' Sam said.

'Shut up, Sam,' Kitty told her brother.

'I'll get some next time,' promised Josh.

'It's my turn to go, next,' Sam said. 'I asked Reg this morning.'

'You think there's going to be a next time?' Martha frowned. 'After the blast Josh got from Dad?'

'Oh, it'll blow over,' Josh said breezily. 'They can't keep us locked up in the village for ever.'

'I don't think you're going anywhere,' Martha insisted. 'I think Dad's serious about us not leaving the village.'

'That sucks,' Sam said with feeling. 'I've been waiting my whole life to get out of this stupid village. Hang on, does this mean we won't be able to take our bikes out?'

Josh nodded. 'I guess so.'

'That sucks,' Sam repeated.

It was the first time they'd all been together since before the outbreak. They glanced at each other – they all looked tired. Martha and Sam still showed signs of the illness, each with faint red patches where the buboes had been, and they were a little hoarse. Sam had the remains of a shallow cough too and neither could walk too far without finding themselves short of breath.

Sam broke the ensuing silence. 'So *do* you think anyone else survived?'

'They must have done,' Kitty replied.

Josh frowned. 'After what I saw in Guildford,' he began, 'and what Dad said, I don't think anyone survived. Not unless they had the vaccine.'

'What do you think, Martha?' Kitty asked, looking to the older girl for assurance. People tended naturally to look to Martha for guidance. Like she was the one with the answers.

Martha shrugged. 'Dad said he was the only one left in the lab. No one else had the vaccine.'

'So that's it? Everyone's dead? The Queen? Lady Gaga?'

'Wayne Rooney?' Sam suggested.

'Maybe,' Martha said. Sometimes she didn't have any answers. There was a pause then, which Josh broke.

'Are you...?' he began, his voice croaky. He coughed and tried again. 'Are any of you having dreams?'

They all nodded.

'I dream about the barricade,' Sam said quietly.

'I dream about Gran, mostly,' Kitty said. 'And Dad.'

Josh was still having occasional nightmares. Awful, horrible dreams, hard to remember. Gruesome scenes he was appalled by.

'What did your mum say when you brought the dog back?' Kitty asked, changing the subject, trying to lighten the mood. She touched Josh's shoulder lightly and he smiled at her. She smiled back and Josh felt his heart skip a little.

'She wasn't too happy about it,' he said. 'She said we'd discuss it when Dad got back. But as it was he was so busy yelling at me about going to Guildford, the subject of the dog didn't really get mentioned.'

'So you're keeping him?' Kitty asked.

'You bet I am,' Josh said. 'He'll pay his way – we need a guard to watch out for foxes. And, anyway, Winston stood up for me against those other dogs. I think I owe him something in return.'

'Why did you call him Winston?' Martha asked.

'You know, Winston Churchill? It's cos he's got this big jowly face, and because he stood firm. It's a strong name, don't you think?'

Martha shook her head. Josh was an idiot sometimes. Kitty giggled.

Josh had a bad night. Legions of the black-haloed dead haunted his dreams. He was almost grateful to be woken in the small hours by the sounds of his father shouting in his sleep. Wordless, terror-stricken noises.

He lay awake for a long time. Nights in the house had been cold, dark and silent since the outbreak. Gone was the background hum of a dozen electrical items. Josh cowered beneath his blanket, a tiny, warm cocoon at the centre of an empty, cold universe. He was anxious about returning to the death-filled land of his dreams, but hating to be awake, alone, in the dark. The real world was scarcely less terrifying than his dreams, though. He thought of the armies of HAV3N victims out there, all over the world. Two billion dead in China alone. The numbers were too big. The scale too great.

He finally dropped off to sleep as the welcome fingers of dawn light crept under the blue curtains, to remind them that a new day was approaching. The world was not quite finished yet. The Earth was not quite dead.

Josh slept late and his father had left for the church by the time he came downstairs. He wanted to try and clear the air with him, so he bolted his breakfast and headed into the village. He didn't find his father, though – just the vicar, Jim Halfdene, chatting with Sam and Kitty's mother.

'Hello, Josh, how are you feeling?' the vicar asked.

'Fine thanks, Reverend,' Josh replied.

'I hear you've been off shopping,' Monica said.

'What? Oh, yes. I went with the foraging team to Guildford on Saturday,' Josh replied.

'Now, Josh, I know it's all very exciting at the moment,' Halfdene said. 'But you mustn't go off like that without permission.'

The back of Josh's neck prickled with embarrassment. If Sam were here he'd say something clever and funny. Josh just felt like a little boy, being ticked off for breaking a window, or something.

'You listen to your father, Josh,' Monica Hilfenhaus said, looking like she might wag a finger. 'He saved this village, he saved us all. We must all show him some respect.' Josh had never really got on with Sam's mother. She tended to blame him every time Sam got into one of his scrapes so Josh had always preferred Sam's father and, in that, he wasn't alone.

'OK, I know, I know,' he said, wanting to turn and

run away from the well-meaning admonishments. 'Where is he, anyway?'

'He's off inspecting farms with Mark,' Monica said.

'Mark? Is he on his feet?' Josh was glad. He hadn't been able to help feeling guilty.

'He's on crutches, but getting around,' the vicar said with a smile. 'There's work to be done, Josh.'

Josh had the feeling that he'd missed something during his trip to Guildford. It wasn't as if he'd been sitting around doing nothing. He was struck by the sense his father was punishing his absence by electing to take Mark on his inspection instead of Josh.

'Anything I can do while I'm here?' Josh asked.

'Oh, yes,' Monica said. 'Come with me.'

She led Josh down into the crypt where he was surprised to find half a dozen people packing food into cardboard boxes. He recognised Harry Waldock who ran the local cricket club. Harry waved at him. Mark's mother was there too, dressed in black, mourning her husband but turning up to help nonetheless. Josh felt even more guilty now about sleeping in.

'You can start labelling these up,' Monica said. 'Here's a list of all the people in the village. Everyone gets a box. If there are three people in a house, they get three boxes. Label them all and take them up into the vestry – we're going to ask everyone to collect their own box this afternoon.'

Josh nodded and got to work.

He caught up with his father eventually at lunch. Michael was crunching his way through a tomato salad and rubbing his head. Josh noticed a half-empty packet of painkillers on the table.

'Still got your headache?' he asked. Michael nodded, wincing slightly. 'Dad, could I come and work with you this afternoon?' Josh asked after helping himself to some food.

Michael hesitated. 'Well, I've got Mark with me at the moment. Aren't you helping Monica with food distribution?'

'Sure, but I just thought you might need some support with the planning side of things.'

Michael sighed. 'I don't want you to feel I'm cutting you out here, Josh. It's just that ... Mark's injured, so he can't do much else at the moment, and he has valuable skills. I need his help.'

Josh nodded.

'Besides, he's ... upset. He's lost his father,' Michael said. 'He needs to be kept busy. I'm afraid his mother isn't much help. She's a shell of a woman.'

'Everyone's lost someone, Dad,' Josh said. 'Everyone's a mess.'

'I know, Josh,' Michael replied, sighing, 'but I can't help everyone. It's like that ... that baby I saw. I had to bury the poor thing. Completely pointless, except that I felt I was doing something, do you understand?'

Josh nodded. So Mark was a project?

'If I can help Mark through this difficult time, then I'll feel as though I've accomplished something.'

'You've accomplished loads, Dad,' Josh said. 'You're helping everyone.'

Michael waved away the compliment and munched on a mouthful of lettuce.

'I'm not trying to get Mark fired,' Josh said. 'I just wondered if there was something you wanted me to do as well.'

Michael frowned.

'At the moment, Josh,' he said, 'I think you should keep doing what you're doing. We have some plans about getting the Gardeners' farm up and running, so I'll need your help on that. But just for now, Monica needs strong backs and legs with the distribution. OK?'

Josh nodded, trying to hide his disappointment. How long was his father going to keep this up?

20 OCTOBER, 7.02 P.M.

'Have you seen Josh?' Kitty asked Judith, who was pouring drinks at the Harvest Supper in the church. She was worried she'd miss him, or that he wouldn't even bother coming. He'd promised, though, before everything. He'd said he'd see her here.

154

'He's probably in the churchyard,' Judith said. 'I told him he had to leave Winston outside and he's been checking on him every five minutes.'

Pews had been cleared and trestle tables arranged in a rectangular formation. Everyone in the village was there, even Gloria Hansen, who hadn't been seen since her baby daughter had died during the outbreak. Thomas Butcher and Amir had been in charge of the cooking in the church kitchens, and had produced enormous vats of butternut-squash risotto. There was fruit and cake for dessert.

Everyone had been given a large box of canned goods to take home as well as plenty of fresh produce. The atmosphere was reserved. Everyone was grieving, but there was a sense of gratitude as well, a feeling that life just might be able to carry on. Reverend Halfdene had given a short service of Thanksgiving before the meal. Now the church was full, and buzzing with noise. It was possible to forget for a moment that the world outside was empty and silent. Someone had put up a big poster over the stage. KEEP CALM AND CARRY ON, it read.

Martha had seated herself on Kitty's right, but the girls had hardly had a chance to talk at all. Mark was on Martha's other side and had been chatting to her nonstop about the plans he and her father had been drawing up for the village.

'You seem to be getting on well with my dad,' Kitty heard Martha saying.

'He's a brilliant man,' Mark replied. 'He saved us all. And he's a natural leader, you know? God knows we need one.'

Across from Kitty sat the portly Mrs Hutton who'd already had two slices of the Victoria sponge resting on a plate in the middle of the table. Reg and Clive Mitchell had brought a portable generator to the village and, under Mark's supervision, had hooked it up in the pub. Mark still kept his crutches to hand.

'Things never seem so bad when there's a slice of Victoria sponge in front of you,' Mrs Hutton gushed at Judith, who smiled and nodded. Meanwhile Kitty had pushed back her chair and made off towards the side door.

Kitty had been delighted when she'd first entered the church, even though she'd helped set everything up. It looked so romantic, perfect for meeting Josh later. Without electric lights, Judith had resorted to candle power. All the light bulbs in the old chandeliers had been removed and replaced with fat, white candles looted from Tesco. The effect was stunning – a soft, yellow light suffused everything, gentler and sweeter than the white neons installed during the last refurbishment a dozen years ago.

Kitty slipped out between the heavy double doors and stood, looking for Josh. She heard Winston bark and trotted towards the sound. She found the dog easily enough, tied up under a tree with a bowl of water and some dry dog biscuits. Winston was delighted to see her and she crouched to scratch his ears. Kitty loved dogs anyway, but this was Josh's dog. So she loved him all the more.

A footstep behind her and she stood and turned, expecting to see Josh.

'Kitty?'

It was Mark. He was good-looking, but she didn't know him well, even though he'd lived across the street from them. He'd once tried to befriend Kitty on Facebook but she'd ignored the request.

'Oh, hi, Mark,' she said, trying not to let the disappointment show in her voice.

'What are you doing out here on your own?' he asked. 'It's cold.'

'Oh, just . . . just wanted some fresh air.' *Stop being nosey*, she thought.

'Yes, hot in there, isn't it?' he answered. 'Look, I'm sorry about your dad.'

'Oh, thanks,' Kitty replied. 'Sorry about yours.'

'Yeah, it's not easy, is it?'

'No,' Kitty said, shivering a little. She appreciated his concern, but found herself hoping he'd hurry up and say what he had to say. Her thin cardigan wasn't enough for the chilly autumn air.

'Anyway,' Mark said, 'I think you should be careful, wandering around on your own like this.'

'Careful of what?' Kitty asked.

Mark shrugged. 'I'm not trying to scare you or

anything, but remember, there's no police now. No CCTV cameras. You should stay safe, be careful who you hang around with, you know?'

'Er, OK,' Kitty replied, confused. What was he on about?

'You know, we were all talking,' he went on. 'In the pub the other night. I mean, the adults were discussing what might happen. Some people started saying how it was important for there to be stable relationships and all that, as the village teenagers – y'know, you four – would have to be, y'know careful, so that things didn't get all messed up.'

Kitty screwed up her face. 'What are you talking about?'

'Nothing really,' Mark said quickly. 'It's just there aren't many of us around the same age...'

'We're not the same age,' Kitty said. 'You're much older than us.' The wind seemed suddenly colder and more insistent, working its way through the thick cotton of her dress.

'Not *that* much,' he laughed. 'Martha's only four years younger than me.'

Oh, Kitty thought. *So that's what this is about. He likes Martha?*

'Is that what the adults have been talking about in these meetings? Getting us all married off?'

Mark laughed and held up his hands. 'It's not like that. It's more about making sure that... stable relationships are formed. If this village is to survive, we

158

must think carefully, plan carefully...'

'Isn't it a bit soon to be thinking about this?' Kitty asked.

'Michael Pirbright doesn't think so,' Mark said.

'I see,' Kitty snapped, her face growing hot as her anger rose. 'So he wants to get his daughter married off, does he? To you?'

'Now who's jumping the gun?' Mark said, smiling infuriatingly. 'Come on, let's go back inside.'

'You go back inside if you want,' Kitty said. 'I'm waiting for Josh.'

'Josh?' Mark said. 'I saw him in the church just now, helping old Reg with something.'

Suddenly Kitty felt deflated. Defeated. Her anger ebbed. Why had Josh sent her that message if he didn't want to see her tonight? She sighed. Everything had changed.

'So anyway,' Mark went on, 'we just think you four need to be careful, that's all.'

'OK,' Kitty sighed. 'I'll be careful.'

'Good,' Mark said. Then he took Kitty's elbow and gently walked her back to the church.

That night Josh was woken from his terrors by the sound of someone else screaming. It was Michael again. He went into the corridor, listening.

'I've killed them all, I've killed them all,' he heard his father saying before his mother's comforting tone broke in and Michael's screams turned to sobs. 'Oh

God, Judith,' he cried. 'My head. It hurts. It hurts so much.'

Michael went back to sleep eventually. But after returning to bed, Josh lay awake for what seemed like hours, staring at the ceiling, imagining what it must have been like for his father, to see what he'd seen. To feel what he felt. A vision of the doctor in the isolation room forced its way back into his mind, crawling out from the dark place he'd tried to lock it away in. He could see his father had been forced to make a choice, an appalling choice. To abandon the attempt to save the world in order to save his family and their community. Realistically, there had been no option but to do what his father had done. Who would do otherwise? But it still couldn't have been easy. How many more lives could Michael have saved had he chosen to stay at the lab and make more of the vaccine?

21 OCTOBER, 7.41 A.M.

'I doubt very much that my father wants me to marry Mark Rogers,' Martha said. 'I think you must have got the wrong idea.'

'Fine,' Kitty said. 'Don't believe me, but that's pretty much what he said. From the sound of it, they think we should all get married sooner rather than later.'

'Even you?' Martha said.

'Why not me?' Kitty replied, slightly hurt.

'You're only fifteen!' Martha replied.

'Well, you're only seventeen,' Kitty said.

They sat on Martha's bed. It was the morning after the Harvest Festival and Kitty had come over before work – they'd been told to report to McGoverns' farm at nine a.m. sharp. She'd come to tell Martha about the events of last night. If Josh happened to be around, she intended to ignore him, let him see how it felt. As it happened he had already left for work when she got there.

'Shall we listen to some music?' Kitty asked.

Martha shrugged. 'Sure.'

Kitty plugged her iPod into a set of battery-powered speakers and put on Lady Gaga. 'Gonna need some new AAs soon,' she tutted.

'We'll have to talk to the foraging committee,' Martha said. 'Ask for batteries and tampons.'

'Oh God!' Kitty said. 'You do it, I am *so* not asking Reg to get tampons for me.'

'OK,' Martha said, still thinking of what Kitty had told her and raising an eyebrow at the idea of either of them being married – but particularly Kitty, since she was so young.

'I am really glad they got the water back on,' Kitty said. 'I was getting sick of sponge baths.'

'Oh, I know,' Martha said.

They lay about for a while, just listening to the music, trying not to think about anything else.

'I didn't even think Mark knew who I was, really,' Martha said. 'Then he just sat down last night and started chatting.'

'Do you like him?' Kitty asked.

'He's handsome,' Martha said. 'Lovely eyes, but maybe a bit scary? Did you see the way he looked at Sam last night? Like he hates him.'

Kitty grunted. 'No. I didn't see Sam *or* Josh last night. But Sam did say Mark has a temper. Nice bum, though.'

'I am not seriously considering it!' Martha shrieked, rolling her eyes. The boys hadn't said much about what had happened on the barricade, but Josh had hinted that the gunshot wound to Mark's leg hadn't been entirely accidental. When Mark turned up last night, however, he'd made a point of thanking Josh for bringing back the life-saving antibiotics and the two had shaken hands. Mark had blanked Sam, who hadn't seemed that bothered.

'So who *would* you marry?' Martha asked. 'If you had to marry someone from the village?'

'God knows – I mean goodness knows,' Kitty said. Her mother had told her off that morning for blasphemy.

'*I* know,' Martha said, with a cheeky grin.

'Who?' Kitty asked sharply.

'Reg,' Martha said.

Kitty laughed out loud and rolled across the bed to kick Martha, who grabbed her leg and twisted her so she fell to the floor with a great thump. Kitty descended into a further fit of giggles, and for a moment everything was all right again.

5 November

Michael brought Mark home for dinner.

'We've been working so late these last weeks that poor old Mark's been missing meals,' he said in response to Judith's raised eyebrow. 'He's still recovering, you know.'

'He's had time to go home and put some aftershave on, though,' Martha muttered to Josh with a grin.

'Nice shirt too,' Josh whispered back.

Dinner was an awkward affair, with stilted small talk during the first course. Michael wasn't helping – he said nothing throughout but just watched the others, eating little himself.

Judith poured wine, first for the adults and then, despite a faint tut from Michael, for the teenagers too. Gradually tongues loosened. Mark seemed to have a few things he wanted to talk about. Though Josh and Mark had shaken hands, it was clear that Mark was still stewing over the events on the barricade.

'I can't stop thinking about it,' Mark said, smearing paté over a cracker. 'If only I'd been there when Dad came back. Maybe things would have been different.'

Josh shook his head. 'I really don't want to talk about it.'

163

Mark looked up at him steadily. 'That's the problem, though. No one will talk about it. I still don't know exactly what happened.' He took a gulp of wine. 'I mean, who pulled the trigger?'

'Mark, this isn't the time or place,' Judith said. 'We understand you're upset, but dredging up painful memories isn't going to bring your father back.'

Mark dropped it, and Josh and Martha were relieved when the conversation moved on to the work being planned. It turned out that Mark and Michael intended to build a fence right round the village.

'But what for?' Josh asked.

'To keep out wild animals,' Mark replied, as though it should have been obvious. 'Wild dogs, foxes.'

'Foxes?' Josh said. 'They'll just dig under it.'

'Josh,' Michael said, breaking his silence. 'We're building the fence.'

Josh looked over at his father as he sipped a glass of water. It was almost as if Michael was deliberately siding with Mark over him, his own son. Was this about more than Josh sneaking out on the trip to Guildford? Josh looked across at Mark, who in turn was watching Martha.

After dinner, Michael asked Josh to help him with the washing-up. Josh wanted to stay – he wasn't sure he wanted to leave Martha alone with Mark.

'Josh,' Michael said insistently.

'And you too, Judith,' he said, as Josh stood reluctantly. 'We could use you as well.'

Judith stared at him. 'You need three people to wash up? It was boil-in-the-bag.'

'Judith,' Michael said.

Judith rolled her eyes. 'Actually, I'm going outside for a cigarette.'

Josh saw his father watching her go through the back door. Michael hated Judith smoking. It had taken him years to get her to stop, and now it seemed she was back on. Josh darted a look at Martha, who rolled her eyes at him slightly. Josh was relieved to see she wore a slightly amused grin rather than the look of mortification he'd been expecting.

Josh washed and Michael dried.

'I can't believe Mark wanted to talk about the barricade,' Josh said.

'He speaks about it a lot,' Michael said. 'It's important to him to know what happened.'

'What happened on the barricade stays on the barricade,' Josh replied. 'That's what we agreed. It doesn't matter which of us pulled the trigger.'

'You're not even going to tell your own father?' Michael asked.

'No, Dad, and I wish people would stop asking about it,' Josh replied hotly. Josh felt that if he told his father it had been Sam who'd killed Mr Rogers then the information would find its way to Mark soon enough.

Michael sighed.

'Mark just needs a sense of closure,' he said. 'It's

important that we can put these issues behind us.'

'Well, exactly,' Josh spluttered. 'That's why we should just drop it. Mark's just trying to stir up trouble...'

'Now now, Josh. I won't have you speak about Mark like that; he's a good man.'

'Look, I feel bad about him being shot and everything, but you didn't see how he behaved on the barricade, Dad,' Josh said, shaking his head. 'He tried to kill Sam.'

Michael glared back at Josh. 'I've got to know Mark very well over the last few days, Josh. I really don't think he's capable of that. I—'

'You weren't there—'

'Don't interrupt,' his father said sharply.

Josh blinked in surprise. His father had been increasingly snappy since he'd returned. The headaches were continuing too. Judith had told her husband to stop and rest for a few days but he wouldn't listen. Josh was on the one hand full of respect for his father and gratitude for what he'd done for them, but on the other hand his dad seemed a different person. He'd never been this moody and irritable before. And whilst Josh had always had a feeling that his father was disappointed in his lack of scientific ability, he'd always been supportive of Josh. Now it seemed that Michael was pushing him away, ignoring him in favour of Mark.

'Easy, Michael,' Judith said calmly, coming back in after her cigarette.

'You can't just go round making empty accusations, Josh,' Michael carried on. He closed his eyes and rubbed his temples, an increasingly familiar mannerism.

'I'm not the one who brought the subject up,' Josh pointed out. He couldn't believe how unreasonable his father was being. He grabbed a glass and rubbed it vigorously in the hot, sudsy water.

'Oh, and, Josh,' Michael said, 'I want that dog of yours tied up during the day.'

'What? Why?'

'He might get out of the garden. I don't want him running off down to the McGoverns' farm and worrying animals.'

'He wouldn't do that...'

'They lost a lamb last week, you know.'

'Well, that's not Winston. That'll be foxes.'

'Do as I say or he'll have to be destroyed,' Michael said sharply, and Josh didn't like the look his father shot at him. They held one another's gaze for a few seconds more, then taking a deep breath Josh turned away and walked out of the kitchen.

6 NOVEMBER, 5.21 A.M.

Martha sat up with a rushed intake of breath, her nightie damp with sweat. She'd been having a nightmare. She'd been on McGoverns' farm and been asked to kill a warehouseful of cackling chickens. She had to stuff them into a white sack and pump gas inside, holding the top closed until they stopped struggling. But every time she opened the sack she'd find it contained not dead chickens, but dead babies.

Martha shivered and tried to block the memory.

She lay in bed and her thoughts turned to the conversation she'd had with Mark after the others went through to the kitchen. Did Mark really like her? If Kitty was to be believed, the adults seemed to have been planning weddings for them all. Mark had never shown interest in her before, so was this some kind of arrangement between him and her father? Surely they wouldn't be so Byzantine.

Part of her welcomed the attention – Martha hadn't really ever had a proper boyfriend, and it was good to know that someone was interested, even if the pool of competition had been somewhat reduced. And Mark was good-looking. Despite herself, Martha couldn't help but be a little attracted by the slight hint of danger he gave off.

Still, there was something a little creepy about him. It wasn't just the dark hints Josh had given about his temper. During the conversation there had been a couple of things which made her nervous. And however much things had changed, post-HAV3N, she was still only seventeen! The thought of being married, to anyone, was terrifying.

'I've been getting on very well with your father,' Mark had said. 'We've got great plans.' Then he had smiled at her in a way that suggested he wasn't just talking about the village. 'Some of the adults think it wouldn't be the worst idea if the youngsters started thinking about...the future. And sooner, rather than later.'

Martha had taken a sip of water so as to avoid replying.

'Your father is one of those people,' Mark went on, as if worried Martha might have missed his meaning.

Martha had observed the way her father seemed to have been cutting out Josh, giving him unimportant jobs while Mark drove around with Michael like some gun-totin' deputy.

She realised it was her turn to talk. 'Kitty mentioned there'd been some conversations about... marriage and babies.' She felt weird saying this to him. 'I think it's a bit soon to try and get everyone married off, don't you?'

Mark frowned and shook his head. 'No, Martha, I don't. I think we're lucky to be alive. And if there's any future for this world, it lies with us. Those of us around child-bearing age.'

Martha felt herself flushing a little. 'Sounds like it's all been planned,' she said.

'Nothing wrong with a bit of planning,' Mark had replied.

Even though it was still dark, she got up and crept

169

downstairs. She put on a heavy coat and went outside, where she found a delighted Winston, also wide awake. Martha took the dog's lead but didn't bother attaching it. At this time of the morning there was not going to be anyone else up so Winston could run about.

She was due down at the farm for her day's work in a couple of hours, but just now – like Winston – she was free to walk and to breathe fresh air, instead of the stink of cow dung. Martha and Winston set off out of town along the Guildford Road, the way dimly lit by the remnants of the harvest moon.

Winston zipped off through a gap in the hedgerow and she could hear him racing through the thick grass of the field beside the road. As she walked, Martha tried to clear her head of the vestiges of the horrible dream. Over the last couple of weeks, since the Harvest Festival, the mood in the village had been strange. More of the *Keep Calm and Carry On* posters had appeared, and people seemed to be getting on with their new lives.

Everyone had been given a job. The pub was still full every night and Martha had heard her father complaining to her mother about the rowdiness of the Wheatsheaf crowd, as he referred to the regulars there. From what she could make out, the core group were Bryan Fletcher, Reg Walker, Amir Mansoor and Clive Mitchell. Apparently they'd made a foraging trip of their own, without telling anyone, to get fresh stocks of alcohol. Even before the outbreak Michael had never been much of a drinker, and though respected in the village, he had never been one of 'the lads'. Her father had wondered out loud if they wouldn't be better off without the pub, for now.

Judith had barked with laughter.

'Oh, leave them alone,' she'd said. 'A few drinks in the evening isn't going to hurt anyone. People need to relax and socialise, especially at a time like this.'

Martha had noticed her parents disagreeing on quite a few things over the last week or so. Michael had even taken to sleeping in the spare room. They'd said it was to help them both sleep better, but Martha wondered if there was more to it than that. Her father looked so tired, and he didn't smile much. Judith had tried to make him relax, but even when he was at home he'd spend all his time in the garden, or doing odd jobs. It was as if he couldn't stop moving, couldn't stop working, trying to fix things.

It was good to get out in the fresh air with just Winston for company. Martha had an opportunity to lose herself in her thoughts; she was so busy during the days, and so tired at nights that she didn't have any time to just walk and reflect on the strange course her life had taken. Just a few weeks ago her main concern had been finding time to study for a physics exam; now all of a sudden she was 'a future leader' and perhaps soon to be engaged. She was a farm hand, and would soon be a crèche assistant too

– for those few young children living in the village. She missed her old life. Her friends, her teachers. But she was glad to be alive, proud of her father for saving them. She knew they'd been lucky. And they had food and warmth, family and friends.

Suddenly Martha's thoughts were interrupted by a growl from Winston. She called out for him and the dog burst through the hedge and came to stand beside her. He looked down the road and growled at something. It was dark. High clouds were dimming the crescent moon.

'What is it, Winston?' she asked. 'A fox?' Then the clouds parted briefly and she saw a pair of eyes reflected in the moonlight a couple of dozen metres away. 'Yes, there he is.'

Winston growled again and Martha was surprised to see the fox approaching. She was even more surprised to see another pair of eyes behind the first, then two more.

Winston stiffened, his hackles rising, his growl now deep and full.

'Those aren't foxes,' Martha realised. 'Come on, boy, we're going back.'

As the glowing eyes approached and the clouds cleared further, Martha saw the dark shapes of a pack of dogs walking towards them.

Martha began backing away, keeping her eyes on the pack. 'Come on, Winston,' she called softly. Reluctantly Winston followed her, stopping to turn every so often, watching the pack as it came. Even in the gloom, Martha could see the dogs were thin. They came on, following, curious, hungry.

'Don't run,' Martha told herself. 'They'll chase if you run.'

She walked in an awkward sideways fashion, head turned so she could see the pack. She had to call Winston softly along as he'd stop to watch the approaching dogs and growl again.

As they neared the first house of the village, one of the dogs suddenly made a rush and Martha panicked. Some primal instinct took control and she found herself sprinting for the house about fifty metres away. She'd hardly travelled ten when she felt something grab her leg, and she was down, grazing her leg on the Tarmac. She heard a snarling from behind her and something heavy was on her back. A sharp pain in her shoulder and she rolled and threw the attacking dog off. As she looked up, she saw Winston in the midst of the pack, snapping and charging as three dogs worried at him.

The dog which had attacked her had recovered and she saw the dark shape leap at her again. She twisted to one side and felt its teeth slash across her wrist. She kicked out, instinctively, and caught the dog a blow to the ribs. It grunted, fell back on to the road and almost instantly was on its feet again preparing for another rush. Martha froze with terror as she saw the flash of the dog's fangs in the moonlight. *Oh God*, she thought, *not like this, not like this* ...

But then a gunshot cracked the morning air and the pack ran, all except one – the one which had been attacking Martha. It fell heavily to the ground, dead. Winston, sensibly, decided not to chase the pack but instead came running up to her and licked her wrist. Martha sank to her knees and hugged the dog. Then she heard footsteps and someone was there.

'Martha? Is that you?' It was Mark, carrying a hunting rifle. He knelt down and helped her to her feet. 'It's OK,' he said softly as she started to shake. 'You're safe now.'

6 NOVEMBER, 8.14 A.M.

'This...*this*,' Michael Pirbright said, pointing to Martha's bandaged shoulder, 'is why I said the children shouldn't leave the village.'

Judith sighed and looked away. Jenny Stephenson had just left, along with Mark and a worried Josh, who hadn't wanted to leave his sister but had been sent off to work by a furious Michael. Mark had brought Martha straight home, before rushing off to get Jenny.

'But, no, I was being over-protective, you said,' her father now went on, pointing a finger at Judith. 'I was being *repressive*, that was your word, I think.' Martha sat, mortified that she should be the cause of so much trouble, hating to see her parents rowing like this.

'You're over-reacting,' her mother said.

'Am I? *Am I?*' he yelled. He stalked over and stuck his face up close to his wife's.

'Dad, please!' Martha was suddenly frightened.

'We're building a fence,' he said to Judith, wagging a finger at her while she looked back at him,

175

impassive. 'I don't care if you think it's a waste of time and resources. It'll keep the animals out,' he said. 'And it'll keep them in,' he added, jerking a thumb towards Martha. Then he left, slamming the front door.

'Sorry, Mum,' Martha said after a pause.

'It's not your fault, Martha,' Judith said, rubbing her tired face. 'He's not...been himself lately. He's not sleeping. He—' She stopped and looked out the window into the back garden.

'I've heard him in the night,' Martha said. 'He's having nightmares.'

Judith nodded.

'Is that why he moved into the spare room?' Martha asked.

'That's one of the reasons,' her mother replied. 'Don't worry, sweetie,' she planted a kiss on Martha's forehead. 'Things will blow over. He'll come back to us.'

Martha looked up at her mother, hoping she was right.

'He just needs time,' Judith said.

Sam roared down Highland Terrace and turned left onto the Green, a narrow road which ran around the green itself, where they played cricket in summer. Sam opened up the throttle past the pub. He was on his way out to the car pool and was running late for work. He'd been told not to go to the farm today but instead to help build the fence – he didn't really mind, as he hadn't been enjoying the farm so much, and at least he got to ride his bike over to the construction site. Sam had never had a very clear plan about what he wanted to do with his life. But whatever it was to be, it *would* have involved a lot of riding about on motorbikes. It probably *wouldn't* have involved working on a farm. It was hard work. A lot of mucking out and dragging heavy things about the place. The only plus side was that he'd been taught to drive a tractor and had only crashed it twice so far.

Suddenly there was a figure on the road before him. He hit the brakes and smeared black rubber across the Tarmac, stopping a metre or so before the figure, standing still in the middle of the road.

'Too fast, Sam,' Michael Pirbright said, his face pinched and pale in the dim morning light.

'You're here early,' Sam replied cheerfully.

'Never mind about that,' Michael replied, irritable. 'The council allowed mopeds and small bikes in the village on the understanding that the riders would maintain low speeds.'

'Sorry, President Pirbright,' Sam said. 'I was running late.'

'If I catch you speeding again, Sam, I will make you regret it.'

'What will you do?' asked Sam.

'You don't want to find out,' Michael said darkly. He turned to go, then stopped and looked back at Sam.

'By the way, Sam. On the barricade, it was you who shot Mark's father, wasn't it?'

Sam hesitated. Why was Josh's dad bringing *this* up? Sam still had nightmares about the barricade, but during the days at least had mostly managed to stop thinking about it.

'It was you, wasn't it, Sam?'

Sam rolled his eyes. 'OK, fine, if you need to know so badly, then yes, it was me. Happy now?'

Pirbright didn't answer, but just stared at Sam impassively for a few seconds more, then turned again and walked back towards the church.

Sam gave the bike some revs and crawled off, feeling shaken by his encounter with the president who, frankly, was getting more and more creepy by the day.

6.01 P.M.

Martha had been given the day off work to let her shoulder recover, though in truth it really wasn't too painful. She spent most of the day helping her mother around the house or reading. She'd asked the foraging committee for more books, and although her father had told the foragers to only bring back useful reference books, Reg had been secretly bringing her novels too. Martha was upstairs reading George Orwell when her father returned just after six. She knew it was him because she heard voices raised a few minutes later. She shook her head and tried to block the sound. Sometime later her mother called her downstairs.

'Come into the sitting room, please,' her father said, and her parents followed her in and closed the door, the signal that there was to be a long discussion.

Martha observed her parents as they sat on the sofa opposite the armchair she'd chosen. Her father looked tired, but determined. Judith looked tight-lipped and Martha could tell that she was seething about something so Martha guessed she was going to find out what the argument had been about. She got the impression that Judith had finally reached her limit. Over the last few days her father had been increasingly moody and irrational and Judith had become less and less patient with him. Martha had been wondering how long it would be before Judith snapped and started giving him what-for.

'Martha,' her father began, 'I'm not revealing any secrets when I say that the world we live in now is very different to the old world. We face an uncertain future. A struggle to survive. And now our immediate survival has been secured, we need to start thinking about the long term. About rebuilding this world. Rebuilding the human race. The responsibility for that will largely fall on the shoulders of the youngsters in this village. And of those youngsters, you teenagers, and the few twenty-somethings we have, will be the new generation of leaders. You two girls, you and Kitty, have particularly important roles.'

'No pressure, then,' Martha said.

'Don't joke about this,' her father said. 'I'm very serious.'

He looked over at Judith, who remained silent and avoided his gaze.

'Your mother and I have been discussing ... your future,' he went on. 'We feel it is important for you to settle down sooner rather than later.'

Martha said nothing, waiting for him to go on. She knew what was coming, but she wanted to hear him say it.

'Mark Rogers is a good man. And over the last couple of weeks I've got to know him well. He's told me that he finds you ... engaging.'

Martha tried not to laugh. 'Engaging?' Had she suddenly woken up inside a Jane Austen novel?

'And Mark asked me if I would object if he were to ask for your hand.'

'Oh my God,' Martha said. She was embarrassed and shocked, even though she'd been expecting something like this. 'Really? This is just ... a bit soon, don't you think? Look, it's only been a few weeks since the ... since HAV3N.'

Judith sucked in her breath and finally spoke. 'I agree, Martha.'

Michael shot Judith a look that suggested she'd veered from the approved script.

'And remember, it's your choice, Martha,' her mother went on. 'You're very young; your father is not trying to push you into anything.'

'Your mother agrees with me,' Michael said in a measured tone, 'that the future of the community, and possibly the entire human race, will rest on the bonds and relationships formed by the younger generation over the next few years. We've been making a few projections and . . . well, frankly we're going to need children. Lots of children. And soon.'

Suddenly Martha felt not just embarrassment, but fear as well. Just what was her father expecting of her? 'So this is some kind of . . . breeding programme?' she said. 'Like with chickens?'

'It's not like that at all,' her father replied hotly. 'I'm talking about you getting married, in the sight of God. We are not animals, Martha.'

'Again, Martha,' Judith said quietly, 'no one is going to force you to do anything.'

The two of them sat there and watched her expectantly.

'Can I have some time to think this over?' she said, feeling a little sick.

Her parents nodded.

'After all,' Martha said, 'he hasn't even asked me, yet.'

**Minutes of the meeting of
the Interim Little Sheen Parish Council
St Andrew's Church
7 November**

Present

Michael Pirbright (President)
Keith Tucker (Chief Mechanic)
Mark Rogers (Electrical Engineer and Security)
Monica Hilfenhaus (Inventory Manager)
David McGovern (Agricultural Manager)
Clive Mitchell (Foraging Manager)
Amir Mansoor (Structural Engineer)
Emily Green (Secretary)
Jennifer Stephenson (Medical Officer)

Previous minutes

The minutes of the previous meeting were read out.

New business

It was decided that the members listed above shall continue in their acting roles until such time as formal elections can take place to confirm or replace each incumbent. Reg Walker asked for a date to be set for this but it was felt that at present the village had more pressing concerns.

President Pirbright began by acknowledging complaints from some members that he did all the talking at meetings. He therefore handed the floor to Reg Walker as representative of the 'Wheatsheaf group', to make an address, recorded and reproduced here in verbatim:

Ladies and Gentlemen, welcome to this meeting of what we're being asked to accept as the new government of our small community. As was suspected at the time of the first meeting, the virus known as HAV3N seems to have caused the deaths of the vast majority of the planet's population and has removed the previous government here in Britain. It falls upon us to continue the proud traditions of democracy and the rule of law here in Little Sheen.

We have not yet found other survivors, though it is our belief that there are likely to be others. We also feel strongly that we are not doing enough to make contact with them.

But whether we find other survivors or not, it is important that we begin as we mean to go on. We must govern according to the fairest and most scientific methods available. Whilst respectful of the faith of many of our citizens, especially at such an extraordinary time, the Bible is not the place to look for our rules, laws or morals. The body of law that existed before HAV3N is largely still appropriate to us, murder is still wrong, stealing is still wrong, the rights of personal possession and individual freedom still apply and must be protected at this time when the temptation may be to look towards a more collective, and more restrictive society.

Mr Walker was thanked for his contribution and the meeting then received updates from various Officers.

Firstly Amir Mansoor explained how the water supply had been successfully restored. As Little Sheen is considerably lower than the aquifer which serves the village there should be no future difficulties maintaining the flow, though periodic maintenance would be required. Mr Mansoor was given a round of applause from all present.

Clive Mitchell listed the following recent acquisitions: 2 lorries full of canned and dried goods; 2 dozen milking cows; 4 sows, 3 piglets and one pig; 1 tractor; 6 sacks of seed potatoes; a range of vegetable and herb seeds; 4 small portable generators; 2 large, permanent generators; 1 petrol tanker; 4 Range Rover 4WD vehicles. As yet no live chickens have been found, and the concern is that the cull carried out by the government during the outbreak was all too effective.

A permanent foraging committee has been established to make short day trips, and, going forward, longer weekly expeditions. Canned goods are less of a priority now as we have established significant stocks in the village and located a supermarket distribution centre in Basingstoke which holds many years' supply of dried, non-perishable goods.

Reg Walker proposed that a Contact Group should be formed to make a longer excursion to attempt to find other survivors. President Pirbright suggested this might be a task to be left until summer, and that the village had more pressing concerns. A vote was held and Mr Walker's proposal was defeated.

The agricultural manager, David McGovern, presented his plan for sustainable fresh-food production. It was agreed that there was sufficient land for the immediate needs of the community if the existing McGoverns' farm was extended to encompass the surrounding farms of the deceased Brown and Corrigan estates. The defunct Grover farm on the other side of the village, now owned by Susan Gardener, offers further possibilities and a feasibility study is to be carried out to ascertain what needs to be done to make that farm serviceable next year.

Mark Rogers, who in addition to his duties as electrical engineer has been asked to take over security operations for the village, outlined the new plan to build a perimeter fence which is projected to be completed before Christmas. A works team has been assembled and Clive Mitchell has acquired the necessary materials for the job. Mr Rogers explained that, after discussion with President Pirbright, it had been decided no children, defined as anyone under 21, should be allowed beyond the perimeter fence for the foreseeable future. It was argued that the future of the village and of humanity rests on them. They must be kept safe from wild animals and other potential perils.

Monica Hilfenhaus, the inventory manager, listed the current stockpile of food and medicine supplies (see separate sheet). Part of this stockpile is currently at the

Wheatsheaf, some is at Freedman's Convenience Store and the remainder is in the crypt at the church. There was a representation from Mrs Hilfenhaus, who argued strongly that all food stocks and general supplies should be permanently kept at St Andrew's. This is to be put to a vote at the next meeting.

Keith Tucker, chief mechanic, updated the council on the establishment of a motor pool at the former BP Garage just outside the blockade on the Guildford Road. It has been agreed that it is preferable that vehicles should be kept outside the village except for deliveries. We want our streets to be safe for the children. An exception was made for the President's own vehicle, where needed for urgent council business.

Emily Green is establishing a crèche, for children of all ages, in the church. She's collecting names of volunteers and will establish a rota. The crèche will serve two functions; on the one hand we need a reliable child-care service, to allow mums as well as dads to help out on the farms and perform other duties. Secondly there are plans in the future to develop the crèche into a school. Mrs Green is currently putting together a full curriculum, to be approved by the council in due course. Whilst that is being organised the children will be taught basic reading, writing and Bible studies.

Finally Mark Rogers, in his capacity as chief electrical Engineer, explained how the two large generators had been installed in the church and the Wheatsheaf as the two main centres of the community and also the two buildings with large enough storage areas for the stock-piles of food. Freedman's Convenience Store has been provided with a generator for their smaller cold storage area. Extra fridges and freezers have been moved from empty houses into the church and pub. The other genera-tors are to be used for the milking machines at McGoverns' farm, and at the car pool, while the remaining generator will be kept as reserve. Most houses are now cooking using portable gas stoves, and it is hoped that at some stage in the future larger, more permanent generators will be brought to the village to provide electricity for all.

The floor was then opened to all questions. Discussion was heated and the legitimacy of the council itself was questioned. A faction, led by Reg Walker and Bryan Fletcher, strongly felt that it was inappropriate for any interim government to be established in the church, and invoking authority from the Bible. It was pointed out that of the former six-member parish council, only three were still alive and that the PC had not been established with such a situation in mind and therefore had no legitimacy. Mr Carter reminded the meeting that the surviving members of the PC were elected and therefore had a democratic mandate. The meeting ended with no resolution being found other than to discuss further at the next meeting.

8 NOVEMBER, 3.33 P.M.

'*Zeus gave his daughter Pandora a sealed vase,*' Martha read. '"*Don't look inside,*" *he told her.*

187

Secretly Zeus was sure that Pandora's husband, Epimetheus, would break the seal and look inside the vase, curiosity having got the better of him.'

She looked up and smiled at the half dozen children, sitting cross-legged on the carpet. Three times a week, Martha was relieved of her farm duties in order to help out at the crèche. She loved it, and the children seemed to like her, especially story time, where she'd read old fables and myths from the dog-eared collection at the church library. The intensity of their interest in the familiar old stories awed her a little.

'But it was Pandora who was more curious. She desperately wanted to look inside the vase, but Epimetheus shook his head. "Don't open it," Epimetheus warned. "Your father is trying to trick you."'

As she read, the door opened and Bryan Fletcher entered. His daughter Ellie was a quiet girl of six, whose mother had died running towards the barricade. She and her father lived quietly in a pretty house just a few doors down from the church. Bryan smiled as Martha carried on with the story.

'Pandora couldn't stop thinking about the vase, and one day, while Epimetheus was out, she thought I'll just take a little look. Pandora broke the seal and removed the cork. Whoosh! Out came twisted black shapes: plague, sickness, hate, jealousy, fear. Such terrible things, new to the world. Pandora plugged

the vase up again quickly, but it was too late! The horrible things escaped through the window and scattered to the four corners of the world.

'*Epimetheus returned to find Pandora crying. She told him what had happened. "I was curious, I couldn't help myself." Epimetheus opened the vase again to look for himself, only to see that the vase was not quite empty. There was one thing left, right at the bottom.*'

Martha looked up. 'Does anyone know what it was?' The children shook their heads, gripped.

'*It was hope,*' Martha said. She caught Bryan's eye. He was looking at her, a smile on his lips and a small tear in his eye.

9 NOVEMBER, 9.02 A.M.

'What did you dream about last night?' Kitty asked. They were sitting in a pew waiting for the rest of the congregation to come in and sit down. The girls had come along early, at Monica's request, to distribute hymn books, freshen the flowers and generally tidy up. Now they were bored and impatient for the service to start. Martha's wounds felt itchy as they healed – Jenny had checked them again the previous evening and seemed happy there wasn't any infection.

'I dreamed about my father,' she answered. 'I've had this same dream a few times. He was travelling through a desert, alone. He was trying to come to me, but he couldn't. There were all these ... dead people. Ghosts, I suppose. They were blaming him for their deaths and dragging him back.'

'Sounds horrible,' Kitty said, shuddering. 'Sam keeps dreaming about our dad.'

Martha looked at her. Kitty was biting her lip. She looked tired, and worried. 'How do you know?'

'He wakes in the night and calls out. "*Dad!*" he says. "*Stop. No!*"'

'Poor Sam,' Martha said, turning round to see that Josh and Sam had just arrived outside. The boys had taken Winston for a walk that morning, managing neatly to avoid helping out at the church.

Bryan Fletcher walked past with Ellie, who smiled at Martha and pulled on her daddy's hand to stop him.

'Would you like to sit with me?' Martha asked. Ellie nodded and hopped onto the pew. Bryan grinned gratefully and sat on the pew across the aisle. Martha had a real soft spot for Ellie. Before the outbreak, she had been a boisterous little girl, but since her mother's death she'd become shy and reserved.

Kitty's mother came over to say hello.

'Thanks for helping this morning, girls,' she said. 'Martha, your father just told me about what happened with the dogs. How horrible. Why didn't you tell me, Kitty?'

Kitty shrugged; she'd found it difficult to approach her mother lately.

'If I'd known I wouldn't have had you rushing

about this morning.'

'It's fine, Mrs Hilfenhaus,' Martha said. 'Mrs Stephenson said there didn't seem to be any infection. I'm not going to let it stop me.'

Sam sloped in with Josh just before the sermon started. He sat, arms folded, feeling drowsy in the warm sunshine filtering through the stained glass ahead. Once Reverend Halfdene had finished, Monica stood to say a few words and Sam shook his head. He'd noticed a gradual change in his mother since HAV3N. Always a committed church-goer, she'd become even more involved. Like Michael Pirbright and Mark, Mrs Hilfenhaus now spent most of her time there, mostly helping to sort and distribute the supplies, but also taking responsibility for a hundred little jobs, from washing cassocks to replacing the candles.

Sam wondered what his mother was planning to say. She was vehemently opposed to the idea that the new council should be established in the pub, and so he assumed that was what she was going to talk about. There'd already been muttering at the back from Camp Wheatsheaf when she stood.

'I'd like to talk today about the children,' Monica began. 'The children are, now more than ever, the future. Our role as adults is to support them in this difficult new world, to nurture and protect them, and to guide them onto paths that will allow our community to continue and grow in God's light.'

Mrs Hilfenhaus was a good speaker. She knew how

to work an audience, with pauses and intonation. But not everyone was impressed. Behind Sam, Clive coughed and muttered something to David McGovern.

'There are no babies in the village,' Monica said. 'And just three toddlers. Then there are Georgie and Alfie Nicholls, aged six and four, and there's Ellie Fletcher, six, and Hugh and Tamsin Gregory, at eight and six. Then, of course, there are our teenagers,' she finished, beaming at them.

Sam found himself flushing as the congregation turned to look at them. As one the four tried to sink down into the pews, wishing the stone flags would open up and allow them to slip down into the dark crypt beneath.

Monica continued. 'There are only nine people in their twenties in the village and only another eight in their thirties. Just twenty-nine out of eighty-two are under the age of forty. So many of our young people were away when the virus struck. At work, or at college, or travelling.

'Not many young ones. Though, of course, we hope there'll be more soon. We need to keep them all safe and happy.' Now Monica took on a more serious expression and lowered her voice quietly. Sam noticed the congregation leaning forward ever so slightly, not wanting to miss any of this.

'And so we've introduced a few new rules for our new society. Not just for the children – these rules apply to all of us as we must set a good example.

Some of the rules you will all already know about and the others are just common sense, but we thought it best to make them formal and write them down.

'Rule One: no children are to leave the village unless being accompanied by an adult, and I mean someone at least twenty-one.'

'Heard it,' Sam muttered.

'Rule Two,' Monica continued. 'All villagers must attend church every Sunday, and refrain from blasphemy, and children must do as they are told at all times by adults.'

Kitty snorted. Martha shushed her gently.

'Rule Three: we expect all children, from the age of twelve, to help out with the farm, or food distribution, or whatever needs doing. We need all hands to the pump.'

'*Rule Four: no farting,*' Sam said quietly. Kitty giggled, drawing a glare from her mother.

'Rule Four, and this just refers to the teenagers really, especially the girls. We'd like you to talk to us before any of you form... personal relationships.'

'Oh my God, this is *sooo* embarrassing,' Kitty muttered as the adults turned to look at them again.

'It's important we don't have broken homes and unwanted children in this new world,' Monica said. 'Children are needed, but must be the product of stable marriages. We don't have the freedom any more to carry on with whoever we want. A man and a woman, married in God's sight. That's the natural

order of things and that is the only kind of relation-
ship acceptable—'

'Oh, for God's sake . . . !' The teenagers heard Reg
cry out from the rear of the church. 'You'll be forbid-
ding them to hold hands in public next.'

'Mr Walker, please restrain yourself,' the vicar
instructed, standing up at the front. 'Please do not
blaspheme in this church.'

'Fine,' Reg said, now on his feet. 'I'm not going to
sit here listening to this archaic, controlling nonsense
any more. I'll be in the pub, planning how we're
going to feed everyone next year. Who's coming?'

The McGoverns, Bryan Fletcher – beckoning Ellie
to come with him, Mr Tucker and a few others stood
with him and left. Sam wanted to go too and nearly
stood, but thought better of it immediately. He saw
Mark sitting firmly in his seat at the front, eyes
straight ahead. As they opened the large rear doors,
the mid-morning sun shone directly into the church
and down the aisle, lighting Monica Hilfenhaus and
Michael Pirbright, who seemed to glow with an
unearthly intensity as they glared at those departing.

The pub crowd filed out and Monica Hilfenhaus
continued.

'We are merely suggesting that for the good of the
community, certain rules and standards are adhered to.
The safety of the children is the utmost concern for us.'

'Are we not going to vote on this?' Josh muttered
to Sam.

'I think we just did,' Sam replied.

'We must not forget that God has saved us,' Mrs Hilfenhaus went on. 'We don't know why He chose us, or if there are others. But we must take this as a sign. A sign that from now on we must live our lives according to His laws, not ours. According to His moral code, not ours, and—'

Then her face was lit again as the rear door opened once more. She looked up in irritation to see who had interrupted this time and Michael stood as he saw who it was, a look of fury clouding his features. The congregation turned with a mass shuffle and a collective creak to see who had opened the door to go, and Sam craned his neck round just in time to see Josh's mum leaving without a backward glance. She let the door swing closed behind her.

'I forecast,' Sam whispered to Josh, 'a heavy frost at your dinner table tonight.'

15 NOVEMBER, 5.46 P.M.

Martha's shift at the crèche finished when the last parent came to collect his or her child. Today it was Bryan, who'd been out foraging and had got back a little later than expected.

'Sorry to keep you waiting,' he said. He looked tired, with a few grey hairs showing amongst his black curls. Martha supposed he must have been in his early thirties.

'It's OK,' Martha smiled. 'We've been writing a play about a princess and an ogre, haven't we, Ellie?'

Whilst Ellie ran to get her coat, Bryan reached into his pocket and pulled out a small packet.

'Oh,' he said casually, as if just remembering something. 'I came across this while I was in Guildford the other day. Thought you might like it...'

He handed the package to Martha, who found herself flushing a little. It was perfume. Expensive too.

'I love this,' she said, spraying a little on her wrist. 'Thank you.'

Bryan shrugged and smiled. 'Well, it was in the sale.'

Then Ellie came charging back and Martha watched them leave. How lovely to get a gift, even if it was a freebie. How nice to be thought of. She loved her work at the crèche and hoped she could do it full time – she didn't like the work on the farm so much. She'd never considered teaching, or childcare before, but was starting to wonder if that wasn't the right path for her. The first few weeks of farmwork had been fun, almost. But early on, Martha had asked her father if she could go out with the foraging expeditions to collect livestock from surrounding farms, as well as useful tools and supplies.

Michael had shaken his head. 'Too dangerous for girls,' he'd said. There'd been a new rule about it: 'Girls under twenty-one are not allowed on foraging expeditions.' In theory Josh and Sam were allowed out of the village, if accompanied.

'It didn't take long for the patriarchy to re-assert itself, did it?' Martha had said.

'If we survive for a dozen years or so,' her father had retorted coldly, 'then maybe you can start up a new suffragette movement. Until then, we need our women to stay healthy and fit.'

'To breed?' Martha had asked.

'And to work,' her father had said.

Judith had gone along to the next council meeting and argued against the idea that girls should be treated differently. There was a vote, which she lost. Even Monica voted against Judith, and the former friends hadn't spoken since.

Martha grabbed her coat and wandered over to the churchyard where she'd arranged to meet Kitty and Josh. Sam was there too, she saw, wrapped up in one of his dad's old coats, drinking cider. His trousers were spattered with mud and dried splashes of cement. Work on the fence had gone surprisingly quickly and in fact had been finished the day before, but Michael had inspected and told them to re-set some of the fence posts. The job now completed, Sam had been told by Michael he'd start work back at McGoverns' farm on Monday. He looked grumpy.

'What's wrong with you?' she asked.

Sam sighed. 'I have cabin fever, I need to escape.'

'Church tomorrow, of course. But he wants to go out for a ride on Monday,' Josh said. 'I think it's a bad idea.'

'You're a chicken,' Sam said.

'You'll get caught,' Martha said.

'Not if we sneak out and back in again. Reg gave us the code for the gate, so no one will know.'

'And what about work?' Josh asked.

'Simple,' Sam replied impatiently. 'You say you've been asked to help me on the McGoverns' farm, I say I've been asked to help you at the Gardeners'.'

'Can I come?' Kitty asked.

'No,' Sam said firmly. 'You remember what happened last time I let you come on my bike?'

'You deliberately rode over that bump so I'd fall off!'

'It's a dirt bike,' Sam said, rolling his eyes. 'You're supposed to ride over bumps.'

'I don't know, Sam,' Josh said. 'You know what my dad's like at the moment. If we leave the village...'

'Oh, listen to you,' Sam said. 'This isn't the old Josh, Hero of the Barricades. Fearless Sidekick. Don't you want to get out of this place for a few hours? Take your bike?'

'Of course I do,' Josh said. 'But there'll be trouble if we're caught, that's all I'm saying.'

'Well, then,' Sam said, grinning, 'we'll just have to make sure we're not caught, won't we?'

Martha frowned and shook her head.

*

Josh and Sam killed their engines, got off the bikes and stepped over to inspect the gate. At three points around the village, a gate had been built into the fence. Each of these was locked with a keypad, installed by Reg, who'd undermined the whole deal by letting them see what the code was. Josh punched the keypad and they wheeled the bikes through and rode off slowly along a farm road.

'Easy,' Sam said. The track wound its way through a dense wood.

'Where are we going?' Josh asked. As it had been Sam's idea, his friend had taken charge of the route.

'I thought we'd head out along the North Downs Trail. Over towards Hampshire.'

'Why over there?' Josh asked. 'What's wrong with the Bourne woods?'

'Too close to the village,' Sam replied, shouting over the growl of his bike in low gear. 'Someone might hear if we open up the throttles.'

In the wet, grey November, there was little bird-song, but rabbits sprung out periodically, stared at them in gentle surprise and popped back into the damp undergrowth. Once they were safely away from the village, Sam gunned his engine and the bike roared off into the woods.

7

The boys rode for an hour or so. Despite his reserva-
tions, Josh found himself relaxing, and he gloried in
the roar of the engine and the power throbbing
through the chassis of the Suzuki. They couldn't ride
very fast – the track was more suited to walking than
bikes, with twists, turns, bridges and the occasional
stile – but Josh enjoyed the challenge of the difficult
conditions. Sam had brought a land survey map of
the area and they stopped from time to time to make
sure they knew where they were and could find their
way back. They were both used to going out on their
bikes for the day so had thought to bring snacks and
water, they stopped by a stream for a rest and a bite.

'This is brilliant,' Sam said, chewing on a fruit bar.

'We shouldn't stay out too long,' Josh replied.
'They'll miss us if we're not home before dark.'

Sneaking away from work had been easy. Neither
David McGovern nor Mrs Gardener had seemed very
suspicious.

'Come on,' Sam said. 'Admit it, this was a great
idea of mine.'

Josh nodded, despite himself. 'It's not as rubbish as your usual ideas, if that's what you mean,' he said. 'Come on, let's go.'

Eventually they came to a small Tarmac road, mostly clear of weeds. Sam twisted his throttle and shot off up along the smooth surface, enjoying the speed. Josh followed. Sam's bike was slightly more powerful than Josh's and he pulled away slowly and after a few minutes was lost from sight. Josh followed as quickly as he could, slightly worried that Sam might take a turning somewhere and they'd lose each other. But, no, there he was, stopped at the entrance gate to some estate or house. Josh slowed and pulled up next to his friend.

Sam took off his helmet and grinned.

'What do you reckon this place is?' he asked, nodding at a Gothic stone gatehouse within. A simple, modern-looking nameplate read: *Lancaster House*.

'Dunno,' Josh said. 'Let's check it out.'

Sam strapped on his helmet again, started his engine and they puttered slowly down a leaf-strewn drive, through thick woods. As they came out of the trees, Josh caught a glimpse of Lancaster House. An Edwardian manor, vast and tall, its dark windows seemed to be watching them approach, though in a welcoming rather than a sinister way.

The main building was four storeys tall, including the rooms in the eaves. Josh imagined there must be cellars too. There were two wings, aside of the central house with its grand façade of grey, Portland stone.

The boys pulled up on the gravel drive in front, took off their helmets and dismounted, their boots crunching satisfyingly on the pebbles. A few enterprising weeds had poked their way up through the stones, and blown leaves had collected on the steps leading up to the massive double doors, but other than that there was nothing to suggest the building was unoccupied.

'Let's go in,' Sam said eagerly.

'We can't just—' Josh began but then stopped. Of course they could just go in. Whoever had owned this building was now dead. It didn't belong to anyone.

Sam made his way up the stairs and tried the main doors. One opened with a creak. Josh followed. It was gloomy inside, and felt cool though not damp. The sense of abandonment was stronger now. They stood in a stone-flagged hall furnished with sofas, massive oak tables and a reception desk.

'It's a hotel,' Sam said. He peered over the reception desk and grabbed something. 'Look,' he said. 'A brochure.' He handed it to Josh. *Lancaster House*, it read. *Eco Hotel*.

'They have . . . had their own farm,' Josh said, leafing through the brochure. 'Grew all their own food. Solar panels, a wind turbine.'

They explored the ground floor – a great lounge full of comfy-looking sofas, a bar, a hall and signs to a dining room. Doorways ran off to the left, the right and towards the back of the building, and a great set of stairs led up from the lobby to the next floor. They decided to leave the upstairs for now and headed off for the rear of the building. They passed through the large dining hall which was crowded with tables. Dirty plates and cutlery lay scattered on the surfaces, rotten fruit mouldered in bowls and a dull stench of decay ran through the room.

'I stayed in a place like this once,' Sam said. 'In Blackpool.' Then he disappeared from sight with a thump and Josh rushed to help.

'Oh . . . yuck,' Sam said.

Then Josh saw what Sam was yucking about. He'd tripped over a body, a man lying face down, a shock of brown hair masking his features. The hands, dried and shrivelled, poked out of the sleeves of the suit the corpse wore. Palms down, elbows raised, as though the man had been trying to push himself back up even as he'd died.

'Dry in here,' Josh said.

'What?' Sam asked as he got to his feet and backed away from the body, a look of distaste on his face.

'The corpse looks all dry,' Josh said. 'It's a good sign. Shows this building doesn't have a problem with damp.'

'Yeah, but on the downside' – Sam gave a wry grin – 'it's full of rotting corpses.'

Josh went through to the kitchens at the back. He

looked out of the window. 'Look,' he said. 'Chickens, ducks.' There was a large pond about seventy-five metres behind the building. Josh opened the French doors and they wandered down, through the unkempt grass, the ducks watching them carefully, the chickens ignoring them.

'The pond looks like it's fed by the stream,' Sam said, walking over to see. 'Hey,' he said. 'Trout.' The fat fish swam lazily through the clean water, shadows stroking the stony bed of the stream. A flash of movement caught his eye and he looked up, across the stream into a thicket of trees, to see a small fawn deer staring back at him fearlessly.

'This is brilliant,' Sam said, looking up at Josh, his eyes bright.

'Yeah,' Josh replied. 'Wish I'd brought my camera. Let's check out the upstairs.'

They went back inside and raced up the stairs, pushing and trying to trip each other. Long halls led off down either wing of the hotel, lined on both sides with rooms. Sam tried a few doors but found them locked. He ran downstairs again to look for keys. While he waited, Josh looked out of a window over the gardens to the back of the hotel.

'There's an orchard,' he said as Sam returned with a few keys, panting. 'Greenhouses, polytunnels, a chicken house, a duck pond.'

'They have everything here,' Sam said, trying key number 101. The door opened. 'Nice,' he said.

The bedroom was luxurious: thick carpets, linen sheets, a marble bathroom. Sam tried the taps.

'They've got running water!' he said.

'Oh, yeah,' Josh said. 'I read that in the brochure. They have rainwater tanks in the loft, you see. Very handy.'

'I really want to live here, Josh,' Sam said. 'Can we live here?'

'Eh?' Josh said. 'Live here?'

'Why not?' Sam said. 'They have everything we need. We can invite other people to come too. The girls, Reg, Bryan, Clive maybe.'

'Not Mark,' Josh said.

'No,' Sam agreed. He didn't say, 'Or your dad,' but they were both thinking it.

'Come on,' Josh said. 'Let's go check out the farm.'

They spent the afternoon caring for the farm animals still alive. Half a dozen milking cows, and a flock of sheep which they let into a bigger pasture. There were a few pigs too which seemed to have survived by knocking down some fences and eating anything they could find. The chickens and ducks seemed happy enough. They made sure all the animals had access to shelter in the barn. The winter so far had been mild but it wasn't likely to stay that way.

Afterwards they sat on the riverbank watching the trout and munching their way through a pack of biscuits Sam had found in the kitchen and which weren't too stale.

'So peaceful,' Sam said dreamily. 'No one yelling at me.'

Then Josh checked his watch. 'Come on,' he said. 'We've got to get back.'

Sam groaned. 'I don't want to go. Let's just stay here.'

'Look,' Josh said. 'I like this place too. And I think it could be somewhere we could live. But we can't come and set up here on our own. We need others.'

'Why?'

Josh rolled his eyes. 'Because we need people to help on the farm, we need people to maintain the building, the plumbing, the solar panels. We need Mrs Stephenson and Mr Mansoor and Mr McGovern, and Reg and Clive and Bryan and the girls.'

'But not Mark,' Sam repeated.

'I don't know, Sam,' Josh said. 'Maybe we do need Mark too.'

Sam said nothing.

'We can't do this alone,' Josh went on. 'That's all I'm saying.'

It was nearly 6.00 p.m. and dark when Josh and Sam arrived back at the gate. They'd taken a wrong turn on the way back to the village. Sam dismounted and punched in the code as Josh directed his headlight onto the lock. It didn't work.

'Are you sure you remember it?'

'Yes, I'm sure I remember it,' Sam said. 'Six-seven-four-five. The number is six-seven-four-five.'

'The number *was* six-seven-four-five,' another voice said from the darkness beyond the gate, causing them to jump, 'until I changed it.' Mark stepped into view, unblinking in the glare of the bikes' lights.

Josh sighed, his heart thumping from the shock. 'OK, Mark, well done, you caught us. Can you let us in, please?'

'Where have you been?' he asked.

'Thorpe Park,' Sam said.

Mark stared at him, unamused. 'You might think this is a joke,' he said. 'But I am the Security Officer for this village. I need to know who's coming and who's going, and where they've been in the meanwhile.'

'We just went for a ride, OK?' Josh said calmly. 'I know we weren't supposed to, but we were only gone for a few hours. Can't you just let us back in?'

Mark seemed to be thinking it over, but Josh thought he was probably just trying to make the boys sweat. What was he going to do? Leave them out there all night? They'd just go round to the car pool, where there were gates, and Reg would let them in. Failing that, they could abandon the bikes and climb over the fence.

'I think you two had better come with me to the church,' Mark said. Then he stepped forward and unlocked the gate.

Once they'd pushed the bikes through, Sam hopped on his and gunned the engine.

'Slowly!' Mark snapped. 'Go to the church and I'll meet you there.'

'Screw you, Gruppenführer,' Sam said. 'I'm going home.' He shot off.

Josh rolled his eyes. He would have liked to follow Sam's example, but it was better to face the music now. He waited for Mark to get on his moped, and followed it back into the village, the red tail-light bumping lazily on the rough track.

17 NOVEMBER, 7.32 P.M.

Following Mark, Josh walked in through the church and towards the side room where his father had set up his office. He felt like he was eight years old again and facing the head teacher after breaking a window, or fighting in the playground. Mark stopped and motioned Josh to go in. Josh opened the door and walked in.

Michael was kneeling at the far end of the chamber before a brass cross. His head was bowed, close to the ground. Josh stepped slowly towards his father, and as he approached he realised his father was praying, whispering furiously and clutching a Bible. Josh cleared his throat to get his father's attention and Michael looked up.

Josh was struck by how thin his father looked, his

eyes red-rimmed and sunken. He stared at Josh as if
he didn't recognise him. Something about his father
just didn't look right.

And suddenly Josh didn't just feel like a nervous
child before the head teacher. Suddenly Josh felt
properly frightened. Not just for himself, but for his
father, and for all of them.

18 NOVEMBER, 7.28 A.M.

'Mrs McGovern told me they've found some chickens
on a farm over near Compton,' Judith told Martha
over breakfast.

'Oh God,' said Martha. 'Not chickens again. I'd
been hoping they were extinct.'

'Now now,' Judith said, trying not to smile.
'Remember what Monica had to say about blasphemy.'

'Sorry, I should have said, "Oh shit".'

Her mother gave a tired smile.

'Are you and Monica getting on OK these days?'
Martha asked.

Judith made a so-so gesture with her hand. 'I don't
see so much of her any more. She's down at the
church most of the time.' She stopped and raised her
eyebrows. 'Anyway,' she said, changing the subject,
'these chickens – they found quite a few hens and a
rooster. So they're going to start breeding.'

'They'll need more than one rooster,' Martha

pointed out. 'Or else the gene pool will be too small and they'll get sick.'

'Well, I'm sure they'll find more,' Judith said. She took a sip of coffee and regarded her daughter. 'It's important, I suppose, planning a breeding programme?'

Martha nodded, spooning Weetabix into her mouth. At times like this, eating normal cereal – even if it was with long-life milk – with the sunshine pouring in through the dining-room window, it almost felt like nothing had happened. Like they were just about to get into the car and drive to college like the old days. She studied her mother carefully. She had a familiar look about her, that meant she was busy thinking over what to say next, and how to say it, exactly.

'So, how do you feel about what your father said...about Mark?' Judith said slowly.

Martha looked up at her, her stomach pulling into the nervous knots that happened whenever Mark's imminent proposal came into her head. 'How do *you* feel about it?'

Judith hesitated, thinking again, trying not to say the wrong thing. 'Your father has a point. And it's not just your father. There are others in the village who think we must...encourage the younger ones.'

'You don't agree?' Martha asked.

Judith shrugged. 'This is a democracy,' she said.

'That's why you walked out of church the other

210

day,' Martha said. It wasn't a question. Relations in the Pirbright household had been extremely frosty since then, as Sam had forecast. Her parents had stopped arguing and now hardly spoke to one another at all. Martha wasn't sure which she preferred, the arguments or the stony silences.

Judith seemed to be suffering some internal struggle. Martha could see her mother was fighting her own better nature, trying to do the 'right' thing by her husband, by the community.

'I understand, Mum,' Martha said quietly, trying to help her out. 'I...accept that it's important to plan.'

Judith looked down at the table, then up at her daughter, then back down to the table.

'But...Mark?' Judith said eventually.

'Why not Mark?' Martha replied carefully.

Judith paused for a long time before replying. 'I don't like him,' she said. 'I think he's creepy. I don't like what I've heard about his temper. His father was a bully and so is he. Also, I don't like the way he and your father have suddenly become so close, while poor Josh has been cut out.'

Martha waited. Her mother was saying all the things she thought, and she felt a sense of relief. It wasn't just her having these doubts. Someone was on her side.

'On the other hand, he's good-looking, charming, fit and strong,' Judith said, looking intently into her daughter's eyes. 'And there aren't that many fish in the sea these days.'

Martha smiled.

'The important thing to remember, Martha, is that it's your choice. You don't have to do anything you don't want. Frankly, this is your father's idea. Personally, I think you should be just left alone. You should enjoy your youth.'

'But Dad has a point...?' Martha said, half a question this time.

Judith shrugged. 'If, as your father believes, we are the only survivors on the planet, then, yes, the *plan* to get everyone married off, appropriately and quickly, is a valid one.' She spoke carefully and slowly, seeming to be always looking ahead for the best word to use next. Then she stood and took Martha's empty teacup.

'But you know what, Martha?' she said. 'If it were up to me, I wouldn't be trying to plan your lives like this. I'd let you go free, make your own mistakes.'

Martha looked up at her, grateful for the sentiment.

'It's human to make mistakes,' Judith added. 'And what's the good of us carrying on at all if we can't be human?'

Martha nodded and smiled. But as her mother cleared the breakfast dishes away, she sat looking out of the window thinking it wasn't quite as simple as that. Everyone's choices had suddenly been reduced. There was a greater good that needed to be considered. She knew that much of the current conflict between her parents was down to their disagreement over this issue. To reject Mark would be to side with her mother against her father, widening the rift. But could she live with Mark for the rest of her life?

A blackbird hopped onto the fence outside the window, a fat worm in its mouth. It seemed to be looking in at her. Questioning: *What are you going to do, Martha?*

Sam gunned the engine on his bike and bunny-hopped onto the bench overlooking the green. He bumped solidly down on the other side before opening the throttle.

He shot over the grass and headed home. He'd had a rotten day at the farm having spent most of it messing with the milking machine. Somehow, by default, he'd ended up as the chief mechanic there, since he had at least some experience with engines, what with working on his bike. Tucker was always busy with the car pool on the other side of the village and Mark spent most of his time at Michael's heel, or else performing his 'security' duties.

Josh had been at the farm very early and had at first refused to talk about his father's reaction last night. Eventually, though, he'd told Sam about his father's furious praying, about how Michael had been incandescent with fury when he learned the boys had been outside the fence. Josh had said he thought his father was going to hit him at one point and, in fact, Michael had seized Josh by his lapel and pushed him backwards against a wall.

'He was so angry, he was spitting as he talked,' Josh had told Sam. '"*You cannot do this to me,*" he kept saying. "*You will not undermine me.*"'

'I'm glad I went home,' Sam had said.

'He's going to talk to your mum,' Josh warned. But Sam had just shrugged.

'He's losing it, Sam. He's going mental.'

Now, Sam parked his bike, stomped inside and went up to his room. He was trying to figure out a way he could use the electricity down at the farm so he could set up his games console, but the chances of them letting him do that were pretty slim. That might be fun, and fun wasn't allowed these days in Little Sheen. Sam was bored. Bored with his life. Bored with the village. The trip to the hotel had made him realise just how much he hated being stuck here, day after day.

He read for a while, squinting in the lamplight, but was interrupted by a knock on the door. It was his mother.

'Come downstairs, please,' she said. 'I'd like to talk to you.'

Sam tried not to roll his eyes. He got up and followed his mother downstairs.

Monica led him into the sitting room, where he wasn't totally surprised to see Michael Pirbright standing by the window, looking grim.

'Hello, Michael,' Sam said in an exaggeratedly cheery voice.

'President Pirbright!' Monica hissed. Sam ignored her.

'Sam,' Pirbright said, 'do you remember what I said to you a couple of weeks ago when I saw you speeding along the Green on your motorbike?'

Sam furrowed his brow for a moment. 'Did you ask me if I wanted to race?'

'Show some respect!' Monica shouted. Sam turned to look at her and frowned. He didn't like the new Mum.

'I told you that if you were caught speeding, you would regret it,' Michael said.

'I haven't been speeding,' Sam said sullenly.

'No, but you were jumping your bike over a park bench and riding across the cricket pitch.'

'I didn't know I wasn't allowed to do that,' Sam said, realising he was sounding childish but not being in a mood to co-operate.

'And that's not the only rule you've broken, is it, Sam?'

Sam said nothing.

'What else did he do?' Monica shook her head in disappointment.

'He left the village yesterday,' Michael said. 'With

my son, I'm ashamed to say. Unaccompanied by an adult, and without permission.'

Monica gasped, as though she'd just heard that Sam had mugged a pensioner.

Meanwhile Michael took his hands from behind his back, revealing a long, thin cane.

Sam laughed involuntarily. Then shook his head. 'This is not happening,' he said. Why had he even come back yesterday? First thing tomorrow, he resolved, he was taking his bike and heading off with some food and water. He'd come back when he felt like it.

'Sam,' Michael said calmly. 'If this community is to develop into a successful and progressive society, we must all abide by the rules. And when punishments are prescribed, they must be carried out. I am not going to hurt you. I will tap your hand once, as a token punishment, on this occasion. But you must understand that a further transgression will lead to a further and more painful corporal punishment.'

Sam turned to look at his mother again, but she struggled to hold his eye. 'Mum, are you hearing this? This man wants to *hit* me. Do you have anything to say about that?'

Monica struggled with her expression, but kept her lips pursed tightly. 'If you break the rules, Sam, you must face the consequences. Things are different now.'

'Really?' Sam asked.

Monica said nothing.

'Also, I'm confiscating your motorbike for now,' Michael said.

'What?!' Sam cried, outraged. 'You can't do that!'

'It's already done,' Mr Pirbright said. 'Keith Tucker has taken it to the car pool. Josh's too. They'll stay there until you've both shown you can be trusted. You can still ride mopeds to get around.'

Sam shook his head, speechless with fury.

'Hold out your hand, Sam,' Michael said.

Sam looked at him, then to his mother, then back to Pirbright. He hadn't much choice just at the moment. He gritted his teeth and held out his hand.

Michael was true to this word; he lightly tapped Sam's hand, then smiled at him. 'I don't think we'll need to repeat this exercise, do you, Sam?'

Sam stared at the older man. There was something about him that he couldn't quite put his finger on – some change that had come over him recently. A gleam in his eye. A look of manic determination. Sam was looking at that most dangerous of things, a man utterly certain he has right on his side.

Slowly Sam shook his head.

8

18 DECEMBER

As the days and weeks passed, the new life became routine. It was tougher; working all day was hard on their young bodies, and Sam, Kitty, Martha and Josh were all still finding their parents much stricter than before the outbreak. Church was compulsory on Sundays and they had little time to themselves.

Josh would rise early, take Winston for a walk then let him loose in the enclosed back garden before heading off to one of the farms for the day. In his limited spare time, he would take photographs of the village, of the work being done, of his fellow survivors. And if there were more photographs of Kitty than of anyone else, well, what of it? She made a good subject, and smiled for him when he raised the camera. He'd been given permission to set up a darkroom in an empty house on the Green and would go there two or three nights a week, gradually improving the basic skills he'd learned at photography club at school.

On other days, he'd meet with Sam, and sometimes the girls too, in the churchyard. Tucked away behind the giant oak at the rear, they could chat undisturbed for an hour or so before they were expected home. They'd sit, shivering on the cold gravestones, breath frosting as they talked about their day's work. They'd drink Coke that Reg had brought back for them from foraging expeditions, and share their music quietly through battery-powered speakers. Bryan brought them the occasional treat too, mostly clothes and accessories for the girls. Sam couldn't help winking at Martha when the older man brought her a cashmere scarf.

'It's just...I just saw it there,' Bryan said. 'In the shop. Thought you might like it.'

'I love it,' Martha said, wrapping it around her neck.

The weather had been mild that December, as though God felt guilty for all that business with the virus and was trying to make it up to them a little. Taking advantage of the weather, the teenagers assembled in the churchyard one evening to have their own pre-Christmas celebration after their various work days were over. Sam had brought some cider, which the boys drank. The girls had some vodka and cranberry juice that Bryan had handed to them with a wink, brought back from a drinks-company warehouse the foraging team had found near Farnborough. The discussion had returned, as it often did, to the 'breeding programme', as they called it.

'Why do they care so much who's with who?' Sam asked. 'What are they worried about, inbreeding?'

'*Eughh!*' Kitty said, looking at Sam. 'No thanks!'

'I'm not offering,' Sam replied.

'You know what bothers me?' Josh said slowly.

'What's that?' Sam asked.

'It's how no one ever talks about other survivors. Apart from the first few days. No one's done anything to try and contact other groups. Where's the two-way radio?'

'Dad said he was sure there weren't any other survivors,' Martha said. 'We were the only ones who had the vaccine.'

'Oh, come on, the Americans must have discovered it too,' Kitty said. 'Americans can do anything.'

'Or there might be people who hid away,' Sam said. 'Underground, in nuclear shelters.'

Everyone was quiet as they digested this.

'It's almost as if Dad doesn't *want* to find other survivors,' Josh said. 'Like he wants Little Sheen to be this... Brave New World, without any outside distractions.'

They all thought it over. Sam sipped his cider, shaking his head slowly. 'If there are other survivors, then they wouldn't need to be thinking about breeding programmes.'

'Maybe we could go to America one day?' Kitty said. 'To California.'

'California's on the other side of America,' Sam

said. 'We could go to New York.'

'That would be something,' Josh agreed.

'Come on,' Martha said, always the responsible one. 'They'll be expecting us home.'

As they got up to leave, Sam crushed a cider can and kicked it over to Josh, who stopped it with his foot and booted it between two gravestones.

'Shot!' Sam said, but then stopped as he caught sight of Mark standing by the side door to the church, watching them. Josh trotted over and picked up the can, and as they left Mark continued to watch them, his face unreadable.

St Andrew's C of E church
Christmas Sermon, Christmas Eve, 24 December

Rev Jim Halfdene:

As this most tumultuous of years comes to an end, it is inevitably a good time to look back on the progress we have made these last few weeks. Let us give thanks to those who have worked so hard to bring us some great comfort in this darkest time of the year, and this dark time of our history.

Firstly, thanks to Mark Rogers and his electrical team who have brought us generators to run the vital machinery. We do indeed have electricity in the church, which we use for the refrigeration of the food supplies and also for the heating up here. We've decided to keep the candles in the main hall but electric lights are available in the anterooms and the toilets.

Thanks also to Clive Mitchell and the foraging team, who have allowed us to stockpile enough canned goods for two years, enough time for us to get the farms up and running. The farms have now been stocked with sufficient pigs, cows, goats, sheep and, finally, chickens to keep us in meat, eggs and milk indefinitely. There is, of course, plenty of room to expand in the coming years should our population grow as we hope it will.

Thanks to Mark again and the fence crew, who have erected a barrier capable of keeping out dogs, and at least giving the foxes and badgers room to pause before they come in and bother our chickens.

Clive Mitchell is organising a fishing trip early in the new year. He and his intrepid band of brother anglers are intending to make the difficult journey down to Clapton-on-Sea in the New Forest. There is a natural harbour there which should have left a number of boats serviceable. We hope they will stay safe and bring back some of God's fruits of the sea. President Pirbright tells me that Our Lord will be busy replenishing the stocks of fish which had been so distressingly reduced in the last few years of the Old World.

Mr Tucker's car pool now has adequate supplies of petrol, diesel and oil after a foraging trip to a refinery *where tankers were found and brought back. Please see him if you wish to take a car. As has been agreed cars are not available for joy rides or picnics at Winkworth Arboretum. They are for official business, but if there is something you feel the village needs, then you are welcome to take a car, after completing a booking form for this purpose. No cars are allowed in the village, as you know, but there are public mopeds available for short trips around the village.*

Finally, President Pirbright has added a new rule for the teenagers. There is to be no drinking of alcohol by anyone under twenty-one. Unfortunately there have been a couple of episodes of public drinking that have been brought to the attention of the council, and this must stop.

Hymn: 'Hark the Herald Angels Sing'

And now, President Pirbright would now like to make an address.

Pirbright:

Ladies and Gentlemen, it is with humility and gratitude I stand here. Humbled and made grateful by your faith in me, but also by God, who saw fit to spare our lives.

As the vicar has already mentioned, a great deal of hard work has been done over the past few weeks.

And now, on Christmas Eve, it is time for us to stand back and rest, and to look on our work and be proud. We are not completed. Not by a long way. We will have to work hard all through the next year, and the year after that, and on and on until we go to meet our Lord. But there is nothing wrong with hard work, as my father always told me. We must consider ourselves blessed to have survived and further blessed to have the opportunity to mould this new world with our sweat, and our tears, and our blood. We have been given an opportunity, an extraordinary opportunity here. And I do not believe our Lord will allow us to waste it.

We survived for a reason. Our Lord God wanted us alive for a reason. He wants us, no... He has commanded us to build a New Jerusalem here, in England's green and pleasant land. To start afresh, according to the truth and the morality and the law of God himself. We must cast aside the old ways, rid ourselves of our old desires and vices and divest ourselves of our arrogance and sedition.

As you know, we have agreed that any present-giving this Christmas should be kept to a minimum. Most people I've spoken to about this over the last few weeks feel the same way as I in that Christmas had become nothing but a festival of materialism in recent years, the real meaning of Christmas forgotten. So, as you know, rather than everyone scraping around for presents to give each other, we have been collecting suitable items from recent foraging expeditions and these will be distributed appropriately, one per person, by Mrs Hilfenhaus and Mrs Green. A gift from the community to each of its members. Let me make this clear, these will be practical items rather than luxuries or extravagances.

Finally, to mark this transition to a New World, the first act of the new year will be to change the name of this village. No longer do we live in Little Sheen. The name of this village, this community, is henceforth to be known as Haven.

25 DECEMBER

Christmas at the Pirbrights was a low-key affair. There were no turkeys in the village, and the chicken population was still too meagre for any to be slaughtered. Instead, a few calves and sheep had had their throats slit by David McGovern.

Conversation was sparse during their meal of roast beef. There were no crackers or paper hats. Judith ate nothing and drank most of a bottle of wine. Michael ate little and drank water, complaining of a headache. They opened their presents in the sitting room afterwards. Josh was actually quite pleased with his Barbour coat. Martha smiled stoically at her sewing machine. Judith got a set of knives which she found hilarious. Michael got a book on local fauna and flora.

'Who chose these gifts?' Judith asked.

'Mrs Hilfenhaus,' Michael replied stiffly.

'Remind me to send her a thank-you card,' Judith said, inspecting a butter knife.

As Martha brought the pudding through, there was a knock at the door.

'Who'd come round during Christmas lunch?' Judith sighed.

'It's probably the queen,' Josh said. 'Come to give us her address in person now there's no telly.'

'Will you go and answer it please, Josh?' Michael said.

Josh wasn't entirely surprised to find Mark standing at the door.

'Merry Christmas,' Mark said.

'Merry Christmas,' Josh replied. 'Er, come in.'

Judith looked unimpressed when Mark walked in, though Michael seemed delighted, and Josh thought his father's look of surprise was somewhat overdone. Martha smiled non-committally.

'Why don't you two stay in the sitting room?' Michael said.

Martha shot Josh a look of panic.

'We'll join you in a while, once we've washed up,' Michael said. 'Josh, this way.'

As on Mark's previous visit, Judith went outside and soon Josh could see clouds of smoke through the kitchen window.

They took their time washing up, not talking. Josh

could hear voices in the sitting room, but couldn't make out what they were saying. He could sense his father listening too, trying not to clink the cups in the sink. Once the dishes were done, Michael went down into the cellar, returning with a bottle of champagne. Josh raised an eyebrow but said nothing.

But then they heard the front door slam. Michael looked puzzled and went through to the sitting room. Judith came back in and she and Josh followed.

'Where's he gone?' Michael was saying to a teary Martha.

'He left,' she said. 'He was angry. He asked me to marry him.'

'And?' Michael snapped. But Martha's tears turned to sobs and she buried her face in her hands. Judith moved to comfort her.

'Well?' Michael repeated. 'What did you say?'

'She said no, Michael,' Judith said firmly. 'Of course she said no.'

3.13 P.M.

Josh and Martha escaped the house as soon as they dared and went to see Sam and Kitty. Michael didn't want them to leave but Judith told them they could. After Martha's revelation, Michael and Judith had retreated to the kitchen where a rollicking argument had carried on for a good hour. It was clear that Michael blamed Judith for Martha's rejection of Mark.

'It's up to her!' Josh heard Judith say a number of times.

'There's so much at stake here,' Michael had replied.

The Hilfenhauses had had their Christmas dinner with a few other lonely souls Monica invited over. There was quite a full house when Josh and Martha went over and Kitty and Sam were able to slip out unnoticed. They wandered down to the churchyard, but the temperature had plunged and they decided it was too cold to stay. Martha told them what had happened. She was shocked and upset, but holding it together.

'Let's go to the pub,' Kitty suggested. 'You need a drink.'

'Kitty!' Martha replied. 'You know the rule about that.'

'What? Oh, come on, Martha, sometimes you act like you're forty or something. It's Christmas. Let's just go and have a sneaky drink. Thomas won't mind.'

'Someone might see us and tell Dad,' Josh pointed out.

'Oh, so what?' Sam said. 'It's Christmas – one drink's not going to hurt.'

Ten minutes later they crept in through the back door of the Wheatsheaf. The pub was full and rowdy. Everyone was facing their first Christmas without loved ones. No wonder they were all drinking so much, Josh thought. Thomas winked at them from behind the bar and nodded in the direction of the snug hidden away at the back. He came over shortly to take their drinks orders.

'What have you got?' Kitty asked. 'Any alcopops?'

Thomas laughed, 'I do, as it happens.'

'Ale for me, please,' Josh said.

'And me,' Sam added and looked at Martha.

'Half of lager,' Martha said. '...Shandy.'

One drink became two and soon they were laughing, even Martha, the tension of the recent weeks easing gradually under the influence of the alcohol and the comfort they found in each other. There were a few other regulars in the pub, and Clive Mitchell and Amir Mansoor both waved at them. As firm members of Camp Wheatsheaf, it was unlikely they'd go running to Michael. Over by the fire, Josh saw Bryan Fletcher talking to the Reverend Halfdene. That was interesting: the vicar drinking with a founder member of Camp Wheatsheaf.

But then the door swung wide and Mark walked in. Josh's heart sank as Mark looked across and spotted the four of them. At first he looked thunderous to see them. But then he pulled himself together and Josh saw a thin smile play over the electrician's face as he limped across.

'Can I get anyone a drink?' He asked. 'Martha?' No one spoke for a moment, silenced by the awkwardness.

'I'm OK, thanks,' Martha said. 'We're not staying much longer.'

'What about you, Kitty?' Mark said.

Kitty looked up in surprise. She shrugged. 'OK.'

Josh blinked at her in disbelief, but she responded with a 'come on, let's humour him' face.

'I'm not sure that's a good idea,' Josh said stiffly. It wasn't so much that he was worried about Kitty drinking too much, but Mark's presence made him uncomfortable. The electrician was perhaps trying to show there were no hard feelings, and yet Josh always got the impression from Mark that there was some other agenda.

Kitty looked at Josh in exasperation. 'I'd like another drink, but you go home if you like, Josh.'

There was a pause.

'Josh? Sam?' Mark said. 'Another?'

Kitty gave Sam a fierce look, and he nodded and shrugged. 'Sure. Er...thanks.'

Josh nodded too. Mark smiled and went off to the bar.

'That's very generous of him,' Sam said. 'Oh, hang on, I've just remembered – everything's free.'

'It's a nice gesture,' Kitty said. 'Don't be mean.'

'Why are you so keen to be buddies with Mark?' Sam asked Kitty.

'He's trying to build bridges,' Kitty said. 'I think you boys are wrong about Mark.'

'You didn't see him on the barricade,' Josh said. 'He lost it.'

Sam belched. 'He's a massive knob,' he added.

'Give him a break,' Martha said. 'He's had a proposal turned down today, for heaven's sake. It took a lot of courage from him to come over and try to make friends.'

'I guess that's blown the chances of us keeping this little excursion secret from our parents,' Kitty said quietly.

'Might as well have another, then,' Sam said.

Mark came back with their drinks. 'Just going to chat with Clive,' he said. 'See you guys around, OK?'

'I think we should go once we've had these drinks,' Martha said, watching Mark go. 'Josh?'

But Josh had gone quiet. He held a finger to his lips and twisted his head in the direction of the next table, where Bryan and the reverend sat.

'It's like he's the one giving the sermons,' Reverend Halfdene was saying. 'I'm just there to read out public notices. Which he writes.'

It was clear who the vicar was talking about. Josh grimaced, then grinned at the others. It wasn't just the teenagers who were frustrated with Michael. Soon after, the vicar stood.

'See you then, Bryan,' he said. Then turning to the pub he opened his arms. 'Merry Christmas, every-one!' he cried.

'Merry Christmas,' the drinkers chorused, and Reverend Halfdene made his way a little unsteadily to the door.

'Bryan,' Sam called over. 'Come and sit with us.'

Martha shot him a look of disapproval, but she made space for Bryan to squeeze into the snug next to her.

'Trouble in the church?' Sam asked.

Bryan raised an eyebrow. 'Let's just say there a few people concerned about the direction things are heading in,' he said. 'Perhaps I shouldn't say anything more.'

'Don't worry,' Martha said. 'We know what you're talking about. Dad has been...acting a little oddly lately.'

'Yes,' Bryan said. 'It's not an easy subject to raise. Hard to know what to do about it, really.'

'I know what we can do,' Sam said.

'What's that?'

'There's a mansion house on a big estate, not far from here,' he said. 'Called Lancaster House – do you know it?'

Bryan nodded. 'I've been there. For a wedding,' he said. 'They converted it into a hotel a few years ago.'

Sam leaned over the table and spoke quietly. 'Josh and I took a trip out there not so long ago. We had a good look around. We think that it could easily accommodate all of us with plenty of room for, you know, babies and that.'

'They have a farm there, don't they?' Bryan said, his face thoughtful.

'Yep,' Josh said. 'The grounds are well-kept and there are tools and equipment for the gardens.

There's farmland already planted, there are greenhouses and polytunnels. There's a trout stream with fish and fresh water, of course. There's a wall around the grounds for security.'

'Sounds great,' Bryan said, beaming at him. 'Let's go there again, check it out.'

'Can you take us?' Josh asked, looking around to make sure they weren't being overheard. 'We can't leave the village without an adult.'

'I hope you're including us this time,' Kitty said tartly.

Bryan nodded. 'You know what? Why don't we all take a little trip out there? We can go in the new year. I'll get a car from the pool.'

'I would *love* that,' Sam said, with feeling. More than any of them he'd been yearning to get away from the village again, even for just a few hours.

'So what's the idea?' Bryan asked. 'You think we should just move everyone there, lock stock and barrel?'

'Those who want to come,' Josh said. 'Some might want to stay here.' He didn't spell out who they might be.

'We've done so much work here, though,' Bryan said. 'The generators, the farms, the fence...'

'All that stuff is already there,' Sam said. 'We wouldn't need to start from scratch.'

Bryan sipped his pint, mulling it over. 'I like it,' he said. 'A fresh start. A new world.'

'My dad won't be happy about it,' Josh said. 'He'll fight it. Bet you anything.'

'Why do you say that?' Bryan asked.

'Because my father sees this village as his very own Noah's Ark. He thinks we rode out the flood right here. Why do you think he built the fence? Not to keep things out, but to keep us in.' Josh shook his head sadly and went on, 'That's why he took everyone's cars away, and why he monitors who's going where. He can control us here. If we go off out into the big bad world, he loses control.'

Bryan looked at him. 'No. You're probably right, but if we can put a proposal together, win over the majority, then he can't stop us. We would need quite a few to agree to come, though. It won't work unless the majority of the villagers get behind it.'

'Do you think that's likely?' Martha asked.

Bryan frowned. 'I don't know,' he said. 'They won't necessarily make a rational decision. We tried this before when we wanted to form a secular government. We had a chance to build a better world, learning from the mistakes of the past.' He sipped his pint and looked at each of them in turn. 'We weren't saying there was no place for God, or for religion. Just that the way we led our lives should be...well, more...rational.' Bryan looked up at them with a sad smile.

'But we lost the argument,' he said. 'People were scared, and they wanted the safety and authority of the church. And who can blame them? Michael has most of the village behind him. What can we do? We can't argue for a democracy, then refuse to accept majority rule.'

The teenagers sat in silence, contemplating this truth, their cheery mood broken.

'Don't worry,' Bryan said, realising he'd spoilt the party. 'Things will change in time.'

'I'm not so sure,' Josh muttered.

'Merry Christmas,' Sam added, and finished his pint.

5 JANUARY, 11.17 A.M.

Keith Tucker looked uncertain when Bryan turned up at the car pool after church with the four teenagers.

'It's just that Mr Pirbright didn't say anything about this,' Tucker said, wiping his greasy hands on a rag. 'He normally tells me when there's to be an expedition.'

'I booked a car. Do you not have any available?' Bryan asked, looking around the old station forecourt, which was currently filled almost to bursting with cars, trucks and motorbikes.

'It's not that...' Keith said.

'Because I can see my old car, over there,' Bryan said. 'The Rover. It might be good to drive it again.' He looked at Keith, a pleasant, firm smile on his face.

Martha couldn't help but be impressed by Bryan. He was so assured. So confident. She found herself wishing it was him in charge instead of her father. Leader of the secular government.

Keith hesitated a moment longer, but then shrugged. 'OK, go on, then,' he said. 'But I have to make a record of this, including who left the village.'

'Fine,' Bryan said absently, and led Sam, Kitty, Josh and Martha over to the blue Rover. It had taken a little organising, finding a time when they were all free to go off on an expedition together. It had had to be a Sunday, after church, when none of them had work, and a day when nothing else had been arranged. By mutual consent they'd decided not to actually tell anyone where they were going. There was technically no reason they shouldn't be allowed to go off with Bryan, but they suspected that, had Mr Pirbright got wind of the idea he'd have found a reason they couldn't go.

Josh had brought his camera. There were photographs of the hotel in the brochure, but if they were to put together a detailed document selling the idea of moving the entire community there, then it was important to take more detailed pictures of the facilities.

There was a real end-of-term, first day of hols sense as the car sped off down the Guildford Road, brushing through overgrown hedgerows. Kitty clapped her hands together – neither she nor Martha had left the village for three months. Martha sat in the front passenger seat and looked through the glove box.

'There's a CD in here,' she said, and took it out. ' "Queen's Greatest Hits"?'

'Oh my God,' Sam said.

'Don't judge me,' Bryan said, grinning. 'Just put it on.'

Of course, once it was on everyone knew the words. Bryan turned it up and they sang 'I Want to Ride my Bicycle' and 'The Seven Seas of Rye', laughing like drains. It felt like the old days in the warm car, with the music up loud, speeding along the tight roads.

Then 'Bohemian Rhapsody' came on and it all kicked off in spectacular, head-banging fashion.

'Stop it,' Martha cried eventually. 'I'm going to wet myself.' She hadn't known Bryan well before HAV3N, but she felt comfortable with him. She trusted him.

Josh was map-reading in the back. It was trickier getting to the hotel by road, less direct, as Bryan had explained they couldn't take the motorway.

'It's still jammed between both junctions I'd be using,' he explained. 'Maybe one day we can clear it, but for now we have to take these little roads.'

The smaller roads created their own set of problems for the driver, however. Grass and weeds had already started to encroach on the Tarmac, cracking the verge and bursting up through every pothole. The mild winter and the absence of human intervention had unleashed the rampant return of nature.

'It's going to be even trickier by summer,' Bryan said. 'If we're going to move here it would be better to do it soon, or else we'll have awful trouble with these roads.'

It took them well over an hour to get to the hotel. The girls gasped as they approached it down the long driveway.

'See!' Sam said. 'Isn't it great?'

'How many bedrooms does this place have?' Bryan asked.

'Fifty-eight,' Josh replied, referring to the brochure. 'Then there are the staff quarters, the gate-house and various outbuildings.'

'Plenty of room for everyone,' Martha said.

'Indeed,' Bryan said. The car pulled up on the gravel and they got out. Martha felt strangely nerv-ous, like they were doing something wrong. Sam sprinted lightly up the stone steps and, turning to grin at the others, pushed open the door. The rest of them followed. They stood in the hall where it was a little cool and Kitty shivered. Josh put an arm round her and she looked up at him gratefully.

'It's beautiful here,' she said quietly.

'Come on, Josh,' Sam said. 'Let's check on the animals.'

'I want to go upstairs,' Kitty said. 'See the bedrooms.'

'Take keys,' Sam said.

Kitty grabbed some keys at random from behind the desk. Bryan took a brochure and began leafing through it as he climbed the stairs slowly.

Josh squeezed Kitty's arm and headed off after Sam, his camera swinging at his hip.

Martha and Kitty followed Bryan. Room 101's door was still open and Bryan and Martha went in while Kitty rushed down the corridor jangling keys. Martha went to the window and smiled when she saw the gardens. The farm was set to one side of the grounds; on the other side were lawns, with shrubs and flower beds – she could even see a folly half-hidden in the trees, and what seemed to be a small chapel across a lawn. They could hear Kitty down the corridor, trying the other doors.

'This is amazing,' Martha said.

'This place could support us all,' Bryan said, behind her.

Martha was suddenly aware of just how close he was standing. She wasn't sure how he felt about her. He'd brought her the perfume, and the cashmere scarf, and always seemed attentive, but maybe he was just being... avuncular – was that the word? He was so much older than her. Could he feel anything towards her? Did she want him to?

He pointed out the window. 'Look, over there they have a small farm, cattle and sheep, that's all part of this hotel.' He was holding the brochure. 'According to this, they were pretty much self-sufficient – the restaurant here used only ingredients produced within five miles. They even had their own microbrewery. The best thing is, this was an eco-hotel. They have solar panels and a wind turbine. If we could get those working again, we can have electricity without having to worry about generators.'

He stepped away from the window and leaped onto the bed. 'Everything we need is here, Martha. We could be happy here.' He looked up at her from the bed, his face beaming, excited like a teenager.

Martha now felt even more nervous. Like she had to make a big decision. They were just looking, weren't they?

Kitty came back into the room, puncturing the tension. She had a face on.

'Some of the rooms are ... er occupied,' she said.

Martha looked quizzical.

'By dead people,' Kitty explained, then shuddered.

Later, they met up with the boys and explored the grounds. They walked through the thick, wet grass to the trout stream and stood to watch the fat fish sliding about in the current, gulping at anything that moved.

'We used to come here,' Sam said. 'Near here there's a steam train that used to run down to the coast.'

'Yes, that's right, from Aldbridge,' Bryan said. 'It's still there. The train was running regularly last I heard of it.'

'Wouldn't that be amazing,' Sam said. 'To get the old loco running again, take people to the coast on trips?'

Josh smiled as he thought of Sam wearing a Casey Jones hat and blowing a great steam whistle. 'I'll be in charge of collecting the fares,' he said.

'Nope,' Sam said. 'You'd be shovelling coal.'

'Oh, thanks.'

'What about me?' Kitty asked. 'What would my job be?'

'You could sell ice creams,' Sam said after a moment's thought.

'Yay!' Kitty said.

'I'll collect fares,' Martha said.

'Yes, that's your sort of job. Bryan, you can be the guard.'

'Sounds brilliant,' Bryan said. 'Sounds like a lovely dream that will never happen.'

'Well, why not?' Sam asked. 'Why can't it happen?'

He turned to face them, serious for once. 'Here we are, with an entire world at our disposal. We can do whatever we like. Why are we restricted to one tiny village? Why do we have to check with Napoleon Pirbright before we can go anywhere? Why can't we live here?'

He spun and spread his arms wide, embracing the world. 'And why can't we run a bloody steam train?'

Over the next couple of weeks, the teenagers helped

241

put the proposal together. Martha and Josh explained their plan to Judith who thought it was a brilliant idea.

'I'm so glad you've found a solid project to get involved in,' she said.

It went without saying that they wouldn't discuss it with their father yet. The idea was to put a dossier together, with Josh's photographs, and present it at the next council meeting. It was hoped that the proposal would be sufficiently interesting that the council would at least put together a working party to look into the possibility.

'Surely they'll do that,' Sam said at a meeting of the Lancaster group at the Pirbrights. 'At least they'll go and check it out.'

'I would have thought so,' Bryan said.

Bryan and Reg returned to Lancaster House on a foraging trip a few days later and made copious notes. Acreage, number of fruit trees, livestock, number of rooms, the condition of the wall and so on. Back in the village, Martha and Judith typed up the notes onto Kitty's laptop which had been charged using the generator at the Wheatsheaf.

Josh and Kitty spent most of their evenings that week in Josh's darkroom, Josh dipping sheet after sheet of photographic paper into the pungent chemical baths, inspecting the results in the dim red light, then pegging them up to dry. Kitty was 'helping', or 'chattering' as others might have called it.

Josh didn't mind – he liked having her there, and if she noticed that a lot of the photos were of her, she didn't say.

It was good to be doing something productive, Josh thought. Not that working on the farm wasn't helping the community, but this was the chance he had to help do something to advance all their prospects. His father would have to be impressed by that, surely?

**Extracts from the minutes of the meeting of Haven Council
St Andrew's Church
19 January**

New business

A request was heard from Emily Green that dogs be allowed in the village. Mrs Green explained that her poodle had recently died. As there were so many strays still roaming the countryside, could more passive breeds be captured and kept as pets?

Mark Rogers argued against the notion, pointing out that the stray dogs ran in packs and were by now feral. The more passive breeds would likely have been killed by those more savage. After a vote, the request was denied.

Mrs Green made the point quite strongly that President Pirbright's son Josh had been allowed to bring back a stray soon after the outbreak and that this dog still lived in the village. President Pirbright said he would consider the matter and revisit it in due course.

A proposal was made by Mark Rogers to restrict teenagers and children from leaving the village at all, without express permission from the council, even if accompanied by an adult. This follows a recent excursion in which all four teenagers left the village for an entire day, accompanied by Bryan Fletcher. It was pointed out that had there been an accident, the new generation of Haven residents would have been left leaderless. President Pirbright reiterated the importance of protecting the teenagers in particular. Without them, the future is bleak for the community.

Judith Pirbright, Reg Walker and Bryan Fletcher then presented a proposal to move the community to a different location. The three submitted a lengthy dossier presenting the argument in favour of moving to Lancaster House, a former manor house, more recently converted to a hotel.

At this point there was a long and detailed discussion. President Pirbright and the other members of the council argued strongly that the village should remain the cradle of our new society, that it offered all we could need and had been the life-long home of many of our older residents. Mr Carter asked if all our hard work was to be wasted. The exchange grew heated and there was a vote. Those in favour of remaining in Haven won comfortably, and a number of those in favour of moving became disruptive and were asked to leave.

The dossier is too lengthy to attach to the minutes but President Pirbright holds the copy in his office should there be enquiries.

PART 2
THE BEGINNING

9

Josh straightened up and stretched, his back killing him. The sun seemed to have decided to drop its full spectrum of radiation on him this morning, and yesterday's burned patches on the back of his neck and calves already tickled with the new day's sun.

The rows of young wheat slid across his sightline and led off towards the hedgerows between the field and the village. In the other direction he could see Mrs Gardener's farm. Or Ms Young as she had recently begun asking him to call her. Josh looked down at the sack of weeds, nearly full again, and glanced behind him to see how many rows he'd done. Three and a half. He counted how many rows he still had to do, and stopped at eighteen, his age now. Martha and he had had to endure a pretty lame, and alcohol-free, public birthday party in the church hall, suggested by their father and organised by Monica Hilfenhaus when Judith made it clear she wasn't going to do it.

There were balloons. And lemonade.

Judith rectified things the next night by inviting

Sam and Kitty round for dinner, handing them a couple of bottles of wine and just leaving the four of them to it.

Josh sighed. Why wouldn't his father allow them to use weedkiller? Surviving the next winter was going to be hard enough without denying themselves the use of technology. He knew it was pointless asking, though. His father would say the same thing he always said.

'Science got us into this mess, Josh. Hard work, and God, will get us out.'

Clive Mitchell had apparently pointed out at an ill-tempered council meeting that cars and tractors were the developments of science, as was the petrol they ran on, but Josh's father was immune to reason these days. The Lancaster House proposal was the last time anyone had tried to argue with him. When Judith, Reg and Bryan had returned to the Pirbrights' after that meeting, they had been shaking their heads in bemusement and anger.

'He just didn't want to know,' Reg had said.

Bryan had nodded. 'Wouldn't even look at it. He was clearly furious that we'd even suggested it.'

'But what about the others?' Josh had asked, desperately disappointed. Martha had looked sanguine, as thought she'd expected this.

'It never had a chance,' Judith replied with tight-lipped fury. 'I don't like to say it in front of you two, but I think your father has lost it. He's…he's a megalomaniac.'

'He did say we may revisit it in due course,' Bryan had said gently.

Reg snorted.

'He's not going to revisit anything. And the rest of them, they just go along with whatever he says.'

As Bryan had said at Christmas, it was clear that most of the community supported Michael. He was the saviour of the village, after all. In the eyes of most, he could do no wrong. In fact, for most of the residents, Camp Wheatsheaf represented what had been wrong with the Old World.

That said, the rift hadn't stopped people drinking in the pub, not least the vicar, much to Michael's annoyance. The teenagers had all been banned from the pub since word had got out about their Christmas Day visit. In fact, they'd been told they'd be caned should any of them be caught drinking, though Sam still had a secret stash. The council had also decreed that no teenagers were to leave the village without express permission from Michael, even if accompanied by an adult.

In church the previous Sunday Michael had used his now-weekly address to fulminate against intensive farming methods from the Old World. 'In one farm in Bedfordshire,' he had said, 'a hundred thousand turkeys were held in one shed, pressed up against each other, pecking one another, desperate for space, for air, for some kind of life. If a virus gets loose in a hell-hole like that, it will evolve, regenerate, re-invent itself a dozen times over as it battles against the turkeys' immune systems, until it finds a form which the poor creatures cannot fight off.

'These sheds were the Devil's laboratories,' he'd thundered. 'Seemingly designed with one purpose in mind, to create a superbug that would kill everyone on the planet.'

Michael had lowered his head and waited for the cloaking silence in the church to lend his words even more gravity.

'If an evil genius had developed a plan to destroy the human race, he couldn't have come up with a better way of creating and spreading the seed of our destruction than intensive farming methods like those. Now I accept my responsibility for helping to create that state. That is a cross I must bear every day of my life. I know I sinned.'

Why this meant they couldn't use weedkiller Josh was a little unclear, but he'd learned not to argue with his father, or with any of the God squad – Mark, Monica, Mr Carter. Strangely enough, the vicar, Jim Halfdene, seemed uncomfortable with the new-found religiosity of some of the others. The fire and brimstone sermons came increasingly from Josh's father.

It had been eight months since the outbreak and his father's return to the village. The teenagers had hoped that over time the strict, god-fearing phase their parents were going through would ease off and they'd be cut a little more slack. But, if anything, the opposite had been the case. Neither Josh nor Sam had been given their motorbikes back. This was mostly because the two of them had tried to cut church one day, and they'd also been given a 6.00 p.m. curfew in their rooms for a week that time as punishment. They'd literally been allowed out only to work in the fields.

Kitty had also been grounded for a week for sneaking out after dark to go and see Martha. Josh had missed her terribly. Seeing her pretty, freckled face after work was one of the few things he looked forward to every day. Sam had told Josh his sister had regular screaming matches with Monica, and that her mother had slapped her more than once.

Martha had become more philosophical about it all. She'd accepted the new ways, in every sense. Josh felt his own attitude had changed as well; though Sam still argued and answered back, Josh found it easier just to go along with everything.

There was plenty of work too. He'd asked his father a number of times if he could be given some greater responsibility, and eventually Michael had put him in charge of getting the Gardeners' farm in operation. Susan Gardener and her husband had been no farmers, but as she was in occupation of the farmhouse and had made it clear she wasn't moving, Pirbright and the council had decided that Josh and Susan should begin planting. Wheat, to begin with.

Josh removed his battered straw hat and wiped the

sweat from his forehead. It was going to be halogen-hot today. He looked up into the deep of the sky, breathing it in. The birds in the hedgerows were going mental. Since the demise of the human race there'd been an explosion in the local bird population. Badgers and foxes too. Dogs hadn't been a problem since the fence had been put up, but the smaller animals would dig under it periodically and get into the chickens.

Sam was over on the larger and more developed McGoverns' farm, on the other side of the village. Josh suspected the council had split the two of them up deliberately, to keep them out of trouble, but the reality was that there wasn't too much to do here yet and he could handle it on his own.

'Could do with some help with these damn weeds, though,' he muttered to himself.

As if answering his plea, the slim figure of Mrs...no, Ms Young appeared at the edge of the field. She didn't come closer, but instead waved him towards her. Welcoming the distraction, Josh began trudging through the crumbly soil towards the farmhouse.

'So, sixteen, eh?' Martha said. 'All grown up.'

'Yeah,' Kitty replied, reaching carefully under an incredulous-looking hen and deftly extracting a warm, brown egg. 'Just think, in five short years, I'll be allowed to drink alcohol.'

'What are you going to wear to the party? Sorry, I should say *your* party?' Martha asked. 'Too warm for Uggs.'

'Thought I'd wear these,' Kitty said, looking down at her chicken-shit-smeared overalls.

Martha tipped her head to one side, appraising the creation.

'It's you, there's no doubt about it.'

'I may accessorise with some cow dung,' Kitty continued, striking a pose.

'Pig swill is in this year,' Martha reminded her.

'Oh, I don't know,' Kitty said. 'It's so annoying that all my decent clothes from . . . before are slightly too small for me. Everything's just a little too tight.'

'I know someone who seems to appreciate it,' Martha said, nodding at Kitty's chest.

'Oh, why did you have to mention him?'

'Sorry.'

'Your mum really wants you to marry him, doesn't she?' Martha asked.

'Everyone does,' Kitty replied. 'All the adults, anyway. I'm convinced he's going to propose at my party tomorrow. What will happen when I say no, I have no idea.'

The girls finished the row of nesting boxes and, carrying their baskets, walked out into the hot sun. They had to take the eggs to the church for counting and distribution before returning to the farm later that afternoon to muck out the pigs, the worst job of the week.

'I'm going to pop over to the Gardeners' before we go to the church,' Kitty said. 'Drop off Ms Young's eggs; she was too busy to collect her ration yesterday.'

Martha glanced at her friend. Kitty had changed a lot in the last few months and was sometimes hard to read. Martha knew, for example, that Kitty found Mark attractive – and she flirted with him terribly. Kitty clearly felt awkward admitting it to Martha, which was unsurprising as it was just six months ago that Mark had proposed to her friend. But Martha also knew something else about Kitty that the two hadn't actually discussed. She knew that it wasn't really Mark who held Kitty's heart, but Josh. Though the girls were close, this had long been a subject that had remained unexplored. Martha had tried to steer the conversation in that direction many times, but Kitty always deftly steered it away. Martha had never been very good at all that deep and meaningful stuff, anyway. She imagined if Kitty wanted to talk about it she would. Martha said nothing now and they walked on, the only sound the scratching of their sandals on the dusty track.

Martha thought back to her own rejection of Mark's proposal. Though he had quickly moved on, Michael hadn't. Since then her father had hardly said two words to her. It was around that time that he effectively, if not officially, moved out of the family home.

256

Judith had largely kept out of council affairs since the Lancaster House proposal had been rejected. Martha felt she was biding her time, waiting for the moment when she could act, do something to reverse their route on this disturbing path her husband was leading them along. Knowing Judith, she was calculating, planning, thinking about exactly how it was one led a revolution.

'Are you sure you'll say no?' Martha now asked Kitty as they walked along the dusty track. The Tarmac had started to break up with all the weeds pushing through, and she marvelled at how quickly it had all changed.

'Yes! Mark's definitely not right for me,' Kitty said, a little too quickly. 'And, besides, I don't care if they say everything's changed. I'm still too young to get married.'

'Oh, it's not so bad,' Martha said, holding up her hand to display her ring.

'Sorry,' Kitty said. 'I didn't mean that you . . . I don't think that . . . oh, you know what I mean!'

'It's OK,' Martha said. 'I hadn't thought I'd be married at eighteen, but then again I never thought virtually the whole human race would be wiped out by a virus.'

'My mother keeps asking me if you're pregnant,' Kitty said, smirking.

'It's none of her business,' Martha sniffed.

'I don't think she's the only one who wants to

know,' Kitty said. 'I heard Mum gossiping with Mrs Rogers and Mrs Green the other day. They're all desperate to start knitting booties.'

Martha laughed.

'Have you spoken to your dad?' Kitty asked. 'I bet he's got your first-born on a work rota already.'

Martha shook her head. 'I haven't seen much of him since the wedding.' Bryan and Martha's wedding had been a low-key affair in the church at Easter. Michael had made no secret that he disapproved. Bryan was, of course, a firm member of Camp Wheatsheaf. Michael had come to the wedding, but hadn't been involved in the planning and hadn't come to the wedding breakfast at the Wheatsheaf, either. Martha had not asked him to give her away.

'He doesn't own me,' Martha had said. 'No one does.'

Judith's eyes had twinkled. She had seemed a little surprised when Martha had told her about Bryan, but Martha could also tell that her mother got it. She understood why. Bryan was a good man, he was handsome and kind and his daughter Ellie needed a mother. And though Martha had rejected her father's choice of a husband for her, she hadn't entirely rejected his reasons for feeling she should marry sooner, rather than later. Martha accepted her duty.

'Shit happens,' Kitty said, looking around to make sure nobody had heard. Swearing was very much frowned upon these days. A month earlier their neighbour Mr Carter had overheard her in the churchyard telling Sam to 'sod off', and word had gotten back to her mother. Kitty had been given an extra shift at the farm as punishment.

Martha grinned at her.

'And he's a good man, your husband,' Kitty went on.

'Yes,' Martha said. 'Yes, he is.'

At that moment Sam was in one of the barns on McGoverns' farm hitting a generator with a hammer. The logical part of his brain knew that simply hitting it couldn't possibly fix whatever it was that had gone wrong. The more pragmatic part of his brain knew that hitting it had often worked in the past and that it was therefore worth a try today.

On this occasion, though, logic won and he realised he needed to get help. The cows were due in for milking in an hour or so and they were reliant on the machines – a fact which Pirbright conveniently ignored during his periodic rants in the church about the evils of Old World technology. Sam had become quite proficient in maintaining the generators, but right now he needed a proper mechanic. The only qualified mechanic in the village was Keith Tucker, who Sam knew was on an overnight foraging trip to Basingstoke, looking for car parts.

Sam had been trying to get on an overnight trip for months, with no luck yet. In fact, other than the trips to Lancaster House, he'd only left the village once since the outbreak, and that was just a two-hour round-trip to Godalming with Clive to get coal from the big yard there. There was a fishing trip planned for the last week in June, which Michael had already told him he couldn't go on, but he hadn't entirely abandoned hope just yet.

He sat on a pile of potato sacks due to be filled in October and considered the broken generator grumpily. There was only one thing for it. He'd have to go and get Mark, who'd become adept at fixing the generators in the last eight months.

Sam hated Mark. Mark hated Sam. Relations between them hadn't improved in the last six months. Sam was particularly irritated by the fact that everyone else in the village seemed to think Mark was wonderful. Mark had also remained close to Michael, and although Josh said he wasn't bothered and was happy working on the farm, it seemed clear that Michael had chosen Mark as the future leader of the village.

Sam had noticed even Kitty was a Mark-fan these days, since his courteous gesture in the pub at Christmas. Sam was puzzled by his sister's behaviour. He'd always thought she and Josh would get together. It was pretty obvious she liked him, and vice versa. But who knew what went on in girls' minds? He didn't like the thought of being Mark's brother-in-law, but it wasn't really his choice, was it? He'd just have to make an effort to get along with the electrician if so. Mark's mother had replaced Judith as Monica's close friend and the Rogers seemed to spend more time at the Hilfenhaus' than at their own home.

No point putting it off, he thought to himself. He stomped out of the milking shed and hopped onto his moped, revved the little engine and headed up towards the village.

He ran into Mark sooner than expected. The electrician was wandering along the Green carrying a rifle.

'What's going on?' Sam said, slowing down.

Mark carried on walking, ignoring him.

'Mark, tell me,' Sam said.

Mark stopped and turned to him, looking him up and down, thinking. He seemed to reach a decision, and spoke.

'David McGovern's lost some sheep. OK?'

'Inside the fence?'

Mark shook his head. 'No. The McGoverns have been using a meadow outside the fence for grazing during the day. The sheep got cut off from the rest of the flock and stayed out overnight.'

'Let me help you.'

At first Mark's face twisted in contempt, and he looked as though he were about to say no, but then he visibly forced himself to smile. He nodded.

'Yeah, you know what? I could do with some help. Leave your bike.' He turned and walked off, the barrel of his rifle swinging behind him.

Sam blinked at the retreating Mark. Maybe he'd decided to make an effort too.

'Have some more lemonade,' Ms Young said, leaning over Josh to pour so that Josh could feel the weight of a warm breast against his shoulder. His mouth felt dry and he tried not to swallow. Ms Young sometimes invited him in and would make polite chat as he drank the soft drinks she gave him. Sometimes she gave him biscuits as though he were a child. He'd assumed she saw him as a surrogate son but lately, just the last couple of times she'd invited him in, he thought he'd detected a change in her. Her clothes, for example.

He watched her as she crossed the room and opened the sash window. She wore a thin-strapped cotton dress, blue like the sky through the window, and seemed to have done something different with her hair. Normally in a ponytail or a bun, today she had it down, the ends brushing her bare shoulders. As she turned back to him he quickly looked away from her heavy breasts, only just held in by the sheer fabric.

She walked slowly behind him as he sipped the lemonade, feeling uncomfortable. A trickle of sweat crawled down his back, keeping time with the ticking of the wall clock.

'I saw you out there, working so hard,' she said

and laid her hands on his shoulders. 'Your poor back must be agony. Gosh, you're so tense!'

Well, I am now, Josh thought to himself.

She began rubbing his shoulders. Not hard. Gentle, circular motions, increasing Josh's sense of discomfort. Ms Young was very attractive, but she was maybe fifteen years older than him. Surely she wasn't intending to seduce him? But then again, Bryan was fifteen years older than Martha. Was the age difference more acceptable because she was a girl?

He stood and awkwardly moved past her, brushing against her smooth stomach as he went.

She smiled. 'Why don't you come through to the sitting room and I'll give you a proper massage,' she said. She stood with the window behind her, revealing a tantalising view of her slender legs through the dress fabric. Josh hesitated. Ms Young seemed to make a decision. She stepped forward, took hold of his shoulders and leaned in to kiss him. He let her, unable for the moment to think of a good reason why he shouldn't. Her mouth was soft and warm on his cracked lips and she tasted like sugar and mint. He felt her silky body move against his and he responded, pushing forward against her.

She broke off and smiled at him again. 'It certainly feels like you're ready for that massage...'

But then Josh saw something move in his peripheral vision and turned to look.

Kitty stood holding a basket, watching them from across the kitchen, bewilderment on her sun-freckled face.

'Get out!' Ms Young shouted. 'How dare you just barge in?'

'I knocked,' Kitty responded weakly. She looked away from Josh, down at the floor. 'I'm sorry.'

Then she was gone, the egg basket resting on the floor, rocking slowly.

Josh pushed Ms Young firmly away and ran out after Kitty.

'Let her go!' Ms Young called. 'She's just a silly girl.'

Josh ran outside, squinting in the bright sun. Then he saw her, running back towards the village, her sandals kicking up puffs of dust which hung behind her like unanswered questions. 'Wait!' he cried as she sprinted off up the hill, but she wouldn't stop. Josh stood and watched her go.

'Damn,' he said.

He took an early lunch break and went looking for Kitty. He needed to find her and explain. But explain what? He'd hardly been forced into kissing Ms Young. In that moment, when he'd seen Kitty across the kitchen, when he'd seen the look of hurt and betrayal in her eyes, he'd realised two things: that her feelings for him were much stronger than he'd believed, and that his own feelings for her were, if anything, even stronger. He saw now he'd been a fool. Why hadn't he said something to her when he'd had the chance? He'd been aware of her flirting with Mark lately. Part of him wondered if she had been trying to make him jealous. Another part had told him not to be so presumptuous. Whatever her motives, he'd found himself drawing away from Kitty, telling himself she wasn't interested and that he should move on.

Since Martha had married and moved out, he didn't see either of the girls as much anyway. Sometimes they'd meet in the churchyard, but more often than not these days it was just Josh, Sam and Winston.

'I haven't seen her,' Monica said at the door to her house, and didn't invite him in.

Josh bumped into Reg on the way down to the church.

'Have you seen Kitty?' he asked.

Reg shook his head and explained that he was on his way to collect his rations. They walked down together.

'Sick of the same old rubbish we get in the ration boxes,' Reg said. 'Beans, tinned fish, pasta and rice. What happens to all the other stuff we bring back? That's what I want to know.'

'Like what?' Josh asked.

'Oh, all sorts,' Reg replied. 'Anything that's preserved or in tins. Cured meats, fancy olives, nice oils. I found some black truffles the other day, in jars.

Handed 'em in. Never saw them again.'

'Why don't you just keep some of the best things for yourself?' Josh asked.

'Because that's theft, Josh,' the old soldier growled. 'It's wrong.'

'But you give us things sometimes,' Josh said. 'You gave Sam that vodka the other day.'

'Shh!' Reg said, looking around to see if anyone was in earshot. 'That's different,' he said with a smile. 'You lot need the occasional treat, for morale, like.'

They didn't find Kitty at the church, either, but they did run into Mark and Sam, filling water bottles and looking set for an expedition. Mark carried a rifle.

'Just in time,' Sam said. 'David's lost some sheep and asked for volunteers to go looking. Wanna come?'

'Oh, bloody hell,' Mark said. 'Why don't we just bring the whole village?'

'What's the problem?' Reg asked.

'I just don't want to have to hold two kids' hands, that's all.'

Reg shrugged. 'I'll come too, then,' he said.

Mark rolled his eyes and went back to preparing his kit.

'We're going outside the fence?' Josh said. 'Crazy.' He looked at Sam and raised his eyebrows, tilting his head towards Mark.

Sam shrugged and watched as Mark stood and

266

turned to go. 'He's actually been talking to me,' he whispered. 'We seem to be best buds now.'

'Do you want to be best buds?' Josh asked, with a frown.

'No,' Sam said. 'But it's better than him trying to blow my head off.'

Reg grabbed a water bottle, dropped it into his backpack and took off after Mark.

'That'll be because he intends to propose to your sister tomorrow,' Josh said steadily.

Sam grimaced but said nothing.

And frankly, Josh thought, *after what happened this morning I reckon she'll probably say yes.*

12.01 P.M.

Kitty, at that moment, was sitting in the Hilfenhaus' garage, crying and drinking one of the beers Sam had hidden in an old cardboard box under a tarpaulin. Two more crushed cans lay on the concrete floor. She didn't really like the taste of beer, but drinking alcohol was what you did when you were this upset. She felt like her head was being squeezed in a vice. It wasn't just Josh, and what she'd witnessed. Work was so hard, and Mrs McGovern kept telling her off when she made a mess of things.

Kitty didn't really feel she had the right skill set to be a survivor. Before the outbreak she'd only really been good at one thing and that was computers. Not just social media – Kitty had learned a little about website design at school and was teaching herself at home. She'd created a blog page for her mother, and had taken over the maintenance of her father's personal website. She'd designed her own page but had never got around to uploading it to the web, the cost of the hosting being prohibitive. Everything she'd learned was useless now. She'd got to grips a little with the workings of the farm, she could handle the chickens fine and got on quite well with the sheep. But the cattle terrified her and the pigs knocked her over and the goats wouldn't do what she told them. She never let on how much she hated it, but she'd sometimes cry herself to sleep after a bad day.

And things were getting worse. Her mother was constantly being horrible to her, everyone was expecting her to marry Mark, and now Josh had done this to her. She took another sip of beer and grimaced at the bitterness. Kitty knew she shouldn't really blame Josh. She hadn't exactly been clear with him about her feelings. It had been quite obvious for some time that Mark liked her. She was flattered, even if she did feel like she'd been second-choice, behind Martha. She was actually surprised that he'd even noticed her. She was also surprised, and miffed, that Mark's interest in her didn't seem to bother Josh at all. In fact, he seemed to have drifted away, and now it was clear why – he was carrying on with an older woman.

She stood up, swaying a little, and lifted the can to her lips. But then she changed her mind, and with a sudden rush of anger hurled the half-full can at the rolling door.

A few moments later, when Monica Hilfenhaus came to check on the noise, she found her daughter huddled in a heap, sobbing noiselessly. Monica kneeled down and laid a hand on Kitty's shoulder. Kitty looked up at the touch.

'Oh, Mum,' she said. 'I'm in such a mess.' But she didn't get the comfort she so needed.

'You've been drinking,' Monica replied, white-lipped.

Kitty peered at her through tear-glazed eyes. 'What? Oh God, Mum, don't be cross, I—'

'Don't you blaspheme as well,' Monica said primly.

Kitty stared at her in disbelief and shook her head slowly. 'I thought you might have come to help. To try and make me feel better,' she said. 'But, no. You've come to yell at me again.'

Monica glared back. 'You will not drink alcohol under my roof.'

'Well,' Kitty said, 'maybe I'll just go and stay under someone else's roof, then.' She stood and pushed past her mother, heading unsteadily towards the door.

'Well, that's what we all want,' Monica said. 'But I doubt very much Mark will want to marry you if he knows you're a . . . a drunk!'

Kitty spun to face her mother again, bristling. 'I don't want Mark to marry me,' she shouted.

'Well, you've certainly been leading him on these last few weeks,' Monica snapped.

'So, I'm not allowed to talk to a boy without everyone expecting me to marry him?' Kitty said, incredulous.

Monica walked up to her and Kitty wondered if she were going to slap her, but she stood firm.

'You'd better marry him,' Monica said quietly, dangerously.

'And if I don't?'

'Then you'll be leaving, and won't be coming back,' Monica said abruptly.

Kitty glared at her mother. 'You know what?' she said. 'If Dad were here he'd stop all this. He wouldn't let me marry Mark, let alone try to push me into it. He'd stand up to Josh's dad too. And he'd hate what you've become—'

Monica slapped her, the sound ringing through the cold, brick-built garage.

And for a moment Kitty thought she might just slap back. Just hit her mother and walk out. She could go and stay with Martha, or at the pub, or with the McGoverns.

But then her shoulders slumped. Suddenly the fight was gone from her. She felt tired, and fuzzy-headed. What was the point in fighting? Her mother had changed – she was just like Mr Pirbright, convinced of her own righteousness. All the adults were the same. There was no escape from this new, hateful world.

Turning away from her furious mother, Kitty slowly took herself back into the house and upstairs to her room.

Martha sat at the window of Bryan's house – her house, now – and watched the men troop past, Sam and Josh trying to trip each other up as they went. She heard them panting and laughing as Reg grinned at the back of the group. Mark too had a smile on his face, and why not? The weather was beautiful, they were safe, and they had enough to eat.

If a part of her wanted to run out and join them, it was a part buried deep under mounds of duty and layers of safety. It had been her choice to marry Bryan, she hadn't been forced. She'd said yes of her own accord. Nor had she done it to annoy her father. She held no grudge against him, even now when he still refused to speak to her.

If there was a part of Martha that had said yes to Bryan because Ellie needed a mother rather than because Bryan had wanted a wife, then that part too was buried deep.

Ellie came running in, looking madly beautiful. Now nearly seven and just stepping onto that long threshold from little girl to pre-teen, Ellie had called Martha 'Mummy' for the first time the week before, and Martha, until that point unsure of how she'd react to such an event, had said nothing but, 'Yes, sweetheart?'

Indeed, why not smile? How could life be better?

Twenty minutes later Josh watched a bead of sweat drop in slow motion from the end of Reg's long nose. It disappeared into the crimson grass surrounding the mutilated remains of the ewe. Josh's legs were scratched and red from walking through the long grass, and he wished he'd worn jeans despite the heat.

'Dog,' Mark said, glancing around the meadow and answering a question no one had asked, at least not out loud.

Reg hunkered down, giving an old man's groan, to inspect the corpse. He clucked his tongue. 'Lots of dogs,' he muttered.

'Could have been a pack,' Josh suggested.

'Odd that they didn't eat more,' Reg said, looking up at him. 'Why kill a sheep and leave half of it to rot?'

Mark answered. 'They're not wanting for food. Plenty of sheep wandering around the area still, wild.'

Reg looked down at the tattered, crimson wool at his feet. 'They've gone savage,' he agreed.

Mark looked at Sam. 'This is why children shouldn't be allowed to leave the village,' he said.

Sam rolled his eyes. 'Oh, here we go, Uncle Mark's health and safety lecture...'

'Screw you!' Mark snapped. 'As far as I'm concerned you can leave whenever you like and have your throat torn out. But Kitty stays in the village, you hear me?'

Josh felt a pang at the sound of her name. Surely she couldn't be marrying Mark, with his temper and his attitude towards women.

'Kitty can make her own decisions, and her own choices,' Sam fired back.

Reg kicked at a splinter of bone, firing it back into the sheep's open ribcage. *Goal!* Josh couldn't help thinking.

'Mark does have a point, Sam,' he said. 'We're in a savage world now. It's wild out there.'

'Whose side are you on?' Sam asked.

'I'm not on anyone's side,' Reg replied.

Mark reached into his pack and pulled out a cardboard box. Rat poison. He sprinkled it liberally over the sheep's carcase, drowning it in the grey powder.

'That should take care of a few of the bastards,' he said.

'What's the point?' Josh asked. 'There must be thousands, hundreds of thousands of dogs roaming around. You can't poison them all.'

Mark's smile was sinister. 'I can try.'

24 JUNE, 7.26 P.M.

Mr Carter sniffed the punch for the twelfth time and

nodded. Sam stood by, looking hurt at the implication he might have been adding vodka.

'Where would I even *get* vodka?' he asked. Sam had been reported after his shed stash had been uncovered; his hand still showed red welts from the caning he'd received for that. Mr Carter smiled half-heartedly and made his way off towards the back of the church hall. On his way he passed the *Keep Calm and Carry On* poster, which Sam had earlier adjusted to read: *Keep Calm and Party On!*

The church was tripped up good for Kitty's celebration, with flowers in garlands, tasteful decorations created by the children under the controlling eye of Sam's mother. The room was well-lit by the obligatory candles, though this time in a rainbow of colours.

At the last festival committee meeting, Sam had made representations, on behalf of all the younger villagers, that they be allowed to install a set of decks and a PA system. Michael had dismissed the idea out of hand.

'You know the rules. Recorded music is allowed at a reasonable volume in one's own home, but we are trying to discourage Old World music and won't allow it in public, especially at volume. We have a perfectly good folk band, which has been practising for weeks.'

Sam watched the band cavorting on the stage. Trying to avoid Old World music had been difficult apparently, as most of their tunes were based on familiar songs, just rehashed with a few added flourishes and a new verse or two. They were currently playing a weird new version of Leonard Cohen's *Marianne*. Sam shook his head in disgust. Still, the crap music hadn't kept Kitty off the dance floor. She'd been on with Mark most of the evening, stopping only to dance with Reg.

Josh had been floating around, watching. Sam had seen him dancing with Ms Young earlier and now he couldn't see either of them. After what Josh had told him about the lemonade incident, he wasn't too surprised. It was pretty clear Josh was messed up about Kitty marrying Mark, but there wasn't much Sam could do about it.

Reg walked past. 'Have you seen Josh?' Sam asked the older man.

'Nope,' Reg replied. 'Not for a while.'

Sam frowned. He needed to talk to his friend. He'd decided, at the last minute, that he was going to try and blag his way onto the fishing trip that was leaving in a couple of days. He was going to attempt to convince Josh to come along too. They needed to get away, and to hell with the consequences.

Then Sam saw his sister coming over to the punch table. He poured her a glass and she took it gratefully, her skin shining with sweat. She had an odd gleam in her eye and a fixed smile. Sam had seen her like this before on occasion; she could be bloody-minded when she wanted.

'Are you OK?' Sam asked. He'd not seen her since this morning, when she'd calmly told her family about her engagement. Monica had been delighted, needless to say, and had rushed around to Linda Rogers' house to start on the wedding plans. Kitty nodded, not looking at him. She drained the cup and handed it to him absently.

'I might go outside to cool down,' she said. 'Come with?' He nodded and followed her to the rear doors.

Clouds had come over that afternoon. It had rained around seven o'clock and the air had cooled a little, offering merciful relief from the day's heavy blanket of heat.

Kitty looked around as they stepped out into the churchyard. With the rain had arrived the cloying scent of manure, filling the air. Sam breathed deeply.

'Ah,' he sighed. 'Who knew utopia would smell of pig shit?'

She didn't reply, just carried on gazing about.

'Who you looking for?' he asked, though he knew the answer.

'No one,' she said. She wandered round the side of the church, Sam trotting along after her.

After a while she stopped and turned to her brother.

'Did Josh bring Winston tonight?'

Sam shook his head. 'No. Josh thought it wasn't fair for him to be sitting out here listening to all the fun inside, so he took him for a long walk today and left him at home.'

Even in the weak moonlight, Sam could see her disappointment.

'This didn't work out last time, either,' Kitty said cryptically.

'Kitty,' Sam began. 'What's going on?'

'I don't know,' she replied. 'I don't know what's going on at all.'

'You're not making much sense tonight,' he said, laughing. 'Look, are you still into Josh?'

Kitty stared at him; she looked mortified. 'You know about... my feelings for Josh?'

Sam rolled his eyes. 'I think there's a blind and deaf guy on Primrose Street who doesn't know about it, but the rest of us are pretty clear.'

'But I'm marrying Mark,' Kitty said.

'Yeah, that's got me puzzled,' Sam said. 'But, hey, it's your life.'

'Is it, though?' Kitty said sharply. 'Is it my life? My choice?'

Sam blinked. 'Well, of course, you don't have to do anything you don't want—'

'Don't be so naïve, Sam,' Kitty said. 'It's time you grew up.'

Sam didn't know what to say. He just stared, trying to figure out just what she was going on about.

'You don't know what it's like,' Kitty said. 'All the adults dropping hints. Mum taking me aside and telling me I need to settle down. Mark's mum coming around bringing gifts. I just feel, I just feel... suffocated.'

Sam nodded. That feeling he understood.

'And what's the point of having free choice, if you can't have the one thing you really want?'

'Josh?' Sam asked. He was feeling a little confused. Of course he'd known for ages that Josh and Kitty liked each other, but he hadn't realised their feelings were this strong. He'd never really spoken to her about this sort of thing, and felt uncomfortable, especially as it was Josh they were talking about but, well, there was no one else around.

Kitty turned and walked away. She sat on a tombstone and sank her head into her hands. Sam could hear laughter and music from inside the church. The gentle breeze flickered its way through the trees at the far end of the graveyard. The air smelled sweet and clean.

'You know he likes you too, don't you?' Sam said.

'He has a funny way of showing it,' Kitty replied, muffled.

Then Sam saw someone walking up the path towards the church and heard a woman's laugh. It was Ms Young, and she was with someone. He squinted in the dim moonlight, expecting to see Josh with her, but then he realised it wasn't Josh. It was Harry. He watched them until they disappeared from view, behind a corner. If she was with Harry, then where was Josh? Maybe he'd been a little hasty assuming they'd been somewhere together.

'I think, maybe, that you and Josh should at least talk, yeah?' Sam said eventually.

'I wanted to talk to him tonight,' Kitty replied. 'But now I can't find him. I think he might be with that woman. Mrs Gardener, or Ms Young or whatever she's calling herself now.'

'He'll be off walking Winston,' Sam said. 'Trust me.'

'Oh, Sam,' Kitty said. 'Everything's such a mess.'

10

After work the next day Josh let himself into the back garden and discovered Winston was gone. He popped into the house to find his mother sitting at the kitchen table looking grim.

'What's wrong?' he asked. 'Where's Winston?'

Judith blinked and looked up at the ceiling.

'A chicken was killed today,' she said. 'Over at the Nicholls' house.'

'Well, it won't have been Winston,' Josh said, guessing where this was heading. 'He wouldn't hurt a fly. Besides, how would he get out?'

'I believe you,' Judith replied. 'But your father has his own ideas.'

'He's taken Winston?'

'Mr Carter, actually, according to Mara next door.' Judith sat with her hands out in front of her, as if trying to think what to do with them. 'They came while I was out. Carter and Mark.'

Josh stood for a moment or two longer, trying to control the rising fury.

'Josh,' his mother began, but it was too late. Josh

280

was gone, back out into the sultry afternoon.

He passed Mark as he entered the church.

'He's busy!' the electrician called, but Josh ignored him and pushed into his father's office. Josh hadn't seen his father for a few days, as to all intents and purposes Michael and Judith were now separated. Josh was surprised when he walked in to find his father had shaved his hair short. So short in fact that his pale scalp could be seen through the remaining hair, shining in the candlelight. He looked thin, bent over the desk, scribbling furiously on a yellow legal pad.

Michael looked up at his son as he entered.

'How dare you just barge in like this?' he said.

'Where's my dog?' Josh asked, his voice quivering with emotion.

Michael dropped his pen and rubbed his temples, eyes closed, the pain clearly visible on his face. 'Josh, your dog killed a chicken today,' he said, without opening his eyes.

'Oh, rubbish.' Josh knocked the idea aside with a sweeping gesture. 'Winston wouldn't kill a chicken.'

'Then what did?' Michael asked, finally opening his eyes and looking at his son. 'Your dog is the only one in the village since Emily Green's poodle died.'

'It was probably a fox,' Josh replied.

'There are no foxes in the village, Josh. We built a fence, remember?'

Josh sighed. 'Dad, I keep telling you, the fence is

useless for keeping out foxes. Feral dogs, yes, but the foxes just dig straight under it. I told you about this and you ignored me—'

'Don't backchat me,' Mr Pirbright said sharply. 'Mark said it must have been Winston—'

'Oh, *Mark* said?' Josh cried. 'Well then, it must be true, if *Mark* said.' Josh was dimly aware of someone, probably Mark, behind him.

'Anyway, it's already been dealt with,' Michael added, returning to his work.

There was a long silence.

'Dealt with?' Josh said quietly. He hoped he was misunderstanding. 'What are you saying?'

'The dog has been destroyed,' Michael said. 'No more dogs in the village, understand?' He stood and pushed in his chair. 'Now, I have urgent business to attend to. So if you'll excuse me . . .'

But Josh wasn't finished. Fury rose within his chest. 'Hold on a minute. You're telling me you've killed my dog today? And you're just going to leave, like that?'

'Josh, you know there was bad feeling in the village about you being the only one allowed a dog—'

'That was your stupid rule,' Josh interrupted. 'I don't see why everyone couldn't have a dog—'

Michael banged the table, making Josh jump. 'We are not going to revisit old arguments,' he said. 'It was not fair that the president's son should be the only one to have a dog. This was the fairest outcome.

There should not be seen to be any favouritism.'

Josh's jaw sagged. 'I can't believe what I'm hearing,' he said. 'Favouritism? Don't make me laugh.'

Michael stood and glared at his son. 'I don't like your tone.'

Josh stalked up to the table and stuck his face close to his father's, challenging him. 'And I don't like the fact that you've killed my damn dog!'

Michael slapped him.

Josh stared back, face stinging, beyond fury now. 'That's the last time you hit me,' he spat and swung for his father. But the desk was in the way. Michael leaned back and Josh's punch missed, then someone had grabbed him from behind around the neck.

'Get him out,' Mr Pirbright said.

Rapidly Mark bundled Josh into the church proper and closed the office door behind them. He shoved Josh roughly onto the ground. By the time Josh had regained his balance and stood up, Mark was on him and punched him sharply in the jaw, knocking him back down onto the hard floor.

'You've got to be kidding,' Josh said, rubbing his face. He felt dizzy. Then fury took hold again and he leaped to his feet and swung for Mark, who twisted his head back and out of the way just in time. Josh's fist pounded into the electrician's chest.

Mark grunted, but recovered quickly and grabbed Josh by his shirt-front, lifting him up. Before Josh could react, Mark swung him round and slammed him hard against the wooden wall of the office, winding him.

My father's in there, Josh thought. *Listening to all this, and doing nothing.*

'So much for a new, peaceful world,' he gasped.

'You don't get it yet, do you?' Mark whispered, his face up close to Josh's. 'Things are different now.'

Josh stopped in at Sam's house on the way home. He was shaking and his shoulder ached from where Mark had slammed him against the wall. Monica sniffed, but let him in, and he ran up the stairs to Sam's room.

'Hey,' Sam said, without looking up from the book he was reading. 'So, you going to come fishing with me tomorrow?'

'I don't think so,' Josh said quietly and Sam, detecting something in his tone, turned round quickly.

'What's wrong?' Sam asked. Josh looked white, shaken and furious.

He took a deep breath to quell the tremble in his voice before speaking. 'My father killed Winston today.'

'What?'

'And when I went to confront him about it, he got Mark to rough me up.'

'Jesus Christ,' Sam said. 'Are you OK?'

'Not really,' Josh said. He sat down and told Sam the whole story. The act of talking it through helped him feel a little better.

'Those bastards,' Sam said when he'd finished. 'Would you rather I didn't go on the trip tomorrow? Sounds like you could do with some support.'

Josh shook his head. 'No, you go,' he'd said. 'Have fun. I'll be all right.'

'What happened to you last night, anyway?' Sam asked. 'You disappeared from the church.'

'Oh, I came home,' Josh said. 'Didn't feel like celebrating, really.'

'Yeah, well, about that,' Sam said. He stopped talking and moved to the door, peering outside. The coast clear, he shut it and spoke in a hushed tone. 'Thing is, I was talking to Kitty, about her marrying Mark.'

Josh grunted. 'Do I want to hear this?' he asked. The last thing he wanted right now was to hear a run-down on the wedding preparations.

'I think you might,' Sam said.

'Go on, then,' Josh sighed.

'She doesn't want to marry him,' Sam said softly.

Josh raised a sceptical eyebrow. 'So why'd she say yes?'

'Because she's a girl, and girls often do the opposite of what you'd expect.'

Josh said nothing, but something moved deep inside him. Could Sam be right?

'I just think you should talk to her,' Sam said.

'Now?' Josh asked.

'Probably best not,' Sam said. 'Not here. The walls have ears, you know what I mean?'

Josh thought for a bit. Then he spoke. 'If I write her a note, can you make sure she gets it?'

Sam nodded, and smiled.

26 JUNE, 8.07 A.M.

Sam was early at the car pool and first on the bus the following morning. He slunk to the back and slumped down into his seat, shades on. He'd already thrown his holdall into the trailer. Now, as long as he didn't make himself too obvious, he figured he had an excellent chance of going unnoticed until they were halfway to the New Forest.

James Freedman, who used to run the shop in the village, got on next, along with Amir Mansoor.

'So he's just lying there, on his back,' James was saying. 'Legs up in the air. Everyone's trying not to laugh, Monica's trying to help him up and then Judith comes...' James stopped as he saw Sam. So much for remaining undetected.

'All right, Sam?' Mansoor called. 'You're not down to come on this trip, are you?'

Sam thought about lying for a moment, then shook his head. Everything was regimented these days. He wasn't going to be able to fool them all.

'I was kind of hoping you might...overlook that fact,' he said limply.

'Fine with me,' Amir said and sat down. James winked and sat next to Amir.

Sam blinked; that was easy. James and Amir were members of the Wheatsheaf crowd, of course. Maybe they were only too happy to ignore the president's orders.

This was the third fishing trip the villagers had been on. It was mostly a Camp Wheatsheaf enterprise. Organised from the pub. It had been suggested, by some of the women left behind, that this was nothing more than a lads' weekend away, with all-night drinking, go-karting and lazing about on the beach. But it was true that the men did bring back a heck of a lot of fish, and the village needed the protein.

Michael had let it be known he was in two minds about the value of the trips. On the one hand, it seemed unfair on those who were left behind to toil in the fields; on the other hand there was the matter of the fish, and also it was good for the menfolk to get away and let their hair down once in a while. When Judith, at an early council meeting, had suggested a similar trip for women only, Michael had hummed and haahed and promised to 'get back to her on that'.

Although Michael had agreed to the trips, he always made sure someone from the council was represented. Mr Carter was due to come along on this trip and he might prove more of an obstacle to Sam's plan than the Wheatsheaf men.

Sam was desperate to go somewhere, anywhere, away from the village. He didn't much care for fishing, but, oh, what bliss to be away from his increasingly strict mother, and that damn milking machine and those awful, stinking cows. Sometimes at night, even after he'd showered, scrubbed and deodorised, he could still smell the heavy, clubbing stink of cow manure oozing from his pores and seeping out from his hair.

Clive Mitchell got on next, followed by Harry Waldock. They saw Sam immediately and Harry waved. Clive looked surprised to see him and came to the back of the bus.

'Are you sure you're due to go on this trip, Sam?' he asked.

Sam nodded. 'Yes, I spoke to Mr Pirbright about it. He said I needed a holiday as I'd been working so hard.'

Clive looked doubtful. Sam held his breath. Then Clive winked.

'All right, Sam, welcome aboard.'

But then his stomach sank as, over Clive's shoulder, he saw Mark get on the bus. Since when had he been going on this trip? Now the gig was definitely up – Mark would move heaven and earth to get him thrown off the bus. Since Josh had told him last night about Mark roughing him up in the church, Sam now eyed the electrician warily as he sauntered down the aisle.

Clive turned and saw Mark. 'Where's Carter?'

'He's ill,' Mark said. 'Michael asked me to come along instead.' Then he spotted Sam and eyed him coldly.

Damnit, Sam thought. *So close.*

'Sam's coming along,' Clive said firmly. 'That OK with you?'

Mark looked at Clive thoughtfully. Calculating.

Then he smiled. 'Yeah, let him come,' he said. 'He deserves it.'

Sam blinked. What was Mark up to? Was he trying to ingratiate himself with Sam? After the incident with the dead sheep, he doubted it, somehow. Mark was up to something. He resolved to watch his back.

The last to arrive was Ben Nicholls, a quiet member of Camp Wheatsheaf who Sam didn't know very well.

And as the minibus pulled out of the old garage forecourt and headed out through the Guildford Road gates, the men began to sing a dirty version of 'Two Little Boys'. Sam sat back in his seat, stunned. He'd be slaughtered for this when they returned. Grounded for a month, caned and probably made to work overtime at the farm for good measure. But that was for the future, and just at that moment, Sam was as happy as he'd been the last time he'd been fishing. With his father.

Sam hadn't known what to expect on the journey. He'd imagined the cars all rusted, and weeds growing up through the road, like in films, but things didn't look that different really, if you didn't look too closely at the blood-splattered windscreens of the stopped cars, or the occasional sack of skin and bones lying beside the road.

'If they're outside, like that one,' Harry told him, pointing to the corpse of a woman slumped over the bonnet of a white Peugeot, 'then birds will pick out the eyes, and maybe the tongue and even the liver if they can get to it.'

'Nice,' Sam said.

'The maggots and insects will swarm and multiply under the skin, consuming all the muscle and soft tissue, leaving just the bones, cartilage and the skin itself. That's why they look like sacks of bones.'

'That's revolting,' Sam said.

'Not at all,' Harry insisted. 'It's nature's little cleaning service. Very efficient. Without it, we'd be up to our eyeballs in cadavers.'

An hour later and they'd arrived. They picked their way through the narrow streets and pulled up in front of a whitewashed seaside inn.

'Right,' Clive said, standing in the aisle to address them. 'Here we are. This is our home for the next four days. Some of us are returning for the third time, others are virgins...' He winked at Sam. 'But don't worry, we'll go easy on you first time.'

Everyone roared and Harry ruffled Sam's hair as the teenager blushed red to his roots.

As they unloaded the bus, Clive explained matters to Sam.

'We tell everyone back at the village that it takes

four days of fishing to fill the trailer, and a trailer full gives us three months' supply of fish. But really, it only takes two half-days at most – the rest of the time we mess about, get drunk and race go-karts down at the track at Beaulieu.'

Sam frowned. 'Is Mark OK with that?'

'You mean, does he go blabbing to Pirbright about it? No. At least, I've not heard any comeback. Carter's the same when he comes. Keeps his mouth shut about exactly what we get up to. They're not stupid, they know they're on to a good thing.'

Sam grinned.

'There's really only one rule of Fishing Club,' Clive said, looking stern. 'What happens on the trip stays on the trip. Got it?'

Sam nodded. 'Got it,' he said, but the smile faded from his face. He felt a shiver run down his spine as he was suddenly reminded of the barricade. They'd had the same rule and Sam had broken it.

There were plenty of rooms in the old, rambling pub and Sam chose a nice little room at the top, with a view of the harbour. He sat on the bed and listened to the seagulls screaming in hunger outside. Boats bobbed gently in the enclosed harbour, and for a while it seemed like everything was as it used to be.

He unpacked and changed the sheets, as Clive had instructed. This room hadn't been used on the last trip, and after nine months, the bedclothes were musty. Downstairs he heard the familiar sound of a generator being started up. He flicked on the bedside lamp and grinned idiotically at the warm light.

11.34 A.M.

'Hi, Reg!' Ellie shouted, running up the pathway. Martha followed behind.

'Oh, hello,' he said, grinning. 'I was just about to knock at your door.'

'Well, now you don't have to,' Martha said with a grin. 'Were you looking for Bryan? He's off foraging.'

'I know,' Reg said. Actually, I came to see you.'

She let them in and Ellie ran upstairs while she ushered Reg through to the kitchen to make him a cup of tea.

'It's amazing in here,' Reg said, taking off his cap and looking around at the pretty kitchen. Martha had asked Reg to bring back paints and wallpaper from his foraging. She'd made changes when she'd moved in, careful not to completely obliterate memories of Ellie's mother but to add her own stamp to the house.

'Well, thanks for bringing me the materials,' Martha said, popping the kettle on the gas hob. Most houses cooked with bottled gas these days.

'It's not just the décor I was talking about,' Reg said. 'I mean ... well, it wasn't so long ago you were just a girl, off to school, running about with your mates. Now ... now you're a mum, and a wife.'

292

Martha shrugged. 'We've all had to grow up pretty fast,' she said.

'Too fast, I reckon,' Reg said, looking down at the floor.

'Look, Reg,' she said. 'I'm happy. I love Ellie, and Bryan. This is what I wanted.'

He nodded, after a moment. 'Of course it is, sorry. I didn't mean to...Anyway, that's not why I've come.'

'Oh?' The kettle whistled and Martha went to pour water into the cups.

'It's about your mum,' Reg said, gripping the brim of the cap he held in his hands.

'What about her?' Martha asked.

'Have you seen her today?' Reg asked. 'I popped round there earlier to see her but she wasn't in.'

Martha shook her head. 'No, why?'

Reg shrugged. 'It's just that, well, she went off at your dad last night at the town meeting.'

'Did she?' Martha said. 'I can't say I'm very surprised. They've not really spoken properly for months.'

'It was about Josh's dog. Or at least, that's what set her off, I think.'

'What about Winston?' Martha asked, handing Reg the cup.

'Couple of blokes went round to your mum's yesterday. Took the dog. It's been destroyed.'

'On what grounds?'

'They said he'd killed a chicken.'

'Winston would never kill a chicken,' she said.

Reg shook his head. 'No.'

Martha suddenly felt sick. She didn't need to ask who had ordered this. *Of all the petty, vindictive acts . . .* Feeling light-headed, she sat down and then, remembering herself, indicated that Reg should do the same.

'He must be devastated,' she said.

'No way it was Winston killed those chickens,' Reg said. Martha shook her head in agreement.

'Anyway,' Reg said, 'Judith proposed a vote of no confidence in your father. Said he was sick and exercising poor judgement. She said he needed to rest and someone else should take over for a while.'

'Wow! What happened?'

'Well, I seconded the motion. I agree with your mum, but they refused to allow us to vote.'

'What did everyone else do?' Martha asked. She felt a surge of pride in her mother. Judith was fighting back.

'A few spoke up and said they thought we should have a vote on it at least. Clive said he'd been worried about your father for a while and quite a few agreed, but most of them just sat there gawping,' Reg said. 'Like they always do.'

'He's got a lot of support,' Martha said.

'He's a hero,' Reg muttered, only slightly sarcastically. 'So, anyway, your mum screams and runs up to the front and gives him a good old shove. He goes arse-up, off his chair.'

'Good for her,' Martha said, laughing.

'Yeah, but she's now banned from attending meetings,' Reg said.

'I'll go and see her.' Martha looked out of the window at a flock of swallows swooping and diving over the fields.

'By the way,' Reg said, between sips of tea, 'you haven't seen Sam around, have you? Ran into David McGovern on the Green, said he didn't show at work today.'

Martha shook her head. 'He must be ill, or something.'

Reg nodded. 'Yeah, that's probably it.'

2.57 P.M.

Harry and Sam spent the afternoon wandering round the town.

'We had to clear a lot of bodies out of there,' Harry explained as they passed the church. 'For some reason, most of the people congregated here and died all together. Made things easier for us. We shifted them down into the crypt, laid them in rows and sealed them up.'

Sam felt relieved to hear that. He'd been imagining rotting corpses behind each of the doors they'd passed. It was a pretty seaside village of a few dozen houses, a pub and a church. They sat on the hot steps of the church and enjoyed the on-shore breeze. The seagulls called to each other and he could hear the ringing of the mainsheets slapping the hollow aluminium masts of the boats in the harbour.

'Were you in the team that cleared Little Sh— I mean, Haven?'

'You can call it Little Sheen while we're here. Pirbright's not around, remember.'

Sam grinned at Harry.

'Yeah, we went round door-to-door, checking if anyone was dead,' Harry told him. 'There were a few.'

'From the virus?'

'Two from the virus – an old man, and Mrs Hansen's baby.'

Sam could see James and Clive working on one of the boats in the harbour, checking and preparing it for the trip tomorrow.

'Just the two, though?'

'A few people had killed themselves. Two overdoses and one old boy had shoved a couple of shotgun barrels into his mouth. That took a bit of cleaning.'

Sam shook his head. 'Must have been tough. Especially the baby.'

'Yeah,' Harry said, deep in his memories. 'You know what, though? The one I found most awful was Mrs Clare.'

'I remember Mrs Clare,' Sam said. She was that old lady who used to walk back and forth between her house and the village, three or four times a day, grinning madly at everyone. 'Sweet old bird.'

'Yeah, we had to break in. Awful stink. She'd been there at least a week, probably much longer.'

'Right at the start of the outbreak?'

Harry nodded. 'I suppose everyone was so caught up with the news reports that no one came to check on her. Government said to stay indoors, so she didn't come out for her walks. Didn't die from the virus, though. Not sure what, she was just lying on the sitting-room floor. Alone.'

'There must have been thousands who died like that,' Sam mused. 'Not from the virus. Just . . . normal things. No one to help them.'

They sat and stared out to sea for a while.

'In those early days,' Sam said, after a while, 'did you hear anyone talking about a breeding programme?'

'Eh?'

'You know, about getting everyone married off so we'd have loads of children.'

'Oh, yeah,' Harry admitted, slightly uncomfortable.

'What did they say?' asked Sam. 'Who was it, discussing?'

'Everyone, really,' Harry said. 'It was a bit mad. Michael had a sheet of paper, he was doing all these calculations.'

'What sort of calculations?'

'Well,' Harry said. 'If all the women in the village between fifteen and forty had three children over the next five years, then say twenty per cent of them died as infants, then there'd be, I don't remember the exact numbers, but around thirty people of child-bearing age in twenty to twenty-five years. Then of those thirty, fifteen would be women. If they had five children each, minus twenty per cent infant mortality, there'd be sixty. Thirty of those would be women and have five children, and so on. The point was, though, that everyone had to start right now. Settle down and start breeding, within a year or two.'

'So Pirbright's plan is to double the population every twenty-five years?'

'Yeah, except it wasn't just Pirbright,' Harry said.

'Who else?'

'Everyone. Clive, Mr Carter, Ms Green, Bryan—'

'Bryan?!'

Harry shrugged. 'Everyone was a bit drunk. Everyone had just started to think they might survive. They wanted to make plans...'

'Plans...' Sam said, shaking his head. So it hadn't just been the God squad. Camp Wheatsheaf had been in on it too.

'What's wrong with that?' Harry asked. 'Don't you have plans?'

Sam looked over at him, squinting in the sharp sun. 'How do you mean?'

'I mean, are there things you want to do with your life?'

Sam considered. 'To be honest, I've been so busy working I haven't really had time to think about that. I suppose I'll just marry someone and have kids. Maybe fix up an old farm somewhere.'

'Do you like farming?' Harry asked.

'No,' Sam said. 'I hate it.' And they both laughed.

'There must be something you want to do, something outside.'

Sam nodded. 'I'd like to go travelling.'

'What, on a boat?' Harry said. 'Like Christopher Columbus?'

'Yeah, someone needs to discover America again. Do it properly this time.'

'You don't need to go that far. What about Spain, Ibiza?'

'That's it!' Sam said, sitting bolt upright, a broad grin spreading across his face. 'I'm going to Ibiza.'

'Can I come?' Harry asked.

'Sure,' Sam said. 'Why not?' He paused and looked out to sea, sober again. 'But to be honest, I don't care where I go. Anywhere would be better than the village.'

Judith was quiet and reflective when Martha went to see her. She'd normally have brought Ellie, who loved Martha's mother and called her Auntie Judith. But now Winston was gone and she didn't want to have to explain his absence to the little girl. She'd waited until Bryan got home so he could baby-sit. It was a warm evening, without a breath of air, and she found Judith sitting on the terrace behind the house, looking at the garden. It was overgrown since Martha's father had moved out. Josh wasn't yet back from work.

'Planning your next assault?' Martha asked.

Judith laughed, but without much humour.

'I don't know what to do, Martha,' she said. 'How can I help him?'

'Do you think he wants help?' Martha asked.

'I'm not sure,' Judith admitted. 'All I do know is that he's not the man I married.'

A squirrel popped out of the overgrown grass on the lawn and peered at them quizzically, perhaps surprised to find there were still some humans alive.

'But then again, I know that man's in there somewhere,' Judith said. 'I can see in his eyes that he's frightened. Torn up with guilt. He needs help, rest.'

'How did he change so much? So quickly?' Martha wondered. 'When he first got back he was . . . he was my hero. He saved me. All of us. I thought he was an angel.'

'Everyone did,' Judith agreed. 'Most of them still do. I guess that's why he's been able to carry on like a little dictator. People like strong leaders, Martha.'

'But he's not a dictator. He's my dad,' Martha said in a small voice.

Judith looked over at her. A teardrop formed on Martha's eyelash and hung trembling, threatening to fall.

'He is,' Judith agreed. 'And I still believe we can reach him. I believe we can save him. You mustn't give up hope, Martha.'

'Is he still having the headaches?' Martha asked, sniffing and wiping her eyes.

'I think so,' Judith said. 'He looked terrible when I saw him last night.'

'Oh, Mum,' Martha said. 'I wish I knew what to say.'

'Nothing you can say.' Judith replied. 'Anyway, tell me about you. How's Ellie . . . and Bryan?'

'They're fine, Mum.' Martha smiled at the thought of her little family. 'Though sometimes I do feel a little left out.'

Judith looked over at her daughter, waiting for her to continue.

'Sometimes Bryan won't talk to me about things which happen at the meetings,' she said slowly, thoughtfully. 'Like he sees me as a child, who needs to be protected from things. I married him because he didn't treat me like that.'

Judith shook her head. 'I thought he was different. This idea that you teenagers need to be protected at all costs. It's stupid. It's wrong.'

'It's Dad, isn't it?' Martha asked. 'His influence is everywhere, poisoning everything.'

Judith nodded. 'But what can we do about it?'

That night the men sat out on the seafront, eating pasta and tinned tuna and drinking ale from a cask they'd brought with them. Sam sipped his pint, delighted to be one of the lads as they laughed and insulted one another.

'Can you swim?' Mansoor asked Sam.

Sam nodded, 'Sure.'

'That's good, cos we don't have any life jackets,' Mansoor said.

'We're taking two boats,' Clive said. '*The Merry* and *The Porpoise*. Sam, you go on *The Porpoise* with James, Harry and Mark. Amir and Ben can come with me on *The Merry*.'

Sam felt a little uncomfortable about being on the same boat as Mark. Despite some signs that there might be a thaw in relations, he wasn't at all convinced Mark didn't hate him. He looked up at the electrician and their eyes met briefly.

'Don't worry, Sam,' Mark said, winking. 'I'll look after you.'

'I think next year,' Mansoor said, 'we should try the north for fishing.'

'Cod!' Mark shouted. 'I'd give my left nut for some cod.'

'We can use your left nut as bait,' Mansoor suggested.

'Scotland?' Clive asked, contemplating the idea. 'Highlands?'

'Nah, it's gotta be deep sea, maybe out of Aberdeen,' Harry said. 'I worked the trawlers up there for a few months, beautiful fishing there.'

The men went silent for a few seconds, imagining what it might be like, then Clive clapped Sam on the shoulder. 'Another one, Sam?'

Sam nodded.

Anxious to be part of the group, he sought for a new conversation. 'There was a trout stream at Lancaster House. Big fat fish in there. What do you think, Amir? Time to dust off the proposal to move from the village?' he asked.

Amir frowned and was about to speak but was interrupted by Mark.

'Don't start this again,' Mark said sourly. 'It was a stupid idea and Michael said no.'

'No,' Sam said. 'I thought Mic— Mr Pirbright said it wasn't the right time. It was going to be looked at again.'

'We're not going to Lancaster House, and we're not going to Aberdeen, either,' Mark said, glaring at Harry. 'Even if there is cod.'

Clive came back carrying a tray of beers and sat and listened to the exchange.

Sam shrugged. 'Seems silly, though, that we've got this whole planet to choose from, and we all just decide to stay in our own homes. There's got to be better places. Why *don't* we visit Scotland, or go over to France? Even just for a holiday.'

'What, all of us together?' Amir asked, laughing.

'Security, isn't it,' Mark said flatly, staring at Sam. 'Too dangerous, especially for the *children*.'

Clive shook his head. 'It's not going to happen, Sam,' he said. 'We tried to establish a new society based on science, rationality and common sense...'

Mark snorted.

'...But people didn't want it. They wanted to cling to the old ways. Superstition, religion, the parish council.'

'It's your lot that wanted to go back to the old ways,' Mark said. 'It's Michael who's the visionary.'

Clive sighed. 'Let's not have this battle again,' he said. 'Pirbright and the church crowd won the argument, the pub crowd lost. More of them than us. That's democracy, and we have to go with the majority.'

Mark seemed to be about to say something, but held his tongue. Sam looked out to sea and wondered how long it would take to sail to France. Or Scotland.

27 JUNE, 10.05 A.M.

Kitty looked at the note again: *Meet me by the milking shed at 10.00 a.m. J*

It was now 10.05 a.m. and he wasn't there. She was supposed to be working on the McGovern farm that morning. She wasn't too worried. She knew Mrs McGovern, and though not exactly a member of Camp Wheatsheaf she didn't hold much regard for President Pirbright, or Mark for that matter. Kitty would explain her absence later. Considering the fuss that was going to be made when it emerged that Sam had gone off on the fishing trip, it was likely that her transgression – and Josh's – would be overlooked.

But where was Josh? Had he not been able to get out of work? It was another perfectly still summer's day and she could feel sweat pricking her back under her light cotton dress. She ducked under the shade of the deserted milking shed, and waited.

Soon enough she heard the sound of a motorbike approaching. Her heart skipped a beat at the familiar sound. In the old days she'd often sat by her window in the early evenings waiting for Josh and Sam to come roaring back home after a day at the track or in the woods. They'd pull up outside the Hilfenhaus', covered in mud, and Josh would pull off his helmet and talk with Sam for a while, curly hair plastered all over his head, handsome as the sun.

Then Josh would put his helmet back on, look up at her window and wave, before roaring off down the road. She heard that roar again now and it matched the roar of her heart. Josh pulled up alongside Kitty and took off his helmet, just like in her best memories. He grinned.

'Your dad gave you your bike back?' she said.

He shook his head. 'Nah, I just took it.'

'You'll get in trouble,' Kitty said.

'I don't care any more,' Josh replied.

'Josh,' she said, suddenly ablaze with nervous emotion. 'I just wanted to s—'

But he spoke over her.

'You don't have to say anything,' he said gently.

He got off the bike and stood before her, suddenly looking nervous.

'Sam told me about the conversation you had in the churchyard,' he said.

Kitty felt herself blushing.

'I'm an idiot,' he said. 'I always...well, I always liked you too, but I never said. I didn't think you might be interested in me, in that way. Anyway, you're my best friend's sister...'

'Do you think Sam's bothered about that?' she asked.

He shook his head.

Kitty thought she must look like a lunatic, her grin was so wide. She tried without success to control it. *Just kiss me*, she thought. And it seemed Josh could read minds, because before she knew it he'd reached around her waist and his mouth was on hers, his warm lips soft, his breath sweet. She'd expected the nervous speech-making to carry on for a while longer. But one kiss later and all that could be thrown to one side. Perhaps Josh was just now realising how much time he'd wasted and wanted to make the most of the now. She melted into him, his leather jacket hard and unyielding. Then he got off the bike and unwrapped a bulky parcel strapped to the pillion. There was a jacket for her, and a helmet which she put on. Then he handed her a backpack.

'You'll need to wear this, I'm afraid. Hold my waist as we go.' She smiled and did as he asked. Then slowly, smoothly, they moved off back up the bumpy path. Josh turned left at the road and headed away from the village. Soon they came to a smaller track and Josh slowed to a crawl as the route became very bumpy indeed. It took a while but eventually they reached a gate in the perimeter fence. They got off while Josh punched the code and wheeled the bike through, locking it behind them.

'Good old Reg,' Josh said, and they puttered along the trail. The lake was perfect, and once they'd dismounted, Kitty sat staring at it for a long time, shaking her head.

'How can it be that such a lovely place so close to the village could have been hidden away like this?' she asked.

'It was on private land,' Josh said. 'Locked away.'

'There's no such thing as private land anymore, is there?' Kitty replied.

'Not outside the village, anyway,' Josh said 'Out here we're free.'

He sat beside her and put an arm round her warm shoulders, and for the first time Kitty's thoughts turned to her fiancé. 'Should I feel guilty about this?' she asked. 'It seems wrong, being happy.'

'I don't think you should feel guilty about anything,' Josh replied, and kissed her again, longer this time.

They ate after that, and Josh snoozed, saying he'd go for a swim afterwards. Kitty stretched on the warm blanket and rolled over to look at Josh across the debris of their picnic lunch. She knew the contours of his face so well, and their familiarity was comforting and exciting at the same time.

She was so happy. She'd wanted to be with Josh for so long, and now they had the rest of their lives together. They could go anywhere, leave Haven, settle in a little cottage by a lake, just like this one, and raise chickens and children.

A dark cloud floated in the background of this perfect vista, though. Mark would not be pleased about her breaking off the engagement. She dreaded even the thought of telling him. And it wasn't just Mark – the entire village wanted this match. Haven was suddenly home to eighty-odd wedding planners.

But love conquers all, she thought to herself. *They'll understand that.*

Sam awoke feeling nervous but excited, the first one up. He'd slipped away from the drinking session soon after it got dark. He'd felt a little wobbly after the third pint and the men had been drinking heavily, roaring with laughter, their conversation becoming a bit crude, especially when they started talking about Mark and Kitty, and what they might get up to on their honeymoon.

Sam had been pleased to hear Harry asking the others to tone it down, though his pleas hadn't had much effect. The men had gone inside after a while, though, and their voices had been drowned out by the slapping of the sea against the harbour walls.

Sam set about cooking eggs and bacon, alarm-clock smells. He made a big pot of coffee which was gratefully consumed by the others as they came down, one by one, rubbing their heads. Mark's hangover seemed to be the worst and he sat at the table with his head bowed, groaning.

'I want you on every trip,' James said through a mouthful of eggs, pointing a fork at Sam. 'You have hidden talents.'

'You should see me Zumba,' Sam said.

Harry disappeared upstairs briefly and came back with a bottle of pills, giving one to Mark. 'This'll sort you out,' he said.

Mark peered at it mistrustfully. 'What is it?'

'Something I got from the hospital on the last foraging trip. Good for hangovers.'

Mark shrugged and popped the pill. Sam watched him. Mark seemed different away from the village, away from Michael. More rebellious, perhaps. Sam was not at all sure this was a good thing.

Half an hour later the two little boats were chugging their way out of the harbour, Clive and James the two pilots – grinning like schoolboys. Harry showed Sam the ropes, literally.

'It's not hard. James finds the fish on the SONAR, you drop the net and drag it along for a while and then we pull this rope here to close the net, while Mark pulls that one to lift it. I haul it over the deck and you let go. The fish slip out over the deck like a shower of shit and we sort them out. Chuck back the little ones and the jellyfish and that. The others we knock on the head and chuck 'em into the hold with the ice.'

'What could possibly go wrong?' Sam said, grinning. The wind plastered back his hair and his eyes streamed. This was brilliant.

'*Woohoo!*' Mark yelled, standing at the prow like a deranged Kate Winslett.

'What was that pill you gave him?' Sam asked.

Harry grinned. 'He'll be fine. He'll just be in a better mood than usual today.'

'OK, Sam?' James called down from the cockpit. Sam nodded and gave him the thumbs up.

Twenty minutes later and James had something on the SONAR. He swung sharply to port and they were off, *The Merry* following behind.

'You know, they found the captain of this boat still behind the wheel,' Harry shouted over the roar of the wind and the rumble of the diesel engines below. 'His bones had been picked clean by the gulls.'

Sam looked up at the cockpit where James stared intently ahead before suddenly shooting out an arm. 'There!' And as Sam looked ahead, he saw a shimmering, almost a rustling, just beneath the surface. As they drew closer, he saw a dark mass in the water, running away from them, switching direction. Gulls screamed and wheeled overhead; one dived down, scooping the water, and came back up carrying a fat silver shard.

'Net!' James screamed, gull-like himself in his shrillness. Mark pulled a lever and a boom swung out over the starboard side. The net dropped and spread itself wide as the weights dragged the bottom down. James gunned the motor and they sped through the broiling mass of fish.

'Mind the boom after the net's been released,' Harry said. 'Mark was careless with it the first time I was out with him. It nearly knocked me overboard. He thought it was hilarious.'

'Cod!' Mark yelled, peering over the bow. He looked up and grinned maniacally. 'It's bloody cod!'

'There's no cod in the English channel,' Harry replied. 'Too warm.'

'You've obviously never been swimming in it,' Sam said, remembering old holidays to Devon.

'It'll be pollock or something,' Harry said.

'It's cod!' Mark yelled back, irritated.

'Just get 'em up whatever they are!' James shouted down. 'We'll be through in a sec.'

Mark gave the signal, and Sam and Harry pulled their ropes. Usually this would be done by one strapping hand, but such was the weight of the fish that there was no way just one of them could manage. Sam hauled with all his might and still it seemed like the net would never come up, but then it was there, hanging by the boat like an upside-down balloon, thrashing with grey and silver as the confused fish searched frantically for an escape.

Mark pulled the boom back over the deck and gave another signal. Harry let go and the deck was awash with their first haul. What seemed like a thousand fish slid and flapped their way across the slick wood, mouths opening and closing in apparent astonishment at their new environment.

'There's definitely no cod here,' Harry said.

Mark scowled and let go of the boom lever. It swung back quickly and Harry had to duck to avoid being hit.

'Mark! I told you last time,' James yelled down, furious. 'Lock that boom before you let it go!'

Harry wore thick gloves and had already begun throwing unwanted sea life back overboard.

Jellyfish, tiddlers, inedible fish and seaweed. There was also the occasional man-made item such as a carrier bag or a crisp packet, which he threw into a rubbish bin attached to the rail. Sam dropped to his knees and joined in, following Harry's lead. Mark began picking up larger fish, knocking them senseless with a small cosh and dropping them through the hatch into the ice room below. James idled the engine and came down to help. Peering over at *The Merry*, Sam could see them doing the same. They worked steadily for an hour or so before the deck was cleared.

Despite the warm sun, it was cold out over the water, the wind was relentless and the spray kept them constantly damp. They huddled together in the small cockpit and ate tinned stew for lunch. James gave Sam a tot of whisky, which burned his throat but warmed his cockles. 'You don't have any more of those headache pills, do you?' Mark asked Harry. Harry nodded and gave him another, struggling to keep a straight face.

Then it was back out for a second run. They found a shoal almost immediately. Pirbright had been right about the renewed bounties of the sea. Sam stood up, stretching. His back ached like someone had been pounding on it with a sledgehammer.

Harry noticed and tossed him the bottle of pills. 'One of those will make the pain go away,' he said.

Sam thought about it, but then he saw Mark arsing about, swinging from the net while James yelled at him.

'No thanks,' he said, but Harry had turned away so Sam put the pills in his pocket.

The net came up, even fuller than before, and Mark dragged the boom over again. Once more the haul flopped across the deck, and Sam, his back feeling like it was going to snap, got down on his knees again. Why had he thought fishing might be a welcome break from weeding? Still, he was away from the village, away from the stench of the cows. He took a deep lungful of the tangy sea air and felt his spirits lift.

'Sam, there's a cod,' Mark yelled, pointing over to the far side. 'Go and grab it.'

Sam moved over to look at where Mark had indicated, but couldn't see it – just mackerel and sardines twisting around a Tesco carrier bag.

'Can't see it,' he said and turned round to see the boom come flying towards him. Then suddenly he was in the freezing water and the shock of the cold rushed over him, stopping his breath. He felt sluggish and heavy like cement. The Solent pulled at his lead-weight legs, dragging him down as though he were in quicksand. He saw Harry's horrified face at the rail and there behind Harry was Mark, gripping the side and leaning over.

Mark winked at Sam as he went under.

Kitty stuffed her towel into the backpack – Josh had thought to bring one for each of them – then put it on and swung a leg across the bike. She slid her hands under Josh's open jacket and stroked his muscular stomach. The months of hard farmwork had strengthened his body. The jacket felt rough and hot against her skin which had been cooled by the dip in the lake.

Josh moved along at a sedate pace and Kitty wished he'd speed up a little so she could benefit from the slipstream. Cool and relaxed from the swim, she didn't want to arrive home sweating. She'd have some explaining to do regardless. She intended to tell her mother she'd been lying in the cool of the church-yard reading, had fallen asleep and lost track of the time. Josh had slowed further, though, and seemed to be inspecting the woods to their left.

'Did you see something move in there?' he called.

Kitty glanced over into the trees. 'No,' she called back. 'Just the wind, probably.'

But then Josh stopped altogether and put one foot on the ground. He was staring intently into the trees. Kitty tried to see what he was looking at. Josh killed the engine and the silence cloaked them. There was no wind. If Josh had heard something...

'Come on—' she began to say when she was stopped by a rustling, cracking noise in the woods. Kitty's heart skipped. What was it?

'There's something in there,' Josh said.

'Probably a cow, or a sheep,' she said, trying to convince herself. 'Come on, we're in enough trouble as it is.'

The rustling had stopped. Josh waited for a while longer but nothing happened. He switched on the engine again and they moved off.

But then they saw something, a sapling swaying. Leaves tumbling.

'What *is* that?' Josh said, stopping again. 'I'd better check it out.'

But something made Kitty cry out, 'No!'

Josh turned awkwardly to look at her, surprised. For an instant time hung. It was just the two of them, in the hot afternoon, standing astride a bike on a deserted road in the silence.

Then the low bushes to their right exploded and something, some *thing*, barrelled out and shot down the slope towards them.

Kitty let out an involuntary squeal, then, 'Go, go! Josh!'

Josh switched the engine back on and in an instant they were moving again, but slowly, the bike weighted down, Josh careful not to accelerate too quickly for fear Kitty would fall off.

As Josh concentrated on riding, Kitty looked behind. The lead dog came through the trees already sprinting but tripped and stumbled as it hit the road. It was some kind of terrier. A Staffy or a pit-bull.

But it wasn't alone. A pack of snarling hounds followed it out of the woods as the leader lunged towards them, even as they moved away. The attacker missed them by inches, and Kitty heard the chomp of its jaws behind her as it stumbled again briefly. She watched it scramble to its feet, overtaken by its fellows coming racing after the fleeing bike.

The bike bounced hard on the uneven track, but it was built to withstand this kind of thing and they sped up, gradually.

'They're still coming!' Kitty called in a remarkably calm voice. 'Faster, if you can.' She looked over Josh's shoulder to see where they were going.

The track stretched out ahead of them, cow parsley and nettles by the wayside, still in the hot air. She took a deep breath, telling herself to keep calm. They were now easily outrunning the dogs, which were already looking tired. They were a mangy shower, perhaps finding it difficult to survive in the wild new world. But survive they had, and they looked mean.

'What's the plan?' she asked as they came to a smoother stretch, and Josh sped up, putting more clear air between them and the pack.

'We'll be back at the village in a few minutes,' he said. 'We'll go to the pub and find Reg. He'll know what to do. Organise a hunting party, maybe.'

Kitty looked behind, relieved to see the dogs a hundred metres behind now. A couple had even given up and were sitting, watching the fleeing humans.

'Uh, oh,' Josh said.

'What?' she replied, turning to look ahead.

'Uh, oh,' she echoed.

She could see what Josh was worried about. He'd re-locked the gate as they'd left. They'd have to stop and dismount. The pack was certain to catch up with them if they did.

Josh tried going off the track and drove a little way along the fence, but though the bike could handle it, the terrain was just too rough for them to get any speed up.

'They're getting closer,' Kitty called. It was true – the dogs, sensing the humans' hesitation, had sped up again and were sprinting, jostling one another out of the way.

'Any good at climbing fences?' Josh yelled.

'If I'm being chased by a pack of wild dogs, yes!' Kitty replied, trying to sound more confident than she felt.

Josh pulled up by the chain-link fence and killed the engine as Kitty got off. He leaned the bike against the fence.

'Use the bike as a step,' he said, grabbing her by the waist and hoisting her up lightly onto the seat. Despite the situation, Kitty was reminded of her old gymnastic lessons. *Pretend it's a beam*, she thought to herself, trying not to wobble. She reached up and could just grab the top of the fence. She twisted to look behind.

'Hurry!' she called. 'They're coming!'

'Don't look,' Josh said, exasperated. 'Just get up.'

Grabbing her ankles he helped push her over. Ridiculously, Kitty blushed at the thought he could see up her dress. Then she was scrambling over. She hung down the other side and dropped, heavily but without injuring herself. She sat up. Josh was already on the bike seat but it was too late.

The lead dog leaped at him and grabbed hold of his jeans. His leg pulled back, he slipped and tumbled to earth. The pack was on him in a second. Kitty screamed.

But Josh didn't stay down. He rose to his feet, a dog hanging off each arm while two others snapped at his legs. Swinging round, he managed to get each of them off and proceeded to kick at those at his feet. His heavy motorcycle boots crunched bone, and cleared a path for him to leap back onto the bike, which wobbled, but didn't fall. Then Josh was scrambling up the fence to safety. Heart in mouth, Kitty watched as he clambered up. *Oh, please*, she thought. *Not now, when we're together at last.*

But then a dog a little smarter than the others sprang up onto the motorbike seat itself.

'Josh!' Kitty screamed. 'Watch out!'

Josh looked down, but it was too late – the dog clamped its jaws onto his calf. He screamed in agony as he felt the teeth sink in. He couldn't let go of the fence without falling back into the pack, so he had no option but to carry on clambering up, the dog hanging from his leg and growling furiously. Josh paused and kicked his leg, with difficulty, but the dog hung on. It looked to be part-terrier, bred to never let go.

'Josh!' Kitty cried.

He hung for a moment, thinking. The only way he could get over the fence was if he brought the dog with him. But what then? Kitty was on the other side of the fence – he couldn't put her in danger. Josh felt his sweaty hand slipping. The pack below snarled and spun waiting for him to drop. A second dog scrambled up onto the motorbike seat and he gave it a kick with his free leg, knocking it off again.

'Josh!' Kitty cried again. He looked up and fixed her gaze. Should he just let go? But he couldn't do that, with her watching. He couldn't let her see him being torn to pieces.

'Come on, Josh,' she said, loud and clear. 'You can do it.'

He nodded, his mind made up. Straining, pulling, somehow he managed to drag himself up to the top of the fence. He swung his free leg over first, then, with enormous difficulty, the leg with the dog attached. He dropped, feet first, onto the other side of the fence, ensuring he landed with his free foot on the dog's ribcage. A satisfying crunch was the result and the dog let go but immediately got to its feet and turned to face Josh, wheezing and obviously in pain. A trickle of blood licked its way down Josh's cheek.

There was no time to investigate his injuries, though. He kept himself between Kitty and the dog. The pack ran up and down on the other side of the fence, barking bravely now they were safely out of the fight.

Josh watched the dog, and the dog watched Josh. It was a mongrel, with perhaps some border collie must be there. A running dog. A sheep killer. This had been someone's pet not so long ago, he thought. Then its world had been ripped apart, like everyone else's. This creature wasn't evil. It was just trying to survive, like they all were. Josh felt a twinge of sympathy for the beast for a second.

But only for a second. Stepping forward, he launched a huge kick. The dog seemed to know what was coming and whimpered slightly before Josh's heavy boot caught it in the throat. It fell back, windpipe crushed, gasping for breath. Josh quickly rammed his heel down on the dog's throat, speeding its death.

2.43 P.M.

Josh lay on the floor of the pub. It had taken him and Kitty nearly forty-five minutes to hop and stagger their way back to the village, Kitty supporting him all the way. He'd collapsed onto the carpet in front of the fire and someone had rushed off to fetch Jenny Stephenson. While they waited, Thomas Butcher gave him a large glass of brandy. Josh took a gulp. The liquid warmed him and doused the shivers a little, if not the pain.

Jenny arrived soon after and cut away his jeans to reveal the wound. The teethmarks were clearly visible, as was a nasty gash in his calf. The sight reminded Josh of the corpse he and Reg had seen near the hospital.

Throughout all this, Kitty was sitting beside Josh, holding his hand and crying quietly.

'Looks like the motorcycle gear helped protect you for the most part,' Thomas said. 'It's the leg that looks nasty.'

'I can get this stitched up OK,' Jenny said. 'But Josh'll need antibiotics to stop any infection.'

'Do we have any left?' Thomas asked. He kneeled by Josh, mopping his brow.

Jenny shook her head. 'I understand they're quite easy to make, though, from compounds. President Pirbright will be able to produce some, but we'll need some supplies from the hospital in Guildford, I think.'

As if in answer to his name, Pirbright came in at that moment. He looked thinner than ever, his blood-shot eyes sunk deep into his shaven skull.

'Why is he here?' he asked. Josh watched him cautiously. Would his father be sympathetic? Or furious?

Jenny looked up, confused, not understanding the question.

'He should have been brought home, or to the church.' Pirbright leaned over and took the brandy glass away from Josh, hurling it into the empty fireplace angrily.

That answers my question, Josh thought.

'He needs antibiotics,' Jenny said. 'We thought you could maybe go to the hospital and make some up. I don't think it's—'

'Poison,' Pirbright spat. 'Poison that poisons our children. No more chemicals, no more drugs.'

'But—'

'Enough! Help me,' he said to Thomas, leaning down to slip an arm under Josh's shoulders. Jenny had finished bandaging the leg now. Thomas looked doubtful, but did as he was told. Kitty stood up to follow.

'You get home,' Michael snapped at her.

'But I—'

'Your mother needs you. Josh will be fine,' Michael said.

'I don't want to go,' she said. She clutched Josh's arm.

'It's OK,' Josh said. 'I'll see you soon, OK?'

She was clearly unhappy about it, but on Josh's insistence, Kitty left, with a parting glare at Michael.

Between them the two men carried the wincing teenager out of the pub and down the street to the Pirbrights' house. Then helped Josh up the stairs while Jenny followed along and then laid him on his bed.

'Thank you,' Josh's dad said, turning to the others. 'You may leave.'

They looked at him in surprise. 'But don't you need help?'

'No thank you, you've done enough.' They moved reluctantly down the stairs as Josh's father closed the bedroom door.

Josh looked up at his dad ruefully. 'Sorry?' he said. But he could see it wasn't going to do him any good. He could see the look of malevolence on Michael's face.

'You will be,' his father replied.

6.13 P.M.

Sam woke in his own bed, back in Haven, with a skull-splitting headache. He could hear a rushing sound. The sea. The sea, grasping at him, dragging him down. Memories of the trip came back in a flood. The boat, the fish. The boom swinging towards him. Mark winking... Sam waited for a while, but no one came, though he could hear his mother downstairs. After a few false starts, he managed to sit up. He sat for a while, waited for his head to stop spinning. He felt sick and fought back the urge to vomit. He didn't have the strength to call out.

Been here before, he thought. *I'm either lucky to keep narrowly avoiding death, or unlucky to keep nearly getting killed.*

He swayed as he stood and made his slow way down the hall and to the top flight of the stairs. His mother passed, looked up, saw him and stopped dead. Sam was expecting her to tell him to get back to bed. She said nothing, merely glared.

'How did I get here?' Sam asked.

'They had to cut their trip short, to bring you back,' she said. 'Jenny Stephenson checked you over. She says you'll live.'

'You don't sound very happy about it,' Sam said.

'There's to be a meeting about this. About you,' she said frostily. 'Seven thirty tonight. President Pirbright wants to see you beforehand. Seven p.m. sharp in his office. You're in a world of trouble this time. All you teenagers. I'm ashamed of you two.'

'Any chance of a cup of tea first?' he asked.

Monica just glared back at him. Sam sank down and sat on the top step, resting his balloon-tight skull against the cool of the gloss paint on the banister. 'Or aspirin?'

'I suppose you really want one of these?' she asked, holding something up. Sam saw it was the pill bottle Harry had given him. He shut his eyes and groaned.

'You should count yourself lucky they brought you back at all. If it wasn't for James jumping in after you, you'd be at the bottom of the Solent right now.'

'Do they have aspirin there?' Sam replied.

'I know what you did,' she said.

'Which particular thing?' Sam replied.

'On the barricade.'

'What did I do on the barricade?'

'You killed two men.'

'Oh, that,' Sam said. 'That's old news. Move on dot-com.'

Monica glared at him. 'One of the men you killed was Mark's father.'

'Good thing too,' Sam replied. 'He was a twat.'

Monica sucked in her breath sharply.

'Don't act all outraged,' Sam said. 'What did you think we were doing there? Handing out leaflets?'

'You were seventeen years old,' Monica said. 'A child. You killed two men and never told me?'

Sam shook his head. 'At that time you weren't being very supportive. You spent your days crying into the Bible. Dad would have understood.'

'We don't need to bring him into this. Michael Pirbright was right about you,' she said. 'He told me you were no good.'

'Ah, how is Napoleon? Marching on Moscow again?'

'Don't you speak about him like that,' Monica said in a dangerously quiet voice. 'He saved your life.'

'Where's Kitty?' Sam asked, changing the subject.

'She's in her room, where she'll be for the next week.'

Sam rolled his eyes. 'Oh, right. Her too. What's she done? Sneezed without using a tissue? Laughed on a Sunday?'

'Rather more serious than that,' Monica replied frostily. 'Adultery.'

'Eh? Who with?'

'Joshua Pirbright.'

'What?' Sam said, brow furrowed. It felt like a demon was sitting in his brain, stabbing at the back of his eyes with a pitchfork. 'Neither of them are married – however much you've tried to force it.'

'She's engaged, Sam,' Monica said through pursed lips.

'OK, I officially pronounce you as insane as Michael,' Sam said. 'I'm off.'

'Where are you going?' she snapped as he stepped gingerly down the stairs. 'We should have dinner first and then we'll go together. We'll face this as a family.'

'Actually, I'd rather go on my own,' Sam said. 'Don't worry, I will go to the town meeting, like a good citizen. But first I'm going to go and see Reg to find out if he has any sodding aspirin.'

6.24 P.M.

'How could you do this?' Monica asked. '*Why* would you do this?'

'I'm sorry, Mum,' Kitty said in a small voice. 'But I don't love Mark. I love Josh. I've always loved Josh.' She lay on her bed, curled into a ball while Monica sat at the end.

'So why did you say yes to Mark?'

Kitty sighed. 'So many reasons, Mum, it's impossible to explain.'

'Well, try.'

Kitty thought about it for a while. 'No, Mum, I don't think I will.'

'Talk to me!' Monica said. 'I'm your mother.'

Kitty sat up and glared back at her. 'You stopped being my mother a while ago. I hate you!'

Monica lifted her hand as if to slap her again, but held it, her face tight with anger.

'There, you nearly hit me again,' Kitty hissed. 'Is hitting me your answer to everything now?'

Monica stood, clenched her fists and rocked back and forth on her heels. She stood like that for a long time, then turned to go, stopping in the doorway, her back to her daughter.

'I'm going to the church,' Monica said. 'I'd thought we should face this as a family, but Sam's decided he wants to go off on his own. Frankly I'm sick of both of you and now I think you should stay here. You know your brother's going to be punished tonight? If I had my way, you'd be there alongside him.' Monica slammed the door behind her. Kitty lay down again and cried and cried.

6.36 P.M.

Sam walked slowly towards town, stopping from time to time to rest. He had little option but to go and

328

face the music later – things would be worse for him, for them all, if he didn't – but there was no hurry. He stopped at Reg's house and explained the situation. Reg gave him two codeine tablets and made him a cup of tea.

'It's not right.' Reg thumped his fist on the table. 'They can't treat you like this. It's time something was done.'

Sam shrugged. 'Things are different now. It's OK, we get that.'

'Listen to you,' Reg said. 'That doesn't sound like the Sam I know. Where's the fight gone?'

Sam shrugged. 'I'm tired, Reg,' he said. 'My head hurts. Maybe I should just go along with it all.'

'No,' Reg said. 'Now's the time to start fighting, not to give up. When it was about protecting you. Imposing some rules to keep you in line and to . . . you know, get you off on the right foot, that's fine. But it's gone too far.'

'It's Pirbright,' Sam said. Closing his eyes and wondering if the codeine was starting to work. 'He's more and more mental by the day.'

Reg nodded. 'He needs to be brought down a peg or two.'

'OK,' Sam said. 'I'm game. Want me to punch him in the nose?'

'I don't think we need to bring violence into this,' Reg said. 'That's Pirbright's way. If we want to hurt him, we just need to take away what he values most.'

'What's that?' Sam asked.

'Control,' Reg replied.

7.07 P.M.

'Sam, you knew the rules,' Mr Carter said, clasping his hands. 'You chose to disobey them and now you must face the consequences of that action.'

'But the rules are unreasonable,' Sam replied. 'I consider it my duty to disobey them.'

Mr Carter coughed and looked down at his notes, unsure how to cope with this unexpected non-compliance. The vicar sat beside him, looking embarrassed about the whole thing. Pirbright said nothing. The three of them formed the disciplinary panel Sam had found himself in front of when he'd presented himself at the church.

Carter spoke again. 'There is a reason the rules exist. Most importantly, they are there for your protection, and quite right too. Look at what happened – you could have died.'

'Only because Mark tried to kill me,' Sam said.

Carter rolled his eyes.

'We've spoken to James Freedman,' he said. 'He has told us it seemed to him that it was an accident. Mark was under the influence of painkillers which affected his judgement. Painkillers which you gave him—'

'What?' Sam cried. 'I didn't give him the drugs . . .'

'Well, he says you did,' Mr Carter said. 'And they were found in your possession.'

'He's a liar! Harry gave me those pills. I didn't even take one. Ask him.'

Mr Carter sighed again. 'Look, Sam. Mark Rogers is a respected member of the community. He does *not* want to kill you.'

'We think the blow might have...confused you somewhat,' the vicar added.

'Why are there different rules for different people around here?' Sam said, not really caring any more. 'Why does Mark, who's only four years older than me, get to go wherever he likes while I'm imprisoned in the village? Why is he believed while I'm patronised? And while we're on the subject, why does he get to marry my sister when she loves Josh?'

'Enough!' Pirbright shouted. 'I've heard enough.' He stood and walked slowly over to a large brass cross. He regarded it and spoke without turning.

'It's not just leaving the village without permission,' he said. 'It's not just abandoning your duties, putting the survival of the village in jeopardy. It's not just the drugs found in your possession. It's more than that, Sam.'

Pirbright now turned and walked towards Sam, who felt uncomfortable sitting while the man towered over him. Sam noticed the unhinged look Mr Pirbright had had for some time was now replaced by a look of total clarity.

331

'It's your general demeanour. Your air of insouciant rebellion that is the real problem here, Sam,' Pirbright said, speaking quite gently now. The vicar and Carter leaned forward to hear. 'That kind of attitude is infectious, I'm afraid. A rebel here and there wasn't such a problem in the Old World, perhaps. Though there are those of us who believe that it was partly our lax response to the undercurrents of our society that led to its destruction. Either way, I'm afraid we can't allow such luxuries any more.'

Pirbright closed his eyes and smiled. 'I think you need to be taught a lesson,' he said. 'And the village needs to see this lesson being taught.'

'OK,' Sam said. 'I'm sorry to have to be the one to break this to you, but you are officially Loony McTunes.'

'Six strokes of the cane,' Pirbright said, ignoring him. 'To be administered at the public meeting this evening.'

Sam laughed uncertainly. 'You're not serious?'

'Really, Mr Pirbright. I don't think corporal punishment is the answer—' began Halfdene. But Pirbright suddenly exploded and grabbed hold of Sam, dragging him across the room. Surprised, Sam lost his footing and scrabbled for purchase on the polished wooden floor.

The vicar stood. 'Michael, stop!'

'Be quiet, Reverend Halfdene,' Pirbright snapped. He opened a wood panel and shoved Sam through.

Though still unbalanced, Sam was nonetheless able to give Pirbright a hard kick in the shin as he went through. Pirbright grunted in pain and slammed the door. Sam heard a lock slide across. He rammed against the wood with his shoulder, but it was solid.

Looking around Sam saw he was in an anteroom. Three cassocks hung on hooks, and there were two narrow wooden cupboards and a table. Otherwise the room was empty. There was one high window which he might have been able to reach by standing on the table. But iron crossbeams suggested he'd need a hacksaw to get through it.

Sam was trapped. Unable to believe this was really happening, he slumped against the wall and sat down, head in hands. He felt tired and defeated. Even if he could get out of this room, where could he go?

Then Sam heard the church bells start to ring.

7.22 P.M.

Ellie's bedtime routine was disturbed by the ringing of the church bells.

'What's that?' she asked as Martha was forced to interrupt the reading of *The Famous Five* book, *Five on a Secret Trail*.

'It's the church bells,' Martha said, getting up to peer out of the window. 'Must be a town meeting.'

'Can we go?' Ellie asked, jumping out of bed and coming to look.

'No, you can't,' Martha said, ushering her back to bed. 'I expect your father will go. He'll tell you all about it in the morning.'

Coming downstairs a few minutes later, she saw Bryan closing the door on Amir Mansoor.

'Town meeting,' he said. 'Don't much feel like it.'

'What's it about?' she asked.

He hesitated.

'Bryan,' Martha sighed. 'Really, this has got to stop.'

'What?' he asked defensively.

'You never tell me anything,' she said. 'You treat me like a child.'

'That's not true,' he said, walking over to give her a hug.

She ducked out of his grasp and held up a finger. 'Tell me what this meeting's about,' she said.

Bryan sighed. 'It's Sam,' he said. 'He left the village, on the fishing trip. He's to be punished.'

'What?' Martha asked. 'What do you mean by *punished*?'

Bryan walked off into the kitchen. Martha followed and stood waiting for an answer. Bryan poured two glasses of wine as he spoke. 'He's going to be caned.'

Martha stood speechless for half a minute before she spoke again. Bryan stood, holding out a glass towards her.

'And you're just going to accept that, are you?' she said.

He sighed again. 'I don't know what you expect me to do.'

'Protest!' she said. 'Argue! Say no!'

He was still holding the glass of wine out towards her. 'I don't want it,' she said.

He set it on the surface and sighed.

'What good would protesting do?' he asked, taking a big gulp of his own wine. 'What good did it do your mother?'

Martha shook her head sadly. 'I thought you were different to the others. I thought you were on our side.'

'I am,' he said.

'No, you're not,' she said. 'You're just like everyone else, going along with whatever my father says, because it's easier. Have you not noticed he's mad?'

'Look,' Bryan said. 'He's got issues, certainly, but he's done a lot of good things for this community. Since the day he came back he's been working for us all. Organising, planning...'

In her anger, Martha found herself asking a question she wasn't sure she wanted the answer to.

'And you, Bryan?' she said. 'Were you planning too, back then, in those first days?'

'What do you mean by that?' he asked, eyes narrowing.

'I know there were discussions, plans drawn up, about who should marry who...'

Bryan looked back at her, angry himself now. 'How dare you?' he said quietly. 'My wife was out there, lying in that road in a pool of blood.'

'I'm sorry,' Martha said, as she realised how offensive she'd been. 'I didn't mean to...It's just that... something happened in that first week. We know people were talking about us. About the future...'

'There were discussions, yes,' Bryan admitted, taking another swig of wine. 'Everyone was in shock. There was too much drinking. After your father came back, when we realised we might survive. That's when everyone got excited. Started talking about how we could...carry on. The human race.' He stopped, and looked at her, as if wondering whether he should say more.

'Why are you being so cagey?' Martha asked. 'What are you hiding?'

'Nothing. I mean...well, it just seems a bit distasteful in hindsight, the discussion we were having. We talked about you and the other children...I mean, the younger ones. Michael said we had to protect you all. Someone, I think it was Clive, started on about genes and bloodlines, and how we had to be careful, you know, about who married who. That was all it was.'

'So this is where the idea of the breeding programme came from?' Martha asked coolly. 'Not just from my father, but from all of you. Camp Wheatsheaf, the so-called scientific faction?'

'Like I said,' Bryan replied softly, 'it was distasteful.'

The bells continued their sombre summons, filling the silence between them. Bryan finished his glass. 'I'd better get down there. We can discuss this when I get back.'

'No,' Martha said.

'What?'

'I'm going to the meeting. You stay and look after Ellie,' she said, and turned to go, leaving him staring after her, open-mouthed.

7.25 P.M.

Josh lay on his bed feeling nauseous. One eye wouldn't open properly. His father had caned him. At first it had just been on the hand, quite lightly. But then Josh had lost his cool and shoved his father in the chest. Michael had turned white with fury and punched his son in the face repeatedly, hence the swollen eye and split lip.

It marked a change in Mr Pirbright – up to now he hadn't been violent, not seriously. He'd left that to Mark. But it seemed now that a line had been crossed. Throughout the ordeal, Josh kept thinking, *But I'm injured. You can't hit me when I'm injured.* He was beginning to realise that his father was properly insane. Whatever vestige of sanity and reason Michael Pirbright had brought back from his lab had by now drained into the pit of guilt and self-recrimination at the centre of his soul.

Half an hour after his father had left, he'd heard his mother come in downstairs. He found himself hoping she wouldn't come to check on him. If Judith saw his face, she'd know who'd done it and would go charging down to the church. So when she called out his name, he didn't answer. He lay there, in pain. Planning, thinking, wondering.

Then he heard church bells. An odd peal. Out-of-kilter. It didn't sound like Jim Halfdene's usual Sunday cackle. Why bells, anyway? It was Friday. No, Saturday. Certainly not Sunday. *They must be calling a town meeting*, he thought. He lay a while longer, listening for the door, wondering if his mother would go down to the church to see what was going on. He heard nothing. Judith refused to set foot in the church these days, and ignored public proclamations.

He sat up, feeling groggy. He wanted to go and see Kitty, but was fearful of the consequences if he was found with her again. Not for himself, but for her. They wouldn't hit her, would they? He couldn't bear the thought of them using the cane on sweet Kitty.

He gazed at himself in the mirror. He looked even worse than he felt. His left eye was open just a glimmer and a purplish bruise covered that side of his face. He slipped on a pair of sunglasses. That hid some of the damage. Then he opened his top drawer and took something out, something heavy, wrapped in an old pair of underpants. He tucked the object into his coat pocket and limped as quietly as he could down the stairs. He heard the flick of a page as his mother read in the sitting room, and snuck out through the kitchen door, across the garden to the back passage and towards the church.

11

27 JUNE, 7.26 P.M.

Usually at council meetings, the members sat at a long wooden table brought in for these occasions. Tonight, though, Pirbright had chosen to stand at the altar, his intent clear. He was here to sermonise.

Sam sat, as defiantly as he dared, on a hard wooden chair to one side. He could see Martha at the front; she gave him a wan smile. Reg sat a few rows back and winked. Of Josh and Kitty there was no sign – where were they? Under lock and key? His buddies from the fishing trip stood at the back of the church, arms folded, looking grim. He wondered if he might count on them for support, but they were outnumbered by the others: those who supported Michael in everything he did. He could hear Jim Halfdene speaking in an urgent, hushed tone with Michael. It was clear the vicar was unhappy with developments.

'Not in my church,' Sam heard Halfdene hiss.

'This is not *your* church, Reverend,' Michael shot back. 'It belongs to the community, and to God.'

Reverend Halfdene made to speak again, but Michael brushed past him and stepped up to the altar.

'Thank you for coming, everybody,' Pirbright began. He spoke slowly, his voice husky. 'Once again, I see it's taken a village crisis to fill up the pews. Might I say that if more of you came to church regularly, for Sunday service and for village meetings, that we might have been able to avoid this latest crisis?

'Because this *is* a crisis,' he continued, palms down. 'We must pause to reflect on, and discuss, this issue. Our children's future is in danger. And I firmly believe that it is our casual attitudes that are responsible. We cannot pin all the blame on the children themselves. Just about the first thing we discussed, the *very* first thing, was the protection of our children and the new rules we needed to keep them safe. Just eight months later and we have adultery, drugs, runaways and near-tragic accidents.'

Michael shook his head. The congregation sat, silent, rapt.

'People, this is not good enough. And it stops here!' he shouted, banging his hand on the lectern. 'Mothers should know where their sons and daughters are. Fathers should be instilling discipline and obedience, and, yes, I include myself in this. I have clearly been remiss in disciplining my children and that will be rectified, let me assure you. The elders should be protecting our children, not taking them on illicit trips to drink and…and fish.'

'Hypocrite!' Reg called from the back.

Michael glared at him. A murmuring broke out in the pews.

'Do you have something to say, Mr Walker?'

Reg stood. 'You abandoned your own children,' he said clearly. 'Replaced your son with a lunatic. Disowned your daughter because she didn't do your bidding. Now you have the nerve to stand there and criticise everyone else's parenting skills.'

'Yeah,' Sam said.

'Sit down!' someone called. Sam thought he recognised Mark's mother's voice.

'Yes, I think it best if you sit.' Michael could barely contain his anger.

'You're an idiot,' Reg said clearly. There was a murmur from the congregation, and laughter from the Wheatsheaf crowd.

'What did you say?' Pirbright replied in a hiss, white-furious.

Reg stepped up onto his pew and held out his arms. 'I said, you're an *idiot.*'

The congregation rustled. There were further calls for Reg to shut up and sit down, though Clive called out in support, 'Carry on, Reg!'

'You've got it completely wrong,' Reg said. 'There's no Old World. There's just the world. There is no Old Immorality, there's just immorality – which includes hitting children, in my book. There's no need for new rules. The old rules worked fine.'

'Oh, really? Really?' Pirbright spluttered, clearly

imagining he had Reg pinned. 'So why was there so much murder, and . . . and prostitution? So much drug abuse and alcoholism? Why was everyone so unhappy?'

'Probably because of people like you, trying to tell them what to do all the time!' Reg shouted back. 'Because people like you can't just let people be, can you? You can't let our wonderful, charming teenagers just be themselves.'

The old soldier hopped down, stepped into the aisle and held out his arms in appeal.

'For God's sake, is this the kind of New World we want, when teenagers aren't allowed to leave the village? When they aren't free to kiss who they want? When they're forced into marriage before they're ready? Where they can't experiment with drugs, and booze, and listen to loud music? I mean, what the hell kind of society are we building where kids can't turn their music up too loud?'

'If you don't like this society, Mr Walker,' Monica Hilfenhaus called out from a pew at the front, 'then you are free to leave whenever you like.'

'Oh, I intend to,' Reg said. 'I fancy a little road trip, as it happens. I think that lad there might like to join me.'

'You're free to leave,' Pirbright replied quickly. 'But not Sam. Go by yourself, and good riddance.'

'That's not your decision to make,' Reg replied. 'You never had any authority here, as far as I'm concerned.

And now you've clearly gone insane there's no reason why anyone should follow you.'

Pirbright went completely white as the church broke into hubbub.

'This man saved our lives!' Mark shouted from the front. 'He's worked tirelessly to keep us safe ever since. And this is how you pay him back?'

'Bah,' Reg said. 'It's people like him that caused the disease in the first place. People who wanted to control everything, control everyone. I've had enough of this crap. I'm going now, and Sam's coming with me, if he wants to.'

'Absolutely,' Sam said, and stood up.

'Sit down!' Pirbright screamed. 'Sam is not going anywhere.'

'Oh, I think he is,' Josh cried. Everyone turned to look at him, unnoticed until now at the back of the room. Josh stood, and to widespread gasps, revealed the service pistol he'd had under his folded coat.

'Hurrah!' Sam shouted cheerfully. This was brilliant, he thought. Good old Josh.

'You would bring a firearm into God's house?' Mr Carter hissed, horrified.

Josh shrugged. 'Oh, didn't I tell you? I don't believe in God.' He pointed the gun up and fired a bullet into the high, arched ceiling. The congregation flinched as one as the gunshot rang around the chamber.

By the time the echo had receded, Reg and Sam

had walked calmly down to the large rear doors joining Josh, who was trying not to grin, his heart thrashing like a mad drummer.

Pirbright stood watching, open-mouthed, but then recovered his wits. 'Stop them!' he shouted. Mark and Carter ran towards them, but Josh waved the gun at them and they backed off.

Mr Carter held up a hand. 'Look, Josh, we can sort this out—' But he was interrupted by Clive, who stepped forward, getting between him and Josh.

'I think it's best if we let them go,' Clive said. 'Don't you?'

James, Ben, Harry and Amir stepped up behind Clive, making it clear they weren't going to let anyone interfere with the departure of the three renegades.

'Cheers, lads,' Reg said. They walked out and shut the heavy door behind them.

'Told you you might need that,' Reg said, grinning. 'Do you know what you're doing?'

'Haven't got a clue,' Josh replied. 'I hoped you might tell me. Come on, let's go.'

'I've got to say goodbye to Kitty,' Sam said as they walked quickly down the street.

'Me too,' Josh said.

'Meet me at the car pool in fifteen minutes,' Reg said calmly. 'The blue Range Rover's fuelled and ready to go. If anyone tries to stop you, wave the gun at them.' He hopped on a moped and whizzed off towards the barricade, while Sam and Josh trotted down to the Hilfenhaus' place. Neither of them was in particularly great shape, Josh grimacing with pain from his bitten leg, Sam still woozy from the blow to the head.

Inside the church, the noise was indescribable as people shouted, demanding answers from Pirbright.

'Silence!' he screamed, to no avail.

Martha sat alone behind a pillar, not wanting her father to know she was there. Michael turned to Mark and spoke urgently, Mark ran off and darted through a small door leading to the tower. The Wheatsheaf men stood firmly before the door, stopping anyone from leaving. Though she could have used her mother's support, Martha was thinking it was probably just as well Judith wasn't there, as she might have attacked Michael again.

She hadn't been too surprised by Josh's actions. She knew her brother and she knew this had been building for some time. It had taken every ounce of her will to refrain from getting up and walking out with them. She was disappointed with Bryan. It was only the thought of Ellie that had stopped her. She was glad they were going, and had no fears for their safety – Reg would get them away, Reg would keep them safe.

Mark returned. 'They've gone!' he called.

'OK,' Pirbright said, unheard by anyone except Mark and Martha. 'Leave through the side door in my office, here's the key. Find Kitty and protect her. Don't let her leave too, they'll probably go there now. I'll go to the car pool with Carter to make sure they don't steal a car in the meantime.'

Mark nodded. 'I'll get my gun,' he said and turned to go, but Pirbright grabbed his shoulder, staying his departure for a moment.

'I don't want the children hurt.'

'I'm not letting them take Kitty,' Mark replied. 'If that old idiot gets in my way...'

Pirbright sighed, then nodded briefly. 'Do what you have to.'

7.44 P.M.

'So we're leaving, tonight,' Sam said urgently. Josh was looking out the window, which afforded a view up the street in the direction of the church. He saw a few people walking hesitantly towards them.

'I need to pack,' Kitty said, leaping up.

'No, no,' Josh said. 'You're not coming, it's too dangerous.'

'What?' she cried, dismayed.

'We'll come back for you,' Sam said. 'When things have calmed down.'

Kitty danced over to Josh and kissed him hard.

'Dude, that's my sister,' Sam said, looking away.

Kitty pulled back and fixed Josh with a look she'd been practising, for just such an event. 'I'm coming.'

'I don't think that's a good idea,' Sam said, but Josh grinned.

'I was hoping you'd insist on coming,' he told her. 'But no time to pack, OK?' He took her by the hand. They rushed down the stairs only to be confronted by the front door opening.

Mark stood there, looking furious. He saw immediately what was happening and screamed, 'NO!'

'Back door!' Sam yelled and they turned on their heels and sprinted through the kitchen. Sod the latch, *bang!* and they were through and out into the warm evening. They heard the door crash open behind them, but they had a good start and the three of them were down and out through the bottom gate in seconds. Then it was a hard, straight sprint along the path, through the nettles. Footsteps pounded behind them as their pursuer ran. Josh let the others go on ahead and turned, lifting the pistol. Mark slowed and stopped as he saw the gun.

'Go on,' Mark said. 'Do it.'

'Go back to the house,' Josh said. 'Or I'll fire.'

'You don't have the balls, Joshy. If it was Sam, then maybe I'd be wetting my pants. Sam's a murderer. Killed my dad. But you? You're just a pussy.'

Josh aimed the pistol just to the right of Mark's head and squeezed the trigger. The gun went off and the bullet pinged off the back of a shed.

Mark flinched but stayed where he was, saying nothing. Josh guessed he was more frightened by the bang and the flash than he was willing to let on. It had certainly scared the hell out of Josh.

'That was a warning, Mark,' he said calmly. 'I only have one bullet left. I can't afford to waste the last one. If you do not go back to the house right now, I will shoot you in the face.'

Mark stood, calculating, for an achingly long time, staring directly into Josh's face. Whatever it was Mark saw there convinced him the younger boy was serious and he backed off. Josh watched him go all the way.

'I want her back, Joshy!' he called as he disappeared through the gate. 'We will be the future of the new world.'

Josh waited a minute longer and turned to join the others, who were waiting for him a dozen metres further on.

'Was that true about only having one bullet left?' Kitty asked.

'No,' Josh replied. 'I lied.'

'That's a relief,' she said. 'How many *do* you have left?'

'None.'

7.58 P.M.

Martha stopped outside Bryan's house. *Her* house. She considered her options. The front door was closed. If Bryan had heard the gunshot in the church,

349

he hadn't come out to investigate. She was still angry with him. Not so angry that she wanted to rush off after the boys, but angry enough that she couldn't face going home just yet. She heard the roar of a car engine behind her, an alien sound in the village these days. She turned and watched it sweep past. It was her father's car, the SUV he now drove, the only car allowed in the village. Mr Carter was beside him. Where was Mark?

She suddenly realised her mum needed to be told what had happened. She set off towards her mother's house, and on the way heard the unmistakeable crack of a second gunshot. Was it Josh's pistol again? No one else had been armed at the church. She hurried on, and when she arrived at the Pirbrights' Judith was out the front, clutching her arms to herself and looking up and down the street.

'What's going on?' Judith said. 'Was that a gunshot? Where was that car going?'

Quickly Martha filled her mother in on the events in the church. When she heard that Josh had pulled a gun on the congregation, Judith put her hand to her face. She was clearly shocked but Martha saw pride there too. Josh had done what she'd been too uncertain to try.

'So they've gone?' Judith asked, her face shining in the porch light. 'Josh has gone?'

Martha shrugged. 'I guess so.'

Judith's shoulders sagged suddenly. She looked

bereft. 'I'm glad they got away,' she said after a moment. 'I think it was the right thing to do...'

'But?' Martha said softly.

Judith paused a moment, looking down the street. 'But nothing,' she insisted. And visibly she pulled herself together. She turned back to Martha. 'You didn't want to go with them?'

Martha shook her head. 'Part of me did. But I can't leave Ellie.'

'And Bryan?'

Martha frowned. 'Yes, and Bryan.'

'Well, it's your choice,' Judith said. 'It's your life. But if you go, Ellie will be fine, and she and Bryan can always join you later.'

'They might not want to come.'

Judith reached for her daughter's hand.

'So what did your father do, when they left?' she asked. 'He must have hit the roof!'

'He sent Mark after them.'

Judith stopped, staring at her daughter. 'Shouldn't we be worried?'

Martha shook her head. 'They had a good head start. They're with Reg. I think they'll be fine.'

But then, as if to make a fool of her, a rattle of distant gunfire erupted in the distance.

'What was that?' Judith asked, though she must have known.

'Maybe we should check on Kitty,' Martha said.

'Good idea.'

They walked briskly down Highland Terrace, passing a few people who tried to stop and talk to them, but Judith was having none of it.

'Later,' she said to a flustered-looking Mrs Hutton.

As they approached the Hilfenhaus' place, they saw a figure emerge from the Rogers' house across the street. It was Mark, looking grim and carrying a shotgun. He crossed the road. They stopped, shrinking into a rhododendron, not wanting him to see them.

Suddenly there was the sound of the SUV coming back, from the direction of the car pool. It roared up at a mad speed but slowed as it approached Mark. The window wound down and Mr Carter peered out.

'It's Walker!' he shouted. 'He's gone mental. No sign of the boys, we think he's trying to give them time to get away.'

'They've got Kitty,' Mark said.

'Are you sure?'

He nodded. There was a pause while Mr Carter turned to speak to Michael. Then he poked his head back out again. 'We'll go after them. We're going to get rifles – shotguns are no good at that range. Wait here for us.'

The car drove off at speed.

Mark stood, watching it go for a few seconds, then he turned and strode off towards the car pool.

'Go back to the house,' Judith said to Martha, before setting off down the street, towards the church.

'What? Where are you going?'

'I'm going to find your father, my husband,' Judith called back, without turning. 'And I'm going to punch him in the face.'

Martha turned and watched Mark storming off down the street. Thinking, calculating. She reached a decision and headed back towards her mother's house.

There was something there she needed.

8.02 P.M.

They ran across fields towards the car pool so as to avoid the road. Josh knew the route well, he'd played here as a child.

Halfway there they heard a succession of gunshots. They stopped and glanced at one another nervously, then carried on. When they arrived they were relieved to find that Reg was waiting, behind the wheel of a Range Rover, engine idling, rifle on his lap.

'I had this Rover loaded up for a foraging trip I was supposed to be making with James next week,' he explained. 'Full of useful stuff. And I've unlocked the gate.'

'Thought this place would be swarming,' Josh said as they clambered in. If Reg was surprised to see Kitty he didn't show it.

'Pirbright and Carter came down in a car. I persuaded them to go back,' Reg said calmly.

'You shot at them?' Kitty asked. 'Did they shoot back?'

'Yeah!' he laughed. 'But the idiots only brought a shotgun. No range at all on those things. This baby, however...' He patted the gun. 'They knew they were out-gunned and they retreated. They may well be back, though, with more men and rifles. Everyone in? Let's go.'

He gunned the engine and they began to move forward, but then the world exploded and the Rover stalled and jerked. Smoke and glass filled the cabin and something wet coated Josh's face. He tasted salt and wiped his eyes. It took a second to recover, but then he glanced over at Reg to see the old soldier's head had been blown off. Beyond the body, through the shattered window, Josh saw Mark reloading an old single-gauge shotgun.

Josh felt a cold surge run through his body, the world swam and turned grey for a moment. *No*, he thought. *We were so close...*

'Easy,' Mark said calmly.

Kitty screamed as she realised what had happened.

'Drive, Josh, drive!' Sam yelled, pushing Kitty's head down, protecting her.

Easier said than done. Though half-frozen with fear, Josh got a leg over and kicked Reg's foot out of the way, depressing the clutch. Mark looked up to see what he was doing and, distracted, fumbled the cartridge, dropping it onto the forecourt. Josh turned the ignition and the V8 rumbled back into life. So far so good, but getting into the driver's seat was impossible without opening the door and pushing Reg's body out. Josh ducked between his friend's now lifeless legs and pushed down on the accelerator with his right hand. He grabbed the clutch with his left.

'Steer!' he yelled to Sam, before releasing the clutch and pressing the accelerator. The car lurched and seemed as though it might stall, but then he gunned it and it jumped forward.

'Oh, great!' Sam said, realising that it was now his head in the firing line. Nonetheless, he leaned over Reg's headless torso and grabbed the wheel just as Mark finished loading the gun and swung it up.

Another roar and the rear window shattered, showering them with glass again. Kitty yelped. Sam shrieked in pain.

'I'm hit!' he cried and let go of the wheel just as the Rover picked up speed. Then a crunch as they hit something and Josh was thrown forward into the dashboard, cracking his forehead a nasty blow. The car stalled again. He popped his head up and saw they'd crashed into the side of the garage. He turned to see Sam writhing in pain in the back seat. Through the rear window he saw Mark laughing and slotting another cartridge into the gun.

Josh grabbed Reg's rifle, opened the door and got out. The evening sun dazzled him and he held up a hand towards it and Mark, as if to ward off the deadly spray of shot. But Mark was on him – he swung the butt of the shotgun, connecting with Josh's jaw, sending him sprawling. The rifle clattered to the ground. Mark kicked it away, then stepped back, giving himself room.

'Oh, even easier,' Mark said, grinning madly. The electrician lifted the gun and pointed it into Josh's face. He cackled as he squeezed the trigger. Josh closed his eyes, shutting out the painful sunlight and the sight of his own impending death. He clenched everything, waiting for the noise.

It came. A roar that signalled the end of everything. And nothing.

Josh opened his eyes to see Mark on all fours on the forecourt, blood pooling underneath him. He slumped down onto his belly and Josh saw a short pole, about the length of a drumstick, sticking out of the small of his back. Mark breathed shallowly, close to death. Josh peered into the sunlight towards where the shot had come from. A robed figure walked towards him, carrying a cross.

It took him a moment before he realised it was Martha, and it wasn't a cross she carried, it was a crossbow.

'I thought you were Jesus for a second,' he said.

'Lucky for you I'm not,' his sister replied. 'Jesus would have forgiven him.'

They felt bad about leaving Reg lying on the forecourt, less bad about planting a foot on Mark's body and wrenching out the crossbow bolt. But there wasn't time for sentiment, and they could hear a car approaching as they peeled out and headed off up the Guildford Road.

'Oh my God,' Kitty said in the back, half crying. 'This is horrible, this is horrible!'

'Shut up, Kitty,' Martha, who had climbed into the front passenger seat, said sternly. 'You're not helping.'

She found an old towel and a packet of wet wipes and began methodically cleaning up the blood and brain tissue. Sam peered through the rear window. Josh had handed him Reg's rifle. The shotgun and the crossbow lay in the back too.

To make herself useful Kitty checked through the gear Reg had packed for his foraging trip.

'Trail mix, chocolate, beef jerky, water,' she listed. 'Warm clothes, boots, a compass, knives and some road maps.'

'Well done, Kitty,' Sam said. She smiled at him and then remembered he was hurt.

'Oh, God, let me look at that wound!' she cried. Her brother had been hit in the neck by some buck-shot, tearing the skin. There was a lot of blood.

'It's not deep, I don't think,' she said. She took out the first-aid kit and began dabbing at the wound with a surgical pad. Having something to do calmed her, helped her focus.

While Kitty cleaned Sam's wounds, Martha

opened one of the maps and studied it. 'Where are we going,' she asked.

'To the hotel,' Sam said. 'Where else?'

'Where is it on the map?' Martha asked. With a grunt of pain, Sam leaned over and pointed.

'OK,' Martha said after a moment. 'You want the A287, Josh.'

'Got it,' he called. His head ached from where he'd hit it against the dashboard.

'Careful,' said Kitty. Josh was throwing the car about, speeding round corners, crunching the gears of the unfamiliar vehicle.

'How long will it take us to get there?' she asked.

'It was over an hour with Bryan,' Josh said, then he thought for a bit. 'Look, especially with the roads so overgrown, it's just too late to go there now. It's getting dark. I think we should find somewhere quiet to rest up for the night, and head there tomorrow.'

'We should probably go to Guildford and pick up some things,' Martha said.

'Tomorrow,' Josh said. 'We'll do it all tomorrow.'

'So where now?' Kitty asked. She leaned forward and rested a hand on Josh's shoulder. 'We need to stop soon, for Sam.'

Martha noticed that Josh briefly stroked Kitty's hand and shot her a warm smile in the mirror.

'I know somewhere,' Sam said. 'Somewhere close.'

Directed by Sam, they turned off onto a discreet country lane close to Guildford and drove another mile or so until they came to a small track, almost hidden by grass. Sam was starting to shiver.

'Down here,' Sam said, teeth chattering. 'This was where my friend Oliver Graham used to live. I've been here a couple of times; it's a long way back from the road.'

They crawled along the dirt track for a few minutes before they saw the house. Josh drove round the back to conceal the Rover, and they gained access to the house through a small rear window.

Martha searched the house and found a bottle of painkillers in the bathroom. She gave two to Sam, poured some bottled water into a bowl and cleaned and dressed his wound. His shoulder had been peppered with shot but only a few had penetrated the skin. Martha eased the tiny pellets out gently with a sterile kitchen knife as Sam sweated and tried not to scream.

Josh went upstairs and found two bags of bones – all that was left of the Graham family. He wrapped them up gently in bed sheets, carried them outside and laid them carefully in the shed. Meanwhile Kitty hunted for food, finding a few cans of beans and soup. Reg had packed a camping stove, and as it grew dark Josh lit a few candles to cheer the place up a bit. After a while they stopped listening out for the sound of pursuing motors and settled down. They ate heartily and Sam felt much better now his wound was dressed and he'd taken the painkillers. No one mentioned Reg. It was as if that subject was to be hidden away for now, to be addressed later, when they were safe. When they could deal with it properly.

'It feels good to be away from the village,' Sam said.

'Freedom,' Martha agreed.

'No one's going to hit us here,' Kitty said.

Sam lay back on a sofa. 'Those bastards. How could they do that?'

'They're scared,' Martha said, after a pause.

'We're all scared,' Josh replied, reaching out for Kitty.

'I don't think we, the younger ones, are as scared as the adults,' Martha went on. 'You know what I've been trying to figure out?'

'What's that,' Kitty asked.

'Why it is we let them behave that way. Not why they did it, that's easy to explain. What I couldn't figure out is why we just accepted it. Why we thought they might know what they were doing.'

'We were looking for guidance,' Josh said slowly. 'Leadership. Everyone was. That was why everyone accepted Dad as president. Even Camp Wheatsheaf, eventually.'

'It's not just that,' Martha said. 'We all believed that things had changed. That *we* had to change. But things *haven't* changed, at least not for us.'

'What are you talking about?' Sam said. 'Everything *has* changed.'

'For *them*. For the adults. Those people have lost their entire history. Everything they thought they knew is gone,' Martha said softly. She sat forward, her face glowing earnest in the dim light. 'Those people who travelled the world, saw different cultures; for them it's all gone. But look at us – none of us has lived anywhere else but the village. What have we lost? The Internet? Facebook? You know, I look at Ellie, and, yes, she has memories from before, memories of her mother. But she got used to the new situation so quickly. As for the toddlers, they're going to grow up not knowing any different.'

She looked around at her brother and her friends, faces golden in the glow of the candles, circling the light source and talking, like all human societies have for all time.

'No, it's different for the adults,' Martha said. 'It broke them. We have our whole lives still ahead of us and a whole new world to explore; they have nothing. No wonder they were scared for us to leave the village.'

'You're making excuses for them,' Josh said.

'I'm trying to understand,' Martha replied softly.

No one said anything in the flickering candlelight. Shadows fluttered along the walls and an owl hooted outside.

'When we get back,' Martha said, 'it's up to us to heal the wounds.'

'Go back?' Sam said. 'We're not going back.' Josh and Kitty murmured agreement.

'Of course we are, eventually,' Martha said. 'They need us. As it stands our world is broken and it's up to us to fix it.'

Sam shook his head. 'I'm not going back. You can go if you like. We're going to the hotel. We're going to start again there. And then, who knows after that – like you said, there's a whole world to explore. We can sneak back to the village, get more people to follow. Don't you want Bryan to come? And Ellie?'

Martha made as if to speak but Josh cut her off.

'Not now, we need sleep. Let's get to bed.'

Kitty looked up, suddenly worried, but Martha stood and took her hand.

'Shall we share?' she asked. Kitty smiled and looked grateful. She kissed Josh quickly and went up with Martha.

Sam looked at Josh. 'Wanna share?' he asked. Josh laughed, shoved him back down onto the couch. Sam howled in pain and clutched his neck.

'Oops,' Josh said. 'Sorry.'

12

Martha was upstairs in the bathroom, sitting on the loo with the seat down, resting her head against the wall. She held a carrier bag she'd been using to throw up into. Her stomach flipped and she dry-retched. This was the third morning in a row she'd been sick. It wasn't something she could ignore any more.

She heard voices through the window and moved the net curtain aside to see Kitty, Josh and Sam down in the garden behind the house, inspecting the Range Rover.

'I can't get back in there,' Kitty said, shuddering.

'Oh, come on,' Sam said, rubbing sleep from his eyes. 'Josh's driving isn't *that* bad.'

'Oh, shut up, Sam,' Kitty said. 'It still has...bits of Reg in it.'

It was true. The insides of the windows were still smeared with a muddy pink. Through the windows, in the clear light of the morning, they could see bits of gristle and bones they'd managed to overlook the evening before.

'We're going to need some more wet wipes,' Sam said.

Kitty rounded on him, furious. 'Do you have to joke about everything?' she shouted, before running off to the side of the house.

Josh went after her.

'It's just his way of coping, you know that,' he said when he caught her. A morning breeze brought scents of summer to them. Insects buzzed in the long grass of the garden.

'I know,' Kitty replied, falling against him and burying her face in his chest.

'We need another car,' Josh said once they'd returned. Martha had appeared, looking pale. She'd walked a dozen metres up the track towards the road and was staring off into the distance, arms wrapped around herself. Sam was sitting on the bonnet of the Range Rover, whistling cheerfully. He hopped off as they approached.

'Let's get an automatic,' Sam said, clapping Josh on the shoulder. 'You might be able to drive one of them.' Then his face lit up. 'Actually, I've got an idea. How far are we from Guildford, to walk?'

'About twenty minutes,' Josh replied.

'Come on, let's stretch our legs,' Sam said.

7.41 A.M.

'Dirt bikes? Really?' Kitty asked, staring through the

364

display window. The sign overhead read *Guildford Dirt and Road Bikes*. Josh rattled the locked door, then suddenly leaped back in alarm as a figure appeared on the other side of the glass. It turned out to be Sam, who grinned and unlatched the door to let them enter.

'How did you get in?' Josh asked.

'Unlocked window round the back,' Sam replied.

'Bikes are more useful to us than cars,' Josh said as they looked about. 'You've seen the roads, the weeds are tearing them to pieces. These will go anywhere.'

Sam was walking through the rows of bikes, groaning with appreciation. 'A Husqvarna, Josh, look. This is beautiful. Thank you, HAV3N.'

Josh began grabbing gear, gloves, jackets, waterproof trousers. 'Kitty, keep an ear out for cars,' he said. 'Martha, find us stuff that fits.' Then he went off to look at backpacks. Half an hour later and they were ready. Sam had selected two powerful bikes, 750cc with pillion seats and luggage boxes. Martha had helmets and accessories for all of them. Kitty walked around stiffly in her leathers, a look of distaste on her face.

'Please tell me I can take my sandals?' she said, looking at the thick leather boots Martha had given her.

'No sandals,' Josh said, picking up the boots and handing them to her.

Kitty sat down grumpily and began pulling on the boots. Josh was busy tossing useful items into the luggage boxes on each bike.

'Right,' he said. 'That's the essentials – water, food, maps. We'll make another trip out to a local supermarket once we're there. We don't need anything else for the first couple of nights.'

'Change of underwear?' Kitty suggested. While Josh's back was turned, she opened the luggage box and shoved her sandals down inside.

'Everyone ready?' Josh called, grinning.

'Oh, yes,' Sam said. He got on his bike and started it up with an enormous roar.

'Yes,' Martha said when the noise had died a little. She clambered on behind Sam and gripped his waist tightly. Slung across her back was Reg's rifle. Josh had the shotgun. The other weapons they had abandoned, including the crossbow, to Josh's dismay.

'I'm not ready,' Kitty said. But then Josh straddled his bike and she gulped and hopped on behind him.

'We'll be going a bit faster even than when getting away from the dogs. Sway when I sway, all right?' he said, voice muffled by the helmet. 'And when I brake, try not to let your helmet crash into the back of mine. You'll get the hang of it quickly.'

Kitty nodded, immediately knocking his helmet with hers. 'Sorry,' she giggled, despite everything.

Sam roared away, Martha hanging on tightly. Josh kicked the bike into first, twisted the throttle, and they were off.

They'd decided to try taking the motorway. Though Bryan hadn't been able to take his car, they figured the bikes should be able to weave in and out of the dead vehicles. They found their way up the slip road onto the M3 and stopped in horror at the sight which greeted them.

Sam had driven down the A3 on his fishing trip, but had seen nothing like this. On this stretch of motorway, at least, the traffic was literally bumper-to-bumper. The hard shoulder was as blocked as the other lanes. Hundreds of skeletons lay fully-clothed in the gaps between the cars, or on bonnets or roofs as people had abandoned their cars to die. The boys turned off the engines and they stood for a while, the whipping wind the only sound as they gazed out over the sea of corpse-driven cars. Then Josh realised Kitty was crying, clinging onto his waist, hanging on so tightly. He reached for her hand and squeezed it.

They turned round and went slowly back down the slip road, looking for the lanes Bryan had so sensibly taken them on before.

The roads were thickly overgrown now the spring rains and summer sun had been given months to work with. Cornflowers and poppies dotted the route, brightening the mood. Josh was in the lead and pulled up as they approached a crossroads. He studied the map for a while, then tucked it away.

'Well, this is why we chose these bikes,' he called across to Sam, then set off on an even narrower road, almost lost in the wild flowers. Sam followed. The going wasn't too bad, though at one point they had to jump the bikes over a fallen tree that had perhaps come down during the winds they'd had in March. It was annoying for the girls, bumping along with only the boys' waists to hold onto.

They stopped after a couple of hours for a drink and a bite to eat. Sam was complaining of a stiffness in his injured shoulder. He looked pale, and Josh suspected he was in more pain than he was letting on. Josh pushed open a gate into a field, noticing the grass was shorter there, and they saw some white blobs in the far corner. Sheep, who'd done well to survive the winter without shelter.

'It's good to know there's still livestock out here,' Josh said. 'And there'll be wild animals to hunt as well. Deer, and rabbits.'

'We won't go hungry,' Sam said. 'The country's full of canned goods in supermarkets.'

'Canned food doesn't last for ever,' Josh said, munching on a biscuit. 'We'll need to farm, and hunt.'

'We need more people, don't we?' Martha said.

Josh nodded. 'Yes, but let's not think about that just yet. Let's just get where we're going.'

Sam stood and winced as he moved his arm.

Martha noticed too. 'Is it hurting? Let me have a look.'

'It's fine,' Sam said. 'Let's just get to the hotel, and you can have a look then.'

'OK, but I don't think you should be riding,' Martha said.

Sam stared at her. 'Well, I'm not walking.'

'No,' Martha said. 'You can ride pillion.'

She straddled the bike, started it up with a strong kick, then put on her helmet as Sam watched, open-mouthed.

'You can't ride a bike,' he said.

'Actually she can,' Josh grinned. 'She's ridden my bike before.'

'Get on, Sam,' Martha said, winking. 'And you'd better hold on tight. I like to ride fast.'

Martha turned out to be an excellent motorcyclist, though she drove more slowly than she'd warned, not wanting to jar Sam's shoulder. They reached the hotel after another hour or so. Three and a half hours to complete a journey that had taken just over an hour six months earlier. The driveway was covered by leaves but the hard Tarmac had mostly resisted the onset of the weeds. The grass of the lawn before the house had reached a height of at least a metre and the gravel concourse to the front of the house was mostly obscured by grass and dandelions.

They left the bikes out the front for now and walked up the steps into their new home.

The four stood in the great entrance hall, a little breathless, nervous at the silence, scared by what they had done.

'We shouldn't try to do too much on the first day,' Josh said, his voice echoing in the great space. 'Let's sort out bedrooms and cooking facilities. We know there's water and some supplies in the storeroom here, and we have chocolate and jerky so we're not going to go hungry.'

'Good plan,' Martha said. 'Tomorrow we can make a trip to the supermarket in Petersfield.'

'Yeah,' Josh said. 'Other than that, let's just explore, and plan.'

Martha took Sam and Josh into the kitchen and checked their wounds. Neither Sam's shoulder, nor Josh's leg seemed to be infected, but Sam's shoulder was tender. She dabbed on more antiseptic and changed the bandages. Sam took some painkillers and they went to explore.

They found a few empty bedrooms on the third floor. It seemed most of the occupied rooms had been on the second floor and they decided to clean those out at a later date. The water was still running, though they'd noticed in the kitchen that the taps coughed for a while before anything came out. Sam checked the water tanks in the loft and pronounced them full.

That just left cooking facilities, and they were

taken care of when Sam discovered an enormous gas barbecue on an outside terrace. It took a while to get going, but in time he had it boiling water and made everyone a cup of black coffee. They sat outside in the warm afternoon sun, enjoying the rustle of the breeze in the trees and the gentle floating of cumulus clouds in the sky. Their sky.

Afterwards, they wandered around the grounds, heading down to the chapel a hundred metres away across the overgrown lawns. It was a pretty little building, with a stained-glass window at one end behind the small altar. There were half a dozen pews on either side of a central aisle. The walls were hung with tapestries and oil paintings of biblical scenes, dark with age.

Josh found a box of matches and lit a candle. 'For Reg,' he said. Martha came up behind her brother to stare at the steady, pale flame. 'He would have liked it here,' Josh added.

'Do you think they'll give him a proper funeral?' Sam asked.

'Of course they will,' Josh said firmly as though he could make them do it by his certainty.

They wandered back to the hotel. Sam and Josh volunteered to clear out the corpses from the dining room, and wherever else they might be found on the ground floor.

'No, we'll all do it,' Martha said. 'We're all in this together, we all get our hands dirty.'

Josh and Sam smiled, nodding, though Kitty's face betrayed a certain reluctance. But together they worked all that afternoon to collect the skeletal bodies, musty when still but releasing a foul stench as they were moved. They laid them respectfully on a great groundsheet in the long grass behind the hotel.

Each corpse left a brown stain where it had lain. Martha scrubbed the carpets as best she could, wearing gloves and a face mask, then found rugs and throws to cover the remaining discolouration until the carpets could be cleaned properly.

'Now what do we do with them?' Kitty asked when all the bodies were out the back.

'I'm not sure yet,' Josh replied. 'I think we should try and bury them. But we'll need a digger, or something.'

'Maybe we should wait until Clive Mitchell comes,' Sam suggested.

'*If* he comes,' Kitty said. 'And we can't just leave them here, it's not . . . very respectful.'

'I know what we should do with them,' Martha said, coming outside to join the others. 'We'll put them in the chapel.'

8.16 P.M.

There was a holiday feel that night as they tucked into tinned cassoulet warmed over the barbecue in a great black pot they'd found in the kitchens. They opened a bottle of wine, ate, drank and laughed, at ease for the first time in months, putting the horrors of the past behind them, at least for now. They talked about their plans for the hotel. Getting others to join them, getting the farm up and running. Fishing for trout in the stream. Hunting wild deer. Getting the electrics sorted out.

'First things first, though,' Josh said. 'Tomorrow we'll take a trip to Petersfield, to the supermarket.' The others quietened down. The thought of going off on another trip so soon after they'd arrived didn't fill them with joy exactly. Especially into another town filled with the dead. They all remembered the sea of corpses on the motorway.

Kitty noticed Martha had been a little quiet. While the boys discussed plans to collect some livestock for the farm, she asked her if everything was OK.

'I miss Bryan. But Ellie more,' Martha said truthfully, even if that wasn't the main thing on her mind just then. 'I feel like I've let her down. Just when... just when she had a new mum.' The mention of motherhood made Martha want to lay a hand against her own belly, but she held back, squeezing her hand into a fist. She wanted to talk to Kitty about it so much, but it was too early. She wasn't sure yet.

'You'll see her soon,' Kitty said. 'We'll go back, sneak in maybe, get your mum and Bryan to spread the word about this place. They'll come. Lots of people will come.'

'I hope so,' Martha said. 'It's just that Bryan and I had a bit of a row before I left . . .'

'Oh, never mind about that,' Kitty said. 'Rows don't mean anything. Not when you're in love.'

Martha nodded and smiled, glad she had her friend with her.

13

Clouds rolled in during the night and sat oppressively over the world as the teenagers got up the next morning and prepared themselves for their trip. Nervousness hung alongside the clouds and conversation was muted.

'Hope it doesn't rain,' Josh said as they made their way out to the bikes.

'We'll put them in the garages round the back later,' Sam called over, pulling on his gloves. 'They're not locked.'

The trip into Petersfield was surprisingly quick and pain-free. Josh had suggested they take a road through a small wood. The shade of the trees had kept the weeds down and the road was mostly clear all the way, though Petersfield itself was clogged with cars. They'd grown accustomed now to averting their eyes from the front seats of vehicles they passed, and apart from the occasional sun-bleached bag of bones sprawled on the pavements it was almost possible to forget the armies of the dead.

Though gardens were overgrown and the ever-present weeds were busy chewing up the roads in town, the houses appeared clean and looked-after. Like the owners had gone on a long holiday, and would just need to sort the post and mow the lawn when they returned to get things back to normal.

The scrum at the Waitrose supermarket car park seemed to have been just as bad as at the Tesco in Guildford. But when they dismounted and entered the store they found there was still quite a bit of stock on the shelves or heaped on the floor.

'Looks like they'd had a delivery just before...' Sam said, not finishing.

Just before. Martha wondered about the staff here: had they battled to get stock on the shelves, doing their bit to try and keep things going, like the government had asked? Restocking pasta shapes in aisle eight, as desperate, coughing shoppers shoved them aside?

There were three or four corpses in the shop she could see, one of them wearing the green uniform of the supermarket. She wondered briefly if they should try to dispose of the bodies and looked around at the others. Sam was busy stuffing rice packets into a backpack. Josh was checking best-before labels on canned tomatoes. Kitty was kicking a shrink-wrapped pack of diet Coke down aisle twelve. Martha sighed and started packing tinned fish into her own bag.

*

Afterwards they wandered through the town, grabbing a few items from the outdoor shop and stocking up on painkillers and tampons from the pharmacy. Martha made sure the others weren't looking and swiped a couple of pregnancy testing kits. Sam was moving stiffly, his shoulder clearly bothering him. Most of the shops showed signs of having been looted or ransacked, but there was still plenty of stock. Perhaps the disease had hit fast here. Small mercies, Martha thought.

The lowering, darkening clouds told them to leave late afternoon. The wind was picking up, and faint spots of rain stung Martha's face as they returned to the bikes and stuffed as many groceries as they could into the boxes at the back.

'Could be a storm coming,' Sam said, squinting up at a huge black cloud which was headed their way from the south.

They were back at the hotel fifteen minutes later, as the first great drops of the storm splattered against their visors. Josh and Sam dropped off the girls at the front, telling them to put the kettle on, and took the bikes round to the garages at the side of the main building, discreetly tucked away amongst a stand of oak trees.

Josh noticed a few cars in the long wooden building: an SUV that might prove useful, as well as a BMW, a Jaguar and an Audi, though they might have to search through the pockets of the corpses in the chapel to find the keys. These were expensive cars. This hadn't been a hotel for ordinary people.

The boys lugged the bags of food out of the garage, Sam shut the door and they ran awkwardly across to the main building, getting half-soaked.

The girls let them in at the kitchen door and together they unpacked the food, stacking it into the great kitchen larder.

Everyone jumped as a brilliant flash of lightning suddenly freeze-framed the scene. It was followed a couple of seconds later by a great crack of thunder. Martha shivered, both spooked and thrilled by the sound.

'Weren't you going to put the kettle on?' Josh asked.

'I will, I will,' Martha said. 'I'm just going to get dinner underway first – it'll take ages to boil water on that barbecue. Everyone OK with tuna pasta?' She bent to open a cupboard, searching for a pan.

'Oh, look,' she said. 'Poor little thing.' Everyone crowded to see.

It was the skeleton of a cat. Picked clean by ants.

'No one left to feed it,' Kitty said. 'It probably starved to death. What should we do with it?'

'It's just a cat,' Sam said, munching on a biscuit. 'Chuck it out the back.'

'Don't be so heartless,' Martha said crossly. 'It was probably someone's pet. We can't leave it here when we're preparing food. I'll take it to the chapel and put it with the others.'

'Oh, whatever.' Sam rolled his eyes and went off to the lounge.

'Coming, Kitty?' Martha asked.

Kitty peered out through the window. Though only late afternoon, it was nearly dark as night. She shook her head.

'I don't think so,' she said, and followed Sam.

Martha laid the cat skeleton in an empty biscuit box. Grabbing a torch and donning one of the new raincoats they'd got from Petersfield, she went out the back door.

'I'll put the kettle on, then, shall I?' Josh said.

5.46 P.M.

Martha knew that Sam was right, that she shouldn't be sentimental about a cat dead for six months. Not when billions of humans had died. But part of her rejected the idea that sentiment had to be measured rationally. The act of laying the skeleton with the other humans was not done for the cat's benefit, but for hers. She wanted to do it, because she felt like it might help her. Because that's what humans did, they got sentimental about little things. Local, manageable things. The idea that six billion humans had died was just too big to consider. Shedding a few tears as you buried a cat, now that was something she could handle.

Martha was quite relieved none of the others had

379

wanted to come. She wanted to just sit for a while in the reflective atmosphere of the chapel and think about things. Think about the thin line that had appeared on the pregnancy test she'd taken whilst the boys were putting away their bikes. Think about the tiny new life growing within her.

The box she'd found to put the cat's skeleton in got wet as she jogged across the grass so she covered it with her raincoat. Reaching the chapel, she pushed open the heavy door with difficulty, her heavy torch bashing against the stone walls. In a tangle, she half fell in, soaked through, breathing hard.

Then Martha stopped in surprise and looked up, puzzled, as she realised there was already light within the little building. Candles had been lit in the candelabras down either side. She flicked off her torch, bemused. Then her heart seized as she noticed something else. The skeletons they'd left on the floor, wrapped in sheets, had been moved.

They were now seated in the pews.

Leaning drunkenly, with the occasional limb or jawbone missing, the corpses grinned maniacally at the painting of St Peter above the altar.

Martha fell back against a stone pillar, heart pounding. Who had done this? Why would anybody do something so ... wrong?

Feeling sick, she turned towards the door and her questions were answered.

'Hello, Martha,' said her father.

Carrying the tea tray into the lounge, Josh stopped to look out the great bay windows to the front. The rain was thrashing down, hammering on the glass. As he stood, watching, a sheet of lightning lit the sky for an instant and he felt a sudden stab of fear.

For there on the gravel in front of the house, was a car. A four-wheel drive, seen for a micro-second.

There's someone here,' Josh said. He slammed the tray down on a coffee table and rushed to the front door, followed by Sam.

'Josh!' Sam called. 'The guns.'

'Good call,' Josh said. 'Kitty, stay hidden.' She nodded and ducked down low behind the sofa. The boys sprinted back into the kitchen where they'd left the pistol and rifle. Now armed, they returned to the main door and were halfway across the hall when the door handle rattled and began to turn.

Looking back into the lounge, to his right, Josh saw Kitty watching him over the top of the sofa, her face full of concern. She shook her head.

The boys raised their weapons and pointed them at the door as it slowly swung open.

'Mum?' Josh said.

'Judith?' Sam said.

Judith stood in the doorway, drenched, her black hair plastered over her pale face. She stepped inside.

'Could you point the guns somewhere else, please?' she said as Kitty ran up to give her a hug.

'Are you here alone?' Sam asked, peering behind her.

'Where is he?' Judith said, ignoring Sam's question. 'Have you seen him?'

'Where is who?' Josh asked slowly, a knot of fear clutching his insides.

Judith stared back at her son, steel in her eyes. 'Your father. He left the village sometime this morning on a motorbike. He came to find you, and he took a gun.'

The boys looked at each other, mouths open.

'We kept an eye on him the night you left,' Judith said. 'And all the next day. He wouldn't leave the church, wouldn't talk to anyone. We brought Mark's body back, and Reg's...' She paused for a moment, eyes closed, clearly distressed at the memory. 'Then this morning he was gone, slipped out somehow. Mr Carter said he'd had a pistol in his desk and that it wasn't there anymore.'

'We haven't seen him,' Josh said. 'He's not here. We would have heard him coming.'

'Have you been here all day?' Judith asked.

'No,' Kitty replied. 'We went to get food.'

'Where's Martha?' Judith asked, looking around.

The knot of fear in Josh's stomach suddenly exploded, taking his breath away.

'She went to the chapel,' he gasped.

382

'There's a chapel?' Judith said, her eyes widening. 'That's where he'll be. Of *course* that's where he'll be. Show me – where is it?'

They ran to the door, Kitty following.

'Stay here, Kitty,' Josh said at the threshold. 'He could be dangerous.'

'No,' Judith said. 'She comes, we stay together.'

And together, as the thunder rolled around the world, the four ran out into the driving rain, towards the chapel.

5.53 P.M.

'What are you doing, Dad?' Martha asked. Her father had told her to sit down on the first pew. When she'd hesitated he'd shown her a pistol tucked into his belt, a big grey thing she hadn't seen before.

Martha tried not to think about the skeleton next to her. As she'd sat she noticed it was wearing a rather expensive suit. The head was turned slightly towards her, the mouth open in a mischievous grin, as though the corpse was just about to tell a dirty joke.

'What am I doing?' Mr Pirbright repeated. 'I came to visit my children in their new home.' He walked to the lectern and rested his thin white hands on the massive Bible lying there. He looked more sparse than ever, his face grey and hollow. Shrunken almost.

'I knocked on the door,' he said. 'But there was no one home, and when the rain started I sought shelter.'

Martha watched him. He smiled a twisted, sideways smile. Something about him gave the impression of impermanence. That at any moment he'd break down in floods of tears, or explode in a fit of rage. But then, he'd been giving that impression for months now.

'And God, as ever, provided,' he finished, holding out his hands and looking upwards, clearly delighted.

'Why did you come to visit us?' Martha asked.

Michael laughed – a short, sharp bark.

'Well, to bring you back, of course,' he said.

Martha shook her head. 'Who says we're coming back?' she asked.

Michael's expression immediately snapped into one of white-lipped fury. 'I do,' he spat.

'You haven't spoken to me for weeks,' she said. 'Why do you want me back in the village.'

'Things will be different,' he said. 'We're going to be a family again.'

'Ha!' Martha cried. 'You're dreaming.'

He lifted his coat again, revealing the gun.

'Force!' Martha snapped back, suddenly angry. Sick of this insanity. 'Violence. That's your answer to everything these days. Well, that's why we left.'

'I was trying to keep you safe!' Michael screamed, slamming a hand down on the Bible.

'You were trying to control us,' Martha corrected. 'Trying to force us into some stupid vision of a perfect society.'

'Yes! A society based on the principles laid down by our Lord,' Michael said, his eyes almost popping with his eagerness to spit out the argument.

'We don't want that,' Martha said. Michael stared at her, speechless, a fleck of spittle on his cheek, glinting in the candlelight. 'I don't even believe in God,' she went on.

Her father's mouth sagged. 'You're … you're one of them, are you?' he said contemptuously. 'Them in the pub?'

Martha shook her head. 'I'm not one of anything, Dad. I'm just me.'

He looked at her silently. A look of doubt crossed his face. She saw his shoulders quivering slightly.

'It's me. Martha,' she said. 'You know me, don't you?'

He stared at her and nodded, almost imperceptibly. The wind howled outside and the rain hammered on the stained-glass window behind his grey, shorn head. Then suddenly his head was in his hands and he groaned.

'Oh, God. It hurts,' he muttered through gritted teeth.

'Dad …' Martha said uselessly. Part of her wanted to go over and help, lay a hand on his head. Let him know she was there. 'What's happened to you?'

A gust of wind whistled outside in the darkness. Michael raised his grizzled head and eyed his daughter sadly. 'We didn't have much time,' he said. 'When

385

we did find what we thought was an effective vaccine, it was too late to test it properly.'

Martha remained silent, watching him. Waiting for him to continue.

'By that time everyone had gone,' he said. 'All the technicians, the staff, the security. Everyone except me, Powell and Smith.' He closed his eyes and squeezed his temples between his hands, as though trying to crush his own head, to kill the pain. 'We had to test it on ourselves. Powell went first. You remember Powell, don't you? She came to our house once.'

Martha smiled and nodded, though she didn't remember.

'We gave her the vaccine, plus some of the useless antivirals we had, then a few minutes later injected her with a sample of the virus.'

He stopped, shivering. Pain and guilt were written large on his tired features.

'It didn't work?' Martha said.

He shook his head. 'She died. She lasted longer than most, though, so we knew we were on the right track. It was just...it was only...'

'What?' Martha said, prompting him.

'As she died, in that sterile room, she was screaming. Hallucinating.' He looked up at Martha and she saw tears rolling down his cheeks. 'She died in agony and fear,' he said. 'It wasn't the virus. It was the vaccine, causing the hallucinations. We knew there was a compound within it that could cause hallucinations as side effects, but we didn't...we never suspected...'

Martha shivered in the cold air, waiting for him to go on.

'We reduced the dose and tried again. I also made some adjustments to the antiviral treatment. That was vital. To beat a virus, you have to keep the patient alive long enough for the right antibodies to develop. We drew lots. I lost, or won – I'm still not sure. Smith took the altered doses, and again I injected the virus into her. She was calm. Forcing out a joke, even. At that point it didn't really seem as though we'd be able to save anybody, not even ourselves. But we had to go on, do you see?'

Martha nodded. Of course she saw.

The he shook his head sadly. 'She died as well. The hallucinations came again, weaker this time. She lasted longer than Powell, and was rational for some time. She described her symptoms, headaches, flashing lights, visions of soldiers and demons. I was able to adjust the make-up of the vaccine accordingly.'

He was talking faster now, more smoothly, the dam wall had burst and he seemed to want to get it all out.

'She went mad towards the end, and I...finished her off,' he said, miming the cocking of a pistol. Martha tried not to look as appalled as she felt. 'I'd started coughing myself by then,' he continued. 'So I made a few educated guesses, made up another altered vaccine, combined it with the improved antiviral and injected it into myself. I kept working as I waited for it to take effect.'

He stopped talking and cocked his head, listening.

'The treatment worked?' Martha prompted, wanting him to go on, hoping the confession might help bring her father back.

He nodded. 'It worked, but not perfectly. As I continued, as I experienced what the vaccine was doing to my body, my mind, something came to me. A flash of inspiration. A notion I would never have thought of on my own...'

'What do you mean?' Martha asked.

Michael's eyes flicked up to the cross above the altar. He smiled. 'Don't you see, Martha?' he said gently. 'God spoke to me. God gave me the solution to the puzzle.'

Martha stared at him, worried again.

'I'd left out a key ingredient. Something to stabilise the compound, stop it reacting against itself. It was the lack of that element which was causing the hallucinations and the headaches, and reducing the effectiveness of the vaccine. God told me what I was doing wrong. I made as much as I could and left, on my way here. My mission was clear. The Lord had given me a gift and I wasn't going to waste it.'

'But why do you think it was God?' Martha asked. 'Maybe you just thought of it yourself?'

Michael shook his head and looked deep into her

eyes. 'No,' he said simply. 'This didn't come to me by accident. This was divine intervention.'

'Dad,' Martha said. 'Something changed in you when you took that vaccine. You said yourself it was unstable. You're not...you're not yourself. You've gone somewhere, and we want you back. All of us.'

His piercing gaze burned through her, as if searching for the soul within. And maybe he saw nothing. Or maybe he saw his own true nature reflected in her clear, blue eyes. Maybe he saw what he'd become. The candles flickered suddenly, and as they did something passed between Martha and her father. Some note of understanding. Some connection, from before, from when she was tiny, from when he'd carried her on his shoulders and thrown her high into the cornflower sky.

'Dad,' she said, standing slowly. 'Daddy.' She held out a hand to him and stepped forward.

Michael watched her coming, a look of confusion on his face. His mouth opened slightly and his lips moved, as though he were praying, praying for her, or for him, or for everyone. Slowly, ever so slowly, he lifted a hand and held it out towards his daughter's. Their fingertips touched, and at the instant they did there was a loud crash from behind. Michael leaped, the wind howled in through the open door, and in an instant the candles were snuffed out, enveloping them in total blackness.

Martha spun in confusion as someone called her

name. Then she remembered the torch, still clutched in her left hand. She flicked it on and saw her mother, Josh, Sam and Kitty standing at the far end of the chapel, hands over their faces against the blinding bright light. Then she saw a flash of steel as Sam swung his gun up towards them.

Judith was already moving down the centre aisle slowly, determinedly. 'Martha!' she heard her mother call again.

'No!' she heard her father cry from behind her. 'Stay away!'

'Wait,' Martha said. She'd been so close to making a connection with her father. He was still there, the real Michael Pirbright. They could bring him back, heal the wounds within him, within all of them. But then she turned back to face him and saw with a sinking heart that he had his pistol out and was pointing it down the aisle towards his wife. In the light of her torch, she could see her father's finger squeezing the trigger.

And without thinking, Martha stepped between them as the pistol shot cracked and she took the bullet in her own body. She heard her mother scream with rage.

Martha stumbled as the bullet slammed into her belly, hard and cold, as though she'd been impaled on a spear made of ice. Somehow, though, she managed to stay on her feet. She couldn't breathe, and as she stood, blinking in shock, shadows swam across her field of vision, grey curtains drawing closed. As Martha's world darkened she remembered, all too late, that it wasn't just her own life she was sacrificing. Michael Pirbright, with all his grand schemes to repopulate the planet, had not only shot his own daughter – he had destroyed the first new life to be conceived since the outbreak. She shook her head sadly as her father stared back at her, his face a mask of horror at what he had just done.

And then for Martha, everything went black again.

6.01 P.M.

After Michael fired his deafening shot, Sam saw Martha pause, shake her head and then fall backwards to the ground. He raised his rifle, intent on spreading Pirbright's brains, staining more than just the windows. But as Martha fell, her torch went out, plunging them into darkness. Judith was halfway down the aisle and Sam heard her scream, a cry of anguish and anger which twisted into panted sobs as she tried to find her daughter's body in the darkness.

Sam held his fire. Without light he couldn't be sure he wouldn't hit her.

'Get down, Judith,' he called. 'I'm going to fire.'

'Hold it, Sam!' Josh cried.

'Quiet, both of you,' Judith's voice called from the velvet darkness. 'Listen.'

Their ears were still ringing from the gunshot, but as they listened, over the sound of the swirling weather outside they could hear another sound. The sound of a man's agonised sobbing.

'Are you happy now?' Judith cried out in the dark. 'You've killed your daughter. Who's next? Are you going to kill your son? Your wife? The whole goddamn world?!'

But even the blasphemy couldn't bring a halt to Michael's sobs. As Josh heard his mother shuffling forward in the pitch-black, he held out a hand, found a pew and began inching his way forward too.

Then lightning flashed outside and gave them an instant of vision. Michael huddled at the altar. Martha lying on the floor of the aisle, dark blood pooling around her, as if in homage to the black haloed billions. And in that instant of light, Josh saw Judith's hand dart forward and snatch up the torch. He heard her bash her hand against the case and suddenly it flickered into life, illuminating the scene once more.

Judith pointed it directly at her husband, fixing him with the searching light of accusation. St Peter looked on dimly from behind, no doubt writing up Michael's actions in his book.

'Josh,' Judith said. 'Hold this torch on him while I check Martha.'

Josh grabbed the torch and did as she asked. Kitty slipped from behind to help Judith.

'Why don't I just shoot him?' Sam said, sidling up.

Josh was about to answer when Michael made the question academic. He lifted the pistol and jammed it into his own mouth.

'Dad, no!' Josh called.

Michael looked up at him and Josh saw something in his father's eyes that made his blood run cold. Suddenly the cloud had lifted. His father had once more returned to them. Maybe he'd been shocked into this moment of clarity, maybe it was but a brief window. Right now, though, it was clear that Michael was sane and completely aware of what he had done.

Pirbright stared at his son with eyes full of guilt and self-loathing.

Josh took a step towards him.

'No!' he cried. 'Don't do it, Da—'

But Josh's words were drowned by the crack of the pistol as his father pulled the trigger and blew the top of his own head off.

Kitty screamed.

'Oh God!' Josh cried. 'Oh my God!'

'Jesus Christ!' Sam said. He turned to look at Judith. She stared at her husband's body, her mouth open. They stayed in that tableau for a few seconds, ears ringing from the gunshot.

Then Judith looked away.

She swallowed. 'We need to help Martha. She's alive, but she needs attention. Let's get her into the hotel for now, there's more light there.' She took off her cardigan and wadded up the cloth, pressing it against Martha's stomach and putting Kitty's hand over it.

'Hold it there, press down hard,' she said.

Then gently, gingerly, the others lifted the unconscious Martha and carried her, the rain, back into the hotel. Soaked they burst in through the front doors and through into the lounge where they laid her on one of the big sofas.

'Should we put her in your car?' Sam asked. 'Take her back to the village?'

Judith clicked her tongue, examining the wound. 'She's in a bad way. I don't know if all those bumps would be good for her. Even with the four-wheel drive it took me a long time to get here.'

'I could go and get Jenny,' Sam said. 'On my bike. I can take the trail. Even going there and back it probably wouldn't be any longer than taking her in the car.'

Josh looked as though he were about to say something, but Kitty kicked him. 'You stay here,' she whispered, 'with your family.'

Judith considered, then nodded. 'Go, then. Bring back Jenny, bring bandages, antibiotics, painkillers, stitches, everything. Just go, *now*.'

And Sam went at a sprint. The front door banged and a few minutes later they heard the roar of the bike outside and saw the fierce glare of his tail-light disappearing down the drive.

Kitty knelt next to her friend and took her hand. Josh stood behind Kitty and rested a hand on her shoulder. Martha murmured and moved her head, without opening her eyes. Judith mopped her brow.

'Hang in there, sweetheart,' Judith said softly. 'Just like you did before.'

Josh kneeled before the three newest graves in the churchyard at Little Sheen. Kitty would be arriving soon. He'd heard hints that the wedding dress was going to blow his socks off, and his stomach churned in anticipation. For now, though, there was time to lay three roses.

Sam sauntered over. He hadn't been keen on holding the wedding here. After his mad dash back from Haven, as it was then called, with Jenny, he'd declared he was never going back to the village again. But the thought of getting married in the chapel at the hotel, with its grim recent history had horrified Kitty, and, of course, she'd had her way.

'It's like a victory for the God squad,' Sam had said, when Josh had told him. 'Wasn't this what we were escaping from?'

Josh had shaken his head. 'I don't think so. I'm not against marriage, or being settled. I just didn't think that anyone else should have a say in who it was I was marrying. It's about choice.'

Sam had sniffed, unconvinced.

Besides, this was an excellent opportunity to bring the two communities closer together. In the first month or so after they had moved to the hotel, a steady trickle of people had followed them from the village: Judith and Clive, James Freedman and his wife. Ben Nicholls, Bryan and Ellie. There were others too, until the two communities were roughly equal in size. Relations were strained at first. Mr Carter took over the running of the Haven council, along with Jim Halfdene. Monica took a back seat, and gradually relations with her children improved as Michael's corrosive influence wore off.

There was a certain amount of coming and going between the hotel and the village, even trading – or, at least, swapping. A few people had moved back and forth a few times, as there was room for everyone to come and go as they wished. Things were comfortable there at the hotel now. They had electricity and hot water, fresh fish and venison. Sam had been arranging fishing trips from Hayling Island, and was already talking about making a trip to France in a fishing boat.

Josh laid the first rose on his father's grave. Some had thought the body should not be interred here. They'd called Pirbright a monster. Mark Rogers' body, in fact, had been buried in a field a few miles away – after what he'd done to Reg, few were willing to stand up for him. Only Jim Halfdene and Mark's own mother had attended his funeral.

Where Michael Pirbright was concerned, though, most agreed that despite his failings, Michael deserved his grave here, as he had saved the village, after all. And if he'd been sick, he was at peace now.

The second rose Josh laid on Reg's grave, diplomatically positioned well away from Michael's. Josh fought back the tears – Kitty would not want him to have red cheeks in the wedding photos. Harry had been appointed official photographer and Josh had given him the Leica to use.

Sam watched as Josh then walked over to the third grave and stood before the simple headstone. He stayed there, head down, for a long time, until Sam could hear the joyous squeals of the bridal party approaching across the green.

Then, finally, Josh leaned forward to lay the third rose, before turning and walking towards Sam, wiping away a tear.

'I miss that old dog,' he said as he passed.

'What the hell are you doing?' a coiffured Martha shouted at them from the side door of the church. On her hip, wearing a pink, silk dress, was Josh's niece, Lily, now five months old. 'She's supposed to keep *you* waiting, not the other way round!'

That Martha had survived the bullet had been extraordinary enough; that she'd gone on to carry the baby to term had been nothing short of miraculous. Lily was, therefore, a miracle baby, everyone agreed – even Lily's father, who didn't believe in miracles but who had nonetheless been seen in the church a few times when it had been touch-and-go.

'Come *on*!' Martha repeated, waving them inside.

Josh and Sam looked at each other and grinned. And then together, side by side, the boys walked into the church.